# Servant of a Living God

## A Novel of Ancient Egypt

# Jason R. Abdale

Publisher's Cataloging-in-Publication Data

Names: Abdale, Jason R., author.
Title: Servant of a living god : a novel of ancient Egypt / Jason R. Abdale.
Description: Flushing, NY: JRA Books, 2025.
Identifiers: LCCN: 2025904896 | ISBN 979-8-9928724-1-5 (hardcover) |
979-8-9928724-2-2 (hardcover collector's edition) |
979-8-9928724-0-8 (paperback) | 979-8-9928724-3-9 (ebook)
Subjects: LCSH Egypt--Fiction. | Egypt--Civilization--To 332 B.C--Fiction. | War--Fiction.
| Historical fiction.| BISAC FICTION / Historical / Ancient | FICTION / War & Military

Classification: LCC PS3601 .B33 S74 2025 | DDC 813.6--dc23

# INTRODUCTION

Ancient Egypt has always been fertile ground for artistic expression. An incalculable number of paintings, sculptures, books, plays, operas, movies, TV shows, and even children's cartoons have been set in the fabled kingdom on the Nile. This land seems to excite the imaginative muse, and this allure is unlikely to go away as long as the pyramids still stand.

In popular imagination, ancient Egypt is a place synonymous with fantasy, where everyone had perfect tans and walked in that peculiar way that was seen in the Bangles' music video. The land of the pharaohs seems to be a mystical mythical place, a kingdom more fitting with the gods and super-human heroes of legend than reality. Stories of booby-trapped tombs, mummies' curses, and Biblical plagues have only served to cultivate this "other-ness" that seems to be applied to Egypt but to no other place in the ancient world. However, the people who lived in ancient Egypt were very real. They had their lives, their problems, their joys, and their sorrows. They had to contend with today and think of tomorrow. During some parts of Egyptian history, day-to-day life was very precarious, and danger and death were ever-present companions. This book is set during one of those times.

While this book is a work of fiction, there are nevertheless several real historical persons from ancient Egyptian history who appear within these pages. They include Queen Sobek-Neferu, King Sheshy, King Heribre, King Nebsenre, King Wahibre, and King Sekheperenre. All of the other characters in this story are entirely fictitious, and any resemblance that these characters may have to any other persons, living or dead, factual or fictional, is purely coincidental.

One thing should be stated at the outset – the title *Pharaoh* never appears within this book. The word *Pharaoh* is descended from the Egyptian word *Perah*, meaning "the great house" and was the name of the royal palace; the royal title essentially means "the person who lives in the big house". The title *Pharaoh* first appears in the written records during the reign of Akhenaten who ruled Egypt during the middle 1300s BC. Prior to this, the Egyptian monarchs were referred to as *Nesu*, meaning "King". Since this book takes place two centuries prior to that time, *Nesu* is the title which is used.

I would like to thank April Cox for all of her help in getting my novel published. I would also like to thank James Abbate and Sarah Holz for reading my story prior to publication and offering their tips on how to improve it. Finally, I wish to thank my parents for fostering my love of history and for putting up with me during the arduous research and writing process.

This book is dedicated to my father, Jeffrey George Abdale (April 30, 1954 – March 14, 2025), a lover of history and classic cinema. You set me upon the path that I would follow.

 # CAST OF CHARACTERS 

**Seshrab of Hebron** – A Canaanite scribe

**Sihon** – King of Hebron

**Ariyak** – King of Gaza

**Iuniyrapet** – Chief overseer at the "Hathor's Mountain" turquoise mine

**Nakhtibre, later crowned as Nebsenre** – A general in the Lower Egyptian Army who made himself King of Lower (Northern) Egypt

**Shaweneiti, later crowned as Khemshawre** – Nakhtibre's son who became King of Lower Egypt following his father's death

**Queen Meret** – Wife of King Nebsenre

**Queen Neferet** – Wife of Shaweneiti

**Montunakht** – Shaweneiti's half-brother

**Atentjehenet** – Shaweneiti's daughter

**Horemheb** – Chamberlain of the Palace

**Captain Nebikhamu** – Commander of the Royal Palace Guard

**Colonel Ankharis** – Commander of the Sapmeh Regiment

**Colonel Horahauty** – Commander of the Khaset Regiment

**Colonel Mebydos** – Commander of the East Ament Regiment

**Nesbit** – The rebel governor of West Ament

**Wahibre** – King of Upper (Southern) Egypt

**Sekheperenre** – Governor of Inebu-Hedj and lord of the cities of Giza, Ankh-Tawi, Saqqara, and Dashur

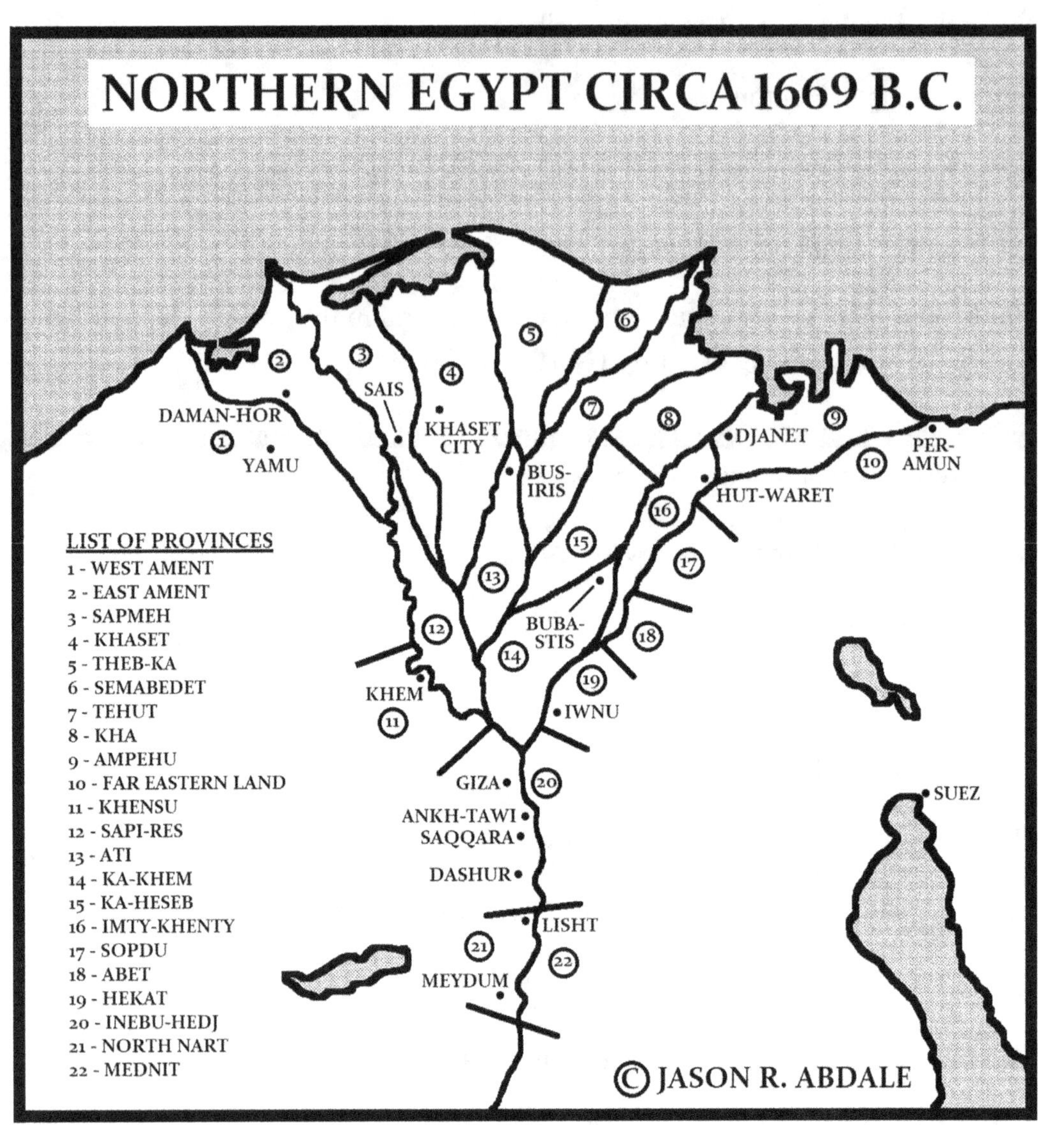

NORTHERN EGYPT CIRCA 1669 B.C.

DAMAN-HOR
YAMU
SAIS
KHASET CITY
BUS-IRIS
DJANET
PER-AMUN
HUT-WARET
KHEM
IWNU
GIZA
ANKH-TAWI
SAQQARA
DASHUR
LISHT
MEYDUM
BUBA-STIS
SUEZ

LIST OF PROVINCES
1 - WEST AMENT
2 - EAST AMENT
3 - SAPMEH
4 - KHASET
5 - THEB-KA
6 - SEMABEDET
7 - TEHUT
8 - KHA
9 - AMPEHU
10 - FAR EASTERN LAND
11 - KHENSU
12 - SAPI-RES
13 - ATI
14 - KA-KHEM
15 - KA-HESEB
16 - IMTY-KHENTY
17 - SOPDU
18 - ABET
19 - HEKAT
20 - INEBU-HEDJ
21 - NORTH NART
22 - MEDNIT

© JASON R. ABDALE

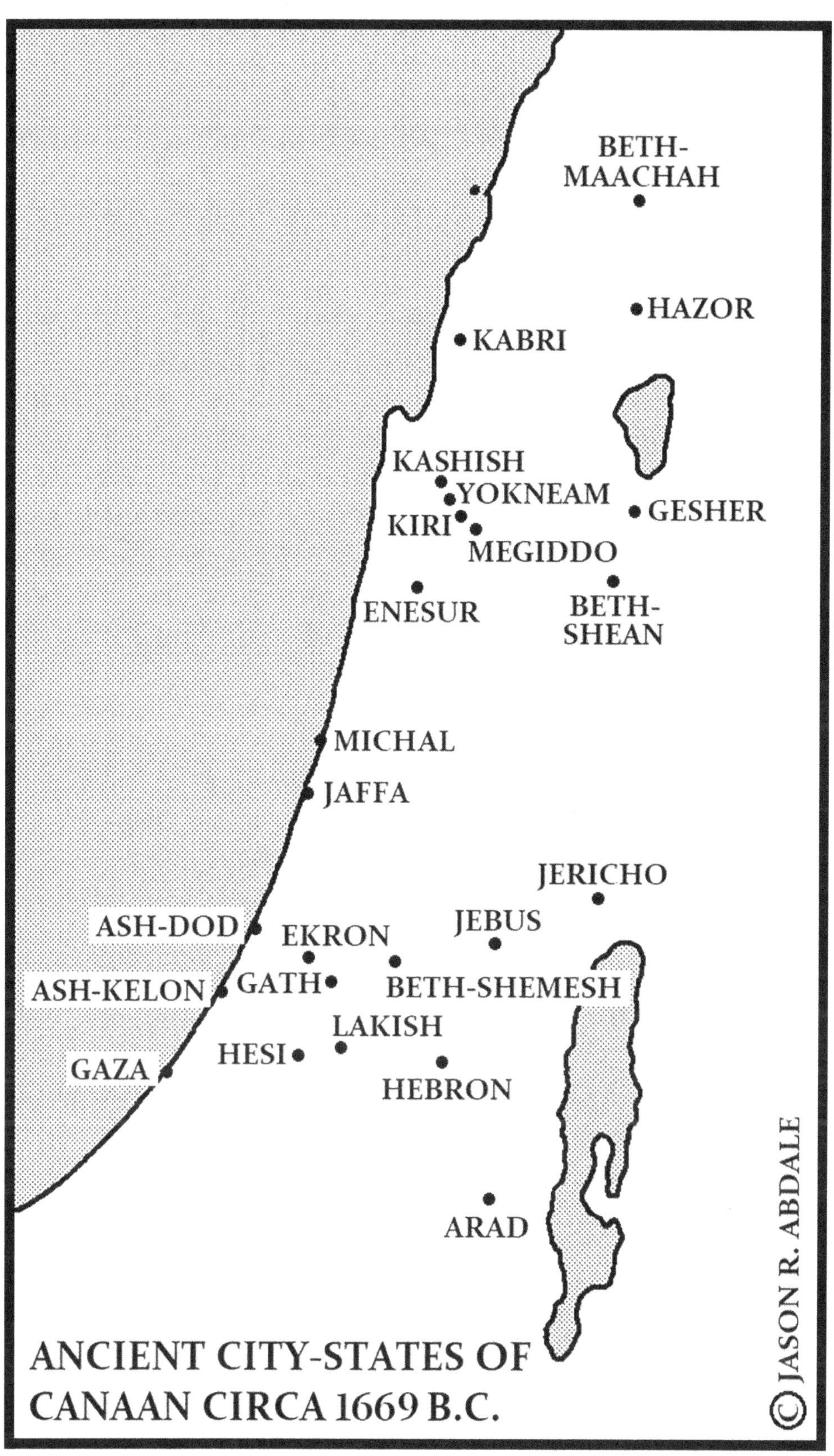

BETH-MAACHAH
HAZOR
KABRI
KASHISH
YOKNEAM
KIRI
GESHER
MEGIDDO
ENESUR
BETH-SHEAN
MICHAL
JAFFA
JERICHO
ASH-DOD
EKRON
JEBUS
ASH-KELON
GATH
BETH-SHEMESH
LAKISH
HESI
GAZA
HEBRON
ARAD
© JASON R. ABDALE
ANCIENT CITY-STATES OF CANAAN CIRCA 1669 B.C.

*I, Seshrab of Hebron, formerly Chief Scribe to His Divine Majesty the king of Lower Egypt, am hereby setting pen to paper to write a history of the reign of my master, Nesu Horus-Khemshawre, ruler of Lower Egypt by the grace of the goddess Wadjet, Son of Ra, Horus Incarnate, Living God of Egypt. I became resolved to write this tale on that terrible day that the capital fell in order to preserve the memory of my former master and his lost dynasty. My bride Neferet, formerly the wife of King Khemshawre, requested that I compose this chronicle to serve as a testimony of what was gained, what was lost, and what is needed to rebuild, and also to warn future generations of the terrible price of power and ambition. I shall write of kings and queens, generals and warlords, victories and defeats, loyalty and betrayal, of the innocents who suffered and the unknowable gods who passively watched it all. And thus, I begin my story...*

Egypt. The year 1669 BC.

The glorious kingdom upon the Nile lay in ruins. For the past ninety years, civil war had torn the country apart. Everywhere was famine, disease, blood, and death. It seemed that the gods had abandoned their people.

For almost two and a half centuries, the rulers of the 12th Dynasty had reigned over a united Egypt and presided over a golden age of prosperity. Then in 1759 BC, the reigning monarch Queen Sobek-Neferu died without an heir, and the throne was open to whoever was strong enough to take it. Hundreds of would-be monarchs asserted their self-created claims to the crown and clashed with each other from the Nile Delta to the borders of Nubia, and battles were fought without pity or mercy with great loss of life and much destruction of the land. So taken were the various lords, princes, and generals with their hunger for power that they did not hesitate in committing the most savage barbarities or defiling the most sacred of places.

Out of this roiling tumult, two factions emerged as the most powerful. The so-called 13th Dynasty, who spuriously claimed to be the direct heirs of the previous royal family, ruled Upper Egypt from their capital in Lisht. Meanwhile, the 14th Dynasty, whose leaders were of no more royal parentage than the nearest plowhand, ruled over Lower Egypt in the north, their capital in Khaset City. A bloody back-and-forth see-saw of attack and counter-attack raged between the two sides. Yet after many years of struggle with no progress made by either side, the two kings agreed to an uneasy truce. Both recognized each other's lands as independent states, and acknowledged each other as equals and the legitimate sovereign rulers of their respective realms.

But then, the Nile River, the sacred lifeblood of Egypt, did not rise. Without the nutritious silt brought by the floodwaters from the south, crops failed and people starved. It did not help that the king was believed to have the divine power to make the Nile flood. As so often happens in history, from hunger sprang resentment, and from resentment sprang rebellion. Egypt once more collapsed into chaos as the regional lords carved up the land into their own mini-kingdoms. From then onwards, the monarchs of both Upper and Lower Egypt ruled over their respective domains in name only; the warlords were the *real* power in the land now. A king's advisor once told his sovereign, "Within the walls of your palace, Your Majesty, your rule is unquestioned. Beyond these walls, you are invisible". Sensing weakness, foreigners migrated into Egypt from all directions. Previously, the nation's borders had been sternly defended with all outsiders kept at a safe distance. Yet now, with the government in a state of dormancy and with the nation not as well-guarded and well-maintained as it once was, Egypt's former enemies penetrated the country *en masse*, and there was little that anyone could do to stop them. With the impoverished state of the country, the famines from the lack of flooding of the Nile, the collapse of centralized government, the fragmentation of the nation into a gaggle of quarrelsome city-states, and with an unstoppable influx of foreigners, it was no wonder that this period was referred to by the Egyptians as "the Second Dark Age".

To the Egyptians, although the king had no governing power, he still *was* a living god and had to be respected. However, that respect was not given, but earned. If the king did not do what was expected of him, he was assured that his reign would be cut short by the hands of hired assassins or by ambitious usurpers eager to place themselves upon the throne.

And that's exactly what happened a year ago when General Nakhtibre, Lower Egypt's most famed and respected military commander, declared war on his own country.

Nakhtibre, whose name meant "Ra's Heart is Strong", was in his late 50s, which to the Egyptians was quite old. His face was like toughened leather with dominant cheekbones and wrinkles around his mouth and brow. Most Egyptian men had faces like this; only the fat pampered rich had full faces with soft skin and light complexions. General Nakhtibre and his famed warrior son Shaweneiti were definitely *not* those sorts of men. They were working men, fighting men, men who weren't afraid to get their hands dirtied and bloodied.

Nakhtibre had entered military service as a teenager during the reign of King Sheshy, who was without question the strongest ruler of the 14th Dynasty, and he became a dominant influence on Nakhtibre's personality and career; Nakhtibre himself called him "The greatest man that I ever knew". King Sheshy was a fighting man, and with the help of his army he violently crushed all opposition against him. Under his rule, the Royal Army of Lower Egypt was transformed from a mediocre gaggle of armed men into a crack fighting force exhibiting a level of professionalism and tactical expertise unheard of elsewhere. In battle after battle, siege after siege, the royalists crushed any foe. The awesome power of King Sheshy's army, and his ready willingness to use that army in response to the slightest provocations, made his adversaries very wary of antagonizing him, and they were grudgingly cowed into submissive obedience. Envoys were dispatched throughout all of northern Egypt bearing the official scarab seal of His Divine Majesty, demanding loyalty and homage...*or else*. The mere threat of the army being sent was enough for some warlords to voluntarily submit to the king's will. For those who stubbornly refused to accept King Sheshy's demands, the end came for them the way that it came for *all* of Sheshy's enemies – swiftly, mercilessly, and with overwhelming violence.

As a young soldier in King Sheshy's army, Nakhtibre quickly gained a reputation for his lion-like ferocity and almost lunatic courage on the battlefield. Yet he also wished to instill order and discipline amongst his fellow soldiers and imbue in them the same sense of duty and patriotism that he himself had. *His Divine Majesty* recognized talent and ability when he saw it, and he had need of such men as unit commanders. After one particularly gruesome battle against one of the king's enemies, a battle in which Nakhtibre once again lived up to his image as a mighty warrior, King Sheshy called the army to assemble into ranks upon the corpse-covered battlefield. Then, in front of all of the onlookers, the king personally promoted Nakhtibre to the rank of Captain, and was commissioned as both a unit commander and a military instructor.

The newly-promoted Captain Nakhtibre worked tirelessly to train the recruits to the same high standards that the great and almighty *Nesu* demanded of all of his men. Nakhtibre, already renowned for his battlefield prowess, now acquired the dubious reputation of being a strict disciplinarian who wasn't afraid to use the lash upon his officers and common soldiers alike. According to Egyptian justice, all people with the exceptions of the king and slaves were treated equally under the law, and he gave no favor to rank. "Learn well and learn quickly", he said, "because war is a strict teacher, and it has no patience for students who learn their lessons too slowly". Captain Nakhtibre's job may have been to teach recruits the lessons of war, but he was learning lessons too. Under King Shehsy's tutelage, Nakhtibre gradually turned into a stone-hearted ruthless man who viewed the club and the axe as the surest ways to gain and maintain order. Administration, politics, and diplomacy were all well and good, but both of them knew "might makes right" was how the *real* world worked.

For a time, King Sheshy compelled all of the lords of Lower Egypt to pledge their allegiance to him. He had also negotiated an alliance with the formidable Nubian kingdom of Kerma, whose lands lay to the south of Upper Egypt; Sheshy even married a Nubian princess to seal the deal. The southern Egyptian king knew that his realm didn't stand a chance in a two-front war sandwiched in between such daunting adversaries. Sheshy also negotiated trade agreements with the Canaanite city-states in which Canaanite raw materials were sent to Egypt in exchange for Egyptian manufactured goods. Likewise, he established non-aggression pacts with the Libyan tribes to the west to keep his western frontier safe. Things were looking up.

King Sheshy ruled Lower Egypt for thirty-three years, the longest reign of any of the northern kings. Under his rule, which was maintained through royal authority, personal charisma, and the liberal use of brute force, order and stability were established and maintained. Some began to wonder if the Second Dark Age had at last come to an end. Yet it was not to be. In 1706 BC, when Capt. Nakhtibre was in his early 20s, King Sheshy died, and the iron-fisted control that he had exerted over the regional warlords died with him. Lower Egypt was plunged into chaos practically overnight as district governors, royal courtiers, and even highly-ambitious peasants fought and slaughtered each other to place the crown on their heads. King Sheshy's son was promptly crowned as the next king of the 14th Dynasty following his father's death, but he was murdered just three days later.

Captain Nakhtibre was an army officer, not a politician, and he had no aspirations to become Lower Egypt's monarchic figurehead. He fought for his country, regardless of whichever pretender sat on the throne. Because of his steadfastness and loyalty, he was promoted up through the ranks to General, and was afterwards appointed to being the supreme commander of the Royal Army of Lower Egypt...which at the time barely numbered a thousand soldiers, but the title was still very prestigious. However, Gen. Nakhtibre could not prevent several of the kings that he swore allegiance to from being ousted from power or murdered. During the thirty-seven years following King Sheshy's death, thirteen men had claimed the title "King of Lower Egypt".

By 1670 BC, the popularity of the reigning Lower Egyptian king, a man named Heribre, had plummeted as low as it had ever been due to consistent crop failures, rampant crime and brigandage, and the unhindered invasion of outsiders. In a meeting with the king's leading officials in the palace's council room, Gen. Nakhtibre voiced his concerns…

"Our nation's borders are being breached from all directions by our enemies: Nubians, Libyans, Canaanites, and the nomads of the desert. It won't be long before they have enough of their own men on our side of the border, and then they can begin a systematic seizure of the entire country from within, carving up our nation like a roasted goose. There are already an unprecedented number of foreigners residing on Egyptian soil, people who have been allowed to enter the country unhindered, people whose loyalties are questionable, people whose intentions are unknown. So far, our *living god* has failed to realize the glaring danger that is present in our country from the presence of so many foreign invaders. We have fought against these people for generations. Now, are we to understand that we should simply open our gates, tear down the walls, and let our enemies into our homes? These people bear no love for us, they don't wish to be our friends – they wish to sabotage us through subterfuge. If our king knew of what was really happening within our country, with the land sinking further and further into anarchy, with the provincial governors seizing absolute power for themselves, and with our enemies encroaching with ever-increasing boldness onto our sacred native soil, I am certain that he would take strong direct measures in combating these threats to our way of life and the salvation of our country. But as of yet, we are forced to take matters into our own hands, and we therefore need to summon our collective will to face these threats head on. Our unified mentality has been crippled, and it is because of this that we have allowed these unfortunate circumstances to occur. In order to prevail, we must once again unify mentally, and I promise that not long after that, we shall also unify politically".

"Here here!" shouted one of the councilors.

"Gentlemen", countered the vizier, "I am willing to hear anything that our esteemed commander would have to say concerning matters of war and defense. However, I wish to say that it is not his place to make any judgments or proposals concerning how this country is to be governed and administered".

General Nakhtibre squirmed in his chair trying to restrain himself. He hated having these meetings with the king's courtiers and government staff, yet as the supreme commander of the Army, he had no choice but to attend them. He detested the back-and-forth verbal tip-toeing and the delicate sensitive ways which he always had to bring up serious matters. He'd have to spend days persuading, negotiating, and adroitly bending them around to his way of thinking. By the gods, it was tiresome! The Army was not a debating chamber – orders were given and obeyed. The general's son, Shaweneiti, who served as his obedient second-in-command, was so much better off than him in this regard. Shaweneiti had no clue about palace politics and the invisible wheelings and dealings that went on behind closed doors. He didn't have to put up with these smarmy bureaucrats who always talked too much and did too little. Thank the gods he wasn't here to see any of this – he'd probably go out of his mind.

"Sir, I am speaking of the very survival of our nation" said General Nakhtibre. "Does the fact that I am a soldier and not a politician make everything that I say completely irrelevant?"

"I wish to say, General, that you should confine your statements and your proposals to your assigned position. Let military men such as yourself worry about military matters, and let politicians concern themselves with political matters. Do I make myself clear?"

Nakhtibre glared. "Yes, my lord".

Arguments and heated language were exchanged between the two sides for the remainder of the day. As the sun set with seemingly nothing having been accomplished, Gen. Nakhtibre was about to leave when he was stopped by one of the members of the royal council. "General, I wish to apologize for the conduct of some of my colleagues. I fear that, like our king, they don't realize the gravity of the situation. You're the one man who has enough respect and personal determination to take us out of the hole that we're in. Whether you realize it or not, there are many in this country, including some in the palace, who are willing to follow you, wherever you may lead us".

There were, in fact, many people who had become intensely loyal to Nakhtibre over the years, and he knew it. His glorious battlefield victories had made him a living legend, but his success and popularity had also earned him enemies in court. But politicians didn't command armies, generals did, and there was no denying whatsoever that Nakhtibre's soldiers were fanatically loyal and devoted to him. If the soldiers were to choose between following their king and following their commander, they would without hesitation choose the second option.

Little by little, as General Nakhtibre became aware of just how much loyalty and support he had from the people, the government, and especially the Army, and knowing how inept and incompetent the present ruling head-of-state was, and believing that the situation was either going to remain unchanged or would only get worse, he started to entertain the idea of putting a more worthy person on Lower Egypt's throne – himself. At first, such thoughts were nothing more than idle musings, but as time went on, and as his infuriation with the present system grew and grew, he began thinking about it more seriously. Bit by bit, the pieces were lined up. There were confidential meetings in darkened rooms, opinions were aired, pledges of loyalty were sworn, and finally, plans were made. Secret orders were dispatched to the unit commanders. As soon as everything was ready, it would happen.

Unfortunately for Gen. Nakhtibre, it would happen a lot sooner than he wanted. True, many in the palace supported him, but others didn't. Politicians and dignitaries were coming and going in and out of the palace at a frenetic rate, but then they mysteriously vanished. When questioned about their absence, they all dispatched replies citing poor health, or family emergencies, or "pressing engagements", whatever that meant. Shipments of supplies had been inexplicably re-routed away from the capital, despite seemingly nobody knowing why. There was also word that the army commanders were dramatically ramping up their training, especially regarding sieges and the house-to-house carnage of urban warfare. When questioned about what was happening, the respondents' answers were unnervingly and suspiciously evasive.

Eventually, King Heribre's supporters were able to add 2 and 2 together. The king decided to act first and he sent assassins to murder Gen. Nakhtibre before he could put his plans into action. They failed – the general's loyal soldiers intercepted them, and after extracting through torture what their mission was, Nakhtibre knew that the time for planning was over. The day after the failed assassination attempt, the order was given. It simply consisted of one word – *NOW*.

There was a battle, and it ended quickly. The king's troops, after seeing that the fighting was not going their way, turned tail and fled with Nakhtibre's men chasing them down and cutting them to pieces. If this was all the fight that *His Divine Majesty* had in him, then the war would be over soon. After this embarrassing loss, King Heribre withdrew the remainder of his forces back to Khaset City with orders to defend the capital at all costs.

Khaset City, the capital of Khaset Province, was very old – even the Egyptians considered it to be ancient. Nobody is exactly sure when it was established, but the consensus was that the settlement already existed prior to the unification of Upper and Lower Egypt centuries ago by King Narmer, which would make Khaset City one of the oldest cities in the entire world. Khaset City was renowned throughout all of Egypt for its excellent grape vineyards, and it was *the* major center in the country for wine production. Beyond the town's walls, grape vineyards stretched for hundreds of acres in every direction. The largest building in the city was the royal palace. Although large, it wasn't as grand as the palaces of previous dynasties. Egypt's iconic royal palaces were in the cities of Waset and Ankh-Tawi, with each palace occupying several acres and made entirely out of dazzling white limestone. These were the two major palaces that the king traditionally occupied, with smaller minor palaces dotted up and down the Nile which the king stayed at when travelling. The royal palace in Khaset City had formerly been one of these smaller royal lodges, but now it served as the official residence of the kings of the 14th Dynasty.

With King Heribre ensconced behind Khaset City's formidable walls, Gen. Nakhtibre had no choice but to lay siege, but he knew that his own men were just as likely to suffer as his enemy. While the king and his royalists were safe inside with water and bread, Nakhtibre's men had to find their own. He didn't want to weaken his position by continuously sending out foraging parties, and he also made it clear that the city's pride and joy, the grape vineyards which grew outside the walls, were not to be damaged under any circumstances. If he was to win, he would have to take Khaset City by storm. He decided to do it under the cover of darkness. Launching a night attack would give him a slight advantage over the large royalist force inside.

Finally, the moon had gone into its death state when it would not be seen in the sky. Now was the time to attack. The order was given.

The battle for Khaset City was fierce and bloody. Both General Nakhtibre and his son Shaweneiti nearly lost their lives and their men suffered many casualties. As the fighting raged, strategy was utterly abandoned, and the battle turned into a gory festival of slaughter that Sekhmet, the bloodthirsty lion-headed goddess of rage, would have reveled in. When the rebels finally broke into the city, they chased the defenders to the royal palace where the king and a handful of followers were making a desperate last stand. In the end, Nakhtibre himself was the one who struck King Heribre down.

The victorious Gen. Nakhtibre immediately proclaimed himself to be the new king of Lower Egypt, and his first task in solidifying his claim to the throne was to be declared a god, as all coronated Egyptian kings were acclaimed to be. Being officially sanctioned by the priesthood as Lower Egypt's legitimate ruler would further secure his position. Traditionally, coronations took place within the Temple of Ptah in the city of Ankh-Tawi, but that was far to the south within enemy territory. So, the chief priest of the Temple of Ra within Khaset City was forced to carry out the ceremony right then and there, surrounded by soldiers with their weapons drawn. After hurriedly performing some prayers and half-improvised incantations, he loudly proclaimed that Gen. Nakhtibre was now *Nesu*, the new monarch of the 14th Dynasty, Horus Incarnate, Living God of Egypt. It was the tradition that a king upon his coronation and transfigurement from a man to a god must take a new name to identify himself. For his coronation, the general-turned-deity assumed the name *Nebsenre*, meaning "Ra is the Lord of the People".

His next task was to reinforce his authority by marrying a woman of appropriate rank, and considering that both Nebsenre and his son didn't have a single drop of royal blood in their veins before their conquest, marrying the previous king's daughters gave their rule a little more credibility. Nebsenre forced King Heribre's oldest daughter Princess Meret to be his wife, and to ensure a royal succession, he compelled her younger sister Neferet to marry his son Shaweneiti. The instant the marriage ceremonies were performed, both Meret and her sister Neferet were required to fulfill their feminine duties...whether they wanted to or not. Soon, it was clear that both women were pregnant. To Nebsenre and Meret was born a son, whom he named Montunakht, "Montu is strong", in thanks to the war god for granting him victory. To Shaweneiti and Neferet was born a daughter named Atentjehenet, "the shining sun".

The newly-crowned King Horus-Nebsenre spent the first months of his reign consolidating his power and strengthening Khaset Province, but he had not forgotten his quest to unify the country. Egypt, like the god Osiris' dead body, lay fragmented and mutilated. Egypt was politically dead, and in order for it to rise from its grave and be the almighty world power that it once was, Egypt needed to reunite.

Now that he was no longer General Nakhtibre but was now instead Nesu Nebsenre, no longer a man but god-on-earth, he could get what he wanted and do what he wanted without resistance. No more handcuffs, no more red tape, no more negotiating with troublesome wishy-washy do-nothing politicians, no more begging for support and aid, and no more asking for permission. From now on, orders would be given, and orders would be obeyed. That was the way of the Army, and from now on that would be the way of the nation. That was the way that King Sheshy did things, and that would be the way that King Nebsenre would do things too. *The son of Ra commands it.* Several months after seizing power, Nebsenre conquered the neighboring western province of Sapmeh, and after that his army took control of East Ament. Now, a year into his reign, the great *Nesu* was making plans for his next conquest.

Inside the council room of the royal palace, Nesu Horus-Nebsenre stood before a large table laden with maps and reports. The room was fairly large, rectangular in shape, and the ceiling was held up by twelve stone columns. The room butted up against one of the thick brick walls which surrounded the palace complex, so it did not have any windows. Instead, it was lit by a profusion of oil lamps, either hanging down from the ceiling or propped up on metal stands erected here and there around the room. In the middle of the room was a huge rectangular table made of imported cedar wood from the Phoenician lands to the northeast, which had been stained dark reddish brown and polished with bees' wax, and several wooden chairs. A year ago, this room had been the setting for some of the most severe hand-to-hand combat in the battle to seize the palace. When the general's soldiers burst in, King Heribre's followers who had barricaded themselves inside this room had no means of escape. These trapped men fought with the savagery of caged beasts, but it was to no avail. Some of the square white alabaster floor tiles still bore scars from where weapons had scraped across their surface, and the large wooden cedar table had several deep gashes in it from axes and spearpoints.

The king was a sight to behold in his martial glory, hunched over the table, his hands firmly planted on the table's surface like strong cables bracing a wall or a lion holding down its prey. Despite his advanced years, his muscles were plainly visible through his thin linen garments, and his powerful physique was evident to all who saw him. In Egypt, people wore things which identified what social rank they belonged to and/or what job they worked in. White linen was the fabric worn by virtually every member of Egyptian society, from royalty down to peasants, although the rich had fabric of the finest quality; the peasants wore coarser material. King Nebsenre wore a white linen tunic with baggy elbow-length sleeves, plain on the top but pleated from the waist down, extending down to his ankles. His head was shaved, but he abstained from wearing wigs as other Egyptians did as a precaution against lice. Upon his head, the king wore the *nemes* crown, which wasn't a "crown" in the common sense of it being a decorated metal ring worn atop the head, but was instead a cloth headdress with blue and gold stripes with a large flap draped over each shoulder and tied like a rope hanging down the back. The *nemes* was deliberately structured to resemble the flared hood of a cobra, the symbol of Egyptian royalty. Mounted in the center of the *nemes* was a gold cobra's head curled upwards like an S. The cobra also represented Wadjet, the winged cobra goddess who served as the patron deity of Lower Egypt; the patron goddess of Upper Egypt was Nekhbet the vulture. In addition to the king's golden bracelets and elaborate beaded collar, he wore a necklace with a gold cross-like symbol called an *ankh*. The word meant "life", and it symbolized the gods' power of life and death over mortals. Only gods were allowed to wear this sacred symbol, and since an officially-coronated king was a god on earth, he was the only mortal allowed to wear the ankh cross. For anyone else, even other members of the royal family, to wear the symbol of the gods was an act of treason and sacrilege. Around his waist, he wore a thick leather belt decorated with brightly-colored beads. Hanging down the front was a long trapezoidal flap, again decorated with many colors. Only the king was allowed to wear this special kind of decorative apron, which was made clear to everyone because in the center of the belt was a golden cartouche-shaped plate which bore the inscription *I Belong To The King*. On his feet, the king wore leather sandals decorated with embossed gilded designs.

As King Nebsenre looked over the papers scattered across the table, two greyhounds were lying on the floor: a white one named Osiris and a black one named Set. He had taken them on many hunting expeditions, including the one that earned him his leopard pelt which he liked to wear when going into battle. In his leisure, he would use his dogs in racing contests to amuse himself and his unit commanders. They were also useful as guard dogs, given the uncertain political atmosphere and the fear that there might be an assassin around any corner.

King Nebsenre knew his son was coming even before he heard his footsteps when the two dogs suddenly became excitable and started barking. The door to the council chamber creaked open, and the dogs happily ran to greet their master's son – Prince Shaweneiti, age 37, Son of *Nesu*, Heir to the Throne of Lower Egypt, Vizier of the Royal Court, President of the Royal Council, and Second-in-Command of the Royal Army, as his titles identified him. As a vizier, he wore a plain unpleated and undecorated white tube-shaped garment which wrapped around his chest under the armpits and extended down to the ankles. It was held up by a single strap which wrapped around the back of the neck; the garment had a tendency to sag in the back, and it was not held in place by any kind of belt. He also wore leather sandals and a beaded collar, though not one quite as ornate as his father's. Shaweneiti hated wearing these effeminate clothes. With its slim wrap-around design and plunging back, his vizier's robe looked more like a dress that a society lady would wear to a fancy dinner party. He felt just as ridiculous wearing this court gown today as he did a year ago the first day that he put it on, but this was what a vizier was supposed to wear, and he had no choice but to wear it. His father had commanded it, and he had learned the hard way to *never* disobey his father.

To denote his office, the vizier also carried a long staff called a *madtew*; it was a sign of authority, respect, knowledge, and wisdom. All high-ranking officials carried special ceremonial staffs to denote their office. Mostly, they had a short two-foot handle, crowned with a lotus blossom, and emerging from it was a flat oar-like paddle measuring over a foot long. Very often, on each side of the paddle, there would be an inscription invoking the name of Nesu to act for him with good guidance. These paddle-like scepters carried by Egyptian government officials were called *sekhem* scepters – the word meant "power". The scepter was deliberately shaped like an oar. The kingdom was a ship, and the king was the captain of that ship. Responsible for keeping the ship moving was its crew, represented by the government. Each official in the king's service was given an oar to literally provide the "power" to propel the ship forward. Only one oarsman was not enough to propel the ship, but rowing together, the nation would progress. The Egyptian vizier was responsible for steering the ship of state in the proper direction, towards truth and righteousness, and away from the children of Set: anarchy, chaos, and destruction. In fact, he was even poetically referred to sometimes as "the pilot of the people".

"How soon can the army march towards West Ament?" asked the king in his loud commanding military voice from across the room.

Prince Shaweneiti began to walk forward, the two greyhounds prancing close behind, smiling and panting, their claws clicking and ticking on the stone tile floor. "As soon as we're re-supplied, which should be within two weeks, the army should be able to move", replied his son.

"Good", he said, looking back at his maps. "The sooner we can secure our western border, the better. That way we can concentrate entirely on the east".

"Speaking of which", said his son, "we've received another message from the Prince of the North".

"Oh gods, what in Duat does he want now?" said the king in an exasperated tone, rolling his eyes upwards.

"The same old nonsense he always says – saying how *he* is the true ruler of all of Lower Egypt, demanding that you pay homage to him, so forth and so forth".

"Just throw it in the refuse pit like all of the other letters that bastard sent", responded the king, dismissively waving his hand in the air. "I'll deal with him in good time. First, we strike west, then we move on the east, and then we'll see just how cocky that puffed-up son of a bitch is when he sees *my* army encamped on *his* doorstep".

"What about the Libyans?"

"What about them?" asked the king dismissively, his eyes still fixed on the papers lying on the table.

"Once we change direction and move on the eastern provinces, it will place our western domains in jeopardy".

Now the king looked up. "We'll worry about that only *after* my army sleeps inside the walls of Yamu. Our first task is to take the province of West Ament, and once that's done, then we can worry about whether the Libyans will attack. At any rate, I'll need to fortify the western border. I can't move on the eastern provinces until I'm certain that my ass is protected".

Shaweneiti smiled. "I'll go see about those supplies", and began to walk off.

"Right. And get that Canaanite scribe in here – I want to talk to him".

Shaweneiti bowed and left. The two dogs wanted to follow him, but Shaweneiti cautioned them. "No, no, my boys. Stay with Father", he spoke in a soft voice, and walked out the door. They whimpered and slunk back towards the table with the papers strewn across it, and flopped onto the floor with a tired depressed look.

He was a good son – respectable, capable, intelligent, diligent, and dutiful, everything a father could ask for. For the hard-as-stone General Nakhtibre, a man who had won many great victories, the birth of his son was the proudest moment of his life. He named his child *Shaweneiti*, meaning "I am the light of my father". His mother died of disease a few years later.

Shaweneiti had been taken on campaign by his father since he was 5. From this young age, "the boy", as he was affectionately called by the soldiers, served almost like an army mascot. Each of the troops took an immediate shine to the youth, and the child enjoyed play-fighting against the much larger infantrymen with a miniature shield and wooden axe. General Nakhtibre didn't have his son present during the actual battle for fear of his safety, but when the fighting was over, he would fetch him. The young boy saw it all – the field of mutilated hacked-up corpses with puncture wounds, axe cuts, and with their skulls smashed in with clubs. Shaweneiti found it to be disgusting and horrifying, and when the soldiers protested at their general exposing the boy to such sights, Gen. Nakhtibre angrily replied, "He must see it all. He needs to know that war is not some playtime game, but a very serious and very deadly thing".

As Shaweneiti grew older, he was entrusted with certain light camp duties such as fetching water, repairing broken shields, and sharpening blades. All the while, he rigorously trained with all weapons to familiarize himself with all of their uses. When he was 13, Shaweneiti experienced puberty, and thus he became a man. In Egypt, there was no such thing as a "teenager" or an "adolescent" – you were either a child or an adult. The threshold for adulthood was the ability to reproduce, and since Shaweneiti's body had now crossed that line, he was no longer considered a boy but a full-fledged man. He was circumcised and his "sidelock of youth", a braid of hair worn on the side of the head to denote childhood, was cut off. Once you were an adult, you were expected to take on all of the responsibilities of adulthood, and that included military service. As such, there were Egyptian soldiers who might be as young as 12, but they were still considered grown-ups.

Now that he was a man, Shaweneiti would be expected to take a more direct part in military matters. At age 14, he fought in his first battle as an ordinary spearman, although he was stationed in the rear on his father's orders. However, like many teenage males, Shaweneiti was full of fire and vinegar, and being posted to the rear didn't suit his temperament. Eager to please his father and prove to him that he was far braver and more adept than the other soldiers, and also worried that the men were thinking that the general was giving him special treatment, Shaweneiti pushed his way through to the front ranks and fought with exceptional courage during his first taste of combat. It highly impressed the soldiers, but his actions greatly angered his father. After the battle was over, Gen. Nakhtibre ordered the entire army to assemble into ranks and stand at attention. Then, he called his son forward. Shaweneiti wondered if he was about to be singled out for special praise, the same way that King Sheshy had done with his father years before. He was in for a rude shock. Before the whole army, the general loudly berated his son in the most vehement language imaginable for disobeying orders, for deliberately putting himself in harm's way, and even more grievously, for disrupting the cohesion of the unit for the sake of personal glory and bravado. Such was an act of individuality, an idea that bordered on treason in Egypt. Individuality was something that was *never* tolerated in Egypt, let alone in the Royal Army. In front of all of the troops, Gen. Nakhtibre ordered his son to be whipped.

Shaweneiti, held up by two strong soldiers to keep him from falling down or running away, was given fifty lashes across his back with a leather strap – his father performed the punishment himself. Shaweneiti liked to think of himself as invincible, as many young men do, and after earning glory in battle on that day he had reason to feel cocky. But the sharp pain of the lash was more than what he had expected. He forced himself not to scream out as the whipping continued. With each hard sharp strike, it made the red Egyptian skin even redder. By the tenth blow, he was bleeding. By the twentieth blow, his back was covered with his own blood. Even the soldiers that were holding him up found the treatment difficult to watch and they had to close their eyes. Nakhtibre performed the entire punishment, blow for blow. *Forty-eight...forty-nine...fifty.* By this time, Shaweneiti succumbed to the immense pain and fainted, and had to be dragged away, leaving behind a trail of blood.

After Nakhtibre whipped his son, he ordered that all of the other men in his son's company were to be whipped as well for allowing such an intolerable infraction of discipline to occur. Collective punishment was regularly used in ancient Egypt. When one soldier from one company failed in his duties, the entire company was punished along with him. This demonstrated that it was possible for many people to suffer due to the actions of a single person. Discipline and diligence needed to be maintained, and the consequences of sloppy or irresponsible behavior could be dire.

Following his public lashing, the young Shaweneiti learned his lesson well. He understood that discipline and unity were the keys to victory, and he never disobeyed orders again. As time went on, he became more and more prominent within the Royal Army. Due to constant association with his father, he gained a knack for strategy, and by the time that he was 20, Shaweneiti was the commander of a company of one hundred men. By age 30, he acted as his father's second-in-command, fighting by his side in the front ranks.

When his father Nakhtibre seized control of Lower Egypt, or at least the parts of it that the king held, one of his first actions was to appoint his son as his heir and his vizier. Shaweneiti knew absolutely nothing about law, politics, and a life in court. His father had kept him sheltered from that for nearly all of his life partly to keep his mind focused on military matters and partly to keep his son safe – the great general knew how dangerous the royal court could be. But now things had changed. His father was *Nesu* now, and that automatically made Shaweneiti a prince of the royal house. What did he know about how to be a prince? What did he know about courtly manners and etiquette? What did he know about how to defend the law and to sit in judgment over others? All he knew was marching and fighting. Being a soldier was easy for him – you go where you're ordered to go, you do what you're ordered to do, and you kill who you're ordered to kill. A soldier's uniform was a more comfortable thing to wear than a royal robe.

King Nebsenre was left alone in the council chamber, looking at the maps and documents, silently planning his strategies in his head, and occasionally scribbling down a few short notes. After a while, he heard footsteps in the hallway, and his son stepped into the room bringing the Canaanite scribe with him. The Canaanite was lighter-skinned compared to the king and the prince. His hands were tied together with cord, his garments were soiled, and he hadn't shaved in several days. He was quite thin, which was odd since the man had claimed to be a scribe, and scribes were usually rather pudgy around the middle due to their sedentary job. The two greyhounds Osiris and Set began ferociously barking at the stranger, snarling and baring their teeth. The man was wide-eyed and his body trembled as he wondered if he had been brought here to be torn apart for the king's amusement.

"Here he is, as you commanded", said Shaweneiti.

"Is he carrying any weapons?" Nebsenre loudly demanded over the noise of the barking dogs.

"The guards searched him when he was taken and found a dagger. They confiscated it".

"Good". The king's eyes then snapped at the two greyhounds. "SHUT UP!" The dogs immediately went quiet and laid down on the floor. Nebsenre then turned once more to the bearded man standing there. "Approach!"

The Canaanite hesitatingly walked towards the king. Nebsenre now defiantly stood in front of the ragged bearded man in his royal splendor, his arms clasped behind his back, chest puffed out, chin held erect. "You are standing before a god! *Nesu* is Horus incarnate, and in the presence of the living god of Egypt, *YOU KNEEL!!!*"

The prisoner immediately dropped to the floor, his gaze averted downwards.

"What's your name? And tell me the truth – I execute liars".

"Seshrab, Your Majesty".

"Your *Divine* Majesty", the king corrected.

"Your Divine Majesty", the man repeated.

"You're a Canaanite, correct?", and Nebsenre began pacing back and forth in front of the kneeling man.

"Yes, Your Divine Majesty".

"Ugh, another one". Nebsenre groaned exasperatingly. "By the gods, nowadays there are more foreigners in Egypt than Egyptians! Whereabouts in Canaan do you come from?"

"I was born in Hebron, Your Divine Majesty".

"How old are you?"

"Twenty-one, Your Divine Majesty".

"A dagger was found upon you. Was your intention murder?"

"No, Your Divine Majesty. It was for self-protection".

"Did you steal it?"

"No, Your Divine Majesty. I bought it at the market in Suez".

"You were also carrying a large amount of gold with you when you were taken. All evidence suggests that you are a criminal, at least a thief, maybe a robber, and possibly a murderer".

"I am none of those things, Your Divine Majesty. I'm a scribe. My business is writing, not robbing".

"Where did you work as a scribe?"

"I served as a scribe for the king of Hebron, Your Divine Majesty".

Nebsenre stopped pacing and snapped to attention. "Why did you leave?"

"I was obliged to, Your Divine Majesty. I fled because I was ordered to falsify records in order to benefit His Majesty. I refused to do so, for it would be dishonest. I was imprisoned and was about to be executed, but I escaped during the night. I fled to Gaza, hoping to find refuge and employment there, only to discover that the king of that city wished to establish an alliance with my former master, and I had to run away again. Some nomads encountered me in the desert and brought me to Sinai. I worked there for four years as an accountant for the turquoise mines. But my old master was still searching for me. So I came here, to seek service under you, Your Divine Majesty, in the hope that if I was one of your palace staff, I would not be sent away somewhere where I would be seized and put to death".

"You certainly are full of yourself to think that you could simply walk up to my palace, ask me for a job, and expect me to give it to you!" Nebsenre thought for a minute, pacing back and forth again. At last he turned to the kneeling man, who had been staring at the ground, afraid to look at Nebsenre in the face. "Worry not, little Asian. I have no love for the Canaanites or their insignificant despots. The trade I have with them is merely a matter of convenience – Egyptian manufactured goods for Canaanite raw materials. I have no intention of forming personal relationships with any of you, and that includes your former master. Can you write hieroglyphs?"

"Yes, Your Divine Majesty".

"How many languages do you speak?"

"I can speak, read, and write in Canaanite, Egyptian, Phoenician, and Akkadian, Your Divine Majesty. I can also speak a little Arabic, but only a few basic words and phrases".

Nebsenre was now genuinely impressed. "You said before that you were employed as an accountant. I take it, therefore, that you are skilled in mathematics?"

"Yes, Your Divine Majesty".

Nebsenre thought for a moment. "Hmm. Yes. I believe you could be very helpful to me, if indeed what you say is true…Very well. I am appointing *you* to be my new chief scribe, subject to me and my son. You will go wherever we go and you will be under our protection. Serve us well, and you will be treated well".

The Canaanite was caught off-guard. He merely wanted a job, any job – he wasn't expecting *this*. "Th-Thank you, Your Divine Majesty".

"Pardon me, father, but what about Imhotep?" asked the prince.

"Can Imhotep speak three foreign languages?"

"No".

"Exactly. This fellow…what's your name again?"

"Seshrab, Your Divine Majesty".

"Seshrab is far too smart to be merely an assistant. Imhotep is no longer my chief scribe. From now on, *the Toad* can be *Seshrab's* assistant".

"I doubt that Imhotep will take the news gracefully that he has been demoted, especially to a foreigner", Shaweneiti commented.

"Imhotep will do what I command him to do or he'll have his damned head cut off!", Nebsenre snapped. He then turned back to Seshrab, who was still kneeling on the floor. "I want you to get to work right away". Then Nebsenre inhaled deeply, and got a cringing look on his face. "You stink of goat urine…Forget what I said. I want you to bathe first. You can work on my records later. *GUARDS!!!*" Nebsenre shouted out.

Immediately, six armed men who had been waiting in the hallway entered the room.

Pointing down to the kneeling man, Nebsenre commanded "Take this man to be cleaned. His stench offends the holy nostrils!"

# CHAPTER 2

*As for myself, I was born as a native of Hebron within the land of Canaan. Having been educated in the temple, I was employed as a scribe shortly after I came to manhood. However, I was obliged to quit my position as the result of an action which was true of heart but mistaken in judgment.*

Seshrab stood naked in the small tub in the palace's wash room while the bath attendants worked on him. The rigorous scrub-down which he received was more aggressive than pleasurable because the Egyptians mixed sand into their soap to act as an abrasive. Afterwards, he had his beard and hair shaved off. Then *kohl*, a dark cosmetic powder, was lined around his eyes, giving him the customary Egyptian "cat eye" look. Finally, he was given a simple linen wrap-kilt and a pair of reed sandals.

"Take him to the king immediately", said the chief bath attendant to the guards posted outside the door.

"Canaan" was not a nation but a geographic region stretching from the Sinai Peninsula halfway up the Asian coast of the Mediterranean Sea. North of Canaan was the land of Phoenicia with its many shipping ports and its forests of highly-coveted cedar trees, and north of that was the land of Amurru.

The Egyptians referred to the Canaanites as *aamu*, or "northerners", but they often had more disparaging things to say about them. To the Egyptians, the Canaanites were, are, and would always be "those wretched Asiatics". One Egyptian text had the following to say about them…

*Behold the wretched Asiatic! He is wretched because of the country that he lives in. It lacks water, it is destitute of trees, and its numerous paths wind through treacherous mountains. He does not dwell in one place, but travels the land from one place to the next. Plagued by want, he wanders the desert on foot. Hunger and starvation propel him to always seek new lands elsewhere. His people have been fighting each other since the time of Horus! Incessantly waging war amongst themselves, they neither conquer*

Canaan was divided into a multitude of small city-states which were constantly at each other's throats, and one of these was Hebron. The city lay nestled within the hills west of the Dead Sea over 3,000 feet above sea level. Much of the landscape below was rocky sandy desert with little hope for agriculture, but the hills were cooler and more fertile. Hebron's main exports were figs and grapes, and the town had significant pottery production in order to ship the fruits and the famed Hebron wine known for its distinct mountain *terrois*. Due to its location astride important travel routes, Hebron was a multi-cultural town consisting not only of native Canaanites, but also Amorites, Kenites, and Hurrians. For this reason, Hebron was sometimes referred to as "the City of the Four Tribes". However, wealthy settlements are always targets, and so Hebron was surrounded by a stone wall measuring fifteen feet tall and ten feet thick to protect it against attack from their jealous and aggressive neighbors.

Among those who profited from Hebron's trade was Seshrab and his family. His father was a prosperous merchant, and Seshrab's two older brothers Danel and Yasib had become members of the family enterprise. Seshrab's father attributed his success in life to his devout faith, for he would regularly offer prayers and sacrifices at the Sacred Grove, a small copse of holy trees located just outside Hebron's walls. When Seshrab was a child, his father took him to the Temple of El, the chief god of the Canaanite pantheon, to learn how to be a scribe – an elite position in Canaanite society. Becoming a scribe was usually step-one in getting higher social and administrative positions, including government officials, priests, and army officers. These positions had their perks, mostly wealth. As the old saying went, *No scribe shall know poverty.*

But Seshrab's father had another reason for sending his son to school. Due to their education and skill, scribes held privileged positions within society, and were therefore exempted from performing some of the more unpleasant tasks which one might be expected to do, including compulsory military service. Men were expected to serve in their leaders' armies during wartime, but scribes were almost always exempt from conscription – their skills were too valuable to risk sending them into battle.

The people of Canaan had good reason to be apprehensive of war now even more so than usual. During the preceding few years, there were reports that the

Amorites, those strange people who lived far to the north who worshiped idols of painted antelope skulls, were growing in power. Like the Canaanites, the Amorites were divided into competing city-states, and they had been very busy developing inventive ways to slaughter each other. The region of Amurru was dominated by two super-blocks: the Kingdom of Yamhad which controlled the north and center, and the Kingdom of Katna which controlled the south. Both nations held sway over the neighboring smaller weaker Amorite city-states which were compelled to serve as vassals. Additionally, there were roving warbands of Amorites who, dissatisfied with life under the rule of others, struck out on their own to establish new warlord states in other parts of western Asia. These were not small roving bands of a dozen or so bandits – these were large foreboding heavily-armed military forces, often numbering in the hundreds or even thousands.

The rumors of the Amorites' growing military power became increasingly alarming as the months went by. There were frequent reports that they had adopted a strange new animal which looked like a donkey, but was larger, stronger, and faster. The Amorites called them "horses", and they had apparently come down from some vast land in the north where these beasts roamed wild. Attached to these "horses" were carts, each carrying a driver and an archer. These were fast mobile archers that could not only shoot from a distance but could outrun anything. The Amorites had picked up the idea from the Ashurians of northern Mesopotamia, who called these war wagons "chariots". The bows which the Amorite archers carried were wonders of technology. Other bows were simple pieces of wood and string, but the Amorites had something better. The mysterious northern nomads from whom the Amorites had obtained their horses also gave the Amorites another gift – the recurved bow. The northern nomads discovered that, by altering the shape of the wood, one could increase the bow's strength, thereby delivering the arrows with more speed, distance, and punch. Even from far distances, the arrows easily pierced through layers of leather and wicker shields; body armor was now obsolete. Amorite foot soldiers were also arming themselves with a weapon that was gaining popularity among the peoples of western Asia. It was developed from the double-handed crescent axe, so-called because of the blade's crescent-moon shape, but at some point someone got the idea to make a smaller version which could be held in just one hand. Although this weapon didn't have a name yet, it would in time be referred to by the Egyptians as the *khopesh*. The thing that made the khopesh and the arrows shot by recurved bows so deadly were not their shape but their composition. Recently, the Amorites had made a fascinating discovery – a new metal, one that was far more durable than the copper which everyone else was using to make tools and weapons. The Amorites discovered that by adding a small quantity of tin to the molten copper, it made the copper stronger. They were not exactly sure how this process happened, but they didn't care. This new composite metal was named "bronze", and the militaristic Amorites immediately saw its potential for war.

Giant donkeys, mounted archers, new weapons, and a super-strong metal that wouldn't break. These rumors seemed fanciful at first, but they were repeated over and over, and the people of Hebron became more and more apprehensive. What if one of those nomadic Amorite warbands penetrated further south and encamped themselves outside their city's gates? Large numbers of Amorites already dwelt within Hebron's walls, and suspicions fell upon them as potential subversives who might throw the gates open to the enemy should they ever arrive, despite the fact that these people had called Hebron their home for generations and were just as keen to keep away invaders as the rest of the city's population.

With the looming threat of conflict, it became imperative for Seshrab's father to get his son into school as quickly as possible. But getting an education was expensive, and most children who were to become scribes came from affluent families. There were no schools in the modern sense of the word. Instead, children were educated at temples by priests. Since only those who were well-to-do could afford to send their children to the temples to be educated, and even fewer could afford private tutors who charged exorbitantly high fees, most classes were small, usually consisting of ten students at most.

Seshrab knew what going to school meant, and he wasn't looking forward to it. Going to school was not simply a matter of getting an education. It was also expected to inculcate obedience, discipline, virtue, piety, and all things deemed worthy and character-building in that society. The children were housed in small dormitories built adjacent to the temple, usually living with the priests, for they were expected to always be on call whenever the priests needed them. In addition to their studies, the students were expected to do menial chores such as washing the floors and preparing the temple for various holy services as well as acting as the priests' servants. Like every small boy, Seshrab bristled at the idea of doing chores. His family had servants waiting on them, but he detested being a servant himself.

"My son", Seshrab's father said to him the day before they walked to the temple, "you must understand that I have enrolled you in this school because I love you and I want to ensure that you have a good future. I want you to get a good education and get a good job, that way you won't be forced to do back-breaking work and get next to nothing in exchange. I have seen the miserable conditions of people in other professions, people who toil all day and are beaten with rods when they do not perform their jobs satisfactorily. The labors of a scribe are those of the mind, not of the muscles. If you master writing, you'll be much better off than the men in all other professions. Surely, there is no career that holds more merit than being a scribe! Remember the old saying – *No scribe shall know poverty*".

Temples were the main buildings in each Canaanite community. Even in small villages, there was always at least one temple. Most were built according to the same basic floorplan, with slight modifications here and there. Every temple had a square or rectangular open courtyard in front of the building's entrance surrounded by a wall. The temple building itself would be square or rectangular in overhead view, constructed with thick walls with no windows, and would be divided into two main rooms. There was a large public hall which was open to everyone, with an altar in the center for the people to offer sacrifices. In the rear was a smaller room, the "inner sanctum", which housed the divine idol, the statue of a god, and was accessible only to the priests. Within the larger temples, there might be smaller side-rooms which were used for storing liturgical objects or as sleeping areas for priests.

On the day that Seshrab entered the temple school, his father gave him a few last-minute pointers to remember: Always wake up early, take your education seriously, don't be disrespectful to the priests, keep your opinions to yourself, don't act like a show-off, stay out of trouble, and make sure that there are witnesses who can testify on your behalf just in case you *do* get into trouble. Seshrab braced himself for his studies and took his place sitting cross-legged on the hard tile floor with about ten other pupils. In a moment, one of the priests' attendants handed Seshrab a thin sheet of slate, a stubby piece of chalk, a small cup of water, and a strip of cloth to wipe the slate clean. Writing in ink wouldn't happen until much later when the students were more adept at it.

Naturally, the first task that the children needed to learn was *how* to write. The priests would draw letters, and the students would practice copying them over and over again, possibly hundreds of times. From there, the priests would progress to simple words, and then to more complex ones, then simple sentences, then complex sentences. The process of learning to write and to read what was written would take several years. Right from the first day, Seshrab was following the priest's instructions, learning to copy the unfamiliar markings over and over again.

There were two languages which all of the students needed to be proficient in: their own native Canaanite as well as Akkadian, a central Mesopotamian language which had become the *lingua franca* of the Near and Middle East. All educated people, including those involved in government and especially those who wanted to be in the diplomatic corps, were expected to know how to speak, read, and write in Akkadian. However, Akkadian was a difficult language to master largely due to the script which was used to write it. The people of Mesopotamia wrote in *cuneiform*, or "wedge-shaped" writing, in which sound syllables were represented by characters composed of complex patterns of short and long triangles. A wooden stylus was split to form a pencil with a triangular cross-section, and the end would be impressed into a tablet made of wet clay, which would then be left out to dry and harden. Due to the immense variation of sounds, there were as many as 800 characters that you needed to memorize.

For centuries, the Canaanites wrote in Mesopotamian-style cuneiform. However, the Phoenicians who lived immediately north of Canaan developed their own unique writing style in which a single sound was represented by a single symbol: A, B, C, and so forth. Under this new system of writing, you needed many more characters to spell out an entire word, but there were fewer characters to memorize – just 25 or so instead of 800. All of this made writing much easier, and this new Phoenician-style script, which was called the "alep-bet" named after the first two letters, was catching on amongst the other peoples of the eastern Mediterranean. The students who were being educated at the temple schools would need to master both Mesopotamian cuneiform *and* the Phoenician alphabet.

Education in the temples was not limited solely to writing and reading – other subjects included mathematics, literature, history, philosophy, and theology. There were no exercise books. Instead, children learned from dictation; the priest would orate, and the children would frantically scribble down what he said while he was saying it. If you wanted to keep up, you needed to write *fast*.

Within his class, Seshrab was only a mediocre student in many respects. He struggled with literature, philosophy, and religion, and he had an especially difficult time with history, as learning all of those names and dates quickly became exasperating. However, there were two areas which he excelled in: mathematics and languages. Numbers came easily to him, and he also had the remarkable talent of picking up languages rather quickly. The other students soon recognized that Seshrab was the class math whiz and language expert, and they often asked him for help when instruction hours were over, that is when they could get any free time; there were hardly any idle moments. They returned the favor by tutoring Seshrab in the areas which he was stumbling through.

The government of Hebron paid close attention to the temple schools to see if there were any talented young men that they could put to use. Seshrab had done everything that was expected, and with the help of his peers he scored high marks in all subjects. Word of his academic acumen quickly spread. In fact, His Majesty King Sihon, the king of Hebron, had learned of Seshrab's remarkable talent and he personally requested that Seshrab be appointed as one of his scribes. Of course, Seshrab's father was absolutely thrilled that his son received such a prestigious position and boasted to everyone that the king himself had hand-picked *his* son above all the others. Seshrab was only 15.

Seshrab soon moved into his new quarters in Hebron's royal palace. Room and board were provided for free to the palace staff, and wages were given in the form of physical products like jewelry, cloth, grain, and salt. As a member of Hebron's upper class, Seshrab had always lived a pampered life, but this was taking luxury to an unheard-of level. He marveled at the opulence of the palace and the splendor of the royal court. *So this is what it means to live like a king*, he thought.

But things were not as glamorous as they outwardly appeared. King Sihon was a very unpleasant person to be around. The man had a violent temper and he often became drunk on Hebron's famed wine. Alcohol and aggressiveness do not mix well, and his servants and subordinates were often severely beaten. Everyone who worked in the palace had to keep on their toes, watching what they said or did, always careful not to upset His Majesty. He was also corrupt, often taking bribes and pocketing taxes for himself. While he and his family lived in luxury, many in Hebron were just barely scraping by.

Seshrab had certainly been aware of the difficulties of "the lower sort" even before he was hired to serve in the palace, but that was simply the way of the world, wasn't it? Some people are fortunate, and some others are less-fortunate, right? Thankfully, he and his family had been one of the fortunate ones. But now, it was strangely different. He was no longer detached from the problems of the poor as he had formerly been because he now realized that he was one of those who reaped the rewards of other people's labors. As a scribe, he was privileged and had a higher standing than others who worked in the king's household. He knew that King Sihon's character left much to be desired, but if Seshrab tried to stand up to him now, he would look like a hypocrite. What did he know of the suffering of the poor? If he was to say "What you are doing is wrong", others would reply, "You had no objections to eating fine food, drinking wine, and sleeping on a soft bed while people outside starved and slept on dirt. How can you protest what the king is doing when you have also had a soft life?" No, nothing could be done, not yet anyway.

Seshrab's temper changed when the state of those who lived in the city became more well-known to him. As a member of the palace staff, Seshrab needed to be on-hand to follow the king's commands, but he was occasionally permitted to leave the palace walls to visit his family. However, while he was outside, he also surreptitiously made inquiries among the common folk. Piece-by-piece, he gradually became more intimately aware of the conditions of the poor. Seshrab was disgusted and horrified. How could he have been so complacent while others had suffered so much? How could he eat his fill and become fat while so many were hungry? He ate less and stopped drinking, but he still felt guilty for not doing more, yet what could he do? When he broached the topic with his father and mother, both told him that they sympathized with the people's plight, but why should they jeopardize their own well-being in order to attempt to bring greater well-being to others? Their family had worked very hard over generations to get where they were now. If Seshrab said or did anything which was a challenge to King Sihon's authority, he could use his royal prerogative to seize possession of the family's property and wealth, leaving them homeless and destitute, and the condition of the poor wouldn't be improved one iota. Furthermore, any criticism could be declared treason, and treason was universally punished by death. "I don't want to see you sent off to the chopping block due to a young man's impassioned sense of morality", said Seshrab's father. "Keep your mouth shut and follow all orders given to you, regardless of how unpleasant they are. This isn't about insensitivity – this is about survival, plain and simple".

Then things got worse. Seshrab had completed the tax assessments for that month when he was informed by the king's chief scribe to go back and re-write the records to show that the people didn't pay enough and that they would have to be taxed more. Of course, His Majesty would keep the extra taxes for himself. All tax assessments had to be signed and verified by the scribe who prepared them, so Seshrab's name would appear on these documents. Previously this had not been a problem, as Seshrab had always been extremely careful to calculate his figures correctly, but now this was different. Now he was being asked to doctor the paperwork and then sign his name to official government tax records which he knew for a fact were blatantly false, and other people would end up suffering for it. This was the last straw, and Seshrab finally mustered up his courage and refused to do as he was ordered. Again, the chief scribe told him to doctor up the records, and again, Seshrab refused. When the chief scribe informed King Sihon about Seshrab's sudden defiance, the king commanded Seshrab to appear before him, and His Majesty personally ordered Seshrab to do what he told him to do. Again, Seshrab refused. Well, one does not defy a king and live to tell about it, so Seshrab was thrown into prison and charged with treason. He was scheduled to be executed the following morning.

Soon afterwards, Seshrab's father was informed about these events. He demanded to speak with his son, and was brought to the palace dungeon under armed guard. The meeting between father and son didn't go well. A flash-flood of hot-tempered words were blasted out, and the situation rapidly deteriorated from there. Seshrab's family begged and pleaded with King Sihon, offering to give him whatever he wished in exchange for their son's freedom and his life, but the king wouldn't listen. The royal ego had been offended, and for this, Seshrab needed to pay. He would die tomorrow.

That night, Seshrab lay awake on the floor of his small cramped cell, staring up at the ceiling. He had been crying and sobbing for hours, his face ached and his stomach was twisted into knots. He had been earnestly praying for a miraculous divine intervention. He begged El, king of Canaan's gods, in a choking strangulated voice to help him, and his prayers got increasingly desperate and frantic with every passing minute, promising to do anything, *anything*, if he could get out of this horrific situation. Hundreds of unpleasant thoughts raced through his mind. He thought about his loving family and how he would never see them again. He thought about the immense sorrow that he had put them all through, and he hated himself for it. He thought of his room and all of his beautiful things. He thought about the happy care-free days of his childhood and longing for those simple days once again. It was too much pain and anguish for a human being to endure. Far too much.

Then he heard footsteps in the dark corridor. One of the guards came to the cell, slid the heavy bolt aside, and opened the door. "Out", was the only word the man uttered.

*NOW?!* He thought horrified. *RIGHT NOW?! I was supposed to have more time, a few hours at least! El, El! Help me! I beg you, do something!*

"Sir, *please*", Seshrab begged, his constricted voice barely able to crack out the words.

"Out", the guard reiterated.

Seshrab cautiously rose up, his whole body shaking, and slowly walked towards the door. He could feel the tears welling up again. Even though the lighting was very dim, he was surprised to see his father standing in the hallway wearing a cloak, with a very worried look on his face. He was holding a second cloak in his arms. But before Seshrab could say anything, his father broke in.

"I was not able to persuade the king to spare you", he said, pulling his son towards the passageway's main door, which led out into the palace hallways while the guard closed and re-locked the now empty cell door, "but my purse had much better luck in persuading your jailer. Quickly put this cloak on, and do not say anything of this to anyone, or it will be all our heads. Remain quiet".

The guard then opened the door to the hallway. The hallway was dark – no torches, no candles, no oil lamps. Good. No light, and no moving shadows to give away their presence. Seshrab's heart was hammering and his stomach was in his throat. He knew that the palace guards patrolled the hallways at night to keep a lookout for intruders or assassins. There was one guard in the hallway, but his back was to the three of them, and he was slowly walking away. The three held their breath, and they prayed that the guard wouldn't suddenly turn around. Thankfully he didn't. He kept walking, but then momentarily paused when he came to a corner. Seshrab's heart nearly stopped from terror. The guard in the hallway poked his head around the corner, checking to see if anybody else was there, then rounded the corner and began to walk down that length of the hallway. He was now out of sight.

"Take off your sandals so he won't hear us", whispered the jailer to Seshrab and his father, and all three of them did so. Then, they stepped out, and the man closed the dungeon door.

The three of them cautiously crept barefoot towards the palace's one and only exit, fearful that they might run into someone around any corner. Then as they were making their way towards the entrance hall, they heard footsteps coming *towards* them from the opposite hallway. A *second* guard. *SHIT.*

The jailer pointed towards the door of the reception room, where guests who wished to have an audience with the king waited until they were admitted into the throne room. He opened the door, but the hinges loudly squeaked when the door moved, and everyone there knew that they had been heard. Seshrab and his father quickly ducked inside.

"*Who's there?!*" a loud voice echoed. Footsteps began to pick up pace.

Thinking quickly, the jailer closed the door with himself still out in the hallway. "Who's that?" he said aloud to the voice in the dark.

"Markot? Is that you?"

"Yes".

The footsteps advanced closer until the palace guard was only a few feet away. The man was carrying a large dagger slung through his belt. "What are you doing?" he asked puzzled.

"I thought I heard someone".

The guard looked at the door to the reception room. "In there?"

"Yes. I just checked it – there's nobody inside".

"You sure?"

"I looked around. Nothing. Maybe it was you I heard before".

The guard seemed unconvinced.

"If you're going to be out here, then I'm going to the kitchen to get a snack before I go back to sleep, alright?" and the jailer walked past the guard down the hall towards the kitchen on the far side of the palace. The guard watched the jailer take a few steps down the hall, and then started making his rounds again. The jailer, who had been slyly looking over his shoulder, stopped and watched the guard walking down the hallway. He then silently made his way back to the door of the reception room. The jailer waited until the patrolman was almost around the corner, still within earshot, and then re-opened the door to the reception room as loudly as he could with a sharp wooden *creak*.

Of course, that immediately grabbed the guard's attention and he spun around to see what was happening.

"Just double-checking – you know, just to be safe", and he went inside. Almost immediately, he saw Seshrab and his dad huddled in a corner, petrified with terror. The jailer motioned at the two of them to stay down and stay quiet. Then he walked out. "Yeah, there's nobody here". But he didn't close the door.

The guard huffed. "Don't make too much noise or you'll wake everyone in the whole place".

The jailer smiled. "Quiet as a mouse. I'll just get something to munch, and then I'll go back to bed".

The guard moved off, rounded the corner and passed out of sight.

The jailer immediately bolted back into the room and hauled Seshrab and his father off of the floor. "Quick, move before he or his friend show up!", he hissed out. They whisked themselves out of the room. A wave of relief momentarily swept over Seshrab, believing that the worst was over.

They could not go out of the palace via the direct route through the main door – too many guards. Instead, the jailer led Seshrab and his father up the stairs onto the palace roof. King Sihon's palace was grand, but it was only one floor tall. In front of the main building was a rectangular courtyard surrounded by a stone wall, with a large gate in the middle.

The jailer motioned for the two of them to follow him. They quickly ran along the perimeter wall until they got to a corner, out of sight of the guards which stood in front of the main gate. The perimeter wall measured ten feet tall.

"Take off your cloaks and tie them together" said the jailer. "I will lower you down to the ground outside. Do not take the main road back to your house, because the guards will see you. Go the long way around. Good luck".

And it was done. First Seshrab was cautiously lowered down, and then his father after him. The jailer then waved them off. They had done it.

The two of them raced back home as fast as they could through Hebron's narrow alley-like streets, taking a long circuitous route to avoid being spotted on the main highway. Then, they arrived back at their house.

The door swung open and the two of them barged inside. Seshrab's mother, who had been awake all night along with her two other sons, let out a sudden startled yelp but her husband immediately shoved his hand over her mouth. "Keep quiet woman, or else you will be the death of us all!" he hissed at her. Then he grabbed a burlap sack and flung it to Seshrab. "Grab everything that you can carry", his father said urgently. "Never mind about your idle nick-nacks! Take only what is necessary – food, water skins, your spare pair of sandals, anything that will be of practical use. Anything that you will need to survive".

"Father, why can't we just hide Seshrab here in the cellar or the attic?" asked his older brother Yasib.

"Because, my lovely simple son, that is the *first place that they'll look for him!* As long as he's still inside the city, he's in danger, and furthermore so are we all if they catch him here. Not only will Seshrab be put to death for treason, but likewise we will be executed for harboring a traitor and a fugitive! We cannot keep him hidden here forever. His only chance is to get out of the city and run as far away from here as possible, where Sihon's reach will not find him".

Seshrab had frantically gathered up whatever he thought was useful. "I'm ready".

"Oh, El, why did this have to happen to us?" sobbed his mother.

"There are only a few hours before sunrise", said his father. "There is no time for long eloquently-worded farewell speeches. You must know that this may be the last we shall see each other. I am sorry for the things which I said to you earlier – I hope you can forgive me for it. Now you must flee if you are to live, *my beautiful darling boy!*" and at this Seshrab's father broke down as he flung his arms around his beloved child. The rest of the family instantly piled their embraces upon him. There was heard nothing but wrenching sobs from everyone there. "Now, run, my son. Run away from here and never come back. I love you so much".

Tears streamed down Seshrab's face as he knew full-well that he would be leaving forever. He opened the door to his lovely home, stepped out into Hebron's dark streets with the satchel hauled over one shoulder, and ran for his life.

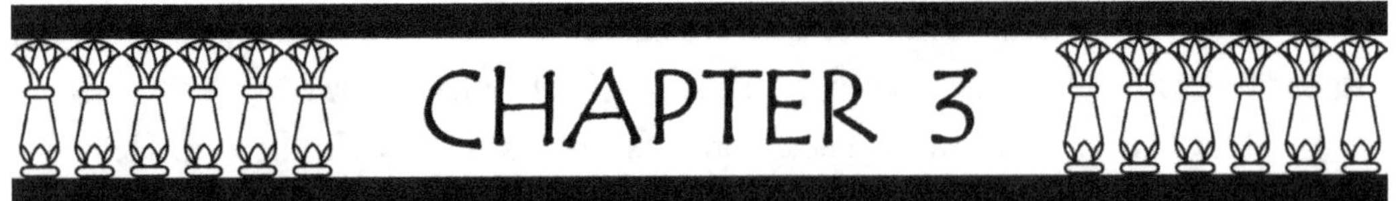

# CHAPTER 3

*After my departure from the service of the king of Hebron, I underwent many trials and misfortunes, though in doing so, I was given a much greater education than any knowledge I received from the temple school. I have endeavored to profit from these lessons as much as I could.*

Seshrab only had a few hours before sunrise. He needed to get as far away from Hebron as possible, so he ran, he ran so hard and so fast that he nearly expired from utter physical exhaustion. By the time that dawn broke, Seshrab was miles away, but that didn't stop King Sihon from sending out his men to look for him. They didn't find him, though. The wind had blown away his tracks in the sand.

Seshrab was now a fugitive, a wanted man, all because he wanted to be honest. His father had said that usually in life the righteous get punished and the wicked get rewarded. Now, he understood what that meant.

Seshrab had absolutely no idea where he was going. He had to avoid the major roads – the fugitive catchers would surely look there first. He couldn't go into the neighboring villages either. The king may have put a price on his head, and the people of those places may be on the lookout for someone fitting his description. Many of them were poor, and if they caught him, they would surely hand him over in exchange for a reward. Seshrab also couldn't flee to any of the city-states that Hebron had any relations with. In his worried panic-ridden state, Seshrab tried very hard to remember all of the places that had some kind of arrangements with Hebron, and he checked them off of his mental list of potential refuges.

Seshrab passed a very unhappy evening that first night, crying as he shivered in the chilly night air. He spent many days in the countryside, living off of the meager provisions that he had taken, or else stealing from isolated farms or whatever wild animals he could catch, usually rats and lizards.

Now Seshrab knew the meaning of the word "suffering". He was always hungry, always thirsty, always tired. He mostly travelled during the night when it was cooler, and would rest during the day. He would try to find rock outcrops where he could sleep in the shade, pulling what was left of his clothes over his head to keep the sun off of him, but sometimes he had to sleep out in the open, which was dangerous.

After what seemed like an eternity of travelling, and being just barely alive, he smelled salty air, and saw a sight in the distance – a city.

Seshrab's clothes were in filthy shreds as he approached the fortified walls on the coast of the Mediterranean. The air was pungent with the smell of salt water and resounded with the harsh squawking of sea birds. Seshrab didn't know which city this was. Even so, he was reasonably confident that he would be safe here. As far as he was aware, Hebron didn't have any relations with any of the seacoast settlements. Using what was left of his strength, the weakened Seshrab approached the gates. By this point he had exhausted his provisions and his satchel was empty. "Water", Seshrab asked the gate guards in a dry rasping voice. "I need water".

The two guards wore leather body armor and carried spears and large round wicker shields decorated with concentric rings of copper studs. One of them handed Seshrab a small leather pouch filled with water, while the other guard continued to point his spear at Seshrab's head. Seshrab greedily drank it all, careful not to spill even a single drop onto the ground, and then graciously handed the bottle back. "Thank you. What city is this?" he asked.

"This is Gaza", the guard replied. "Do you not know this land? What nation do you come from?"

Seshrab was about to say "Hebron", but just before he did so, he became hesitant and decided it would be better to give them some false information about his identity, just in case. *Think fast*, thought Seshrab, even though his head was spinning with hunger. "I come from Jericho. I had a quarrel with my wife, and she kicked me out of the house and took away all of my money. I have no living relatives, and all of my friends are away fighting in the army. I have nowhere to go. I've been wandering in the desert for what seems like forever. Please, may I enter your city? I am very hungry, I need a place to stay, and I need work".

One of the guards was skeptical, but the other took pity on him. "You poor fellow", he said. "I always maintained that women are mankind's worst enemies. You have been wronged too much. Come, have this piece of bread. I know it isn't much, but you can have it".

Seshrab thanked the guard for his generosity and quickly gobbled down the bread.

"What is your name, stranger?"

"Saul", Seshrab lied.

"I doubt that you will find much work here, Saul of Jericho, but you are free to beg in the streets".

Seshrab thanked the man, and entered through the city's monolithic gate.

The skeptical guard looked at his comrade. "You actually trust this stranger?"

"Not for a second", he replied.

And so, Seshrab now lived the lowly life of a street beggar. He didn't like the idea of staying in Gaza. Port-cities like this tended to be dangerous places, being havens for pirates and criminals on the run from the law…like himself. However, at least while he was here, he wouldn't be wandering in the countryside anymore, hungry and thirsty and with little or no shelter. He could beg for scraps, he could root through garbage, and he could take shelter from the rain and the wind. It truly was a miserable existence, but it was still better than death. The other beggars were wary of him, viewing him as competition. Some of them were professional beggars who were too lazy to do work. Others were unlucky souls who had fallen on hard times and were now forced to live on the streets.

Seshrab had no idea what he was doing, and he wasn't at all street-smart. At first, he tried to be polite to the passers-by. "Excuse me, kind sir, but could you spare a few crumbs for a hungry man?" Mostly he was ignored. "Pardon me, gentleman, but could you please lend a few grains to a hungry man who has had some bad luck?" Nothing seemed to work. Either they walked by him, not even making eye contact, or they cursed him for being a parasite or sponge, living off of others' hard work while he did nothing but hold out his hand. One fellow even spat on him!

Seshrab knew that he needed to find work in order to get anywhere, but what could he do? All he knew was writing, and if he ever revealed himself to be a scribe, he might get caught. Most likely, he'd have to get a job scrubbing floors or cleaning out shit pots. He asked around, but no one would give him any encouragement no matter how much he tried to convince them of his honesty and sincerity. He was even threatened a few times.

Seshrab started thinking that he should have just done what his king had told him to do rather than resist him. *I could be back in the palace right now,* thought Seshrab, *in my little room that I shared with the other scribes, drinking wine and eating figs, and looking over the monthly tax assessments. Now look at where you are! You should have done what the king told you to do, and not question it. You could worry about the wrath of El later.*

Seshrab scrounged and scraped in the gutters of Gaza for two months. Then one day, while Seshrab was making his daily inquiry about finding employment, there was heard a great cry. "Stop! Stop that man! Thief! Thief!"

Seshrab saw a man, a beggar that he knew, fleeing through the streets clutching a gold necklace. Instinctively, Seshrab tackled him to the ground and wrested the necklace from the man's grip. The criminal bolted off amidst the crowds. Not long afterwards, six soldiers armed with spears and clubs rushed forward. Seshrab recognized two of them – the two gate guards that he met when he first came to Gaza. But when they saw him, their reaction was nothing like what he expected. One of them punched Seshrab in the guts with the butt-end of his spear which brought him down to his knees wincing in pain. The other soon after struck him on the back of the head with his mace. Everything abruptly went black – he was out before his body even hit the ground.

Not long after that, a fat richly-dressed bearded man hurried to the place where the guards were gathering around Seshrab's body.

"Your Majesty, we captured the criminal. See? He still holds your necklace!" The soldier reached down and pulled the gold necklace from Seshrab's hands, who was now lying unconscious on his belly in the crowded street, flooding with onlookers. The back of his head was bleeding.

"Take him to the prison immediately! He'll be hanged for this!" commanded the Gazan king.

The two guards picked up the man, but then the king saw Seshrab's face. "Wait! This isn't the man who stole my necklace! This is someone else".

"But, Your Majesty, the proof of his theft is there", and the guard pointed to the necklace.

"I saw the thief's face, soldier. This is not the man in question. This fellow must have beaten off the rogue and took the necklace away from him. Who is he?"

"I recognize him, Your Majesty", said one of the guards. "He came here about two months ago. Something about his wife, I can't remember exactly". The second man had nothing to add to it.

The king turned to the crowd that had gathered around to see what was happening. "Does anyone here know who this man is?"

"I know him, Your Majesty", said one of the beggars, approaching, bowing low. "His name is Saul of Jericho, a beggar like myself".

"And no doubt lusty for any shiny trinket that pleases his eye", said the king. "He probably fought the thief not to save my necklace but to steal it for himself. We'll soon know more of this. Take him to the prison. We'll interrogate him there".

Seshrab was brought to a cell, still unconscious, and laid out on the floor. Then, one of the two guards picked up a bucket of seawater and dumped it onto the unconscious man. Seshrab groggily woke up.

"Are you feeling alright?" the other guard asked.

"My head hurts", came the faint weary reply.

"Thank Nasib for that. He's the one that cracked you over the head with his club", turning to the guard, "and after you gave him your water, too!"

"Oh, was that me?" he asked, as he put down the bucket.

"Yes, don't you remember? He showed up here, he told you some damn sob story, and you gave him your water".

"Oh yes, that's right".

"Your memory's terrible".

"Shut up, Maok".

Seshrab groaned. He was dizzy, light-headed, he had a terrible headache, and felt nauseous. The room was spinning around him, and the floor heaved up and down like the surface of the ocean.

"Can you stand up?" asked Nasib.

"No, I…I feel sick".

"Your smell makes everyone sick", commented Maok. "If you're going to throw up, you'd better do it now. The three of us are going to be here for a while, thanks to you".

"Now, tell us everything about yourself and what you're really doing here, Saul of Jericho, if that is in fact who you are", said Nasib.

"My name *is* Saul of Jericho", maintained Seshrab.

"Where did you get the necklace?"

"Sirs, please", asked Seshrab wearily. "Could I not talk now? I feel dizzy".

"I don't care *how* you feel. Now, where did you get the necklace?"

At first, Seshrab didn't understand the question. He wasn't wearing any necklace. Then he remembered. "I took it".

"Ha, you admit you stole it!" exclaimed Nasib, pointing at him.

"No, I took it. One of the beggars stole it, and I wanted to give it back to its owner. So I beat him off and took the necklace from him".

"Do you really expect us to believe that? That you would give back a necklace worth twenty cows? You're either lying or have no concept of value".

"I'm telling you the truth. Whether or not you believe me is another matter".

Maok punched Seshrah hard in the face and knocked him to the floor. He could taste blood in his mouth.

"Easy!" said Nasib. "He just woke up. I don't want him knocked out again, or we'll be stuck here all day!"

"What do you think?" asked Maok.

Nasib scratched his chin. "I'm not sure. He may be telling the truth about the king's necklace, but I still have a feeling he's hiding something".

That grabbed Seshrab's attention. "A king's necklace?" he asked. "That necklace belonged to a king?"

"You look surprised", said Maok. "Didn't you know that you stole from the king of Gaza?"

"No I didn't. Er, I mean that I didn't know that the necklace belonged to a king".

"You just thought he was a nobleman, right? Some prince or aristocrat?"

"No! I didn't steal from anyone! I didn't even see who he was! I was asking about finding work when I heard someone shouting to catch a thief. I saw him, saw what he was carrying, stopped him, and grabbed the necklace out of his hands. I wanted to give it back to its owner, and maybe get a reward for my kindness".

Nasib looked at Maok. "His Majesty did, after all, say that this was not the man who stole his necklace. Do you believe what this fellow says?"

Maok thought for a second, and nodded. "I think I do".

"The king will probably want to see you, Saul. He'll want to hear your story from your own lips".

Meanwhile in Gaza's royal palace…

"This is what I get for going out of the palace!" scoffed the king to his councilors. "Thieves! A thief robs me in broad daylight in front of everyone! What does that say about my city?! And moreover, what does that say about the power of the king? I should be feared and respected, but instead, I'm treated like a buffoon by pick-pockets and street hoodlums!"

Just then, there was a knock on the door. The attending guard opened it, and Maok and Nasib entered with Seshrab. "We have questioned the prisoner, Your Majesty", said Nasib. "He denies stealing your necklace for himself, and says that he wished to return it to its rightful owner. We believe that he is telling the truth".

"Do you, indeed? What was his name, again?"

"Saul of Jericho, Your Majesty", said Maok.

"Let him approach".

Seshrab slowly walked forward, bowing low. He still felt dizzy. He hoped to El that he wouldn't suddenly throw up in the king's presence.

"Well, well. You did me a good turn, Saul of Jericho. It is a comfort to know that in a city of thieves, there are still a few honest people such as yourself. I thank you for retrieving my stolen necklace".

"It was my pleasure, Your Majesty", replied Seshrab.

"Since I have been told that you intended to give the necklace back to its owner rather than pocket it yourself, I shall reward you for your virtue. Here", and the king took off a ring from one of his fat fingers and held it out. "Take it".

But Seshrab shook his head. "No, Your Majesty. I do not want any gifts. I want something else, something aside from jewels".

The councilors murmured to themselves. One of them said, "He dares to defy a king? He dares refuse him?"

The king looked curious. "You turn away a ring of solid gold? Other men would have eagerly taken it. If it's not treasure that you want, then what?"

"Work, Your Majesty. I want a job, and to be paid a regular wage. Is it possible that you could have some use for me?"

The councilors loudly guffawed and snorted at the preposterous request.

"For you, an ordinary street beggar?" asked the Gazan king. "Well, I suppose that all depends. What can you do?"

*Do I dare tell him?*, thought Seshrab. *Do I dare tell him that I'm educated? Do I tell him that I can read and write?* "I can cook, Your Majesty". In reality, Seshrab knew absolutely nothing about cooking. Back home in Hebron, his family's servants did all of the cooking for him.

"I already have a cook", replied the king, "and he's very good. I have no intention of releasing him".

Plan B. "I can be a house servant, Your Majesty. I can clean".

"I already have over a hundred servants working for me, waiting on me hand and foot. I have cooks, cleaners, messengers, and guards. I have washers, tailors, jewelers, and craftsmen of all sorts employed in my service. If you wish to work for me, man, you're going to have to prove that you are essential to me. I think you would be much better off taking the ring, thanking me for the reward, and leaving. It doesn't appear that there is anything that you can do that one of my other attendants can't".

Seshrab was getting desperate. No one in Gaza would give him work. He even tried to join the military, but the soldiers turned him away, believing that he was a spy. Seshrab realized that he had no choice, and so, biting his lip, he uttered "I can read and write".

The Gazan king looked aghast. Even the king himself didn't know how to read and write – he had *people* to handle that sort of thing. "You're lying! You dare lie to a king?! Straight to my face!!! How can you, a filth-covered street beggar, know how to read and write?"

"I learned, Your Majesty", came the blunt but vague response.

"Really?" asked the king, indignant and confrontational. "You there!" he called out to Maok and Nasib. "Fetch me a skin, some coloring, and a pen to write with".

The two men bowed and left. After a few minutes they returned carrying a large leather sheep skin, a bottle of juniper berry juice, and a feather. The two men laid the items on the ground next to Seshrab.

The king pointed to the articles. "You say you are a scribe, that you know how to read and write? Show me. Write my name".

Uh-oh. Seshrab had been living in Gaza for two whole months and never learned what the king's name was. He had never heard it or had any inclination to learn it – he had been focusing on other priorities. With a great deal of embarrassment and hesitation, he asked, "What *is* your name, Your Majesty?"

The king looked completely insulted. Turning aside to his councilors, "What is my name? Of all the impertinence! How long have you been in my city?"

"Two months, Your Majesty".

"Two months, and in all this time, you never once bothered to learn who is master here?! I am the king!!! I am Ariyak, King of Gaza, and you'd better damn well not forget it, peasant!"

"No, of course not, Your Majesty".

"Write my name!" the king commanded, pointing to the leather skin.

Seshrab sat cross-legged on the floor, dipped the feather into the bottle of berry juice, and started scratching the king's name onto the back of the leather skin. When he was done, he held up the skin that had strange-looking symbols on it.

ARIYAK.

There was a great deal of murmuring and muttering in the royal hall when Seshrab presented the skin with the king's name written on it. "Your Majesty", began one of the councilors, "you do not know what these strange markings mean. They could be nothing more than nonsensical scribbling. There's no way that you can know if these symbols really do spell out your name".

"Can you write fast?" the king asked Seshrab.

"Yes, Your Majesty. Very fast". Studying in Hebron's temple school had forced Seshrab to learn this skill.

"Good. I shall dictate a message and you are to write it out word-for-word exactly as I say it". As the king began orating, Seshrab's hand flew across the leather canvas, every now and then dipping the needle into the berry juice. After what seemed like a considerable amount of time, the king finished and the leather skin was covered in purplish-black scrawl.

"Now", King Ariyak said, turning to his councilors, "send for my secretary".

The royal secretary was one of the few men in the palace who knew how to read and write. He would be the best to judge if Seshrab's story was true. After a minute or so, he came through the door.

"You summoned me, Your Majesty?"

"Yes", replied the king, and he pointed to the leather skin which Seshrab had just written all over. "Read that, out loud so that all can hear you".

And he did. To everyone's astonishment, it was word-for-word exactly as the king had orated.

King Ariyak turned to his doubtful advisor. "Does that satisfy your doubts, councilor? Even I don't know how to do what he has done". The king, astonished and amazed, turned to Seshrab, pointing at him. "This beggar, this filthy vermin, this ignominious detestable insect, this walking talking stinking mis-shapen mountain of fetid festering seagull excrement, knows more than the king! This is no ordinary common peasant – this man has brains! This is a man of intelligence and education. Your family must be rich in order to give you such learning. Did they send you away to school? Or did they hire tutors to teach you?"

"I learned on my own, Your Majesty", Seshrab lied.

"By the gods, to do such a feat you must surely be the most intelligent man in my entire kingdom, and you're begging in the streets? No, no! This will not do! Saul of Jericho, you are to be taken into my service. I shall make use of your skills and your intellect as much as you are able to furnish them. It is my royal decree that you are to be made one of my scribes. Furthermore, it is my wish that you use your knowledge and ability to teach me how to read and write so that I may learn what you yourself have learned. If a peasant can learn how to read and write without anyone's help, then surely a king cannot do any worse". He turned to his councilors. "Besides, no man should be smarter than the king".

And so it passed that Seshrab was made the king's personal writing tutor. The king's learning was slow and frustrating, and his lack of progress showed itself in flaring bouts of temper, but Seshrab had the patience of a teacher. King Ariyak realized this, and decreed that Saul of Jericho, as he was known, was to be a teacher for a class of would-be scribes, and also serve as the tutor to the king's three children, teaching them how to read and write plus whatever other useful information that he could impart. Seshrab wasted no time teaching his little pupils not only basic penmanship, but teaching them about math, literature, philosophy, history, mythology, and whatever else he could think of. The king was highly pleased with all of this, and Seshrab became a man of considerable importance within the royal court. He was treated very well and every luxury was placed at his feet. People smiled at him and were friendly with him. As other courtiers passed Seshrab in the palace corridors, they bowed slightly and addressed him courteously. Things appeared to finally be going his way.

All went well for about a year until Seshrab heard something that greatly disturbed him. King Ariyak received a visitor – King Sihon of Hebron.

"Welcome, welcome, noble liege to my house!" the king exclaimed holding open his arms, embracing the man.

Seshrab was passing by in the hallway when he distinctly heard King Sihon's voice. He could *never* forget that voice. It stopped him dead in his tracks and made his blood freeze. *Oh no, not him. Here? Why is he here? Has he found out about me?* Seshrab eavesdropped on the two monarchs' conversation, and all of his happiness instantly drained out of his body like a flood pouring out of a busted dam. Seshrab had served very faithfully and ably as a teacher, but his educational duties had left him no time to attend to other matters. Affairs of state were handed off to other scribes in the palace, and matters of the highest importance were given exclusively to the king's chief scribe and personal secretary. Seshrab was utterly ignorant of all of the political wheelings and dealings which King Ariyak conducted, and one of these involved establishing alliances and trade arrangements with other city-states. And that was why the king of Hebron, the violent alcoholic corrupt greedy man who wanted to have Seshrab executed, was here. Negotiations between Hebron and Gaza had been going on for several weeks, but Seshrab knew nothing about it. As part of the process, King Sihon had come to Gaza to meet with King Ariyak in person in order to address various matters face-to-face.

From what Seshrab could overhear, King Sihon had come here strictly on business, and he didn't seem to be interested in making inquiries about Seshrab's whereabouts. Nevertheless, his presence here and his close association with the king of Gaza put Seshrab in mortal danger. He had no choice but to leave. *Oh no, it can't be! Things were going so well!*, thought Seshrab. *I must be cursed. That's the only explanation. I must be cursed.*

Throughout the rest of that day, Seshrab took extreme care to avoid being seen or heard by King Sihon under any circumstances. Then, without warning or explanation, Seshrab fled the palace during the night, but not before he left a small note in his room addressed to King Ariyak, thanking him for his immense kindness, that he would never forget his generosity or the respect that the king had shown to him, and expressed that it was his fondest wish that the king's three children should be healthy and intelligent and that His Majesty should have a long and prosperous reign. The note, however, gave no word as to why Seshrab left. He carefully and cautiously made his way out of the palace and out of the city, once again towards an unknown fate.

Seshrab briefly considered fleeing north to one of the other coastal city-states such as Michal, Jaffa, Ash-Dod, or Ash-Kelon, but those were the most obvious places that he might run too, and surely those would be the first places that King Sihon would check. No, the only way that any pursuers might lose his trail was if Seshrab fled somewhere they were certain that no sane man would ever go – deep into the Negev Desert, which lay to the south on the border of Canaan and Arabia. Nobody in Canaan thought of actually going *into* that immense expanse of rock and sand, not unless they wanted to die.

Seshrab wandered through the desert, but this time, there was no food to sustain him and no water to drink. After days of travelling through the heaving undulating dunes, he lost all of his sense and collapsed onto the sand. Everything went black.

Seshrab awoke sometime later to the sounds of a strange language. He slowly opened his eyes and found that he was lying on a rug in a tent. Seated nearby were several men dressed in long ornately-patterned robes, their faces covered with veils, only their eyes showing. They were speaking to each other in some unknown tongue. Seshrab correctly assumed who they were – desert nomads, Arabs from the south. He was in a Bedouin camp. Some wanderers must have spotted him and rescued him from the sand.

The Arabs in the tent now saw that Seshrab had awakened, and this caused a great deal of fuss and commotion. One man tried to talk to him, but Seshrab didn't understand a single word of Arabic. "I'm sorry, but I don't speak your language". His voice was dry and hoarse.

When he said that, the men began chatting to each other, as though surprised that this stranger could even talk at all. "You from Canaan?" one of them asked brokenly.

Seshrab's eyes opened wide. "You can speak Canaanite?"

The Arab took off his veil, revealing the characteristic mushroom-style haircut that all Arab men had in those days. He had dark leather-like skin tight from exposure to the sun with clear bone structure, very prominent cheek bones, and heavy sleepy-looking eyelids that gave him a drowsy appearance. "Some words", he replied in his thick Arabic accent. "Who you?"

Seshrab was about to say "Saul of Jericho", since he had been using that name so often it was almost instinctual, but now he realized that he needed to use a new identity, just in case these Bedouins knew of the absence of a man by that name. On the whole, Canaanites were wary of Arabs. Seshrab might have a price on his head, and he had heard stories that Arabs were very greedy people who would slit anyone's throat for a profit. "I am Zacharias of Lakish", he replied. He had to remember that name from now on. "Where am I?"

"Here", came the matter-of-fact reply.

"No, I mean where are we located?"

"Forty miles south of Gaza", the Arab answered. "You almost dead. We find you, bring you here". He held out a plate of palm dates and a cup of goat milk. "Food?"

Seshrab couldn't restrain himself. He immediately gobbled down all of the dates, pausing only to spit out the large seeds, and greedily guzzled down the milk. The Arabs called outside to their comrades, who were tending to their donkeys, probably telling them to bring more food for the hungry stranger.

"Why you in sand? Lost?"

"No", Seshrab answered. "Someone wanted to kill me, and I ran away from him".

"Man no kill, desert will", came the rather dark response from the masked Bedouin. "Where you go?"

Seshrab hadn't thought of that – he had *no idea* where he wanted to go. He was just running. It seemed that so much of his life was unplanned, living from one day to the next with absolutely no thought of the future. "Away from here".

The man then conferred with his fellows. "We go to Sinai. You come".

Seshrab gave a weak tired smile.

Seshrab quickly became friends with the Bedouin nomads. Along the journey southwards, their donkeys carried their supplies and tents while they walked in front, pulling them with reins. They travelled mostly by night, avoiding the hot desert sun, and sleeping during the day inside their tents. Seshrab found their navigation skills to be absolutely amazing. The desert looked all the same to him, just miles and miles of sand and rock, but somehow these nomads knew exactly which routes to take, as if they were travelling on invisible roads known only to them.

Seshrab didn't know how long this journey was going to take – he might be in the Bedouins' company for some time. He felt that it would be good to pick up some Arabic along the trip so that he and his companions could communicate better. So, the man who he had spoken to earlier coached him through some basic words and phrases. As they made their way across the sand dunes, his impromptu tutor put him through his lessons.

"Now, let us try it once more", he began. "Hello".

"Hello", responded Seshrab. *"Ahlen la sahlen"*.

"No, no – *Ahlen WA sahlen*".

"Sorry. *Ahlen wa sahlen*".

"Again".

"Hello. *Ahlen wa sahlen*".

"Good. Now, goodbye".

"Goodbye. *Ma'assalama*".

"Say your name. 'My name is Zacharias'".

*"Ismy Zacharias"*.

"Good! Very good!"

After a long journey, they reached a large bustling port-city on the tip of the Eastern Tongue of the Red Sea. "That is Ezion-Geber", one of them said to Seshrab, pointing to the city that lay before them. "The gateway to Sinai and the sea". It was here that Seshrab parted with his Arab friends. The Bedouins were sorry to see Seshrab leave; they enjoyed his company. Seshrab was tempted to stay with them, but he was not suited to the life of a nomadic wanderer, going wherever the desert wind took you. He liked having roots.

The southern Canaanites spoke in a distinctive accent which was more "hocky" than the mid-lands accent that Seshrab spoke with, probably due to their increased contact with the Arabs to the south. The people of Ezion-Geber, in particular, had a very thick accent, sounding like a peculiar mixture of Canaanite and Arabic, which Seshrab found difficult to understand.

Seshrab made no secret when he arrived in Ezion-Geber that he was an educated man. He didn't want to spend any more time as a street beggar. He had experienced enough of that hard life on the streets of Gaza for two months, and that was far too long. He inquired about finding work, and to his surprise, he immediately found it. An accountant was needed for the turquoise mines to the southwest, and being a scribe who had been educated in mathematics, he was admirably qualified. Seshrab took the job right away, and boarded ship for Sinai.

# CHAPTER 4



*After departing from my home, I travelled throughout a great portion of the land. I dwelt for a time within the kingdom of Gaza, which stands upon the shore of the western sea, where I ascended from low to high, and became acquainted with every level of society. Afterwards, I travelled the desert with the sand-roaming nomads who dwell in tents and have no roofs to cover themselves or have fields to plow, and who are perhaps the freest of all men. Thereupon I came to the southern city of Ezion-Geber, which stands upon the Red Sea, and soon after came to the barren waste of Sinai, where I made myself useful as best as I was able.*

Sinai was a hard harsh place, a barren wasteland devoid of food and water. However, this vast abyss of sand and rock concealed underground treasure: copper and turquoise. For centuries, people have burrowed into the hard stony ground to extract these prized possessions. The great Egyptian king Sneferu, who had lived almost a thousand years earlier, had established the first turquoise mining operations within the Sinai Peninsula. Since then, turquoise mining had become big business for the Egyptians. Turquoise was a highly-valued luxury good, and the Egyptian upper class couldn't get enough of it. However, they hardly ever gave any thought to the people who chiseled these sky-blue stones out of the solid rock. Mining was hard dangerous work, and it was not unheard of for people to be crushed to death in cave-ins or asphyxiated from lack of oxygen. For the unfortunate souls who labored here, swinging their shovels and pick-axes under the beating heat of the sun, or those who went below into the dark with their hammers and chisels, their lives were often miserable and short.

A week after Seshrab arrived in the port-city of Ezion-Geber, a transport ship pulled ashore on the southwestern coast of the Sinai Peninsula. Seshrab stepped down the gangway onto the sandy beach, hauling a satchel over one shoulder, and took a few moments to survey his surroundings. A small ring-shaped fort stood near the beach to guard the port against attack. There was a well-worn path leading into the interior of the country, and standing beside the road was a stone marker. On the top, inscribed in Canaanite letters, were the words MARKHA PORT OF THE MENTIU. Underneath this, the stele was inscribed in a language that Seshrab couldn't understand – blocks, circles, birds, wiggly lines, and other things.

Seshrab was surprised to see many darker-skinned people alongside the Canaanite laborers, although he had no idea what sort of people they were. Perhaps they were Arabs, which was unlikely, or maybe they were Egyptians, whom Seshrab had heard about, but he couldn't be sure – he had never actually *seen* an Egyptian. There was a person on the beach, a red-skinned wiry man who was pointing and giving a lot of directions to various orderlies – the port-master. He was barking out commands in a strange language that Seshrab had never heard before. It wasn't Canaanite or Arabic – it was something else. Possibly the same language that those strange symbols on the stele represented. This fellow eventually caught sight of Seshrab standing there, confusedly looking around, not knowing what to do. The port-master momentarily took himself away from his duties and walked towards this peculiar stranger, who had clearly never been here before. "*Iw tenem tjem?*" he asked directly.

Seshrab knew Canaanite, Phoenician, and Akkadian fluently and he also knew a small smattering of Arabic, but he didn't understand what this person had just said to him. "I'm sorry, but I don't understand you", Seshrab responded, shaking his head puzzled.

"Are you lost?", responded the man, now speaking in Canaanite.

"I'm looking for the turquoise mine".

"Which one? There are several here".

"Uh, the one called 'the Mountain of Hathor'".

"That way", and he pointed up the path. "Go along the path, and bear to the right. It's twenty miles to Hathor's Mountain, but there are rest stops along the way".

"Thanks".

"This is your first time to Port Markha, yes?"

"Yes it is", replied Seshrab.

"Then you have never seen an Egyptian before?"

"No. Never".

"You can go with them", the port-master said, now pointing towards some unfortunate haggardly-looking people with the same red skin as himself. "Those are Egyptians", the port-master explained to him. "They're going to the mines… poor beasts". And then the port-master departed back to his former place to stand and survey the loading and unloading of cargo and passengers.

The mine at Hathor's Mountain was deep within the desolate rocky craggy interior, and there was only a thin winding well-worn path to indicate the way. Finally after an arduous two-day journey, Seshrab arrived at his destination, and he looked around at his new home – the Hathor's Mountain turquoise mine.

His first impression of the place was that it looked like a nest of ants that had been kicked open. Dozens of filthy dirt-covered people milled about, all of them very frail and skinny with sunken lifeless eyes, thin scrawny arms and legs, exposed ribs, and emaciated sunken bellies. Walking about nearly naked, their only article of clothing was a loin cloth which barely covered their privates. Sweeping up the valley, the hillside was festooned with a vast labyrinthine warren of tunnels. Dingy canvas tents of various sizes were scattered helter-skelter over the area, while nearby were innumerable crudely-built stone huts which served as sleeping quarters for the workers. At the top of the mountain stood a small temple dedicated to the Egyptian goddess Hathor which had been erected for the miners to worship at, named "Temple of Our Lady of Turquoise".

Curiously, there was an open wooden door frame perched on the slope, standing over the valley below. Hanging from the middle of the horizontal lintel was a length of rope, and suspended from the end of it was a large copper pipe. A small wooden peg stuck out of the side of one of the vertical posts, and hanging from it was a wooden baton hung with a leather strap.

As Seshrab walked past this peculiar feature and drew closer towards the center of the mining operations, he saw that upon the side of one of the red sandstone rocks which formed the craggy slope were a series of bizarre symbols drawn in white paint. These symbols were very similar to those which he had seen on the signpost at Port Markha. Perhaps this was Egyptian writing, likely another signpost stating that this was Hathor's Mountain. However, Seshrab's hypothesis was quickly proven wrong, for directly next to these symbols, also in white paint, were the following words written in Canaanite:

WELCOME TO IMHET
WHERE SOKAR LIVES


HOPE LIVES ELSEWHERE


In addition to the mine workers, there were several donkeys, either carrying wicker baskets on their backs or pulling heavy wooden sleds filled with rubble. The poor beasts were scrawny nags, with visible ribs and exposed backbones, their hairy coats worn down in patches from rubbing against the rock walls. They snorted and wheezed with labored breaths, barely able to stand, let alone walk.

Seshrab was also surprised, or rather appalled, to see that there were numerous children here, all of them very thin and covered with dust, carrying baskets and buckets of rocks and rubble. Their hands and feet were raw with bloody blisters and many of them had very bad coughs, their throats rasping and wheezing. "My gods", Seshrab lowly muttered to himself. One of the child laborers, a small boy who seemed to be no more than 8 years old, passed by, and his appearance caught Seshrab's attention. The boy's only distinctive feature was a small article of jewelry, if indeed it could be called "jewelry" – a single half of a walnut shell tied with a bit of string hanging around his neck. It was his only personal possession. He ought to have been counted as wealthy amongst his peers, as most of the workers here had absolutely nothing to call their own.

Enough sight-seeing – it was time to get down to business. Seshrab approached one of the lighter-skinned workers, whom he assumed was a Canaanite like himself, who was moving towards him hauling a large wicker basket on his back. "Excuse me, but who's in charge here?"

The walking cadaver didn't say anything. He just blankly stared at Seshrab with dead eyes, and then slowly turned and pointed to a large tent, and continued on his way, shuffling back towards the mine entrance.

Seshrab strode towards the large tent that was indicated to him. Some poor living skeleton sat cross-legged outside the tent's entrance, pulling up and down on a length of rope which moved a large canvas flap back and forth, suspended from the tent's ceiling, in order to fan his master and keep the flies from pestering him. Inside the tent, Seshrab saw a red-skinned man whom he assumed was Egyptian seated at a folding desk, scribbling away on a sheet of papyrus, deep in concentration. The man hadn't even glanced as Seshrab pulled the flap open and stepped inside. The fellow was dressed in a decorated white robe, with a white cloth draped over his head, and he had a closely-cropped goatee. A fly-whisk fashioned from a giraffe's tail affixed onto a short wooden handle and wrapped with leather cording lay on the side of the table.

"Um, excuse me" Seshrab asked.

"Just drop the letters over there – I'll get to them later", said the Egyptian man, not even looking up, dismissively flicking his pen off to the side. Although the man spoke in Canaanite, he was speaking in a "south-lander" accent which was so thick that Seshrab thought for an instant that he was speaking in Arabic.

"Oh, I'm not a messenger, sir. My name is Zacharias of Lakish", Seshrab began. "I was told that you were looking for an accountant, and I was hired by your agent in Ezion-Geber".

"I see", he said, standing up from his desk. "Well, welcome to our little slice of Imhet, Zacharias" and shook Seshrab's hand.

"Imhet? Is that the name of this place? I thought that it was called 'Hathor's Mountain'".

"Well, it's what *we* call it anyway. My name is Iuniyrapet. I'm the chief overseer here. I'll assign a tent to you – it's not much, but it's better than nothing. As soon as you get your things together and refresh yourself, you can get started on *that*", and he pointed to an immense pile of papers stacked against one side of the tent.

"Very well, sir".

And so Seshrab's life once again began anew. A clerk's life is a tedious tiresome business, but at least it's safe…or *relatively* safe, depending on who your employer is. As a scribe, Seshrab was mercifully spared the brutal existence of the mine workers who labored outside his tent's four walls. Still, his experience under the king of Hebron had made him very receptive to the suffering of those poor unfortunates. Many of the Canaanites who labored here were slaves, taken as prisoners-of-war in the never-ending see-sawing conflicts between the Canaanite city-states, and then sold to the Egyptian mine operators for labor. Seshrab looked upon the poor wretches with pity. Praise the gods that he was not "damned to the mines" like these lamentable souls. Seshrab realized that the job offer which he had received in Ezion-Geber to work as an accountant in a turquoise mine was inaccurate. This wasn't a mining camp. This was a prison.

In contrast with Seshrab's empathetic attitude, Seshrab's employer Iuniyrapet seemed strangely proud of the misery which so evidently presented itself to everyone except himself. At one point, Seshrab asked Iuniyrapet if he felt any compassion for the situation of the people who worked here. At hearing this, Iuniyrapet rose from his table. "Get up, Zacharias. There's something you must see". Iuniyrapet took Seshrab by the shoulder and led him outside the tent, taking no notice of the seated man pulling back and forth on the rope which fanned him inside. "Look around, Zacharias of Lakish – what do you see?"

Seshrab looked. "I see only suffering, misery, and despair".

"I see *gold*, Zacharias. Gold, everywhere the glint of gold. That's what this enterprise is all about – profit, Zacharias, pure profit! There is nothing better. With each strike of the pickaxe into the rock, I hear the beautiful metallic chink of gold falling into my purse. This is not a social concern, this is a business, Zacharias, a business. This mine operates for one reason only – to make *me* money, lots and lots of money. Great profits require great labor. Understand?"

Seshrab didn't like it, but he tried hard to conceal his distaste. "Yes, sir. I understand".

In Hebron, too, the people suffered and died at the whims of a man who was concerned only with profit. While he was employed as one of King Sihon's scribes, Seshrab's soul had been wrent by guilt for not doing enough to help Hebron's people. When at last he did stand up to the king, he was sentenced to death for it. The mine boss Iuniyrapet reminded Seshrab of his former master. He insisted on having wine and fine food brought to him every day, while the hundreds of slaves who worked for him were given mere crumbs to sustain themselves after hours of back-breaking labor in the hot boiling sun. Whenever he walked outside, one of the slaves carried a sunshade over his head at all times. Yet despite his regal bearing, Iuniyrapet was not a king, a prince, or a lord. He was just an ordinary man who had been given extraordinary power over the lives of other ordinary men.

Seshrab was always very polite and cordial to the workers he encountered. He wished to make them feel that they had at least one friend here. One day, Seshrab asked one of them a question. "Why do you call this place 'Imhet' if the name is actually 'Hathor's Mountain'? What does the word mean?"

And he was told the answer…

"Imhet" was the Egyptians' version of Hell – an endless fiery wasteland of desolate sand dunes. It was always day, always high noon, with the sun relentlessly beating down on you. Here there was no food to satiate your hunger, no water to quench your thirst, no shady shelter or the cool darkness of night to give you relief from the hot burning sun, and absolutely no end to any of it. Here, the souls of the damned endlessly wandered this endless desert, always hungry, always thirsty, driven to raving insanity by the intense unstoppable heat boiling their brains. The realm of Imhet was ruled over by the god Sokar, known as "the Gatherer of Souls", "He who is Upon the Sand", "the Destroyer", "the Punisher", "the Tormentor", and many other colorful epithets. He was the red-eyed desert falcon who collected the spirits of the damned and carried them off to his barren lifeless world to undergo everlasting suffering and pain.

For several months, Seshrab's life at the turquoise mine continued at a slow plodding boring pace. It was grinding tedious work, but that's the lot of all scribes: documents to copy, letters to write, reports to fill out, day after day, week after week, month after month, each day no different from the next.

And then, one day, something terrible happened.

The whole of Hathor's Mountain had been carved out into tunnels of every size and direction as veins of turquoise were discovered and followed. At the entrance to each tunnel was a plaque inscribed with the tunnel's name, the name of the supervisor who initiated its excavation, and the date that ground was broken. Inside, workers carefully chipped away at the rock walls. They were filthy from top to bottom, and their hands were covered in blisters and sores. There were even several old men in their 50s and 60s. They coughed and gasped from the dust and the lack of breathable air. In some places, the dust was so thick that it looked like smoke. There were also three donkeys who pulled wooden sleds laden with large wooden coffers to haul out the rubble.

In addition to Iuniyrapet who was the chief overseer of the entire mine, there were several junior overseers who worked as "tunnel bosses". Each one was in charge of a specific section of the mine, and there were several of them for each individual section who worked in alternating shifts. The overseer who was on-shift in one of the tunnels that day was all the way at the back of the mine, deep inside the mountain. He was carrying a single oil lamp, the tiny flickering yellow light casting a minuscule glow. Fire needed to be kept to a bare minimum due to the lack of fresh air. Even a single candle or a single oil lamp could significantly deplete the limited amount of oxygen that the workers had to breathe. For this reason, there was only a small number of oil lamps spread out over long distances through the tunnel's length. The areas in between were completely black, and you had to make your way through solely by touch. The roof of the tunnel was propped up with wooden cedar beams. There were no trees for dozens of miles around, so all of the timber had to be imported from elsewhere, which made it expensive. As such, the amount of wood used to shore up the roof was limited to cut costs.

The tunnel boss held the oil lamp close to his face, methodically inspecting the surface of the rock wall, looking for any new veins of turquoise that the workers might have exposed. He carefully examined every square inch of the gritty surface of the pinkish-tan sandstone, looking for the tell-tale shimmering blue glimmer in the twinkling flickering light.

Then he spotted something, very faint, and it stopped him dead. He stared intently at that spot on the rock wall for a few seconds, then wet his finger with some spit and rubbed it against the rockface. In the flickering of the lamplight, the hidden treasure presented itself – a small spot, scarcely the size of a marble, of sky-blue turquoise. The tunnel boss smiled. "Got you".

Then a horrible sound immediately seized his attention. There was a long, drawn-out groaning creak of bending twisting wood, punctuated sharply here and there by a loud attention-grabbing snap. Dust and gravel fell from the tunnel's ceiling.

The overseer swung around, terror in his eyes, and screamed out into the tunnel, *"IT'S BREAKING!!! GET OUT!!! EVERYBODY GET—"*. The roof of the back of the tunnel collapsed and he was instantly crushed by several thousand pounds of stone. The ground shook, and there was a deafening rumbling roar as the roof of the cavern fell in, section by section, steadily moving up the tunnel's entire length, intermixed from within by sudden shrieks of horror which were instantly drowned out. There were panicked cries and yells, and the frantic whinnying snorts of the terrified work donkeys. Men and animals fought and clambered with each other to get out before the tunnel caved in completely. Those who were closest to the tunnel's entrance managed to get out in time, but for everyone else deep within, it was too late.

Outside in the tent encampment, the laborers and overseers had heard the unmistakable sound of the cave-in, they had felt the ground shake, and they had faintly heard the horrible screams of terror echoing from deep within the mountainside, the reverberations sounding like the unearthly howling of Imhet's damned souls. Seshrab, who was working busily in the office tent, had heard and felt it all too, and he quickly rushed outside to see what the hell could have happened. He saw a handful of filthy dust-covered miners run for their lives out of the tunnel's yawning maw, the rumbling roar of the cave-in getting louder and louder, and barely a second after, a forceful blast of pinkish-tan dust and debris shot out of the open mouth of the tunnel like a gigantic siege cannon.

The entire hillside was instantly thrown into panicked commotion. One of the other tunnel bosses who happened to be off-duty at the time raced towards the alarm gong and began pounding on the copper pipe with the wooden baton hanging on the post next to it. The alarm bell was a sound that everyone at the mine feared and dreaded. Once again, one of the tunnels had caved in, and everyone would be needed to dig out the rubble and rescue survivors. The whole hillside echoed with loud urgent crying and shouting as everyone ran at top speed towards the dust-enshrouded mine entrance.

Seshrab ran towards the mine entrance too, the overseers loudly barking out commands and orders to the swarming gaggle of slaves who rushed onto the scene. Slowly the dust from the cave-in began to clear, and Seshrab's ears were assailed by the voice of a man screaming out in pain. As he came closer and as the dust cleared a bit more, he saw a horrible sight. There, trapped in the rubble which blocked up the mine's entrance, was one of the miners, an old man in his 50s, buried up to his armpits in rocks and boulders. His entire body was covered in a thick layer of powdery pink dust. He was helplessly flailing his left arm about in the air. His right arm had been sheared off between the shoulder and the elbow, leaving only a bloody mangled stump, which was even now pouring out blood from the torn ragged flesh. His mouth was full of his own blood, and he howled and screamed in unimaginable agony.

The mine slaves and even Seshrab himself fell to the earth and began frantically digging out the rocks and rubble with their bare hands like a pack of human dogs. All the while the injured man was screaming in a way that Seshrab had never heard a man scream before in his whole life. They managed to clear off the rubble and pulled the rest of him out, and Seshrab knew right away that his condition was *very* bad. "Oh gods!" he cried out when he saw what had happened to the poor old man. Both of his legs had been crushed, all of the bones within smashed into dozens of pieces, the flesh of his legs shredded to bits like he had been mauled by some wild animal. In some places, the bone was exposed. He would surely have to have both of his legs amputated – that is if he managed to live long enough.

While the old man was carried away from the mine entrance, and while the other mine workers desperately worked to clear out the rubble and rescue any more survivors, Seshrab shouted *"Get the doctor! Somebody get the doctor!"*

The slave crouching next to Seshrab looked at him and shook his head. "There's no doctor here, sir".

Seshrab couldn't believe it. He honestly thought for a moment that he must have mis-heard the fellow! "What did you just say?"

"There's no doctor. We're sick, we work. We're hurt, we work. We die, we're replaced and they work".

Seshrab was speechless.

The rest of the workers continued to pull bodies out of the wreckage. There were also badly injured men who, by some miraculous hand, were somehow still alive. Unfortunately, one of those who didn't make it was a young boy that Seshrab recognized. He had been working deep in the mine and wasn't able to get out in time.

More rocks and rubble were cleared away. It was at that instant that something caught Seshrab's eye – a small object poking through the piles of rocks that had been thrown out. Another man was just about to heap another basket-load of debris onto the pile when Seshrab ran over to the spot and quickly threw up his hands. *"Wait! Hold it! Hold it!"* Seshrab practically flung himself onto the debris pile, and pulled out what he had seen, now dangling limply from his dusty fingertips – a walnut shell tied onto a string. "Alright, go". And the work of clearing the mine continued.

Later that day…

"How many?"

"Seventeen", replied Seshrab. "And three donkeys".

Iuniyrapet seemed more irritated than sorrowful by the accident. He turned to one of the tunnel bosses. "How long until the debris is fully cleared out and the beams replaced?"

"Two days, maybe three", the man answered.

"Damn! Two days' work lost!" and he thrashed his giraffe tail fly-whisk. "We'll have to step up production in the other tunnels to make up for it".

"Sir, please!" Seshrab burst out, momentarily forgetting himself, but then realized that he'd better not say anything more.

Iuniyrapet huffed in frustration, and then turned to the tunnel boss. "Give the workers who were in the tunnel the rest of the day off. They get back to work first thing tomorrow. The other workers who are in the other tunnels will keep digging. The work doesn't stop. Understand?"

"Yes sir", answered the tunnel boss, and he left.

Iuniyrapet then turned to Seshrab and repeated "Understand?"

Seshrab knew that he needed to choose his words very carefully, but all he could muster himself to say was "Yes sir".

That evening, the workers held a memorial mass at the temple of Hathor, "Our Lady of Turquoise". Seshrab decided to attend, partly out of respect and partly out of curiosity. Within the temple stood a forest of pinkish-tan sandstone pillars inscribed in Canaanite and Egyptian. Many of them bore appeals from the poor wretches who worked in the mines to the heavenly beings to put an end to their suffering. Others bore lamentations bemoaning their dreadful condition, without any hope that it would ever improve. The miners chanted in Egyptian. Unfortunately, Seshrab had no idea what the workers' choir was singing, as he hadn't learned any of the Egyptian language since he was here. He imagined that they were singing something beautiful.

Beyond the temple was the miners' graveyard. Here were laid to rest the unfortunate souls who perished in the mines or whose worn-out bodies finally gave up the ordeal of living. None of the graves had gravestones marking them. As was customary in that time, grave goods were supposed to be entombed with the dead.

However, for the poor miners who slaved away underground, they often had no personal possessions to be laid with them.

There was one notable exception. For the small boy who was killed in the mine collapse, he was buried wearing his walnut shell necklace – Seshrab had made certain of it. Seshrab also placed into the grave pit a small nugget of turquoise, barely the size of a marble, which he had discovered mixed in with the rubble. He also felt that it would be appropriate to make a remembrance of this young boy who had died far too young, and so Seshrab erected a crude primitive grave marker, consisting only of a simple rock placed at one end. Scratched in Canaanite onto the rock's flat surface were these words…

HERE LIES THE BODY OF A CHILD
KILLED IN THE MINES
WHOSE NAME IS UNKNOWN TO ALL
EXCEPT TO THE GODS

From that moment on, Seshrab resolved that he would do everything possible to improve the miners' condition. At every available opportunity, Seshrab himself went into the mines carrying bread and skins of water to refresh the tired workers. None of this was done in secret. In fact, Seshrab had made certain that his efforts on behalf of the miners were plainly seen by those who were in power over them, especially Iuniyrapet. Hopefully, his merciful work might catch on amongst others. He could not expect to deliver all of this charity alone.

Of course, Iuniyrapet dismissed it. "Being sensible is always preferable to being sentimental", he said. "You are young, and you are full of fire the way that all young men are. You all need a cause to fight in. You'll soon see what the ways of the world are".

Seshrab could see that he wasn't getting anywhere breaking through to him. So, he tried a different strategy. If all Iuniyrapet cared about was money and business, then so be it. Seshrab doctored up the accounts to make it seem that the mine was making more money than it actually was, and used these false reports to convince Iuniyrapet to spend extra money on timber bracing to shore up the tunnels.

"Zacharias, do you have any idea how *expensive* timber is here?" he said exasperated. "Do you know how much that amount of lumber will cost?"

"We can afford it, we've made enough".

"So you say".

"So I *know*. I've gone over the accounts, you're making plenty of money from the sales, you can afford to splurge a little. It will make the tunnels safer".

"Well…"

"It's good for business!" Seshrab exclaimed. "As long as things are done cheaply, the tunnels are going to continue to collapse. Shoring up the tunnels with extra timber will make the tunnels more secure. Time is money. Every time one of the tunnels collapses, you lose time, and you lose money. No cave-ins, no workers getting injured or killed, no time lost in digging out the rubble, and no loss of productivity. A short term cost will lead to a long term gain. Profit, remember boss? Profit".

During his time there, Seshrab had witnessed four cave-ins – all of them were horrible: the ground shaking from the tremor, the thunderous roar of rocks and gravel cascading through the tunnel, the sharp clanging of the alarm bell, the panicked yelling and shouting, the frantic chaos and disorder, the screams of pain.

Iuniyrapet scratched his chin thoughtfully. "Alright", he said. "Alright I'll place the order".

"Thank you, boss".

In reality, the mine was losing money, but Seshrab didn't care. Iuniyrapet was rich and he could afford to take a loss. Seshrab also mocked up a kind of "donkey ambulance", consisting of a pair of donkeys connected to each other by a flexible wooden frame hung with tent canvas. He pressured to have a hospital built in each of the rest stops along the 20-mile path leading from the mine to Port Markha in order to care for the sick and injured who were being transported back home. He was able to get support in this endeavor from Port Markha's harbor master who said it was a good idea. Seshrab also insisted that the mine ought to have a doctor always on-hand to provide medical help to the workers. That took a lot more convincing – doctors were expensive. Yet in the end, Seshrab got his way. After all, healthy workers were productive workers, and more productivity meant more profit. To this, Iuniyrapet eventually consented, and he even went one step further. To Seshrab's great surprise, Iuniyrapet declared without any prompting on Seshrab's part that all of the children and the old men would no longer be employed at the mine, and that the labor would be carried out exclusively by only the youngest and fittest men. "After all", Iuniyrapet said, "the young, the old, and the infirmed are unproductive, and unprofitable".

All of Seshrab's efforts on behalf of the miners to provide them with food, water, medical care, and safer working conditions did not go un-noticed. Little by little, the workers themselves began to warm up to him. "Good day, Zacharias", they would say to him. Seshrab would always politely respond in-turn, and ask how they were feeling, and if there was anything that he could do for them today. For the first time, the men who labored in the turquoise mine were well-fed and well-treated. They were given clean water, sufficient rations of food, and proper medical care, and they were even given one day off from work each week. A day of rest would help them to regain their strength, and a strong worker who was well-fed, well-rested, and well-cared-for was a productive and profitable worker.

Seshrab's efforts had another unforeseen side-effect. His work to make the mine safer and more efficient had actually made the mine more productive than it had been before. Far from *losing* money, the mine was now *making* money. The mine boss Iuniyrapet asked Seshrab if he had any more ideas rattling around in his head, to which he cryptically responded "Always".

Even the mine boss was not unaffected by all of this. Over the four years that Seshrab had worked in the turquoise mine, his boss Iuniyrapet had slowly transformed from a greedy selfish man who was concerned only with profit to being a kind and compassionate employer who genuinely cared about the welfare of his workers. To the immense surprise and shock of everybody who worked there, he even began attending holy services at "Our Lady of Turquoise", and even sang prayers and hymns along with his workers.

In recognition of all that Seshrab had done for them, the mine workers decided to do Seshrab a favor. They agreed to teach him how to speak, read, and write Egyptian. Seshrab was already fluent in several languages, and now he set his mind to learning Egyptian, but mastering this would prove to be more difficult than he first thought. The Egyptian laborers tried to teach him their language as best as they could, but since few of them could read and write, the learning process was difficult. Seshrab learned the language phonetically, listening to the way that a word was pronounced and writing it out using the Phoenician alphabet, which he felt would be more helpful than attempting to write in Akkadian cuneiform. He had to ask his boss, who frequently received letters from Egypt and therefore could read hieroglyphs, to transliterate the words back into the Egyptian alphabet. In this somewhat roundabout manner, Seshrab slowly grasped hold of the Egyptian language.

Seshrab heard many stories about the fabulous wealth of Egypt and how the Nile River brought its wondrous silt every year which could make crops blossom. He was told about its impressive architecture, its colorful markets, its spectacular animals, and all manner of things. Egypt began to sound more and more like a paradise. But the Egyptian miners told other stories as well, stories of hunger, of civil discord, of rebellions and revolutions, of armies and warlords, of battles, blood, and death.

The turquoise mine not only received letters from Egypt, but also from various cities throughout Canaan. Seshrab held his breath every time his boss told him that he had received a letter from the north. He imagined that every Canaanite letter contained an inquiry of whether or not his boss had, at any time, seen a character fitting his description. Such a letter would have word of Seshrab's true identity, of his status as a wanted criminal with a price on his head, and that he would be handed over to those wishing to do him harm. Thankfully, his anxiety was unfounded, so far.

Then, it happened.

One day when Seshrab entered Iuniyrapet's tent, his boss said "Ah, good, you're here. A messenger from Ezion-Geber showed up a few minutes ago. He said that he had come on behalf of the king of Hebron, who has a position open for a scribe in his household, and was inquiring about whether or not I had a scribe in my service of a certain age and meeting certain educational requirements".

Seshrab's color instantly drained from his face. "Did you answer?"

"Yes", Iuniyrapet replied. "This could be a great opportunity for you, Zacharias, if you play this right. But the thing is I don't have anybody who can replace you. The king of Hebron might want you, but frankly, I need you! I don't known of anybody who can match your qualifications. And just because the king of Hebron is asking around for help, that doesn't mean that he's definitely going to choose you – he might pick someone else for that position".

"How long until the message reaches Hebron?" asked Seshrab with a shaky voice.

"I assume three weeks", Iuniyrapet replied.

"I…um…"

"Zacharias, are you alright?"

"I…I need to go". Seshrab left for his tent and started to cry on his cot. He was panicking, hyperventilating. He needed to think of a way to get out of there fast. Then he got an idea.

Seshrab came back to the office tent and said "I've decided. I want to go to Hebron to seek service with the king".

"You should save yourself the trouble. His Majesty would have to approve you, and I don't want you to go all the way to Hebron with the possibility that you'll get rejected. Besides, you're the only scribe here. Where am I to get a new one on such short notice?"

"Well, I've been teaching some of the more receptive workers reading and writing, and they could do just fine as my replacements. You can always get new laborers to fill their vacancies".

Iuniyrapet scratched his chin. "Well, I'll certainly be sorry to see you go. You've done a lot of good work here, but I understand. This is an opportunity that you can't miss. But the next ship bound for Ezion-Geber won't leave Port Markha for a few days".

"I can wait", Seshrab replied.

Later that day, after his work was done, Seshrab counted his wages of salt and grain that he had collected so far – he had hoarded as much of it as he could. He had no intention of going to Hebron, or even as far as Ezion-Geber. But where could he go? He had to go someplace where no one would find him, and even if they did, there would be no way to extradite him and take him to his death. But where was such a place? Then, it hit him – Egypt. The king of Egypt was the most powerful ruler in the world, or so Seshrab believed. *If I could be placed under the personal protection of the Egyptian king, no one could touch me*, thought Seshrab. *I would be protected, free from my pursuers. I will at last sleep in peace at night and live without fear.* Seshrab quickly hashed out the rudiments of a plan – he'd take ship at Port Markha, go up the Western Tongue of the Red Sea, and land on the coast of Africa near Suez. After that, he'd make his way to Egypt, go up the Nile, and seek service in the great king's court. It was desperate, even foolish, but Seshrab felt that he had no other option.

The next day, Seshrab, carrying his belongings and four years' worth of wages in a canvas sack, paid his farewell to his boss Iuniyrapet, who had written him a very glowing recommendation. Ten of the workers had applied for his position as the mine's accountant. He left the tent, said goodbye to the workers, took one last look around the place that had been both his job and his home for the past four years, and left.

Seshrab had the forethought of packing a large quantity of dried provisions and some leather skins of water and made his way down to the coast. It might be a long journey to get from here to the Egyptian court, and he didn't want to run out of food. When he finally got down to Port Markha, there were many boats there of varying sizes, all of which had different destinations. "Which is bound for Suez?" he asked the harbor master, and the vessel was pointed out to him. When he asked the captain of that boat what the fare was, the captain looked at all of the luggage that Seshrab was carrying, and gave a very high price. Seshrab wanted to protest, but given the current circumstances, he decided not to. He paid the captain for the passage and boarded, resigned to his fate, not looking back.

# CHAPTER 5

*In time, I came to the land of Egypt so that I may serve His Divine Majesty Nesu Horus-Nebsenre, Son of Ra, Living God of Egypt. I proved myself to him through the merits of my education, and he promptly appointed me as his chief scribe.*

It took a full day to sail up the Western Tongue of the Red Sea and reach the port of Suez. The city stood upon the border between Egypt and Canaan, referred to by the Canaanites as the *Masar*, meaning "border" or "frontier". Suez was a cosmopolitan city, populated by Egyptians, Phoenicians, Canaanites, Nubians, and even a few Punt-landers from the south. Like many border towns, Suez was a criminal's stronghold with hardly any law and order and was a favorite stomping ground for pirates, smugglers, and criminals on the run. Months of living in the gutters of Gaza had made Seshrab street-smart, and he never forgot the lessons that he learned. He instinctively knew that he had to watch his back. *Blend in*, Seshrab thought to himself. *Be confident and determined. Don't look hesitant, cautious, or confused, or they'll single you out. Don't talk unless you have to. And above all, don't show your money to anyone.* And Seshrab was carrying *a lot* of money on him, four years' worth of wages.

Seshrab had some food and water with him, but it wouldn't hurt to get some extra supplies. He bought some fruits and a small skin of Egyptian beer, always taking care not to show just how much money he had on him. He traded some of his grain and salt for some gold beads, and with this, he bought a dagger for self-protection. Afterwards, he walked due westward. He'd hit the Nile sooner or later.

The border separating Canaan from Egypt was demarcated by an immense salt marsh stretching from the city of Suez northwards to the Mediterranean coast, full of poisonous snakes and disease-spreading mosquitoes. This vast swamp formed a natural barrier against invasion. In fact, the Egyptians referred to this swampland which separated Egypt from Canaan as *Shur*, meaning "the Wall". To further guard Egypt's eastern border against Canaanites or Arabs, the Egyptian rulers of the 12th Dynasty had constructed a line of forts called "the Walls of the Ruler". However during the Second Dark Age, many of these forts had been abandoned and had fallen into ruins, and had become repurposed as holdouts for roving gangs of bandits.

There was a road which ran along the coast of the Mediterranean from west-to-east called "the Way of Horus". This highway connected the easternmost branch of the Nile to Egypt's border fortifications, and even extended beyond them, running along the coastline into the heart of Canaan, reaching as far as the city of Gaza. However, the Way of Horus was many miles away from where Seshrab was, and it ran along the northern edge of the Sea of Reeds; there were no roads which actually passed *through* this vast swamp. Anyone wishing to travel to Suez had to get there by ship rather than by travelling overland. Seshrab would have to find his own way through.

As Seshrab entered this vast marshland, he understood why this place formed a natural barrier. The reeds grew six feet tall and were tightly packed together, so he could not really see where he was going. He advanced slowly through the reeds, pushing his way through, swatting the flies that constantly buzzed in his ears and bit him all over. There was the lurking fear that he might fall into quicksand. There were also a few large salt lakes in the area, with water that was completely undrinkable. His body was covered in scratches and sores from mosquito bites, and he doused them in beer so that they wouldn't become infected. Still, he pushed on. As long as he travelled due west, he would eventually reach the Nile.

After a long arduous journey through the stinking muck and filth, Seshrab managed to break through the vast swampland of the *Masar*, and he came upon a desolate barren country. For a moment, Seshrab thought that he had accidentally been turned around in the marsh and had wandered back into Sinai. However, the path of the rising and setting sun reassured him that he was facing towards the west. He had officially crossed into Egypt.

Egypt was not what he had expected. Seshrab had been told many stories about the bountiful fertility of the Nile River. Yet he saw no greenery, only more of the lifeless windblown wasteland which he hoped he had put behind him. *The river must still be some way off in the distance*, he thought. How far? He hadn't the faintest idea.

Seshrab quickly examined the packs of food and water which he had brought with him. He would need to make every crumb and every drop count if he was to make it as far as the river, however far that may be. His experiences wandering in the desert following his escape from King Sihon's palace, and from his travels with the Bedouin nomads, had taught him many hard-learned lessons. Travel only at night when the air is cool. Cover as much ground as you can before the sun rises. Find a place of shelter, if possible, to take your rest *before* dawn, for it is already too late to look for a place to encamp yourself when the dawn approaches. Do not encamp yourself in a dried riverbed, especially one within a gorge or gully, in case there is a flashflood. Keep out of the sand dunes – it's too straining to travel through sand on foot over long distances. Use dead reckoning to avoid wandering in circles – pick out a spot in the distance, and walk directly towards it in a straight line. Then pick another spot beyond that, and move on. Look for memorable landmarks, if there are any, in case you lose your way.

Seshrab was exhausted, and he was worried about infection from the biting flies which he had been forced to endure. He had gone through the swamps during the daytime because he was scared of travelling through that place by night, lest he should accidentally fall into quicksand. But now that he had passed through the swamps north of Suez, he wouldn't travel in the daytime – far too risky. No, he would stay here on the swamp's edge and recuperate a little from his journey, and try to get some rest if possible. Then, when the sun set, he would begin his march westwards through the coolness of the night. He took off his cloak, suspended it with some reeds to form a primitive sunshade, and waited for nightfall.

It was a longer journey than expected. Seshrab kept his rations to a bare minimum to make them last as long as possible. He quick-walked as fast as he could during the coolness of night, advancing ten or fifteen miles every night, and then hunkered down under his makeshift tent during the day. The sun beat down on him mercilessly like a hammer, and everywhere he looked, it all seemed to look exactly the same – rocks, sand, and dry dead grass.

As he continued advancing westwards, the land gradually turned green and fertile. Seshrab now knew that he had truly entered Egypt. Then a wondrous sight met his tired eyes. Three massive triangular mountains slowly rose out of the horizon. Could it be? Yes! These were the famous "pyramids" that he had heard so much about. The Egyptian turquoise miners in Sinai had mentioned these gigantic structures from time to time, yet Seshrab couldn't believe that such things existed – it was too fanciful. Now, he was seeing them with his own eyes. They were like torch-beacons or lighthouses to a lost ship. Seshrab had been told that these things stood close to the Nile – just walk towards them, and you'd reach fresh water.

Eventually, he came upon the Nile River, a shimmering blue ribbon framed with green. From across the river, the three gigantic stone pyramids, man-made mountains made of smooth white limestone, towered over the whole landscape. All around them were complexes of temples and other small buildings, and laying nearby was a massive stone lion with the head of a man wearing a royal crown.

Yet Seshrab couldn't waste time taking in the sights. By now he had been walking for days through the desert and had been wearing the same clothes since he first set out, and they were getting quite ragged. He also hadn't shaved in weeks. Seshrab was incredibly thirsty, and when he saw the river glistening before him, he dropped his baggage and practically threw himself into the water, guzzling it down as greedily as he could.

"I shouldn't do that if I were you", came an Egyptian voice. Seshrab looked around and saw a man, an Egyptian, standing behind him holding a fishing pole in one hand and a basket in the other. The fellow had a large prominent birth mark on the right side of his face. "You need to boil it first. If you drink the water raw, you'll get sick. There's an evil spirit in the water".

"Thank you, I'll remember that", replied Seshrab in Egyptian. He looked upwards back towards the pyramids across the river.

"Those were built centuries ago", pointed the man, slowly ambling towards him, the end of the fishing pole bobbing up and down as he stepped. "Amazing, aren't they? To think that we used to be able to build things like *that!*"

"Used to?" Seshrab asked, puzzled.

"You're not from here, are you? You're a Canaanite, yes? I judge you to be Asiatic since you have that complexion. There are many of your people who live in Egypt these days".

"Yes, I am a Canaanite", Seshrab replied. "I've come from Suez".

The man's eyes widened. "Suez? You *walked* here all the way from Suez?! But that's over seventy miles away, and there's nothing between here and Suez but empty desert!"

"I know. The blisters on my feet told me so".

"What are you – one of those *wandering lunatics* that I've heard about?"

"Actually, I'm a beggar", Seshrab replied. "Been so for quite some time".

"I see. Well, you'll be in abundant company. You see lots of bums, beggars, and whores along the roads. I imagine you'll fit in just fine".

"Thanks", Seshrab answered dejectedly.

"Anyway, I can't stand here all day making idle chit-chat – I've got fishing to do".

"Are the waters good here?"

"Crap. Utter crap" replied the man exhaustedly. "The Nile's been in a bad way for years".

"Sir, I, uh…I don't mean to be imposing, but…"

"But what? What is it man? Spit it out!" as he cast his line in the water.

"Well, I've come a very long way, and I don't know anybody in this land. So…I was wondering…if…"

By now, the man had slowly turned to face him and had an expression on his face that screamed *Oh hell.*

"…if you could please put me up just for one night, until I can be on my way again".

"No".

"No?"

"No", and he turned back to attend to his fishing.

"Sir, I would really appreciate some place to stay. I'd be very grateful".

"Look, you seem like a nice guy, but I don't let any strangers into my house, I don't care how nice you are! People have been robbed and murdered here. Besides, I haven't caught any fish in days. I don't have enough food to feed my wife and kids, let alone any lodgers I take in. So take your packs and look for some other place to flop for the night".

"Well, if its food that you're lacking…", and Seshrab opened one of his bags, shoved his hand into it, and pulled out a dripping fistful of wheat grain, "…then perhaps, we can come to an arrangement?"

The man slowly walked over, staring, never taking his eyes off of Seshrab's hand for one second. "It seems that begging has become a rather profitable profession lately. Maybe I ought to try my hand at it one of these days". Then he looked Seshrab straight in the face. "Stranger, you just bought yourself a bed for the night", and the two shook hands. "Here, let me help you with your packs".

"Uh, no, thanks. If it's alright with you, I'll just carry them myself".

"Very well, suit yourself. My house is just over there", the fisherman pointed. "I'll take you there, and we'll sit down and have a nice supper".

Seshrab was about to leave when he decided to take one last look at the wondrous pyramids across the river. He had thought that they were merely tales – no mortal men could possibly make something like that. Yet here they were…and here he was.

Seshrab's host walked a few steps when he turned to see if his guest was following, and he saw Seshrab standing there, gazing at the pyramids of Giza. The fellow walked over and stood beside him, sharing the admiring view. "Look well upon it, stranger. Those days are gone forever. We'll never see the likes of *that* ever again…It makes me weep", and the two of them walked to the fisherman's small house.

"We have a visitor!" he called out as he opened the plank door to his small one-room domicile. Inside was a woman, a daughter, and a young boy. Both children were very thin.

*"WHO THE FUCK IS THIS?!"*, shrieked out the wife.

"Please, my sweet", cautioned the husband as he and Seshrab walked into the room.

"I don't want this filthy gutter rat in my house!"

"My dear, please!" entreated the husband, gritting his teeth and forcing a smile.

"Throw him back out into the street with all the other tramps who come around here begging for a handout! As if all of the homeless unemployed derelicts who come knocking on our door every day aren't enough. When they're not here robbing us and cutting our throats in our sleep, the lord's tax collectors come around here and steal the very clothes off our backs!"

At this, the husband suddenly got a fearful look on his face, and began to frantically look around. "My dear please SHUT UP! You have *no idea* who might be listening!"

"And now you've actually brought one of them home, like some lost stray puppy, you addle-brained imbecile! What am I supposed to do? Feed him, wash him, clothe him, and give him a bed for the night? Well feed him with WHAT?! You didn't happen to catch anything in the river this time I suppose? No? No, I thought not, just like you didn't catch anything yesterday, or the day before, or the day before that!"

"But my dear, this man's brought—".

"He's brought fleas and lice and vermin into *my* house, *that's* what he's brought! By the gods, he reeks! And a Canaanite, no less, I see. Well that's to be expected, isn't it – their kind always were a filthy disgusting lot. Shitting and pissing in the streets, no manners, no sense of decency. Just a lot of brutish thugs if you ask me! Dangerous too, always fighting and killing each other. I imagine that before the day is out he'll cut our throats, rape our daughter's dead corpse, and then finish off by humping the neighbor's cow!"

"Excuse me, miss, but I *can* understand you, you know", Seshrab interjected, speaking in excellent Egyptian.

The wife's face abruptly turned linen white and a look of abject horror swept over her.

Now, the husband put on a smug gloating face, and slowly puffed up his chest. "Now…as I was about to say…this fellow has kindly decided to give us some food. He has heard of our condition, and he wants to help us. As you can see from his several packs, this man is a traveller and he has come a long distance. All he wants is a bed for just one night, and then he'll be on his way…Kindly get the children ready for supper".

"Yes, my husband", said the woman sheepishly, and tended to her two children.

The man walked back over to Seshrab who was still standing in the doorway and quickly pulled him outside so that they'd be out of hearing. "Thank you – you made my day! Gods, I wish I was an artist, so I could capture on papyrus the look on that bitch's face for all eternity".

"How long have you been married?"

"Oh, I don't know, I stopped keeping count ages ago. Last year, this year, next year, what difference does it make, it's always the same".

"Very outspoken, isn't she?"

"Old Egyptian saying – *The man rules the family, but the woman rules the house*".

"I see".

"Come, let's get you inside and get some food in our bellies".

The man and his family were grateful for the grain and salt that Seshrab had brought. With these, the wife made a simple flat bread seasoned with a few herbs. It wasn't much of a meal, but at least they now *had* a meal. There were no table or chairs anywhere in the room – everyone ate sitting on the floor. The father looked over at his skin-and-bones son and daughter, who were tearing into the bread like ravenous animals. "Hey! Don't eat so fast, you'll give yourselves a tummy ache".

"You know, for a Canaanite, you speak Egyptian very well", said the wife, now trying to be as polite as possible as they all ate their freshly-baked bread around their kitchen hearth.

"Thank you".

"By the way", said the fisherman, "you never told me your name".

"Zacharias", said Seshrab out of habit. After all, he'd been using that alias for the past four years – it was a hard habit to break.

"My name is Nehem-in-netjeru. It means *Saved by the Gods*". Then the man started chuckling, lowly at first, but then louder and louder to himself.

"What's so funny?"

"Nothing. Forget it", he said grinning and waving his hand dismissively.

Seshrab looked around. The house was a small rectangular one-room affair with walls made of sun-dried mud bricks and covered with white plaster to reflect the sun. The wooden door stood on the far end of one face close to a corner. The fireplace's hearth projected outwards from the middle of the same wall forming a prominent bulge in the wall's surface. There were two small windows: one directly opposite the fireplace and another on a side wall. The floor was made of unglazed terra cotta tiles. A ladder lay propped against the side wall which led up to a trapdoor in the ceiling. A single oil lamp hung suspended from the middle of the ceiling, made of wooden beams with the space in between filled with white plaster. Hanging elsewhere from hooks embedded in the ceiling were baskets, spare fishing poles, and rolled up fishing nets. Copper pots and pans hung from wooden pegs which stuck out above the fireplace's mantel. In the corner opposite the door stood a tall wooden dresser festooned with ceramic plates and dishes and an elaborately-painted water pitcher. In the opposite corner was a bed, which didn't look large enough to accommodate everyone; Seshrab guessed that the children slept on the floor. Underneath the bed, Seshrab caught a glimpse of something – an abrupt change in the pattern of the floor tiles, and it looked like a wooden frame. He correctly guessed that it was a trapdoor hidden underneath the bed, possibly for food storage, or keeping valuables safe, or maybe as a hiding place in case anyone unfriendly should come poking around.

"You have a lovely home", said Seshrab.

The wife suddenly looked nervous.

"Relax, I'm not going to rob you".

"Oh, I, uh, I wasn't thinking anything of the sort! No, not at all!"

"No, of course not, my dear", said her husband, trying hard to hold back a smirk.

Seshrab thought that it would be a good idea to change the subject. "Giza is a splendid place. Those pyramids, amazing things. Does the king live there?"

The two children started chuckling to themselves.

"The only kings that live there have been dead for about 800 years", Nehem-in-netjeru replied. "Pyramids are royal tombs. But if you've got any ideas to cross the river and go sight-seeing, forget it. The priests who prayed at the nearby temples are all gone, and the guards who protected the tombs from grave robbers are gone too".

"Why?"

"Because the guards murdered all of the priests, robbed the tombs, and ran off with the treasure. The only people who live there these days are those who cannot find a home elsewhere, or who are taking shelter from bandits or soldiers. Desperate people do desperate things. If you step foot in that place, you might not make it out alive".

"Oh". Seshrab started to think that he shouldn't have asked. "Well, then where *does* the king live?"

"Why would you want to know *that*?"

"I wish to be employed in his service", Seshrab replied in a matter-of-fact way, as if it was incredibly obvious.

The man looked at Seshrab's haggardly appearance and snickered. "The sun must have gotten to your head, stranger. A good night's rest will set you right by tomorrow morning".

Seshrab decided it would be best not to press the matter any further, and continued nibbling on his bread. He didn't say anything more for the rest of the meal.

After their meager dinner was finished, at dusk, the man pointed Seshrab up to the ladder leading to the trap door in the ceiling. Seshrab went up first, and the man went up behind him carrying a blanket. Once on the roof, Seshrab briefly scanned his surroundings, and observed the other small cottages clustered around in the ever-growing reddening of the sunset. Meanwhile, the fisherman Nehem-in-netjeru ascended, quickly shut the trap door behind him, and spread the blanket on the roof. The two of them sat down. "Keep your voice down", he whispered. "I don't want the family downstairs to hear this. Now, what was all that cow-shit you said earlier about wanting to see the king?"

"I'm sorry if I said something wrong".

"Yeah, well, I'm starting to have second-thoughts about having you sleeping here if you're a spy or an assassin. I'm trying to keep my family safe from killers and the last thing that I need is one under or over my roof".

"I'm not a spy or an assassin".

"Even though you're trying very hard to conceal that dagger which I know you keep hidden inside your cloak? You needn't deny it – I spotted it earlier".

Seshrab now became very self-conscious. He'd been carrying it around with him for so long that he'd forgotten it was even there. "It's for my own protection. As you yourself said, there are dangers here, and I've already had several brushes with death at the hands of evil men".

"So have I. I'm not sure about you. You're a beggar and you dress and smell like a leper, but you're carrying enough food to feed a dozen men, along with several other packs containing who-knows-what. I'm naturally suspicious of outsiders, because the light from a friendly smile often hides a knife in the shadow. But I've promised you a place to stay for one night, and I don't like to break my word. My family's below. Just in case you're entertaining any notions in that head of yours, I don't think that I need to tell you what might happen if you attempt to come inside during the night".

"You needn't worry about me. I'm staying up here on the roof, all night. I promise".

"See to it that you do. And you still haven't answered my first question".

"It's a long story".

"I've got all night".

Seshrab paused, and thought hard, and let out a sigh. "Five years ago", Seshrab began, "I came into some bad company, but I didn't know it at the time. I was young, naïve, and stupid. I was given a job by a rich and powerful man. He gave me food, a bed to sleep in, and some steady money, but in exchange for his generosity, he and his associates wanted me to do things for them, things which involved hurting other people – theft, robbery, fraud, extortion, doctoring up accounts. I knew it was wrong, but I couldn't get out of it – they had too tight a grip on me. Finally, I just couldn't take it anymore and stood up to him. I refused to go along with what he wanted me to do. He didn't like that. He was going to kill me for my defiance, but I managed to get away, at least for a while. He's a very vengeful vindictive person. Every time I tried to hide and build a new life for myself, he found me. I've been on the run since then, going from one place to the next. Now, I've come here, to Egypt. Hopefully he won't find me here, but just in case he does, I want to be somewhere safe, somewhere where he can't get to me. What place is safer than under the king's arm? If I become his man, no matter how lowly I must grovel and scrape, then nobody can hurt me ever again".

"You must be either very stupid or very desperate to come all the way here on a hair-brained notion like that".

"Yes, that's exactly what I am. Desperate. And afraid. And very tired".

Nehem-in-netjeru thought for a minute. "This person who's after your head…Does he know that you've gone to Egypt?"

"I don't know", Seshrab replied. "I know that he managed to track me as far as Sinai. I got out of there before he and his friends could get their hands on me. Maybe by now they've learned that I was in Suez".

"Suez", said Nehem-in-netjeru lowly, thinking. "If I were them, I'd say that there are three choices that you could have made. First, you could have advanced north up the frontier road until you got to the *Wadj Wer*, and then get on a boat to some other place. Or second, you could have boarded another boat at Suez and gone south, and landed somewhere on the coast of the Red Sea. Or third, you could have done the incredibly stupid thing and advance west, through miles of disease-ridden mosquito-infested swamps and then march mile after mile through barren inhospitable desert that would kill most men, until you came here. Now both of us know which option you chose. The question is, which option do you think *they* thought you chose?"

Seshrab couldn't answer.

"Travelling along a major highway is risky because you'd be easily spotted if people were on the lookout for you, and you could be intercepted if you were to make your way to one of the shipping ports on the seacoast. If they know that you landed in Suez, they could check the harbor master's manifest to see if anybody fitting your description recently boarded a ship bound for one of the ports on the Red Sea or elsewhere, and they'd learn the name of the ship, where it was heading, and approximately what date it would land. It would take a lot longer to get you, but they'd be confident that they were on the right trail. So, that leaves only one other option, doesn't it?"

Seshrab could feel the dread rising up inside him.

"If you really have been on the run for years, then hardship is very familiar to you, and they will know that you have undertaken many ordeals. If you were strong enough to make it out of Canaan, and to make it out of the deserts of Sinai, then they'll wager that you could also muster up the strength to make it across the Eastern Desert between Suez and the Nile. Travelling directly west through the wilderness is extremely risky, and only a madman would do it. Nobody would think to look for you coming this way…and that's precisely why they *will* look for you coming this way".

Seshrab's whole body seemed to sink.

"The way things are going for you, the only way to be safe from a big man with a knife is to be under the protection of a bigger man with a bigger knife. Are you serious about asking the king for his protection?"

"Yes".

"Which king? There are two of them, you know".

"What, two? I didn't know that".

"Oh yes, one in the north and one in the south. The king of the south is much closer, in Lisht – it's about thirty miles south of here, just a two day walk. Although he really isn't much of a king – that one town is all that he rules over. The king of the north is much further away, at Khaset City, but he controls nearly one-quarter of the Nile Delta. The guy who rules there is a real hard-ass. If you ask me, though", said the man, leaning in closer, "the person you really ought to get in good with is Lord Sekheperenre. This is his land, you see. Everything from here southwards as far as Lisht is his domain. He controls Giza, Ankh-Tawi, Saqqara, and Dashur, and that's not a minor accomplishment in these times. Even now, he's got his eye on a few other places to add to his realm. The king of the south leaves him alone – he knows that he can't stand up to Sekheperenre's army. He's also as rich as the gods. More gold than any man can know what to do with. Just make sure not to get on his bad side, that's all. Trust me, you *really* don't want to get in his way".

"Sounds like someone I used to know".

"Hey, better him than someone else. The other warlords that rule around here are all alike – just heavily-armed thugs, they come and go, and spend too much time fighting among themselves. Meanwhile, we plain people are the ones who always get the worst of it. I've seen the same small plot of land change hands at least ten times, and who knows how many dozens of people got killed because of it. Our only hope is to be under the protection of a strong leader like Lord Sekheperenre. That's the only way that you can be safe these days. Take my word for it – if you're looking for a strong powerful man to serve as your master, he's your man. His headquarters is at Ankh-Tawi – it's just ten miles south of here, on the western side of the river. If you set out tomorrow morning, you can be there within just a few hours".

It was a lot for Seshrab to take in. "Thanks. I'll think about it".

"I'll head below now", said Nehem-in-netjeru. "Try to get some sleep, and remember, stay up here. Good night".

"Good night", replied Seshrab as he watched the man go to the trap door, climb down the ladder, and shut the door leaving Seshrab alone on the roof.

Seshrab had a lot of thinking to do that night. He needed to make a decision as to what to do tomorrow morning. Yet he was so exhausted and so drained that he almost immediately fell asleep.

The following morning, Seshrab awoke from a full night's sleep – he couldn't remember the last time that he was able to do that. The first thing that he intended was take a bath; he could plainly see that the fisherman and his family thought that he had a foul odor. Well, after all of the walking that he did, how could he not smell disgusting? He hadn't taken a bath since he left Hathor's Mountain, and that was quite some time ago. Nothing would have pleased him more than to plunge into the Nile for a good swim.

From the rooftop, Seshrab gazed at his surroundings. Egypt was a wondrous place, far more glorious in all of its natural splendor than the most richly decorated palaces and temples that he had ever seen. One could almost breathe the very essence of life in the air. The land was good and green, the sky was clear, and one felt an inescapable sense of serenity. The Nile was beautiful and graceful, like a shimmering silk scarf, slowly winding its lazy way northwards in no hurry or rush at all. It could take all of the time that it wanted. Small white sailboats and fishing boats dotted the river like white lotus flowers drifting on the surface of a pond. Locals lined the riverbanks washing their laundry or tending to the fields, their skins burnt a dark rusty red from constant exposure to the sun and wearing white linen dresses and wrap-kilts. The more that he saw, the more Seshrab felt an overwhelming feeling of contentment come over him. It was a calmness for his mind, heart, and soul.

There was a knock on the trap door from inside and it opened. "Good morning", said Nehem-in-netjeru. "Did you sleep well?"

"Yes, very well, thank you".

"Good. Come downstairs, and let's get some bread in our bellies".

"If you don't mind", said Seshrab, "I'd prefer to wash up first".

"That's a good idea. I don't want any vultures circling over my house thinking that there's a dead body on the roof".

Seshrab climbed down the ladder and walked out the door down to the river. He remembered what his host had said to him earlier about not drinking the water, or else he'd get sick. But what about washing? Could the evil spirit invade the body through the pores of the skin? Even Seshrab was offended by his own stench, and without a second thought, he jumped into the river with all of his clothes on. The cool water felt good against his crusty skin. He splashed around for quite some time, thoroughly enjoying himself, and even spontaneously laughed out loud a few times. He was either oblivious or unconcerned with the fact that he was making a spectacle of himself. The neighbors poked their heads out of their windows and doors to see what all of the noise was about.

"Look at him!" said Nehem-in-netjeru to his wife, daughter, and young son, who had gathered outside to see this performance. "You'd think that he had never seen water before!"

Seshrab emerged from the river with a big grin on his face. Egyptians didn't wear underwear, and Canaanites didn't either, and the wet flax tunic clung tightly to his body leaving very little to the imagination about Seshrab's anatomy. Without any concern for the growing audience gawking at him, he pulled off his tunic and wrung it out on the shore, standing stark naked on the river's edge. The reaction of the onlookers was to be expected – the fellow was *obviously* not all there – and they quickly turned away to be about their business and not be spotted staring. Seshrab slapped his tunic in the air to shake off any excess moisture, casually draped it over one shoulder, and calmly strode up to Nehem-in-netjeru as if everything was perfectly normal.

"Excuse me, sir, but do you know where I can find some fresh clothes?"

"Get inside now, you brainless idiot!" cursed the fisherman, pulling him through the door into his little cottage. Nehem-in-netjeru handed Seshrab a spare wrap-kilt and tunic. "Here! Put these on! Unbelievable!"

"Thanks" said Seshrab, snickering to himself.

"I'm starting to wonder whether or not you really are alright in the head", remarked Nehem-in-netjeru. "Are you sure that your trip across the Eastern Desert didn't cook your brain inside your skull? Or maybe you caught mosquito fever? And what about what you said yesterday, all that nonsense about wanting to seek service with the king? Is that truly a plan of yours that you've worked out, or is this just an addle-headed fantasy?"

That final question caught Seshrab off-guard. Plans? Did he *ever* have any plans?

"Whether the sun or some damned fly has scrambled my brain, that I don't know. Madmen never know that they're mad. In their minds, they are the only ones who are sane in an insane world. But this much I do know, and it's not brought about by heat stroke or mosquito fever. I need to do something, no matter how desperate or foolhardy. I'm running out of options. I'm sick of always looking over my shoulder, sick of having every day of my life filled with fear and dread. Last night, sleeping on your roof, was the first time that I slept a sound sleep in a very long time. I'm hoping that it won't be the last. It's a gamble, I know, but I need to make one more throw of the dice".

At this, the man's wife opened the door. "How dare you! Standing out there with no clothes on with everyone staring at you, and carrying on like it was nothing. What in the gods' name is wrong with you?!" she said, sticking her finger in Seshrab's face.

"My dear", said her husband, "we were just discussing that exact matter".

"Well here's *another* matter that I want you to discuss. You promised him a bed for the night, and he paid for it. Now tell him to pack his bags and get out!" and she left slamming the door.

"Remember what I said", reminded Nehem-in-netjeru. "You say you're running out of options? The king might not be the best option to choose. I still say that you should appeal to Lord Sekheperenre for his protection. He's hard and demanding, but if you get into his good graces, no one will dare touch you".

"My mind is made up", said Seshrab. "Today, I will go north into the Delta, to the northern king's palace, and throw myself on his mercy. Within his walls, I will be safe".

Nehem-in-netjeru folded his arms and let out a long sigh. "Very well. But you don't know how to get there, so let me tell you. The Nile River resembles the papyrus stalk – it is a single stem, and then splits into many parts. There are seven branches of the Nile. Take a boat up the fourth branch, and you will see Khaset City on your right. That's where the king of Lower Egypt lives. The royal palace is there. You will see the palace before you see the town".

"Thanks".

"I still say that you're making a mistake".

"Perhaps I am, but I cannot know until I try. Thank you for your hospitality. Believe me, I'm grateful". Seshrab hauled his bags and his host opened the door for him. He stepped outside to see the neighbors looking at him sideways and gossiping amongst themselves. "Thanks again", and Seshrab and Nehem-in-netjeru shook hands. "I'll be on my way now".

Then, as Seshrab began to leave, he barely took two steps when he saw the fisherman's two children. They were so thin, so frail. Last night they had a meal, however meager it may have been. But when would their next one come?

Seshrab turned back to Nehem-in-netjeru and dropped his bags to the ground. "Please get me two pots, or two sacks – *anything* that can hold things in it".

Without asking for clarification, the fisherman instantly went back into the house, grabbed the large cooking pot and a smaller frying pan and then hurried back out to meet Seshrab. Seshrab then promptly opened two of his bags – one carrying grain, and another carrying salt, and dumped them each into the two vessels. "Here", said Seshrab, and he poured out half of the grain and half of the salt which he was carrying. "You and your family have more need of it than I do".

The man was stunned. "But…but why? Why are you doing this? You barely know us!"

"You were kind to me and you need help. I am in a position to help you, and so I shall".

Nehem-in-netjeru was speechless for a few seconds. "I'll never forget you for this. I assure you, I will *never* forget", and he shook Seshrab's hand once more. "You are a good man".

"No I'm not", replied Seshrab, "but I'm trying to be". And then Seshrab was once again on his way.

After a short voyage by sailboat, Seshrab disembarked on the shore of the northern province of Khaset. Soon, very soon, he would be at the walls of the king's palace. Seshrab was in high spirits. He was so close to his goal that he could taste it.

The provincial capital of Khaset City was only a short distance away, easily within a day's march. Seshrab knew that he was getting close when he saw a familiar sight – grape vineyards. His home-town of Hebron had been renowned throughout Canaan for its excellent wine, and Khaset City was likewise renowned throughout all of northern Egypt for its exquisite vintage. As he walked through the trellised vineyards erected on either side of the road, draped with their broad hand-sized leaves, a surge of nostalgia swept over him, remembering the happy days of his childhood, frolicking and playing with his brothers amidst the vines that grew on the terraced hillsides. He could not resist the urge to walk over to the side of the road and casually stroke and caress the grape leaves against his fingertips, remembering days gone by. For a few precious instants, he was back home.

Seshrab reached Khaset City in two hours, long enough to get hot, sweaty, and smelly all over again. It was now that he fully understood what Nehem-in-netjeru had said to him – *You will see the palace before you see the town.* The royal palace of the king of Lower Egypt was utterly enormous. It dominated not only the city but the whole countryside, so much so that it looked like the town which lay around it was being physically suppressed under its power.

Seshrab walked through Khaset City's trapezoidal gate and down the wide processional avenue towards the palace. There was no way that he could possibly get lost, as the central boulevard was wide and it extended in a straight line directly towards the king's house. For the most part, the town's buildings were small unimpressive mud-brick things. There were a few exceptions to this, however: there were two large temples, one built next to the town's main gate and another built next to the palace (or perhaps it was even part of the palace – Seshrab couldn't be sure), and a large mansion which Seshrab assumed was the residence of either the mayor or the provincial governor. The population of the city was also much smaller than what Seshrab had expected. The townsfolk that he saw going about their business did not pay much attention to him except perhaps a passing glance.

Walking up the length of the city's wide central boulevard, Seshrab came closer and closer towards the royal palace of the king of Lower Egypt. A large wall with boxy towers loomed twenty feet upwards. Seshrab didn't know how long each side of the wall was, but the front wall – the wall that he was looking at – was at least 300 yards long. In the middle was a large trapezoid-shaped gatehouse similar to the one he came through only a few minutes earlier. The actual doors looked small by comparison, even though they were ten feet tall. Carved on the large billboard-like façade were monumental depictions of the Egyptian king in all of his majestic regal glory accompanied by hieroglyph inscriptions. The carvings related to a king named Sheshy who reigned several decades earlier, not the present monarch. Looming up behind the wall was a large rectangular-shaped building, which must have been the actual palace itself, with a flat roof.

This was his chance, but Seshrab was suddenly seized with doubt. *Wait a minute, why should I do this?*, he thought. *This is the king of Lower Egypt – who am I compared to him? Why should he give me work? Why should he even look at me?* For a moment or two, Seshrab believed that he had gone on a fool's errand and had wasted his time, but eventually, Seshrab mustered up his courage, grumbling that he had come all this way and that he'd better do something. He slowly walked towards the palace gate, which seemed to grow physically larger the closer he got to it. There was an Egyptian soldier standing guard on either side of the door. The reception that Seshrab got from them was not welcoming at all.

"Stranger!" one of the guards called out in Egyptian. "Who are you?", he snappishly demanded. "Where are your papers?"

The barking command caught Seshrab off guard. Not the demanding tone – he'd expected that – but the actual question itself. "Papers? What papers?", Seshrab replied, also in Egyptian, which would be the language that he would speak from now on.

"Your identification papers, hippo dung!" they snapped at him. "What business do you have at the palace?"

"Certainly he didn't come here to take a bath!" spat the other guard. "He stinks like dog shit".

"What's your name, Canaanite?"

If anyone was still looking for him, he couldn't go by the name of Zacharias of Lakish, nor could he go by the name of Saul of Jericho. But at that instant, his mind went blank.

"Well? Are you mute? Speak damn it! Give me an answer!"

*Think fast, Seshrab.* "Um, Meranat of Jaffa".

"Um?! Did you say '*UM*'?! You mean you actually had to *THINK* about it?!"

"Maybe that's not who he really is. Some trouble-maker no doubt. Maybe even an assassin".

"Meranat. More like 'moron'", commented the other guard. "What are you carrying in those sacks, Meranat, if that is your real name? Contraband?"

"No! My food and supplies", Seshrab responded.

"What about those bottles?"

"Water".

"Poison!"

"And where are your damn papers?!", added the other. "You still haven't answered that question!"

"I don't know what papers you're talking about! I don't know anything about identification papers". Seshrab was getting frustrated and aggravated.

"Everyone in the king's domain has to carry proof of who he is. That's the law".

Proof of identity? "I have a job reference. Here". And, without thinking, Seshrab reached into one of the bags he was carrying and took out the sheet of papyrus that his former boss Iuniyrapet had written on, describing how *Zacharias of Lakish* had been serving as an accountant and record-keeper at the turquoise mine on Hathor's Mountain for four years and had performed his duties with perfection. The guard snatched it out of Seshrab's hands and scanned it. It wasn't until then that Seshrab realized his mistake. *Oh, damn it!* He just hoped that these goons couldn't read Canaanite.

They could.

The guard glanced over the parchment, handed it to the other guard and said to Seshrab, "A job reference is not a suitable form of identification. You need a specific kind of identification".

"And you need special clearance if you wish to step foot onto the royal grounds or work in the palace". After he said that, the second guard began scanning the document.

"What do you want here?" asked the first guard.

"I want a job working in the palace. I'm a scribe. I can read and write. I'm fluent in three foreign languages. I can do math. I worked as a teacher and an accountant. I wish to serve your king. I have never seen a living god before".

"And doubtful you ever will if you don't have the proper identification".

The second guard, the one holding the recommendation letter, interjected, "Now, wait a minute. This man has very high qualifications if what he says is true. If he's so desperate to serve *Nesu*, then maybe we can give him a break".

"It's against the rules".

"Well maybe, just one time, we can *bend* the rules", said the second guard, growling between his teeth.

He got the message and nodded. "Yeah…yeah, maybe just one time we can go easy. Alright, fine".

"I'll show his recommendation to the king".

"Can't I keep that?" asked Seshrab, trying to get it back. "I don't want to lose it. Besides, I think I could present a much more convincing case if I could speak to the king in person".

"No one speaks to the king personally unless they're a member of the palace staff, and you aren't. You don't have the proper clearance. First, I have to notify the palace chamberlain of your arrival and the purpose of your visit. Then he has to decide whether or not you are worthy of the king's attention. If he does, then he'll tell the king that you've arrived, and then the king has to make up his mind whether or not he wants to see you. That's the way it works".

Seshrab knew he had no choice.

"Wait here". The guard turned around and pounded on one of the two doors. It creaked open slightly, and a face peered out. "Let me in – I need to speak with Horemheb. Have someone take my place". The face nodded, and the door opened wider. The first guard left and a new guard stepped outside. The door closed behind him with a heavy echoing boom.

Seshrab felt that he was done for. He stood there, outside the palace gates, not knowing whether he'd be allowed in or not. "So", he said trying to make conversation, "what are your feelings about crocodiles?"

"They won't be hungry tonight if you don't shut up".

*Oh boy.*

After about a half-hour, the door opened, hitting the replacement guard in the back and nearly knocking him over – the other guard had returned. "The palace chamberlain wants to see you immediately, but I think you should wash first before you meet him. You certainly cannot present yourself in the condition you're in. Follow me". Seshrab was overjoyed. He could barely contain his excitement. It had worked! Everything was going according to plan!

The door opened wider, and Seshrab saw that standing with the returning guard were five other armed men. He was led into the gatehouse. It was dimly lit, with only a few oil lamps, and he could barely make out the forms of soldiers leaning up against the walls. He also heard muffled talking, like conversations inside a room with a closed door. Seshrab assumed that there were small rooms inside this gatehouse, presumably storage areas or bunks where the guards slept when taking shifts. The interior doors of the gatehouse were still closed. The returning guard pushed them open, and light flooded in.

"Follow me", he said to Seshrab.

Seshrab was led into the palace complex. The first sight that greeted him was an open dirt courtyard and beyond it was a large multi-story rectangular building.

The walls surrounding the palace formed a square shape. On Seshrab's left and right were long low buildings which took up the entire length of either wall. Seshrab and his escorts walked towards the long building on the right side.

A door was opened, and they brought Seshrab inside. There was a long hallway with a series of locked doors on both sides. One of the guards knocked on the nearest door. It was made of solid cedar panels and had no windows. "Anyone home?" No answer. "Right, leave your stuff out here. Go inside and clean yourself up", and he unlocked the door and pulled it open.

Seshrab was looking forward to getting clean. He dropped his bags of belongings and stepped into the open doorway, but when he looked inside, all he saw to his puzzlement was a bare room. There was no bathtub, no water, no buckets, nothing. Just a bare empty room.

Then, Seshrab was shoved inside and the door was slammed shut behind him. "Hey!" Seshrab screamed out, pounding on the bolted door. "Let me out!"

"Let me out – that's what they all say", replied the guard outside, and the armed men left, carrying away all of his bags.

Seshrab began to cry. *How could I be so stupid, so naïve?* He was a dead man. The king must have read the letter, decided that he was not who he said he was, and had ordered him to be put in the cell as a "suspicious person". Or even worse, perhaps the king was aware that this person was really Seshrab, the wanted scribe who dared to defy the king of Hebron. Was the Egyptian king friends with him, like King Ariyak of Gaza? If so, Seshrab's death sentence was already signed.

Seshrab lay in that cell for two days and nights with no food or water. Only the thin band of light creeping under the door from the outside hallway had given him a sense of time. He was delirious with hunger and thirst. A person can only go for three days without water before they die, but that did not concern him. Frankly, Seshrab didn't care whether he lived or died. He felt that his life was at an end. After all that he had been put through, he just didn't care anymore.

At last, the door was opened, and he saw six guards standing in the hallway. With them was a man who looked important, maybe a high-ranking palace official. He wore a long white robe and carried a tall staff. "You there. Stand up", this fellow commanded. He had a powerful voice, like an army commander.

Seshrab was weak, yet he found sufficient strength to stand. He immediately felt light-headed and dizzy.

"Let's go".

And so, Seshrab was taken away to who-knows-where – to meet the inquisitor, to meet the king, to meet the executioner, he didn't know and he didn't care. The six heavily armed men surrounded Seshrab while the man in the long robe led the way down the halls and corridors of the palace complex. The fellow appeared to be in his mid to late 30s. The fabric of his robe sagged a little in the back, and Seshrab noticed that this man, whoever he was, had his back covered with scars. *He's been whipped*, thought Seshrab, *and rather severely too. I wonder what he did to get such a beating.* When Seshrab served King Sihon of Hebron, the despot often whipped his servants. Thankfully, he had been an obedient servant and had never been punished…until the end, of course.

As Seshrab was taken into the interior bowels of the palace, through hallways which were closely guarded by fierce-looking armed men, he had a feeling that he was being brought to account for himself, and that he'd better tell the truth. To lie might mean an even worse death. Besides, he was tired of pretending to be someone that he wasn't: Saul of Jericho, Zacharias of Lakish, Meranat of Jaffa. He was Seshrab of Hebron, and always would be. He was tired of always running away. His life had been utter misery for so many years. If he was going to die, so be it. If the king should order him to identify himself, he would say, "I am Seshrab of Hebron, and I don't care if I live or die".

Thankfully, *Nesu* wanted him to live.

# CHAPTER 6

*Upon my appointment as Chief Scribe to His Divine Majesty, I became acquainted with the manners and customs of the Lower Egyptian court. I attended on both the father and the son inexhaustibly so that I may further prove my merits to them. My devotion and diligence were rewarded, for Nesu was generous and magnanimous, and he bestowed his favor greatly in innumerable ways.*

*Meanwhile, King Nebsenre was contemplating how to further expand his control over the fragmented parts of Egypt, for Egypt was no longer united as it once was, but was split in two, with a king ruling each half of the country. Moreover, each half was splintered into smaller states, each one ruled by its own strongman who assumed all power within the lands that he controlled, ruling their lands as if they themselves were kings. Nebsenre vowed to restore order as well as unity, and began reunifying the land through military force. He had already managed to assume control of two rebel provinces by the time that I came to the royal palace, and was at that moment preparing to undertake a third campaign with his army.*

"Take him to the king immediately", said the chief bath attendant to the guards posted outside the door, and Seshrab, newly cleaned and clothed, was escorted outside to once again meet with His Divine Majesty, Nesu Horus-Nebsenre, the living god of Lower Egypt.

As Seshrab left the wash room and walked down the long hallway, cleaned and perfumed and dressed in Egyptian style, he was thinking about his "adventures", although he wasn't sure if he wanted to call them that. Adventures were fun, and his experiences were anything but enjoyable. Escorted by guards, he walked back to the council room where he first met the king. The cedar door opened, and he saw the king there with the man wearing the long white robe and the scars on his back. The king's two pet greyhounds, white Osiris and black Set, once again began savagely barking at the stranger.

Seshrab immediately knelt. He had learned quickly.

"Ah yes, that's more like it", said King Nebsenre, carefully examining Seshrab's new appearance. "You may not be an Egyptian, but at least now you *look* like one". He pointed to the dogs. "They won't trust you until they've been around you for a while, and they're much harder to win over than people. At most, they'll merely tolerate your presence. Do you know my son? This is Shaweneiti, Prince of Lower Egypt, heir to the throne, my vizier, and second-in-command of the Army. You are to give him the same respect and obedience that you accord me".

"Yes, Your Divine Majesty".

The dogs kept barking and snarling.

"*SHUT UP!!!*" Nebsenre screamed at the dogs. The two canines abruptly went quiet. "Take Seshrab to the scribe's quarters. Tell Imhotep the bad news and have him give Seshrab a thorough explanation as to what it means to be my chief scribe".

"As you wish, father".

Seshrab needed to speak. "Pardon me, Your Divine Majesty, but may—".

*Nesu's* eyes glared with rage. "You *DARE* to speak to me?! You do not speak to me or my son unless you are spoken to first! Understood?"

"Yes, Your Divine Majesty", said Seshrab shaking.

"Well, what is it?"

Seshrab wasn't sure that he wanted to ask him now.

"Speak up, man! The gods gave you a mouth and a tongue – use them! – and waste no more of my time. Now speak your piece".

"Your Divine Majesty, may I have some food and water?"

"What?"

"I have not eaten or drunk anything in two days, Your Divine Majesty. I am very hungry and thirsty".

King Nebsenre turned to his son. "See to his request. When he has finished eating, then you can bring him to meet the Toad".

Seshrab gorged on Egyptian cuisine: roasted duck stuffed with palm dates, grapes, and diced pomegranates, with some pieces of bread on the side, and a large mug of beer. The duck meat was rubbed with a delicate mixture of herbs and spices and was glazed with a tasty sauce. Seshrab thought that it was the best thing that he had ever eaten in his whole life, unquestionably. The bread, however, left much to be desired. It was very gritty and it felt like eating sandpaper, but he was so hungry that he was in no mood to complain about the bread's texture. The beer was remarkably good but rather pulpy. It was a lot safer to drink than the water, and everyone in Egypt, even children, drank beer. Once he finished guzzling it down, he was told to pick himself up and to accompany the guards to his room in the Servants' Quarters.

The royal palace was not a single building, but rather a complex of interconnected buildings of various sizes which were constructed around a central courtyard and surrounded by an imposing wall, separating it from the rest of the city's architecture. To outsiders as well as to those Egyptians who simply didn't know any better, they referred to the entire palace complex as the *Perah*, "the Great House". However, in truth, only the palace's large main building where the king and his family lived was called by this name. As for the other buildings of the palace complex, they had their own names: "Servants' Quarters", "Guard Barracks", etc. The Servants' Quarters was a long low rectangular building attached to the Perah's left and ran along the length of the courtyard's western side. It consisted of a long central hallway with rooms on either side. The rooms were tiny and were actually referred to as "cells", which did nothing to alleviate the stark prison-like appearance of this place. The maids, butlers, cooks, and other personal servants lived in the cells that were closest to the Perah because they were constantly called in to do work and they had to get to the Perah quickly. After them were the craftsmen and repairmen who either made things for the family or fixed anything that needed fixing. The scribes lived in the rooms at the far end of the long hallway. There were nine scribes including the chief scribe who worked in the palace complex. Most of the time, each scribe was assigned to a specific area of the palace – the kitchen, the barracks, the treasury, and so forth. However, it was not unusual for scribes to be assigned different or multiple duties depending on whatever came up.

Imhotep, a native Egyptian, had been the chief scribe for Nebsenre and his royal predecessors. Many positions in Egyptian society including "Chief Scribe" were hereditary. Imhotep's father had been a scribe, and his father before him, and Imhotep himself had held the position of "Chief Scribe to the King of Lower Egypt" for years, As such, he had grown accustomed to his position and the perks that went with it. Scribes were largely untouched by regime changes due to their skills, so much so that they were practically sacrosanct, untouchable. Because of this, scribes, especially the chief scribe, could afford to put on swaggering airs and boss others around because they would get their way most of the time. Imhotep was one of the few people who worked in the palace who had servants waiting on him. He was very fat with a thick double chin and a small pug nose, and swayed a bit when he walked. On his head, he wore a large black wig with many long curls. As a mark of his higher status, he wore a full tunic, not just a wrap-around kilt around his waist.

When General Nakhtibre and his army stormed the city and took possession of it, changing his name to Nebsenre upon his coronation, Chief Scribe Imhotep was one of the first to swear loyalty to the new ruler of Lower Egypt. He fawned on the royal family, always bowing and smiling and using very flowery language when speaking to them, but his treatment of others was anything but civil. He looked down on others and liked to boss the other attendants around – not just his subordinate scribes, but other servants in the palace, like the maids and the bathing attendants, people who were not technically supposed to be under his authority. He ate snacks every two hours, enjoyed daily massages, flirted with all of the female servants (who, due to their lower standing, were not entitled to resist his lascivious advances), and usually entrusted all of the work to the other scribes, doing little if any work himself.

Previous kings may have been content to allow Imhotep to continue this sort of behavior and were willing to overlook his less-than-appropriate conduct as long as he did his job, which in their opinion was merely to act as a supervisor to the other scribes, delineating work and keeping watch over them like an overseer of a labor gang. That changed when Nebsenre came to power. King Nebsenre and Prince Shaweneiti couldn't stand "the Toad" as they called him due to his fat appearance, his scowling face, and his poisonous attitude. The prince preferred to keep his opinions to himself, but true to form his father wasn't shy about expressing his thoughts out loud. Both men insisted that Imhotep do his share of the work, which Imhotep wasn't accustomed to. Moreover, due to his post of Chief Scribe, Imhotep was expected to actually do more tasks and harder tasks than the ordinary scribes who worked under him. Imhotep, never the one to actually do any work of any sort, tried to explain to Nebsenre that this wasn't what his job entailed, whereupon the king flew into a loud profanity-drenched rage, screaming that his job was to do whatever the king told him to do. He then threatened to have Imhotep court-martialed for insubordination – he specifically used the term "court-martialed" – unless he obeyed the royal will.

Imhotep did what was asked of him, at least when the king and his son were present. When they were out of sight, however, Imhotep dumped his workload on the other scribes and ordered them to keep their mouths shut, and if they told anyone that they were doing work that was assigned to him, he'd make their lives miserable. The subordinate scribes were in no position to resist. Both the king and the prince knew that Imhotep was dodging work, and Nebsenre dearly wished to be rid of the man. However, the main reason why Imhotep had managed to keep his job for so long was because there simply wasn't anyone else who was as qualified as him to take his place.

And then, Seshrab showed up at the palace.

Prince Shaweneiti, Seshrab, and a small group of four guards armed with axes (there was no room for spears due to the low ceiling) walked down the long hallway of the Servants' Quarters. The hallway was wide enough for only four people standing side-by-side. The building itself was pretty bare. It wasn't decorated with paintings or tapestries like the Perah. There were no windows, at least in the hallway; some of the rooms had windows, but only those facing out towards the open courtyard. Instead, the long hallway was lit by a profusion of oil lamps mounted on the walls, which created a lot of smoke. There was so much haze that Seshrab couldn't even see the end of the hallway, which seemed to gradually fade away into mist. He could hear muffled voices as he and his escorts passed by some of the rooms, some male, some female, as they made their way down the long hallway.

As they approached the scribes' rooms which were at the far end of the long hall, Seshrab noticed that the noises began to diminish, and it began to smell better. There was even a slight hint of perfume in the air. It was dead quiet. Seshrab wondered if there was anybody living in this part of the palace.

The troupe made their way down to the very last door in the hallway, and there they stopped. It looked no different than any other door. All of them were bare – no numbers, no names, just bare wood. The prince knocked on the door.

"Oh damn, what is it?" came a mumbling voice inside. It was a heavy voice, the voice of a fat man. There were shuffling footsteps, and the door creaked open.

Chief Scribe Imhotep was startled to see the prince accompanied by several armed guards. "Oh, Your Highness!" He now began frantically looking around his room. He threw on his curly black wig and fussily straightened it, then quickly dashed over to grab his *sekhem* scepter which stood propped up against a wall, hustled back to the door entrance and, standing tall and erect, and with a puffed chest, bowed to the prince in a very outlandish and exaggerated manner. "Your Highness, you do me great honor by coming here to see me. What would you ask of me, my lord?"

"You are no longer Chief Scribe", said Prince Shaweneiti in a matter-of-fact straight-to-the-point tone and a no-nonsense facial expression.

Imhotep's expression, by contrast, abruptly changed.

Shaweneiti put his hand on Seshrab's shoulder. "This man is Seshrab. He is now the king's chief scribe. You will teach him whatever he needs to know, you will answer truthfully and fully any questions that he asks, and you will obey any orders that he gives you. Is that clearly understood?"

Imhotep began stumbling for words. "B-b-but Your Highness, why—?"

Shaweneiti shot his hand up, a signal for him to be silent. "It is not your place to question the command of *Nesu*. You will do as you are told. The king has commanded that Seshrab is to take your place as Chief Scribe, and you are to be his assistant".

*His assistant?* "Your Highness—?"

"And if you protest the word of the living god, you will have your head cut off".

At that, the four guards tightly gripped their axes.

Imhotep saw that he was cornered. "I shall do as the king your father commands, Your Highness", and Imhotep hesitatingly bowed in submission.

"Good. It is settled", said Shaweneiti. "Give Seshrab your ring and your scepter". All important government officials were given gold signet rings, and the chief scribe, as a high-ranking palace official, was no exception.

Imhotep hesitatingly obeyed the command. He gave Seshrab his scepter, and then forcefully tugged the gold signet ring off of his fat finger and handed it over. Seshrab immediately put it on.

Prince Shaweneiti turned to Seshrab. "You are now Chief Scribe by the command of His Divine Majesty, my father. Perform your duties well", and the prince and his guards walked away, leaving Seshrab alone with the now enraged Imhotep.

Imhotep closed the door to his cell, waited a few seconds, and then swirled around and slammed a rock-solid punch right into Seshrab's face, knocking him to the floor, dropping the *sekhem* scepter in the process. "Alright, you little shit", snapped the fat man to the surprised and slightly afraid newcomer, "you listen to me, and listen well, because I'll only say this once. *I* give the orders, and you will do what *I* say *when* I say it. Regardless of what the prince or the king calls you, *I'm* still the one in charge here, and you had best not forget that! I can break you, I can make you wish you were never born! And another thing – this is not your room. This is *my* room! *My* furniture, *my* paintings, *my* food, *my* women! You'll bunk with one of the other junior scribes and sleep on the floor". At that, Imhotep threw the door open. He stooped down and grabbed the *sekhem* scepter off the floor. "Get out!", and he grabbed Seshrab by the neck and dragged him outside.

Seshrab wasn't sure what he should do. Should he call out for help? As if reading his mind, Imhotep barked "Don't bother yelling out. They won't listen to you. And if they do get curious, I'll say that you're a wretched Asiatic and that you tried to kill me, because all of you Asiatics are thieves and murderers".

He brought Seshrab to the next door and banged on it with the butt end of the scepter. Almost immediately, it creaked open, and a young man, perhaps a few years younger than Seshrab, peeked out with a puzzled expression. Without explanation, Imhotep pushed the door open all the way and flung Seshrab to the floor. "This is your new roommate", he said to the young scribe. Then turning back to Seshrab, "Remember, don't cross me, boy, or get in my way, or I'll smash every bone in your body with this", holding his scepter in a very ominous way. "It'll sting – *bad!*" and he stormed out in a huff and slammed the door behind him.

Seshrab was now suddenly filled with immense rage, and charged the door, but was caught and restrained by the young man. "NO! You'll only make things worse for yourself", he cautioned. "Imhotep cannot be stood up to. He is in too good of a standing with the royals. It's your word against his, and assaulting an elite member of the royal court means certain death, even if you have good reason".

Seshrab had no words. He just let out a loud growl of anger and frustration, and propped himself against a wall, bitter. He banged on it once with his fists. It didn't help.

"I'd love to chat, but I have a lot of work to do, and I need to get it finished by tomorrow", said the young scribe, and he returned to sitting on his bed. On it was a large rectangular board and a jumbled mess of papers with long lists of figures. Resting on the board was a small ceramic cup of water and an Egyptian scribe's palette, which was a long piece of wood with a groove cut down the middle to hold the pens, and with a pair of recessed inkwells on one end. One well held black ink, the other red. The young scribe sat down on the bed, careful not to jar it too much so as to spill the water, laid the board on his lap, held the writer's palette in his left hand, placed a sheet of paper on the board with his right hand, removed a pen from the palette, dipped it in water, swished it around in the black ink well, and began to write.

It was a certain comfort for Seshrab to hear the familiar scratch-scratch of a pen against paper. It was a sound that to him symbolized all of the hopes that he had for himself – respect, prosperity, and a quiet uneventful life.

Seshrab wanted to talk more with the young man, hoping that he might find a friend in this strange new land, someone that he could talk to and trust. However, he felt that he should not talk too much, if at all, and that he should not try to make friends because he probably wouldn't find any here.

Seshrab decided not to talk. Instead, he shuffled over to a corner of the room, slumped down onto the bare floor, and tried to fall asleep, letting the rhythmic and methodical scratching of the pen lull him to rest.

Seshrab was shaken awake. "Wake up", he heard someone say.

Seshrab groggily rolled over. His whole body ached from sleeping on the hard floor. He slowly cracked open his eyes and saw a dark shape kneeling over him. For a second, Seshrab didn't know where he was or who this person was, and then he remembered. He recognized the voice of the young scribe that he met yesterday – this was his room.

"It's morning now. Time to get to work".

Seshrab looked up. There was one small window which faced out to the palace's open central courtyard, but it was still dark outside. "Morning?" he grumbled.

"It's almost dawn", the scribe replied. "The king wants business to begin in earnest when the sun rises, which means that everyone has to be up and ready beforehand".

"Is it always like that?"

"Always", the scribe replied. He then opened the door and went outside carrying a piece of straw, and Seshrab saw the warm glow of oil lamps radiating outside in the hallway. The scribe came back a few seconds later, the end of the straw flickering with a small flame, and lit an oil lamp that was in the room. The little glow from the lamp helped to soften the room and make it not as lonely and imposing as it once was. "You don't get much sleep in this place", continued the scribe. "All business is supposed to stop when the sun sets, but I often have to stay up late finishing my work. I didn't get to bed until after midnight, but that's not unusual".

Seshrab tried to sit up. His muscles were sore and his bones cracked. "How long have you been working here?" asked Seshrab.

"A little over two years", he replied. "Come on, get up on your feet", and the scribe yanked Seshrab off the floor. "Clean yourself up. We have to present ourselves in a few minutes for roll call".

"Roll call?!"

"The king used to be a general. Personally, I think that he still thinks he is one. *Nesu* runs the palace like an army barracks. It works like this: At dawn, everyone has to go to the throne room and kneel before him. The vizier reads off the names of everyone who works in the palace, and we must all answer, 'I am here, my lord'. When the last name is read, the king dismisses us, and our work-day begins".

This was entirely different from the way that Seshrab was accustomed to doing things. This regimented routine didn't happen in the palaces of King Sihon of Hebron or King Ariyak of Gaza, but he gathered that he'd get used to it eventually. "What's your name?" asked Seshrab.

"Djoser", replied the young scribe.

"I'm Seshrab".

"Seshrab? That's not an Egyptian name", replied Djoser curiously. "Where are you from?"

"Hebron".

"You're a Canaanite?"

Seshrab suddenly felt uneasy. "Yes", he replied cautiously.

Djoser sat back down on the edge of his bed. "I'm surprised that the king let you in – he doesn't care much for foreigners. You're working as a scribe?"

"I'm supposed to be Chief Scribe".

At that, Djoser let out a burst of sarcastic laughter. *"Chief Scribe?!* Are all Canaanites that stupid? Firstly, you only just got here, and secondly, Imhotep is the chief scribe. What makes you think that you're entitled to his job? What makes you think that you're my boss now?"

Seshrab had thought that this person would be a friend, but now he wasn't so sure. "I came to the palace yesterday, and the king was impressed with me. I can read and write, and I speak many languages, and the king said that I should be Chief Scribe, and that Imhotep was to hand over his authority to me". Then Seshrab remembered the gold ring. "I can prove it – look. The prince gave me Imhotep's gold ring, see?"

"Listen, jackass", Djoser said, pointing his finger right at Seshrab's face, "I've been working here for the past two years, and a few of the other scribes have been here even longer. You came here yesterday, and you think that you're entitled to be higher than us who've actually put in the work?! Don't you think that's a bit *unfair*? What makes you so damn special? Huh?"

Then there was a knock at the door. "Who is it?" barked Djoser in an increasingly aggravated mood.

"Breakfast", came the muffled reply from outside.

Djoser opened the door, and in the hallway stood a young boy carrying a tray of bread rolls, grapes, and dates. An instant later, Imhotep appeared next to him. "Oh good, you're awake", he sneered at Seshrab with an insincere grin. "Did you have a pleasant night's rest, boy?

"I'm no boy", responded Seshrab in a more severe tone than he was used to.

Imhotep shoved the servant with the food out of the way and then smacked Seshrab hard across the face. "If I say you're a boy, you're a boy – got that, you little shit?"

Seshrab attempted to restrain his rising anger. He wanted to lunge at him like a pouncing leopard and strangle this pompous ape to death, but he held himself back, his muscles tight and tense.

"I said 'Got that?!'"

Seshrab took several deep deliberate breaths, and he replied, "Yes, my lord".

"Good, that's better". Then unexpectedly, Imhotep handed Seshrab his sekhem scepter. "Take this, and present yourself for roll call. Must keep up appearances, you know".

"Yes, my lord".

"Get going", and Imhotep shoved him out of the room into the hallway along with the servant boy who was still standing there with the tray of food. "Get to the throne room" he said as he started snatching up the food from the tray and stuffing it into his mouth. "Djoser here will show you the way. Tired, Djoser?"

"I didn't get much sleep last night, my lord", Djoser replied.

"Well that's just tough" he muffled out while chewing. "You work too hard, Djoser!" he said with mock sarcastic sincerity. "You need to take it easy every now and then, like I do. Get up off your ass and present yourself. Show our snotty-nosed newcomer the way. And for Ra's sake, don't yawn in the king's presence".

Djoser stood up. "Follow me, *Chief Scribe*", he said to Seshrab, and the three of them walked down the hallway of the Servants' Quarters towards the Perah.

Seshrab resented the treatment that he had gotten so far, but he had to keep reminding himself why he had come here in the first place. In spite of Imhotep's bullying, Djoser's unkindness, and the guards keeping him in prison for two days without any food or water, he knew that it was still better than being outside. As far as he knew, King Sihon was still looking for him, and it likely wouldn't be long before he caught wind of Seshrab escaping into Egypt. Going after his Canaanite neighbors was one thing, but King Sihon surely wouldn't dare launch an invasion of Egypt. As long as Seshrab was here, he was safe…or so he kept telling himself. However, if he wished to remain here, he needed to be on his absolute best behavior. *No matter what they say*, he thought to himself, *no matter what they do, no matter how badly they treat you, just smile and say 'Yes, sir', do your job as best as you can, stay out of trouble, and live to see another day.*

The throne room was located in the center of the Perah's first floor. It was the largest room in the palace, used for official ceremonies and presentations and as a makeshift auditorium. It was also used every day for the morning roll call. There were three doorways which led to the throne room: one small door on the left, mostly used by the servants, and another small door on the right, mostly used by the guards. These side doors measured four feet wide by eight feet tall. Then there were the two main doors. These were gargantuan things – two enormous cedar doors, each measuring six feet wide by twelve feet tall, and covered with decorated sheets of gold. It was meant to dazzle, impress, and intimidate anyone who *dared* to approach *Nesu's* presence. All three sets of doors were opened to allow the entire palace staff to quickly enter and exit. Seshrab, Djoser, and Imhotep entered the great hall through the main set of doors.

The interior of the throne room was a stunning sight. The room was large, square-shaped, with a floor made of large square tiles of polished white alabaster, and a high ceiling held up by four rows of massive cylindrical limestone columns measuring six feet in diameter. Each column was completely covered with hieroglyph inscriptions and various brightly painted scenes of the king, life in the palace, and images of war and the gods. The walls of the throne room were made of brick and faced with a thick coating of white plaster. All of the walls were covered in painted black hieroglyphs and monumental larger-than-life images, all of which were lavishly and vividly painted with bold bright colors. Arranged around the room were several large alabaster lamp stands fitted with a copper basin on the top, within which were placed flammable oils and sweet-smelling perfumes and fragrances. This oil was set on fire, and it created a glowing orange ambience in the immediate area, something harsh and primal. The flickering of the flames made some of the people in the carvings appear to move slightly. However, the sides of the room, especially behind the columns, were dark and shadowy, and Seshrab had trouble distinguishing just how big the room actually was.

Running up the middle of the throne room from the main doors to the other side was a massive stripe of red granite tiles, with a border of black marble separating the red pathway from the white alabaster. At the far side of the room was the *dais*, the raised rectangular platform which the throne stood upon. The dais consisted of three steps, constructed of brick and faced with black marble. The throne was carved from a single massive block of light grey granite, measuring over five feet tall with a rounded top, with a red velvet cushion on the seat. On either side of the throne was a large standing lamp identical to the ones that lined the main pathway up to the throne.

As he entered, Seshrab let his eyes follow the red granite pathway up to the royal platform. There seated upon the throne was King Nebsenre, his golden *nemes* crown looking like a lion's mane. Firmly clasped in one of his clenched fists, as erectly vertical as an obelisk, was a large shepherd's crook measuring about five feet tall or so, made of solid gold and banded at regular intervals with blue enamel.

The shepherd's crook was the symbol of royal authority as the king's protector over his "flock" of subjects. The torches burning on either side of him gave him an ominous appearance. What was particularly unnerving was that directly above the king's throne, right where the mighty war commander Nebsenre sat, was an enormous painting showing the Egyptian king grasping a kneeling enemy chief by the hair with one hand, and in his other hand was a club. The arm was raised up, a moment frozen in time, just before *Nesu* was about to bring the mace crashing down and smash the enemy commander's skull in. It was a threatening message to any foreign emissary visiting the king's court – *Do not toy with me. Behold the fate of my enemies.*

Prince Shaweneiti stood in front of the growing crowd at the base of the dais on the king's right-hand side, the place of honor, holding a scroll of papyrus listing the palace workers. Seshrab noted that the more prestigious the worker's position, the more gaudy their garments were. Several of the high-ranking officials were carrying their sekhem scepters, holding them straight and erect, like a formation of spearmen.

"Go up front, damn you!", Imhotep whispered to Seshrab. "You're supposed to be Chief Scribe, remember? All of the high-rankers have to stand at the front", and Imhotep gave Seshrab a hard shove.

Seshrab cautiously and awkwardly made his way through the crowd of strange faces. There were a lot of "Pardon me's" and "Excuse me's" as Seshrab squeezed and maneuvered his way to the front of the gathering. Some of them gave him dirty or haughty looks. The closer he got, the more he got a feeling of butterflies in his stomach. He had this unshakable feeling that he was doing something wrong, like a child cheating on a test and hoping that the teacher didn't see it. At last, he came to the front, and saw the full majesty of Nebsenre, the lion of Egypt, sitting barely twenty feet away from him. The ominous colored painting of the Egyptian king about to smash in the skull of one of his enemies didn't alleviate Seshrab's uneasiness.

Then, the time came. "ATTENTION!" called out the prince.

Everyone instantly snapped rigidly upright, as if they were made of stone, terrified to appear even the slightest bit out of alignment.

"All hail Nesu, Horus-Nebsenre, Living God of Egypt. Kneel before the son of Ra!"

At this, everyone fell to their knees and prostrated themselves, bowing down so low that their foreheads touched the floor. Seshrab copied their movements.

Then, all at the same time, they chanted "All hail Nesu, Horus-Nebsenre, Living God of Egypt". Seshrab didn't speak – nobody had prepared him for this.

"Arise! And stand at attention to hear your master's commands".

Everyone in the room once again rose up and stood at attention. Seshrab tried his best to follow along.

"His Divine Majesty has called you here for your day's work. State your presence, so that he may be satisfied that you are here to do your labors".

Seshrab looked around in an uneasy uncertain way, playing everything by ear. He was not really prepared for the obvious ritualism of this performance. Then he thought, *Oh damn, I know I have to say something specific when he calls on me. What was it again? I can't remember! What if he calls on me first?!*

King Nebsenre spoke, "Prince Shaweneiti, my son, heir to the throne, vizier to His Divine Majesty, and second-in-command of the Army, are you present?"

"I am here, my lord", the prince replied, even though he was obviously standing next to him. Still, this was a very ritualized roll call, and everyone had to announce their presence.

*I am here, my lord. That's it*, thought Seshrab. *That's strange. I thought that it was something more complicated than that.*

"Read off the roll of all of those in Nesu's service", commanded the king.

Prince Shaweneiti began. "Captain Nebikhamu, Commander of the Palace Guard".

"I am here, my lord", came a voice off to Seshrab's left.

"Horemheb, Chamberlain of the Palace".

"I am here, my lord".

"Kawaset, Secretary of the Treasury".

"I am here, my lord".

"Imeni, Secretary of Grain and Livestock".

"I am here, my lord".

"Seshrab, Chief Scribe".

That was his cue. "I am here, my lord", Seshrab called out.

There was a lot of mumbling and rumbling amongst the crowd. This man was unknown. Wasn't Imhotep the chief scribe, and had always been so? Who was this newcomer, this foreigner who had gained access to the king's service?

"*SILENCE!!!*" yelled out King Nebsenre. The room immediately became quiet. "I suppose you are wondering who this man is. As you can see from the light complexion of his skin, he is not Egyptian. He is a Canaanite. He is very intelligent, and has only recently entered my service. I have replaced Imhotep as Chief Scribe with this man. He will do well".

Seshrab gulped at the stern implications of that last sentence.

Nebsenre turned to his son. "Continue with the roll".

Prince Shaweneiti bowed respectfully and picked up where he left off, reading off the list of names of every person who worked in the palace. The process took five whole minutes. When it was done, Nebsenre stated "You are now dismissed to do your duty". Everyone bowed and left.

And so it continued for a few more weeks. Although Seshrab had been given an important post, he was not accepted by the other servants and palace officials, partly due to his nationality as a non-Egyptian, and partly due to him being "the new guy". Yet more than anything else, they were resentful that the king had chosen to appoint this newcomer to such a prominent position. Seshrab should have been scrubbing floors or cleaning out the latrines – the tedious menial jobs that all new employees had to do. Regardless of whatever qualifications he may have had, they felt that he had gone up the ladder without doing any of the work necessary to get there. Seshrab was often given dirty looks or even spat on, while others muttered obscene language under their breath whenever they passed in the hallway. The other scribes were openly disrespectful to Seshrab, paying no heed whatsoever to him. Djoser whom Seshrab shared a room with, never let him sleep in his cot – Seshrab *always* slept on the hard floor.

Even the king wasn't all that different. King Nebsenre kept Seshrab close but not too close, and Seshrab was never allowed outside the palace grounds. Seshrab was trapped here and he knew it. It was like being in a prison – a very large and well-furnished prison that you could freely walk about in for the most part, but a prison nonetheless. Nebsenre had Seshrab conduct semi-important assignments, but would never allow him to be present during military discussions, and occasionally Seshrab would receive the king's notoriously foul language due to one perceived error or another. His son, Prince Shaweneiti didn't yell at him, insult him, spit on him, or hit him. He merely ordered him about: "Seshrab, write this" or "Seshrab, catalogue these papers", and such. Seshrab preferred working around the prince because he felt that he didn't have to prove anything. He was given assignments, and he did them.

Seshrab did his best to contain his temper, repeatedly urging himself to bear all of this malice with unconcern. *Suck it up and deal with it*, he kept thinking. He had to keep reminding himself that as abusive as all of this was, it was still better than the alternative. *Being in here is still better than being out there.* As long as this situation remained status quo, Seshrab could not expect things to improve. Seshrab hated Imhotep and the amount of abuse that he inflicted upon not only himself but upon the other scribes as well. He tried to keep it in. Even though his mother had told him not to bottle up his anger, he knew that he had to keep his mouth shut.

And then one day, the straw broke the donkey's back. Seshrab had never let his emotions get the better of him like that before, but it happened, and it changed things. There was a lot of shouting, screaming, fists, the sound of cracking bones, and the sight of red blood splattered in the halls. There were witnesses.

It had all started rather ordinarily in terms of the bullying and derogatory abuse that Imhotep inflicted. He wasn't especially vicious that day more than any other, but for Seshrab, it was just one day too many. It happened in the hallway right outside the throne room, just after the morning roll call. Imhotep made some insulting comment to him – Seshrab couldn't even remember what it was, it was so trivial – but he just couldn't take it anymore. Seshrab went absolutely berserk right there in front of everyone. He let out a loud scream and lunged at Imhotep, taking him completely by surprise. He slammed Imhotep against the wall, which was no little feat considering the man's enormous girth, choking him with one hand and slamming his fist as hard as he could into Imhotep's face, but the man was so fat that it had little effect. Imhotep gained the initiative and began hitting Seshrab. In a matter of seconds, there was a full-fledged back-alley brawl going on inside the royal palace with everyone looking on. Seshrab saw that his own physical strength was not working, so thinking quickly, he grabbed his sekhem scepter that was lying on the floor and swung it at Imhotep. *WHAM!* Right into his guts! The force of the impact knocked the breath out of him and momentarily stunned him. Feeling himself gain the initiative again, Seshrab began wailing on him with his scepter, using it like a club, slamming it down on him over and over again like a metalsmith using a hammer on an anvil. Seshrab's emotions were so worked up that he was completely oblivious to what was going on around him. Even the king and the prince had come out into the hallway to see what all of the raucous noise was about. Someone had called the palace guards to intervene and put a stop to it before someone got killed, but both the king and the prince barred them from doing so – they wanted to see what would happen. The fight turned into a spectator sport. Seshrab wasn't aware of it, but many of the courtiers were smiling when they saw him beating Imhotep into a bloody pulp, especially the other scribes and the female servants, whom Imhotep had abused more than others. Some were even openly cheering him on! "KILL HIM!!! KILL HIM!!!" they shouted gleefully over and over again.

It was at that point that King Nebsenre decided that enough was enough. "STOP! STOP! I COMMAND YOU!!!" he blasted, and he yanked the scepter out of Seshrab's hand and handed it off to his son the prince. He then pointed to Imhotep's bloody crippled unconscious form lying in a splattering of his own blood on the floor. Several of his teeth had been knocked out, he had numerous broken bones, and was bleeding severely. "Take him away". It was a general order to the whole audience. A few of the men nearby grabbed Imhotep and dragged him off somewhere. Nebsenre then turned to the crowd. "It's finished! Disperse! Perform your duties!"

At that, everyone left and went about the day's business. Their fun was over, and it was time to work.

Seshrab was panting heavily. His adrenaline was shooting and his heartbeat was racing. His whole body was splattered with Imhotep's blood from his head to his feet.

Nebsenre momentarily propped the royal shepherd's crook against the wall, and he clasped Seshrab by both of his shoulders with those strong gripping hands of his. Seshrab now fully comprehended what he had done, and he was suddenly seized with great terror. He remembered what Djoser had told him when they first met, when he first wanted to attack Imhotep for bullying and threatening him – *Assaulting an elite member of the royal court means certain death, even if you have good reason.*

But the king was smiling. "You're not the worm that I thought you were! You have *courage*, man!!!" he beamed. "You have just done what I have wanted to do for a long time. I never thought that such a bookish person as yourself would have such ferocity inside you. The warlike spirit of your people is still strong in your heart. You have shown your true self to me, and I am heartily glad of it!" Then, the king took back his crook and walked off.

Prince Shaweneiti handed the battered bloodied sekhem scepter back to Seshrab, a little knowing smirk on his face. "Go to the baths and clean yourself up". Then he looked at Seshrab's blood-splattered white linen kilt. "I'll see to it that some new clothes are brought to you", and then he walked off to join his father. He chuckled a little along the way.

Seshrab was a bit woozy. The adrenaline rush was crashing. *What just happened?*, he thought to himself.

He walked around the corner, and Djoser was there waiting for him. He, too, was smiling. "When we first met", he said, "I asked why you felt that you were so damned special. I was wrong to treat you with such disrespect. You were the only one who stood up to that pompous self-righteous ass. Everyone else had been 'put in their place'. But not you. You resisted, and you triumphed. You have gained my respect, and certainly the respect of everyone here. No one in the palace shall look down on you ever again". He held out his hand. "You are my friend".

Seshrab, smiling, clasped his hand and answered, "You are my friend".

As Seshrab walked through the corridors, Imhotep's blood still splattered all over his face, body, and kilt, others stood by, pointed at him, and whispered to themselves. Seshrab knew that they were talking about him, but he didn't care. He had earned the respect of the royal family and had earned at least one friend, and that's what counted.

At last, he came to the bath room. He had been here once before several weeks ago when the king had sent him here when they first met. Only members of the royal family were allowed to bathe here – the rest of the royal court had to clean themselves with wash basins in their cells. However, when Seshrab had first arrived and was presented before the king, his stink was so awful that His Divine Majesty ordered the scribe to be taken to the royal bath room right away.

As Seshrab walked through the door of the bath room, the chief bath attendant and his five helpers turned around and stared at him. They had all seen the fight in the hallway. Now, the triumphant conqueror, splattered with the blood of his defeated enemy, stood before them, mighty weapon in hand.

"The prince ordered me to come here to get cleaned", said Seshrab in a very plain way.

At first, they just stood there and stared at him, mouths open. Then, the chief bath attendant began clapping, and soon afterwards all of them began clapping and smiling. "Our hero!" one of them shouted out. "Hail Seshrab, smiter of toads!" cried out another. Then they all rushed up to him.

"Welcome, welcome!" said the chief bath attendant, shaking Seshrab's hand. "Let us attend to you in every way! You there!" he said snapping his fingers at the other five men. "Get some hot water at once! And the very best soap, not that cheap sandy crap! Warm soft towels! Do you wish to have music played while you bathe, sir?"

*Sir.* It had been a very long time since anyone had called him that. "No, that will not be necessary, sir", he replied with turn-for-turn politeness. "I just want a wash. Uh, is there someplace where I can put this?" he asked, holding up his scepter.

"Oh, of course, of course! I'll just take it and lay it down on the side over here. Hey! How's that hot water coming along?"

"The fire's coming along nicely", said one of the other attendants.

"Infernal! The man wants a bath *now*, not later! Build the fire up!"

"Right away, sir!"

"By the way, I'm sorry I don't remember your name", said Seshrab to the chief bath attendant. "There are so many people here in this palace that it's hard for me to keep track of who is who".

"My name is Tutmoses", he replied.

"It's very nice to be introduced to you, Tutmoses".

After a minute of waiting, Seshrab climbed into the tub. The hot water felt very good and soothed his muscles. The five attendants were very careful not to scrub him too hard. They treated him as if they were washing a member of the royal family. Seshrab learned all of their names: Ahmose, Djedifre, Keti, Raneb, and Thesh. He asked about their families and about their interests. They all made very pleasant conversation. "By the way, what happened to Imhotep?" asked Seshrab.

There was a bit of silence. "Don't worry about him, sir", answered Tutmoses. "He won't bother you or any of us anymore".

Seshrab decided not to press the matter further.

While Seshrab was taking his bath, Tutmoses got called to the door. There was a boy standing there with a bundle and a small note. "From His Highness the prince", the boy stated, handed both objects to him, and took off.

Tutmoses read the note carefully. He then set both items on the side near Seshrab's scepter, walked over to where the bloody white kilt was laying crumpled on the floor, grabbed it, and dumped it into a pile of other clothes that were scheduled to be washed by the laundry servants. "The prince has sent some new clothes for you", he explained.

After his bath was done and was thoroughly cleaned, he was dried down with towels, had the *kohl* eye liner applied to him, and was sprinkled with perfume. Seshrab thought that all he would be getting was just another plain white kilt to replace the one that got ruined. When the bundle was carefully unraveled, he was surprised to see that there were several items. First was a black Egyptian-style wig. Then, there was a short-sleeve knee-length tunic made of white linen trimmed with dark blue ribbon. Third was a white kilt which was to be worn over the tunic around the waist, folded in such a way that a large flap would hang down the front.

Once Seshrab had cleaned himself up, he took up residence in Imhotep's former cell at the far end of the Servants' Quarters. He wouldn't need to share a room with Djoser anymore, which he imagined Djoser was very grateful for. The cells were already small for just one person, but having two people sharing one was distinctly cramped. The chief scribe's cell was the same size as all of the other cells in the Servants' Quarters, but it was much better furnished. Like Djoser's cell, this one had a small window which looked out onto the palace courtyard and let in natural light. However, unlike Djoser's cell, this window had hinged wooden shutters to block out the light if the occupant so wished. An ornately-pattered rug lay in the middle of the floor. A cabinet of well-polished cedar wood stood in one corner with stacks of papyrus paper, brushes, writing palates, and ink blocks of varying colors on the shelves; the ink blocks were wrapped in papyrus paper and coated with beeswax to keep them from getting wet. There was a small table to serve as a nightstand, and on the shelf underneath its tabletop was a wash basin made from blue faience ceramic and a small ceramic drinking cup. Most importantly of all, at least for Seshrab, the bed was no simple canvas cot but a *real actual bed*, with goose down stuffing, mounted on a solid wooden bedframe with hammock netting for added suspension and springiness, and all covered with exquisite white linen sheets. Seshrab was overjoyed – weeks of sleeping on the hard floor had put a cramp in his back.

One day, late in the evening, Seshrab was walking through the palace about to go back to the Servants' Quarters to get some sleep. As he was walking through one of the colonnaded halls, he passed by a room and could hear voices inside. Several armed guards were standing in front of the door, blocking anybody else from entering. Seshrab continued on his way.

Meanwhile, inside that room, King Nebsenre was discussing the imminent attack on West Ament with his regimental commanders. Back when Egypt was still a united empire under single rule, the army was divided into four divisions of 4,000 men each named after the gods Amun, Ra, Ptah, and Set. However, when the civil war began following the collapse of the government in 1759 BC, the army's structure fell apart. But then during the reign of King Sheshy, the Royal Army of Lower Egypt was re-standardized. The smallest military unit was a squad of ten men. Ten squads formed a company of 100 men, five companies formed a battalion of 500 men, and four battalions formed a provincial regiment of 2,000 men. Three of the regiment's four battalions, 1,500 men in total, were infantrymen, and the remaining fourth was made up of archers. A company of 100 rangers would be attached to each regiment. Nebsenre controlled three provinces so far, which meant that he had a total of 6,300 men under his command – 4,500 infantrymen, 1,500 archers, and 300 rangers.

Egyptian regiments were named after the province that the men came from, and were identified with standards carried into battle. These were not flags, but were instead head-sized gold statuettes mounted on top of a pole. These standards were sacred items, blessed by the priests. Each regiment had its own patron god or goddess who would protect the men or grant them skill or courage in battle, and these statues were representations of gods or items associated with the god. Being the regiment's standard-bearer was a very important position because it was believed that this man embodied the essence of what the regiment was.

First was the Khaset Regiment, under the command of Colonel Horahauty, who had fought with Nebsenre and his son in many battles and whose loyalty and courage were undoubted. The regiment's symbol was a bull and its patron god was the sun god Ra, king of the gods. The bull statuette which was carried by the regimental standard-bearer had a sun disk mounted atop its head, signifying its connection with the lord of the sky.

Second was the Sapmeh Regiment, commanded by Colonel Ankharis, an aggressive man always eager for a fight. Its patron was Neith, goddess of the hunt and the patron goddess of archers. Her symbol, which became the symbol of the regiment, was a green shield over a pair of crossed bows. It was believed that Neith had inspired mankind to make their first weapons during prehistory in order to hunt their prey, and that she protected the bodies of dead soldiers.

Third was the East Ament Regiment, commanded by Colonel Mebydos, cautious but vigilant, a superb strategist, relying more on his wits than his weapons to win his battles. Its patron was Horus, the falcon-headed son of Osiris. Egyptian mythology stated that Horus had exacted revenge for the murder of his father at the hands of his wicked brother Set. The regiment's symbol was a gold falcon.

"We will need to blockade the province to prevent Governor Nesbit from eluding us", said the king.

"West Ament shares a border with the province of Khensu to the south", said Colonel Mebydos. "They may cross the border and seek protection there".

"Knowing your wrath, Your Divine Majesty", said Colonel Ankharis, "I doubt that the lord of Khensu will allow the fleeing West Amentites into his realm".

"West Ament's capital city, Yamu, is located here", and Nebsenre pointed to the map, "about thirty miles away from Khaset City – at least two days' march. It's not far from where this particular part of the Nile branches into two. It's very close to the southernmost tip of East Ament, and we can launch the invasion from there. It's only eight miles in a straight line from the river to the city. We can maybe reach it in one day. We can make a landing…*there*, thereby splitting West Ament more or less in half. As soon as we establish a beachhead, we must advance quickly and take the capital by force. Once we seize control of Yamu, all of West Ament will be ours. Any other questions?"

"No, Your Divine Majesty", they all said.

"Very well. Colonel Ankharis and Colonel Mebydos, return to your home-provinces immediately and muster your troops. Colonel Horahauty, have your men ready themselves for battle. We'll rendezvous with Ankharis' and Mebydos' regiments along the way. Speed will be of the essence in this operation. Your regiments must be ready to move instantly".

"Our regiments will be standing by, waiting for Your Divine Majesty's arrival", said Colonel Ankharis.

Preparations for the campaign were now well underway. To anyone who witnessed the collection of boats and ships of all sizes along the coast of Nebsenre's domain, and the troops perpetually drilling for battle, it was obvious that a new military campaign was about to commence. Such activity was also plainly visible to those on the opposite shore in West Ament. The king wasn't exactly being subtle about his intentions.

Finally, the day came – the army was going to march tomorrow. It was customary that the day prior to the army setting out, the king would offer a sacrifice at the Temple of Ra to ensure victory and good favor with the gods. This temple was the third-largest structure within Khaset City, the first being the royal palace and the second being the Temple of Amun, which was located immediately next-door to the palace. The Temple of Ra was located on one side of one of Khaset's town gates; it was the first building that you saw when you entered the town. The falcon-headed sun god Ra was the patron god of Khaset Province.

King Nebsenre was accompanied by his son and a small troupe of twenty bodyguards. He had performed this ritual twice before when he had conquered the provinces of Sapmeh and East Ament. For the sacrifice, he brought with him a perfectly white bull, unblemished and unscarred. Nebsenre, although a living god, did not like to be carried on a litter like a perfumed aristocrat. He was first and foremost a soldier, and he preferred to march on foot, so he, his son, and the sacrificial bull walked to the temple and his armed men formed a circle around them.

As King Nebsenre, Prince Shaweneiti, and their bodyguards made their way to the Temple of Ra, crowds gathered alongside the road to watch. Normally, the king stayed within the walls of his palace and was hardly ever seen in public; it helped to augment the mystery and awe surrounding *Nesu*. The people bowed their heads to the ground, never looking directly at him.

At last, the group came to the gates of the temple. The Temple of Ra was surrounded by a high brick wall with one large gate, and next to the gate was a large well-polished copper disk, which would be struck to let the priests inside know that someone wished to enter. The party paused outside, Prince Shaweneiti struck the gong, and waited.

The people, who by now had formed a large crowd, began to approach slowly, their heads still bowed, asking for the king's blessing. Nebsenre, always eager to increase his public image, obliged, and he waved his guards away.

"But Your Divine Majesty—" protested one of the guards, but Nebsenre interrupted him with a stern glance.

Nebsenre laid his hands on one of the peasants, a woman. "I, Nesu, living god of Egypt, bless you and wish that you prosper". The woman thanked him and inched away. Another one, a man, came forward and the same blessing was given.

By now the temple's gate had opened and a young priest stuck his head through.

"The king is blessing the people", said Prince Shaweneiti. "Please wait".

The king continued the laying-on of hands for a few more minutes. Another one, a man, came forward and knelt, wearing a large billowing robe of linen, probably a merchant. Nebsenre held out his hands, but then the man suddenly reached into his robe, pulled out a sharpened copper dagger, and slammed it straight into the king's chest, baring his teeth as he did so, and the king fell down to his knees. Screaming erupted from the crowd and the people began to run away. The sacrificial bull panicked and charged off with the rest of the crowd. "Get the prince!" the man shouted, and three other men pulled out their daggers and rushed the guards. The guards were so stunned by the sudden attack that the men barged right through them, the knives ready to come down. Prince Shaweneiti wasn't armed with anything but his ceremonial staff. As one of the men lunged, Shaweneiti blocked him, but a second assassin managed to slash open the prince's arm. By now, the guards regained their composure and fell upon the attackers. They were ready to butcher them right then and there when Shaweneiti shouted "No! Don't kill them! They're no good to us dead. Take them away for interrogation".

Shaweneiti then turned towards his father, and saw him lying on the ground unmoving. "Father? Father! *FATHER!!!*" he knelt down by the body, a pool of blood accumulating on the ground, and shook him. "Father! Father!"

It was no use – the living god of Lower Egypt was dead.

"Oh father, I'm so sorry. I'm so sorry".

As the attackers were forced to the ground, spears were pointed into the back of their skulls, ready to drive them into the murderers' brains if they so much as twitched. One of the guards called out to his comrades to find some rope. As one of them ran off to find something to bind the prisoners with, another ripped his linen kilt into strips, helped the prince up to his feet, and bound the prince's arm to stop it from bleeding. Another guard grabbed Nebsenre's striped *nemes* crown and pulled off Shaweneiti's prince's cap. "What are you doing?!" he exclaimed.

But the guard didn't answer, and he quickly placed the *nemes* atop Shaweneiti's head. Then he fell to his knees and bowed, extending both of his hands upwards in salutation. *"Abrik Nesu Shaweneiti!!!"* shouted the guard.

At that, all of the others joined in. *"Hail King Shaweneiti!!! Long live the king!!! Hail King Shaweneiti!!! Long live the king!!!"*

# CHAPTER 7

*Word spread quickly through Khaset City and through the palace that King Nebsenre had been treacherously murdered while preparing to make his victory sacrifice at the Temple of Ra, and that his son the prince had been severely wounded. Nebsenre's body was brought back to the palace upon a bier, and as the body returned, his guards had to beat off the peasants who dared to approach him, eager to dip their fingers in his sacred blood.*

*King Nebsenre, formerly General Nakhtibre, had reigned as Lower Egypt's king and living god for exactly one year, five months, and twenty days. His son Prince Shaweneiti was immediately acclaimed on the spot by the king's guards as the new king of Lower Egypt.*

*The murderers were brought to the palace dungeon, whereupon all of them except one were put to death in the most gruesome manner – by performing a live disembowelment upon them. Members of the Palace Guard, under the direction of their leader Captain Nebikhamu, carried out the king's command. I myself was not present at these proceedings, the king having judged that my constitution might not be robust enough to endure the sights and sounds of such an ordeal, and instead bade me to attend to other matters. One of the other scribes, who was older and had a stronger stomach for such things, was ordered by His Majesty Nesu Shaweneiti to record any information that the doomed men would cry out whilst being tortured. The report of the interrogation would afterwards be presented to me to look over, and afterwards presented to His Majesty.*

"Oh, get off me!" snapped Shaweneiti to his physician, pushing him away while he was poking and probing the wound. "Great gods, it's just a simple cut! I've suffered worse than this and no one fussed over it as much as you". He was sitting in the doctor's chambers. The king's personal doctor was one of the few staff actually had quarters inside the Perah itself, and not within the Servant's Quarters amongst the other cells where the other workers lived. Outside in the hall, the two greyhounds Osiris and Set furiously scratched at the door and raised an immense racket with their barking and yowling – they instinctively knew that something was very wrong.

"But Sire, the wound may have become infected. The blade might even have been poisoned".

"If it *was* poisoned, I'd be dead by now. And as for infection, that's what alcohol is for. Just wash it out, sew me up, rub some honey on it, and cover it up with a bandage. I'll be fine".

"Do you want any beer to lessen the pain, my lord?"

"I'm a soldier, I'm accustomed to pain. Now get a needle and thread and start stitching. And make sure you stick them in boiling water before you work on me with them!"

"As you wish, Your Highness – I mean Your *Majesty*".

At that moment, the door opened and Seshrab entered the room, trying as hard as he could to bar the two dogs from coming in, which they definitely didn't appreciate. Slung over one shoulder was a satchel bag full of sheets of papyrus paper as well as a portable ink pallet. The physician went off to the far side of the room to heat some water over his small hearth.

"Well, what is it?" asked an increasingly irritated monarch, gripping his wounded arm.

Seshrab knelt, his eyes cast down to the floor. "Your Divine Majesty, I wish to report—".

"Stop there, Chief Scribe", Shaweneiti interrupted. "I'm not divine…not yet. I have not yet been officially coronated and transfigured with the essence of Horus. For the time being, I am merely a king, not both king and god. So do not address me as 'Your Divine Majesty'. Just 'Your Majesty' will do for now".

"Uh, yes, of course, Your Majesty", Seshrab corrected himself, trying his best to keep up.

"Anyway, what did you come in here to say?"

"The prisoners have been questioned in the manner you ordered, Your Majesty. The sole remaining assailant said that the men were hired by Nesbit, the governor of West Ament. It was he who planned and paid them for your father's death, as well as your own. They were each paid a half-pound of gold to do the deed, and were to be paid another half-pound each upon completion of their mission".

"Nesbit…I thought as much. Just one pound of gold to kill a king? My father was worth a higher price than that. One would think with ambitions as high as his, Governor Nesbit could afford to be a little less stingy. Take their gold, Seshrab", ordered Shaweneiti, trying to change the subject, "and use it for my father's funeral expenses".

"Yes, Your Majesty".

"Nesbit...", Shaweneiti muttered to himself. "Praise the gods that the army is ready to move. I'll be gone for at least a week while I deal with him. After the customary three day mourning period is up, my father's body is to be handed over to the embalmers. It will be prepared for mummification while I'm gone. Use the assassins' gold to pay the embalmers for their work".

"Yes, Your Majesty".

"Your Majesty", said the doctor, "the needles have been prepared".

"Good, you can begin your work. Seshrab".

"Yes, Your Majesty?"

"I want you to watch this. You may have need of such knowledge one day".

"I may need your assistance as well, Chief Scribe", the doctor said.

"What do you want me to do, doctor?"

"Just wait a moment". The doctor brought over a few things on a copper tray: a ceramic bowl, a jar of wine, a jar of honey, a sewing needle made from a porcupine quill, thread placed inside a small folded linen sheet, and a roll of clean linen bandages. "Hold the wine".

Seshrab laid his burdens aside, stood up, and took the wine in both hands.

"Your Majesty, will you please remove your hand and extend your arm".

The king did so. Seshrab cringed at what he saw, but the look on the king's face seemed to convey that he had suffered worse and that he considered this to be only a minor injury.

"Alright now", said the doctor to Seshrab, holding the bowl underneath the injured arm, which was already being christened by dribbles of blood, "wash out the wound with the wine. The alcohol in it will cleanse it".

Seshrab already knew that putting alcohol on an injury helped to reduce infection, but he also knew that it would cause incredible searing pain. He hesitated.

"This is no time to be squeamish! Do it, man!" yelled the king.

Seshrab obeyed, and cautiously poured the wine over the open cut, careful not to spill too much. The king's jaw tightened with a sharp deep intake of air between his clenched teeth, followed by a slow exhale through his nostrils.

"Now, put the wine down and take the bowl. I'll do the rest".

As Seshrab held the bowl, the court physician applied a layer of honey to the open wound. The Egyptians recognized that honey had healing properties in addition to being a food sweetener. Then he began stitching. The whole time, the king didn't say a word, even though both the doctor and Seshrab knew that he was in great pain. When the cut was stitched up, the doctor wiped away the excess blood, and then brushed a second layer of honey onto the injury to prevent infection. Finally, a linen bandage was wrapped over his arm.

"Are those the interrogation records?" asked Shaweneiti while the doctor was wrapping him up.

"Yes, Your Majesty" replied Seshrab.

"Let me read them".

Seshrab arose and handed the papers over to his king. As soon as he did, he knelt again.

"There's no need to be so formal, Seshrab", said the king as he began reading the documents while the doctor still attended to him. "Kneeling is very hard on the knees. I prefer my soldiers to stand at attention when addressing a superior officer".

Seshrab immediately shot up and stood as stiff and straight as a spear.

"That's better" he said, not even looking at him, scrutinizing the interrogation transcript…

*Q. What is your name?*
*A. Amunpenefer.*

*Q. Where do you come from?*
*A. West Ament.*

*Q. Why did you kill our king?*
*A. I was paid to do it.*

*Q. Who paid you?*
*A. Nesbit, the governor of West Ament.*

*Q. Why did he want you to kill Nesu?*
*A. I don't know. He didn't tell me.*

*Q. I don't believe you! Tell us why he wanted you to kill our king!*
*A. I don't know. He said nothing to us regarding his reasons.*
*Interrogator hits him.*

*Q. Why did Governor Nesbit want our king dead?*
*A. I said I do not know. I do not know.*

*Q. This purse was found on your body, and others like it were found*
*on the others. Is this the gold that you were paid with?*
*A. That's half of it. Nesbit gave us half a pound of gold to do it, and*
*said he would give us another half-pound upon word of our success.*

*Q. Why did Nesbit ask you and these others to do it? Are you mercenaries?*
*A. No.*

*Q. Professional assassins?*
*A. No. But I am poor and I need money. I have been forced from time to time to take up murder as my trade. I cannot speak for the others who were with me. But I imagine that they are like myself.*

*Q. Describe how you came to be employed in his service.*
*A. Nesbit summoned us, and told us what he wanted us to do. Although I cannot remember his exact words, he told us that he was a kind lord who rewarded his most loyal followers. He said that he wished us to kill two people – the king and his son. I was about to tell him what price I wanted, when he said that it would be he, not us, who would negotiate the price – he would pay us whatever money that he wished, and we were to either accept it or reject it. He gave us each a half-pound of gold, and promised another half-pound for each of us if we were successful in our deed. He told us to go to Khaset and blend in, and when the time was right, strike. After a while, we were informed that Nebsenre would be attacking West Ament within the month of Payni. We sent one of our men as a runner back to Nesbit, telling him of Nebsenre's plans, and he told us to kill him before the pre-war sacrifice. We did as he ordered.*

*Q. Did you see any soldiers in West Ament?*
*A. Yes.*

*Q. How many were there?*
*A. Not many, barely more than the palace guards. Perhaps only 500 men. They were always training with their weapons.*

*Q. Were the peasants drafted?*
*A. I don't think so. I didn't see any being conscripted or being issued weapons.*

*Q. Our army numbers 6,000 men. You are outnumbered 12 to 1. How can only one battalion defeat three regiments and take over the capital?*
*A. I do not know.*

Shaweneiti handed the documents back to Seshrab. "Put these with the other court files", he said. "Make two copies of these documents. Put one with the criminal cases, and the second with those relating to the military. What about the prisoner?"

"I told the inquisitors that he was to be kept alive, Your Majesty, to see if his story was true".

"Good".

"Your Majesty", began the doctor, "I'll need to put your arm in a sling to keep it immobile".

"Very well", replied Shaweneiti, and the doctor got onto his work.

"Your Majesty", interjected Seshrab, "I did not know your father for long, but I wish to express to you personally my sadness regarding his death".

Shaweneiti was touched by this. "Thank you, Chief Scribe", he said, trying to sound matter-of-fact. "I appreciate your kind sentiments. Now resume your duties. And let Osiris and Set in – they've been worrying about me long enough".

Seshrab bowed and opened the door, and the two greyhounds immediately bolted in, whimpering, panting, their tails wagging furiously, and pawing at their master's son. As Seshrab was about to leave, one of the palace attendants entered the room. He courteously bowed to Seshrab as he passed, and in return Seshrab courteously bowed back and walked out the door.

"Your Majesty, several priests from the Temple of Ra and the Temple of Amun have arrived at the Perah. They wish to speak to you urgently".

"Tell them to wait for me in the throne room", said the king while he was petting and stroking his dogs. "I will see them in a few minutes".

The attendant bowed and went back out the door to fetch the priests.

In the empty throne room, the seven priests with shaved heads and garbed in immaculate white linen gowns chatted amongst themselves. Then, one of the side doors opened and the king came into the room attended by four armed guards, as well as the two greyhounds Osiris and Set, their claws clicking on the stone tile floor. As the king entered, all seven priests bowed to him. King Shaweneiti, his left arm thickly bandaged and laying within a sling around his shoulder, ascended the steps of the dais and took his seat upon the throne with the guards standing on either side. The two dogs likewise took their places seated on the dais' steps.

Once again, the priests bowed to him. One of them was the chief priest of the Temple of Ra. His white robe was much fancier than those of the other men. It was a short-sleeved tunic extending down to the ankles. The skirt of the tunic was arranged in three overlapping pleated layers. However, the thing which distinguished him more than anything else was a leopard pelt draped over one shoulder – only the chief priest of each temple wore such an article. "Your Majesty", the chief priest began, "We wish to express our condolences at the death of your father".

"Your condolences are noted".

"I wish to also bring to your attention, Your Majesty, that it is customary for a three-day mourning period to be in place so that the family of the deceased can grieve for their fallen".

"I am aware of that custom", said Shaweneiti.

"Your Majesty, since the king is the father of the nation, the entire country should be in a state of grief. They must mourn for three days. That means that they should do no work for those three days, but give themselves solely to prayer and lamentation".

"I understand".

"And yet, Your Majesty, we see your soldiers fervently training on the parade grounds with their weapons, fetching supplies, and other duties of military camps as though there was no such mourning period in progress".

Shaweneiti didn't answer.

"Your Majesty, it is written in both the state law and in religious law that such a mourning period is to be put in place. You must punish these soldiers for breaking the law".

"I ordered them to continue their training", said Shaweneiti.

"But Your Majesty, your father was the king, and the proper lamentations must be shown. The law must be upheld. It's not just legal considerations that must be addressed here. To not show the proper mourning is an insult to the dead man's soul. As the living god of Lower Egypt, he must be accorded what is proper".

"I agree", said Shaweneiti. "I have no desire to offend my father's spirit. He already had enough enemies when he was alive. But I believe that he would be pleased with me even more if he should see that, rather than stagnating in tears, he should see us readying to take revenge on his enemies".

"But Your Majesty, I—"

Shaweneiti bolted up from his throne, shouting *"AM I NOT THE KING?"*, the thunderous words loudly reverberating within the largely empty hall.

All of the priests were caught off guard by this sudden explosion of aggression. Shaweneiti was always a very reserved and quiet person by nature. His two dogs instantly shot up from their relaxed seated positions and began barking and snarling, their teeth menacingly bared at the priests who had clearly angered their new master.

"Indeed, you are the king, Your Majesty", replied the chief priest meekly, his head bowed.

"And does the king of Lower Egypt have supreme power over all of Lower Egypt?"

"Yes, Your Majesty".

"Do his powers include the authority to write new laws, change existing laws, or discard them altogether?"

"Yes, Your Majesty".

"Then I exercise my royal prerogative now, and I decree that anyone who wishes to mourn may do so, and anyone who wishes to work may do so, and that includes training for war. We are about to invade the land of the man who arranged my father's death. Lord Nesbit does not mourn my father. We cannot afford to be lazy and lie in our beds while my enemies rigorously prepare themselves for battle. Nesbit will be expecting us to be in mourning. He'll be expecting us to be prostrate and lax. We'll go against his expectations, and we will attack him. Is that clear?!"

The priests had been put in their place. "Yes, Your Majesty".

"Get out".

About two hours later, Seshrab came looking for his master, and when he inquired about the king's whereabouts, the palace attendants told him that he was practicing with his troops in the palace courtyard.

Seshrab stepped out into the sun, blinding him for a few moments; he'd been inside for quite some time, lit only by torches, lamps, and the occasional window. As his eyes became adjusted, he saw the men divided into sections, each practicing their own particular fighting style. He heard the rhythmic grunts and utterances of the men as they practiced their maneuvers. The spearmen went from stationary stance to attack stance over and over again, changing from standing upright, their spears pointed towards the sky, to a crouched position, shields braced in front of them, their spears sticking out between the shields. Archers shot volleys of arrows at targets of varying distances. Men practiced off to the side with axes and maces, whirling, blocking, and striking so fast that Seshrab couldn't keep track of their movements.

Egypt's armies were almost entirely militia – fighting farmers who put down their pitchforks and picked up their spears when the king decreed. By law, most men were members of their village militia or *niwt*, obliged to give a certain period of military service each year. As part of their training, men would engage in marching, formations, weight-lifting, wrestling, knife-throwing, and various other martial exercises. Large stores of weapons were housed in the royal armories, and the opening of the armories and the distribution of the stored weaponry was traditionally a day of celebration.

Every soldier, or *ahauty*, in the Egyptian army fought on foot, even the king. Almost all weaponry was made of copper, but mace heads were usually made of very hard stone like granite or diorite. Copper was the most up-to-date metal that the Egyptians possessed at that time; bronze wouldn't be acquired until it was introduced into Egypt by the Amorites from Syria a generation from now, and iron wouldn't make itself known in Egypt for centuries.

Body armor was made of hardened jacked leather, sometimes fitted with rows of copper studs for added protection. However, hardly anybody wore body armor because leather was very expensive, and it could also be detrimental when temperatures could reach as high as 120°F. For the most part, the ordinary Egyptian soldier didn't wear any body armor at all, and instead relied on large shields for protection, and fought *en masse* shoulder-to-shoulder in phalanx-like block formations. Only officers wore armor, and even then, the amount of protection that it afforded was minimal. The armor worn by company commanders consisted of a wide strip of leather, measuring ten or twelve inches wide, which was wrapped around the belly to protect the abdomen from stab wounds, and was held in place by a pair of shoulder suspenders. Higher-ranking officers like regiment commanders wore full cuirasses extending from the armpits downwards, made of overlapping strips of leather, with tassets covering the thighs and groin. Armor made out of copper was extremely rare, reserved solely for royalty. Copper armor consisted of rows and rows of overlapping metal plates that were sewn onto a leather jerkin. Amazingly, *nobody* in Egypt wore helmets.

Every single soldier in the Egyptian army wore a white cloth headband that was wrapped around the forehead and tied in the back. This item had originally been adopted purely for utilitarian reasons, to keep sweat from dripping down into the eyes while fighting or on the march. However, so many Egyptian soldiers wore this, and they had worn it for such a long period of time, that eventually this white headband became one of the identifying features of an Egyptian soldier and it became a part of their uniform. Company commanders were identified by a single white feather sticking up from the back of the head, and regiment commanders carried a baton called an *aba* scepter which resembled a flat hand extending out of a short handle.

Egyptian infantry, the *menfut*, were multi-role soldiers. Their primary weapon was an eight-foot spear carried in the right hand. The spearhead itself was made of copper and had a long narrow flattened spike sticking out of the rear called a tang. The spearhead was fixed onto the shaft by cutting a long notch down the top of the shaft, slipping the tang into it, and then bolting the head into place with two nails, one above and one below. The infantry also had secondary weapons slung across each shoulder with belts that were crossed over the chest in an X. Hanging down on the left hip was a cowhide cylindrical quiver containing six three-foot long javelins, the sharpened points pointing down of course. Hanging down on the soldiers' right side was a small axe or mace, carried in a loop made of leather or canvas. An Egyptian mace consisted of a round wooden handle approximately one-and-a-half to two feet long and one to one-and-a-half inches in diameter. Fixed at the top was the mace head, made of diorite stone with a hole drilled through its center to allow it to be attached to the handle. Egyptian mace-heads came in several shapes: round, egg-shaped, and cone-shaped with a flat top. The mace was also a symbolic weapon of the king's power. Egyptian paintings and wall carvings showed the king smiting his enemies with a mace, symbolizing his power as King, and his ability to dominate all before him and to overpower any foe. The patron god of the Egyptian infantry was Montu, the falcon-headed god of war and battle.

On the infantryman's left arm was carried a large shield made of wooden boards and covered with mottled black-and-white cowhide, and trimmed in a strip of red-dyed leather. The shield measured two feet wide by three and a half feet tall, straight-sided, and with a pointed top shaped like a Gothic arch. The red leather trim was formed into a circular loop extending off of the shield's peak. The shield had two arm straps, one for the lower arm near the elbow and the other to be held in the hand, fastened to the shield with solid copper rivets. In addition to personal defense, these shields were also used to make the surrounding walls of temporary army camps in the field. The tents would be laid out in rows, a large trench would be dug around the camp, and the dirt was piled up as a wall on the inside, so that an attacking adversary had to first cross the ditch and then climb up the earthen embankment to get into the camp. These "Gothic-type" shields would be lined tightly against each other across the top of the dirt wall, and they would be held in position by being braced with long wooden stakes that were split into a small V at the top; one of the points would be thrust through the leather loop at the top of the shield, and the butt-end shoved into the ground. The appearance of these shields, with their pointy tops and the V-shaped spaces between them, looked like the crenellations of fortress walls, and that's exactly what they were used for. Archers would shoot arrows between the gaps and spearmen would thrust over the top, keeping attackers at a distance.

Every regiment had a contingent of archers, known in Egyptian as *megau*, "shooters". Egyptian bows came in two sizes. The more common of the two was a single-piece bow, measuring three feet long, usually made of acacia wood and wrapped with cord at intervals to keep the wood from snapping, with the siyahs strongly recurved, looking almost like hooks. There were no notches carved into the siyahs to hold the bowstring; it was instead looped around the siyah's point and held in place by the thickness of the bow and the strong curvature of the siyah itself, so that the bowstring didn't slide off once it was drawn back. The second type of bow, which was much rarer, was a longbow measuring five feet long or longer, which the Egyptians had copied from their southern Nubian neighbors. These Nubian longbows were precious things, and they were often transported in protective leather cases to keep them from being damaged.

Arrows were three feet long and made of hollow reeds collected from the marshes, fletched with goose feathers, and tipped with triangular-shaped arrowheads made of bone or copper. Sometimes men who owned their own bows and arrows would write little messages along the arrow shafts; this was *never* done on arrows issued from the armory because they belonged to the government and were on loan, and weren't to be damaged or defaced in any way. Sometimes the arrows had the name of the archer, so that he could claim which kills were his and which weren't. Sometimes they were good luck prayers or mantras: "Sun god, guide my strike", "I shall strike my target true exactly where I intend", "I will not falter or fail my master", "Neith's breath is the wind that guides me", "I am the wrath of Sekhmet". Others had less-than-savory messages written by those who had a sick sense of humor, such as "Stand very still", "Look out!", "Give us a kiss", etc. Each archer carried a quiver of twenty arrows. The quiver was not cylindrical, but flattened, and its bottom was rounded. Made of a single piece of toughened leather, it was held together by sewing up one side with rawhide, and then placing a few inch-wide copper hoops at regular intervals along it to help maintain its shape. These hoops had holes pre-drilled into them, and thick cord was used like sewing thread to hold the metal hoops onto the quiver. The curved bottom of the quiver was covered in a single copper cap, so that the sharp arrowheads didn't puncture the bottom. These quivers were made to last, because leather was expensive and you didn't want to keep replacing your equipment. The quiver was carried with a leather strap, slung diagonally across the chest and back, with the quiver hanging down from the right hip, so that the arrows would be within easy reach. Archers had a secondary weapon, usually an axe or a large knife, hanging on their left hip. They carried no body protection other than a leather bracer on their left arm to protect the arm from the bowstring as they shot their arrows. The patron deity of Egyptian archers was the goddess Neith the Hunter.

In many societies, archers were looked down upon by other soldiers as being cowardly and without honor because they preferred to kill their enemies from a distance rather than fighting them face-to-face. However, this was not the case in Egypt. Here, line infantry and archers were regarded as equals, and both groups held each other in the highest respect. Archers praised the infantry for their bravery in battle and their skill in hand-to-hand combat, and the line infantry praised the archers for their skills and their "falcon eyes", the ability to see their enemy from afar. Archers who were especially good shots were regarded as being blessed by the gods, and the infantry never ceased in thanking the archers for "lightening the load" when it came to killing enemy troops before they got too close.

However, both the regular line infantry and the archers were in agreement when it came to their poor regard for the *nakhtu'aa*, "strong of arm", the elite light infantry rangers. The *nakhtu'aa* fought in individual combat, not in firm phalanx-like formations that the regular infantrymen stood in. They were equipped with small round shields made of wicker and covered in leather, battle axes, and also carried a dagger housed in a special leather sheath that was carried on the left forearm, used for the close-in work. In terms of duties, these men would rush outwards from behind the main infantry line to pursue fleeing enemies, as the Egyptians possessed no cavalry yet. Other functions for them were to act as scouts, vanguards of an army's advance, to land on enemy shores and secure a beach-head, and as assassins. They were selected for exceptional physical skills, including speed, stamina, and agility, and were usually kept in the rear since they were so valuable. To be made a member of the *nakhtu'aa* was a great distinction. However, despite their elite status, they were scorned by the regular soldiers, who viewed the rangers as only taking on special assignments and being kept usually out of harm's way while the *menfut* had to deal with the bulk of the fighting and were therefore *always* in harm's way. Some members of the *menfut* commented that the only time that the *nakhtu'aa* actually joined the battle was when the battle was already over. Where were they when the enemy horde smashed into the front ranks and the *menfut* fought for their very lives? It was also generally believed by both the line infantry and the archers that the rangers got too high a share of the credit and the glory when it came to winning the battles. The *nakhtu'aa* rangers accused the regular soldiers of being disrespectful to them, and the regulars accused the rangers of having too high an opinion of themselves and being unworthy of whatever respect they received. The patron god of the *nakhtu'aa* was Wepwawet, the White Wolf. Invocations of his name included "He who points the way, He who leads the way forward, He who clears the path before the army's advance". Wepwawet was the patron god of spies, scouts, commandos, and other recon forces. In Egyptian art, Wepwawet was often depicted as a giant white wolf who was always armed and dressed for battle, and always marched out at the very front of an army's advance. Both Wepwawet and his rangers led the way.

Egyptian battles usually began with volleys of arrows. Afterwards, the infantry would soften up the enemy lines with a barrage of javelins. Then, with the javelins gone, the infantry would bring their long spears to bear upon the enemy. Axes and maces were only used if the spearhead was broken, and were therefore considered "last resort" weapons. Once the enemy had turned tail, the battle-lines would part and the *nakhtu'aa* would spill out like water from a cracked dam, they would chase down the fleeing enemy soldiers like cheetahs going after gazelles, killing them as they fled.

In the courtyard, there was a company of a hundred infantrymen arranged in five lines of twenty soldiers each. The company commander for the line infantry, identified by his officer's white feather pinned through the back of his white headband, shouted his orders. "Attention!"

The infantry, with their large shields and spears, immediately snapped to attention, standing as erect and as straight as stone columns. Their spears did not waver an inch but stood perfectly still.

"Guard!" he shouted

With one fluid motion, all of the men in all five lines stepped forward on their left foot, twisted their bodies to the right to minimize their body profile, swung their large Gothic arch-shaped shields in front of them, and leveled their spears so that they rested in the V-shaped cavities in between the shield tops. It was all done in a single movement.

"Attention!"

The men stood.

"Guard!" The men braced themselves for attack again.

"Stab!"

At once, all of the spears were thrust forward with the full force of their entire right-half of the body.

"Retract!"

The spears were pulled back to their original resting position.

"Stab!"

"Retract!"

"Stab!"

"Retract!"

"Attention!"

The men stood at attention.

"Prepare to throw javelins. Change…javelins!"

The standing men passed their spears from their right hand to their left hand. The shield was carried on the left forearm. The men held their spears in their left hand while at the same time holding one of the two shield straps in their hand as well.

"Javelins!"

The men reached over to their left side and pulled out a javelin from their quivers and held them aloft, as if ready to throw them. The javelins carried in the quiver were always pointed down for two reasons. First, you didn't want to accidentally stab yourself if you wanted to grab one. Second, it made it easier to throw them if they were pointed down. You didn't need to twist your hand downwards to pull the javelin out, as one might pull out a sword (which hadn't been invented yet) from its sheath. Rather, you just reached your hand over to your left side, grabbed a javelin, pulled up, and formed your arm into a right angle, with the javelin perpendicular to your arm, facing forward, horizontal.

"Ready!"

The men twisted their bodies to the right, extended their left arms for balance, and drew back their right arm, ready to throw.

"Throw!"

The men hurled their javelins forward with all of the strength that they could muster. The javelins arced beautifully, travelling silently, and landed about fifty or sixty feet away from the front line with muffled *thuphts* as they landed in the dirt.

"Javelins!" he called out again.

The infantry grabbed their second javelins. Each infantryman carried six of them.

"Ready!"

"Throw!"

"Prepare to change to spears. Change…spears!"

The men put their spears back in their right hands and once more resumed their default stance of being ready at attention.

"Guard!"

The men leveled their spears, ready for attack.

"Stab!"

"Retract!"

"Stab!"

"Retract!"

"Advance!"

Now the infantrymen marched forward in perfect synchronous stride – left, right, left, right, slowly advancing across the courtyard. Their spears were perfectly horizontal, like the teeth of a giant comb.

"Double time!"

The infantry now jogged across the field, still keeping pace, still with their spears leveled.

"Stop!"

The men abruptly halted.

"Attention!"

The men stood.

"About face!"

The men whirled around in their own respective positions so that they now faced the opposite direction.

"Guard!"

"CHARGE!!!"

The men now broke into a flat-out run, the full weight of their bodies under the charge putting so much weight behind their deadly shafts. They didn't scream or shout – they knew better than to waste such energy. All the while, they maintained their synchronous steps.

Seshrab was awed. He had never witnessed such precision before. When the Canaanites attacked, they just swarmed their opponents in massive human waves. No wonder that Egypt was the most militarily successful nation in the world. It made his war-like Canaanites look like a chaotic mob of barbarians.

At last, he spotted his master. The king was on the other side of the courtyard, practicing hand-to-hand combat with other soldiers armed with axes and maces. He had just suffered a severe injury earlier that day, and yet, he was still out on the parade ground drilling with his troops. His personal doctor stood nearby just in case his wound opened up again and had to be tended to. The king had thickly wrapped his wounded arm with layer upon layer of bandages, and then covered it further with a leather archer's bracer, just to be safe. King Shaweneiti had abandoned his ankle-length tunic for a shorter one that came to just above the knees – the better for movement, such as marching and fighting. Seshrab slowly made his way across the practice field, taking care not to get in anyone's way or put himself in danger. Shaweneiti was surrounded by five men equipped with large shields and weapons. The blades of the axes were fully sharpened, not blunted, despite the risk of accidentally harming the king – Shaweneiti insisted that they were to be "real" weapons. The king himself had no shield or body armor and only had his stone-headed mace for protection; five physically fit and fully-armed men against one man, and he was already wounded. To Seshrab, it seemed an uneven contest. But Shaweneiti was far more experienced in hand-to-hand combat than these men were, and in no time at all, he had brought all of them to the ground. He used his whole body – his arms, legs, and torso – in addition to his club as tools to his advantage. The other men, relying solely on their shields for defense and their weapons for attack, did not know how to combat his maneuvers. "You are too limited in your capabilities", he told them. "Your axe is not your only weapon. Your body can be used as a weapon as well. Dodge blows rather than trying to block them – your opponent will have wasted his energy, and you will have avoided getting broken bones. Grab his weapon arm, if you can, and sharply twist it backwards so he will buckle, provided he doesn't smash your rib cage with his shield. Your shield can be a weapon with its pointed top. If brought upon your enemy with enough force, it can easily break bones, rupture organs, and cause internal bleeding. If you strike your enemy on the head and he's knocked unconscious, do you abandon him and fight another opponent, or do you finish him off right there?"

"That depends, Your Majesty", said one of the men.

"Explain".

"If your formation is broken up, you finish him off, but if you are solid and under attack, you can't because you're pre-occupied fighting his comrades. Besides, Your Majesty, if he's knocked out, he can't hurt you, provided he doesn't rouse himself, so there's no need to distract yourself by dealing the killing blow when someone else is trying to do the same to you".

"Exactly right. But what if he's not unconscious? What if he's fully aware? What if he's just wounded?"

"Kill him", came the unanimous response.

Shaweneiti turned around and saw Seshrab standing nearby, observing with interest. "Keep practicing with your weapons and shields", he told his companions. Then he turned and walked over to his scribe. "What is it?" he asked flatly.

"Your Majesty, I copied those documents as you asked and put them in their proper places".

"Good", he said, tucking his mace under his armpit and wiping the sweat from his brow. The whole weapon was two feet long. The butt-end of the handle flared out slightly to prevent it from being pulled out of the hand, and the grip was wrapped with leather. The mace head, carved from dark grey diorite stone and measuring four inches, was somewhat egg-shaped, fat towards the top and tapering toward the bottom. Diorite was harder and more durable than copper, and was so hard that Egyptians often used chunks of it as hammers to break up other types of rock, like limestone or granite. The surface of the mace-head was carved to look like overlapping bird feathers – a reference to the falcon-headed warrior god Horus, the smiter of evil – and was well-polished so that it shimmered in the sun. Directly underneath the stone mace-head was a gold strip inscribed with hieroglyphs saying *The King's Own Skull-Breaker.*

As King Shaweneiti wiped the sweat from his eyes, he paused for a moment in thought. "You realize that, as my chief scribe, you are to go wherever I go".

"Yes, Your Majesty".

"Do you know that I am about to lead the army to attack West Ament?"

"Yes, Your Majesty".

"Then you shall come with me. I want you to pack for a long journey. You are to record everything that happens during this campaign".

"Yes, Your Majesty".

The sounds of the drilling carried. Dust arose in the air and sweat dripped on the ground. Men blistered their hands gripping their weapons and strained under the weight of their shields. "Have you ever been in a battle before, Seshrab?"

"No, Your Majesty".

"Have you ever witnessed a battle, or seen the aftermath of one?"

"No, Your Majesty".

Shaweneiti paused. "Have you ever been to a butcher shop or slaughter yard?"

"Yes, Your Majesty. Several times".

"Well that's something, anyway".

Later that day in the Perah's council chamber, King Shaweneiti met with Colonel Horahauty, the commanding officer of the Khaset Regiment. They were finalizing the preparations for the upcoming campaign. "How are the men coming along?", Shaweneiti asked.

"The veterans are fine, Your Majesty. I have no doubt that they will perform as expected", replied Col. Horahauty. "But the new recruits need work. We need more time".

"We don't have time. The longer we delay, the more our enemies will be able to prepare themselves. If we are to win, we must strike Nesbit immediately. We attack, plain and simple, and at the earliest possible moment. Is that clear?"

"Yes, Your Majesty".

"Get your soldiers ready, Colonel", ordered the king. "We march tomorrow".

Later that day, King Shaweneiti gathered his entire palace staff into the throne room. His wife Queen Neferet and his father's widow ex-Queen Meret were there with him. Shaweneiti had no love for his wife. Her marriage was merely one of political convenience, just like Meret's marriage to his father. The king and queen didn't sleep in the same room, and they hardly ever spoke to each other. It was as if she or her older sister didn't even exist. They floated through the corridors like ghosts in the palace. By contrast, Shaweneiti did show affection to his daughter Princess Atentjehenet and his step-brother Prince Montunakht.

"Tomorrow, I and the troops of the Khaset Regiment will depart from the capital to attack the man who slew your former king. The remainder of our forces will join us on the way. While I am gone, my wife Queen Neferet and my father's widow Meret are to be cared for and obeyed as if they were me".

"Understood, Your Majesty", they said.

"I realize that there are still two more days left for my father's mourning. After the customary three day mourning period is over, hand over his body to the embalmers. Tell them to spare no expense in preparing him for the afterlife. I've already asked my chief scribe to write out a detailed description of the funeral goods, and also which tomb goods are to be placed in the burial chamber along with my father's mummy. I've left the document next to the body so that you take it with you when you bring the body to the embalmers. Use the assassins' gold to pay the Men of Anubis for their labors".

"Understood, Your Majesty".

"Nebsenre is to be buried in his tomb within the city's necropolis".

"Understood, Your Majesty".

"I intend to return within a month. By that time, the mummification of my father should be half-complete. See that everything that I command is carried out. With the grace of the gods, I'll return to you alive and in victory. That's all, you're dismissed".

The palace staff bowed and left, but then, "Seshrab, come here", he called out after his chief scribe.

Seshrab approached the dais. "Yes, Your Majesty?"

"Have you packed yet?"

"I was going to do so now".

"Be sure to take a spare pair of sandals, an extra tunic, dried food, and as much paper and writing equipment as you can carry. I'll give you no special treatment and you are expected to shoulder your share of the burden. I don't want to hear you complain or moan during the entire journey. You're to travel with the baggage train along with the other attendants and camp staff. Is all that understood?"

"Yes, Your Majesty".

"I am going to the Temple of Ra", Shaweneiti said. "My father was never able to perform his sacrifice to ensure victory in the war. I'll go there now and ask the gods for their blessing upon my troops".

It was a short journey from the palace to the Temple of Ra, but Shaweneiti travelled with fifty heavily-armed soldiers; he didn't want to go the way of his father, and he told the men beforehand that the crowds were to be kept at a distance. Shaweneiti, in contrast to his father, wished to be carried on a litter, bourne by four large muscular men. The royal litter was made of two thick wooden poles laid horizontally with a platform in the center. Underneath were four short straight legs. On the front end of each carrying pole was the carved head of a bull with a sun disk in between the horns – the representation of the prosperity goddess Hathor – while the back ends were flared out to look like lotus blossoms or papyrus tops. The whole thing was plated with gold and the carrying poles were decorated with black enameled trifoil designs like three-leafed clovers. Upon the central platform was a wooden chair for the king to sit in, and over this was a canopy frame draped with red velvet curtains edged with gold fringe.

The bull which Nebsenre had wished to take to the temple earlier had broken free and escaped when he was attacked by the assassins. Thankfully, the bull was later caught and returned to the palace. Now, Shaweneiti brought it along once again to fulfill its holy duty, pulled along by two attendants. Along the way, just as before, people lined the road and bowed, and thankfully no one approached any closer, or else things could have taken a very grim turn.

King Shaweneiti, with his men and his accompanying white bull, came to the temple gates, where he saw a disturbing sight – the blood of his father was still there on the stones. The king's blood was believed to be sacred, and no one had dared scrub the dark brownish-red stain away. The priests believed that Nebsenre's blood, the blood of a living god, had sanctified the temple and had granted it even more holiness than it already had.

The temple's gates were firmly locked. Egyptian temples were not open to the public; anyone who wished to make a sacrifice at the temple had to ask permission to be let in. Priests were not intermediaries between the mortal and divine worlds, but were rather guardians, protectors of the holy mysteries. The priests had sacred knowledge that was to be kept secret, and nobody was allowed within without their approval.

King Shaweneiti, seated on his litter, commanded one of his guards to strike the large copper gong several times to get the attention of the priests inside. It was done.

Several priests worked in the temple. There was the chief priest who performed most of the rituals, the orator who chanted the magic spells and prayers, the "priest of sacrifices" whose duty was to thoroughly inspect any offerings to see if they were suitable, and various low-ranking clerics who did purification rituals and attended to various temple duties.

After a few seconds, one of the two doors slowly creaked open, and the face of a bald-headed man, perhaps in his early 20s – a priest new to the religious order – appeared in the gap. He saw an impressive sight – the king, carried on a throne litter bourne by four large men, accompanied by fifty infantrymen, and a splendid white bull. There was no need to ask questions. The gate was immediately opened, the young priest stood aside, and bowed to the king as he entered the sanctuary. The men carried the litter across the small sand-filled courtyard towards the temple itself. The young priest closed the wall gates behind and rushed towards the temple door, where a second priest of the same age was waiting. The royal litter was set down, and the king walked towards the door, accompanied by half of his guards. The remaining guards stayed behind at the litter, guarding it and the sacrificial bull. "I have come to make a sacrifice of victory to the god Ra" he said to the priest waiting at the door.

The doorman nodded and went inside to get the sacrifice inspector, and the young priest went inside with him. The bull would not be allowed to actually go inside the temple until it was deemed worthy enough to enter. After a few moments, the doorman returned with the sacrifice inspector. This priest was a much older man than the two young lads that Shaweneiti had seen so far. He was at least 50 years old, and had a wealth of experience in his particular duty. A man in his profession had to have the eyes of an eagle, able to spot the most minute unnoticeable flaws. The man carefully inspected the bull from all sides and all directions, carefully caressing its skin, feeling for imperfections in the surface. He inspected its horns to find cracks or signs of wear. He looked at the hooves, the teeth, the eyes, the ears, everything. The priest of sacrifices looked at the younger priest holding open the door, and nodded to him. The bull was acceptable.

Shaweneiti turned to his men. "All of you, wait outside". Only the man performing the sacrifice was allowed to enter. Everyone else had to remain where they were, for fear that they might contaminate the sanctity of the ritual, and also to prevent too many people from seeing the interior of the temple. Shaweneiti, the bull, and the two priests entered, and the doorman closed the door behind them.

The temple's interior was an eerie dark space lit by the faint orange glow of oil lamps while incense and perfumes hung heavily in the air. There were many large columns arranged in lines, spaced out at regular intervals throughout the room. As they made their way down the column-lined room the dim glimmering light to go into the inner sanctuary, their footsteps echoing all around, the king was momentarily surprised to see somebody *else* in the temple - a man lying on a reed mat, sound asleep. The man was almost certainly a "dreamer", a person who slept inside temples at night because he wished to receive a dream from the gods so that he may be given divine enlightenment. The group continued down the hallway.

The young priest knocked on the door the inner sanctuary, and then the door slowly creaked open, but just barely enough for a single eye to peer out from inside. "The king wishes to make a sacrifice", the young priest said. The door slowly opened wide, revealing the room's forbidden interior. The inner sanctuary, unlike the rest of the temple, was brightly lit. The walls of the rooms were covered with hieroglyphs and paintings. In the center of the room was a large stone altar decorated with hieroglyphs carved into the stone and then gilded with gold leaf. At the back of the room, behind the altar, was a fifteen foot tall white limestone statue of the falcon-headed sun god Ra, standing up, holding an *ankh* in one of his hands and a staff in the other, with a large flat disk atop his head meant to represent the sun. Within the room were the chief priest garbed in a leopard pelt, the orator, and a few other low-ranking priests. The whole party entered and the doors were quickly closed behind them to prevent anyone out in the hallway from looking inside.

"You are to speak of nothing that occurs in this room", the chief priest said to the king. "Begin the purification", he said to one of the other priests.

The young man, holding a gold vessel, washed the bull four times with holy water. Each time that he did so, the orator priest annunciated, "You are purified in the sight of Ra, to make you pleasing to his eyes".

Afterwards, the bull was sprinkled with holy oil four times, the orator priest once again saying "You are purified in the sight of Ra, to make you pleasing to his eyes".

The bull was then garlanded with a wreath of lotus flowers. The chief priest handed King Shaweneiti a knife made of obsidian, a glass-like black volcanic stone. "Speak to the god".

"O Ra", began the king, "almighty sun god, King of Heaven, extend your hands upon my army and myself, touching all of us with your blessing, just as the sun extends its golden rays upon the earth and warms all that it touches. Grant my army victory in the coming war. Do not let my enemies stand victorious over me. Let them be destroyed in the battles to come".

Using the sharp stone blade, Shaweneiti slit the animal's throat, and the blood flowed into a large gold basin that was held by one of the priests. When the blood stopped flowing, the "blood collector" held out the bowl, and the chief priest dipped his hand in it. Then, he sprinkled some of the blood across the altar's polished surface. Afterwards, he used his fingers to color Ra's stone sun-disk. On all Egyptian paintings, the sun was shown as being red, not yellow, and coloring the lifeless white stone its intended color was meant to give "life" to the stone, to make it appear as it appeared in reality. Blood was given to Ra, who had grown pale, in order to give life back to him and the sun he embodied.

The sacrifice was complete.

The next day.

Seshrab waited inside the throne room for the king to appear. Most of those going with Seshrab were cooks and craftsmen who would prepare the food and see to the soldiers' weaponry and kit. Accompanying them was also the king's personal doctor and one medical assistant. Seshrab's friend Djoser was also coming with him to act as an assistant scribe. One of the priests from the nearby temple of Ra was also there, acting as the army's chaplain. Seshrab and the others had been waiting there for almost an hour, shuffling around, occasionally making light chit-chat, but mostly absorbed in their thoughts of what was going to happen within the next few days. Some were wondering to themselves if they were going to make it out alive. True to the king's command, Seshrab carried a large leather portfolio filled with papyrus paper, ink blocks, brushes, anything that might be needed. In a canvas bag slung over one shoulder, he carried a spare tunic, an extra pair of reed sandals, and a small pouch of dried fruit and hardened bread.

Suddenly, there was a great groaning creak as both of the enormous gilded doors were pushed open by a pair of strong muscular arms. Seshrab and the others whirled around at the sudden sound in time to see none other than the king himself performing the deed with militaristic purpose, a stern and hardened tone on his chiseled face. And what a sight to behold Shaweneiti armed and ready for battle as he shoved the great doors aside and revealed his form! He looked more like a mighty warrior chief than the refined and courtly monarch that they had known. Had he not been wearing his striped gold-and-blue *nemes* crown, they might not have even recognized him! On his body, he wore a short-sleeve knee-length tunic, but not the traditional white linen that he always wore. This one was a bright vivid royal blue, and the neck, sleeves, and hem were trimmed with an inch-wide gold ribbon. Upon his body, he wore a cuirass of shimmering copper scales sewn onto a leather jerkin – the look was meant to evoke the feathers of Horus. Topping it all off was his father's leopard pelt, with the animal's front legs tied around his neck and with the back legs tied around his waist.

"Wow", Seshrab exhaled.

"Wow is right", commented Djoser.

The king strode into the room, his heavy footsteps echoing in the mostly empty chamber. A respectful distance behind him was a man carrying the king's shield and his diorite mace – his personal weapon-bearer. He surveyed the men before him. "Is everything ready?" the king asked Seshrab.

"Yes, Your Majesty. Your army is assembled on the parade ground and awaits your orders to march".

"Are all of you ready?"

"Yes, Your Majesty", they responded in broken unison.

"Follow me".

Seshrab and his company followed the king and his servant out of the throne room and into the hallway. Directly across the hall from the throne room was a smaller rectangular room, an entryway room used when receiving arrivals. This room connected to the outside. Both the forward and rear doors were open. On either side of the king's path of advance, the whole palace staff and the two royal ladies lined in formation, waiting to bid farewell to their monarch as he left for the war. As the king passed with the attendants following behind him, the whole body of people bowed in respect.

The large entranceway doors of the Perah were fully open as well, so that there would be no pause or hesitation as the king made his way outside. As the full blinding light of the sun hit Seshrab, his eyes gradually adjusted, and he saw the troops of the Khaset Regiment, numbering 2,000 men, standing rigidly in perfect formation, waiting for the arrival of their king and their commander. The other two regiments from Sapmeh and East Ament would rendezvous with them along the march.

Colonel Horahauty, the commanding officer of the Khaset Regiment, armored in leather fitted with copper studs, walked up to the king and saluted. "Your Majesty, all men and provisions are accounted for. The regiment is assembled and awaits your instructions".

"Thank you, Colonel. Return to your troops and await my order to march".

The regimental commander saluted once more, turned around deftly on his heels, and strode back to his awaiting men. Meanwhile the king said to his attendants, "All except my bearer, take your appointed place among the baggage, quickly".

"Yes, Your Majesty", Seshrab and the others said, and then jogged over to where the donkeys were located, carrying on their backs all of the logistical needs of an army on the march. A vast caravan of pack animals was needed to haul all of the army's supplies – tents, medical equipment, spare weapons, dried food, bottles of water, beer, and wine, paper and ink to write orders, inventories, and messages, etc. Wagons had not been invented yet.

As soon as everyone had gone to their appropriate place, Shaweneiti strode forward a few long steps towards the center of the men gathered in front of him, his armor bearer remaining behind. He overlooked his troops. Many of them were veterans with the scars to prove it. Some had been on more than a dozen military campaigns with him and his father. Others were new recruits who had just been drafted and had never been in combat before. The men were barefoot, their fragile reed sandals hanging around their necks to keep them from wearing out and fraying apart on the hard pebbly roads. Some had good luck charms hanging around their necks. Each man also carried a small leather satchel on his back for personal belongings.

Shaweneiti stood before them, not being carried on a litter like a king, but with his feet firmly planted on the ground like a soldier, prepared to march with them and spill his own blood along with theirs.

"Today, my brave soldiers", he called out to the vast assembly, speaking loud enough to ensure that everyone could hear him, "we march forward to strike at our enemies to the west. Once again, we leave behind our homes and our sense of comfort and safety in order to avenge a great wrong that has been committed. The murder of your former master, my father, cannot go unpunished. An example must be made of he who sent men to slay my father and myself, the man who hired assassins to do his bloody work because he was too much of a coward to do it himself. What does this say of the man? He has no courage! He does not stand in the battle line along with his men as I do, but looks on from afar from a safe distance where he cannot be hurt. He does this because he is afraid.

"You too, I know, are afraid. This is more so for the ones who are not schooled in battle, those who are unfamiliar with its sights, those who are not yet re-molded into the psyche of the collective. For many of you, this will be your first battle, and you are afraid. You do not want to leave the comforts of your surroundings behind, the land that you know well and that you feel safe within. You do not want to leave your homes. But I wish to state that you are blessed, for men such as yourselves have the fortune of being able to distinguish yourselves with glory and victory, and not live your lives in mediocre insignificance as you would if you remained on your farms and in your workshops. Yes, here at home you are safe and at ease. You wake up with the sun, do your work, eat your meals, and go to bed, and think nothing of it. This you do from day to day, and it is all familiar to you. You feel comfortable within the walls of your cottages, or behind the benches and tables of your craft shops, or with your bare feet touching the plowed soil on your farms. But surely you were not put upon this earth for such an obscure fate, to be just one more face among the multitudes, he who shall be forgotten when the gods draw his *ka* out of him.

"Some of you are afraid that you will die. Such things are expected in life. Death is a part of life. In the past, men were afraid to go off to war because if they died on foreign soil, and were buried on foreign soil, their souls would not be allowed to enter Heaven, so all of the dead were brought back here to Egypt. My fellows, you need not worry about such things, for this is all Egypt! One cannot say that we fear to tread into foreign soil. It is all our soil, every last inch of it. The land that we march to is Egyptian land. Do not fear your fate, for you are not in foreign lands, and you will not be barred from entering the afterlife.

"Only war gives men the opportunity to show that they are better and nobler than the position that they occupy. They are not mere peasants laboring on the land or in their shops. Only in battle can you earn the chance to get an everlasting reputation as a man of valor, so that your name will be remembered throughout history instead of forgotten like so many others. To win for yourself a glorious name is a very high honor which cannot be merely awarded as a gift, but must be earned by your actions. Prove your steadfastness, your discipline, your unwavering resolve, and you shall receive all of the accolades that you deserve, and if you perform exceptionally well, if your courage stands when all others' have fled, you shall be singled out among your brethren, and I shall say to you, 'You are my brother, my shield, my strong arm'. Only in war can such honors be won.

"In exchange for that high honor, the gods demand an equally high price. Boldness and courage are virtues accompanied by risk, and every time you pick up your spears or your arrows, you engage that risk, the risk of your own deaths. Why should you fear harm? Do you fear for your family's welfare? Do you not know that I am your king and your father, and that all of the people are my children? Is it not the father's duty to protect his children? Do not fear that your family shall know hunger or poverty. As long as I reign in Egypt, with the grace of the gods, no one shall suffer want. If you should fall, your wives and your children shall not fall with you. Do you fear that you shall never see your loved ones again? Why should you fear this? Is your wife good to you? Are your children obedient? Why then should they be denied paradise when the time comes for their *kas* to be drawn out? Your fears are unfounded! And I assure you that every man of virtue and courage, by his actions, if he should die, shall unquestionably earn himself a place in Heaven. Now I ask all of you, do you fear?"

"NO!!!" came the great reply.

Shaweneiti pointed to one of the infantrymen, and walking straight up to him, demanded "You, soldier! If my enemy raises his hand against me, will you help me strike him down?"

"Yes, Your Majesty".

He turned to another one. "You! Will your shield protect me when I stand in the lines with you?"

"Yes, Your Majesty".

"You! Do you doubt that my own shield will fail you?"

"No, Your Majesty".

"Soldiers, men of Egypt, do you think that I fear?"

"No, Your Majesty", they all shouted in unison.

"Why don't I fear? Why am I not afraid?"

"Because you are *Nesu*, and the king fears no man!" came a reply from within the ranks.

"The king is protected by the cobra goddess Wadjet herself", came another reply, "and no enemy spear shall touch him".

"Wrong!" said Shaweneiti. "I do not fear because I know that I shall stand beside *you*. Yes, you! You, men of Egypt! I do not fear because I am in your company, in the shadow of your shields, protected by your spears, standing side-by-side with you in the foremost of the battle lines. If my enemy shall raise his hand against any of you, I shall strike him down! If my enemy raises his hand against me, I know that you shall strike him down! You veterans of my past campaigns, you who fought alongside me and my father, have I ever failed you?"

"Never, Your Majesty!" came the reply from the scarred veterans.

"And I shall not fail you this time either! I shall not waver, but I shall stand firm and steadfast. When the enemy rushes forth, I shall not take a single step backwards. Will *you* step back?"

"No, Your Majesty!"

"And that is why, my children, I do not fear!"

All of the men huzzahed and cheered in one loud deafening voice. Seshrab, too, was caught up in the emotional power of the king's speech, and he too cheered, smiling.

King Shaweneiti turned around to his bearer and indicated him to approach, and the man quickly hustled forward. As the troops continued to cheer, Shaweneiti took from the bearer his shield and his diorite-headed falcon feather-decorated mace. The sight of the king taking his weapon and shield made the troops cheer louder. They knew that the king meant what he said about standing right there in the front ranks with them, that he was no coward, that he would fight just as ferociously as they would, and even more so. It would not be long now. They would march any second. Many of the soldiers began rhythmically shouting out his name over and over again, jabbing their spears up in the air with each roared-out syllable. *"SHA-WA-NEI-TI!!! SHA-WA-NEI-TI!!!"*

Shaweneiti purposefully walked in between the two large squares of men standing on either side of the courtyard, moving towards the great monolithic gate of the palace complex, being cheered and praised the whole way. This was Shaweneiti, "the boy", the son of the mighty General Nakhtibre, whom the soldiers had seen raised to war from the time he was a child. For years, this man had fought beside them in the civil wars. He had never let them down. He had never lost a battle. He had given them victory after victory, and with the grace of the gods, he would give them victory once again.

Nesu Shaweneiti turned towards the assembled mass of men, and raised his war mace into the air. "Soldiers...MARCH!!!"

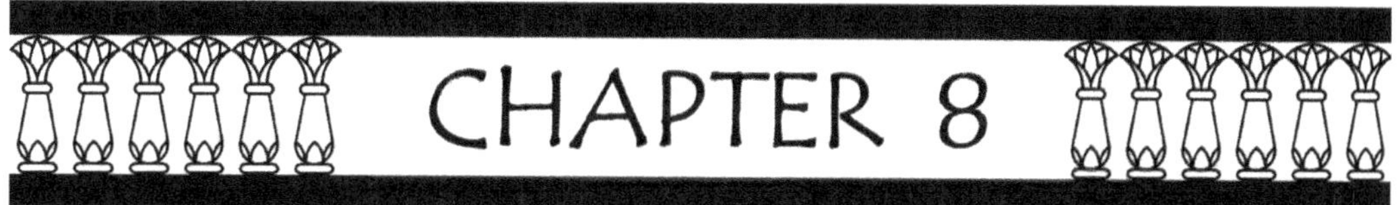

# CHAPTER 8

*His Majesty led his army out from Khaset City to do battle against the dastardly and villainous Nesbit, the governor of the rebel province of West Ament, who had ordered the murder of His Majesty and his father. His Majesty's army numbered over six thousand men, and it took several days to reach our destination. I accompanied the army upon its march into West Ament. Upon arriving at the rebel capital city of Yamu, a great and lamentable battle was fought.*

At the king's command, both sets of doors of the gatehouse were opened and the army began to march out of the palace and along the broad parade boulevard out of Khaset City. The king himself led the march. The doorway through the palace gatehouse was very narrow, so only a few soldiers could march abreast at any one time. For all 2,100 troops and the supply caravan to march out of the palace courtyard, it would take a few hours.

As King Shaweneiti exited the gatehouse with his troops marching behind him, erupting into song and unleashing their masculine military hymns from their throats, the townsfolk of Khaset City lined either side of the wide procession-way to give their king and their army a good send-off. Women and children closely crowded onto the very edges of the road, cheering, waving, and clapping the whole way.

After they exited Khaset City, which took the better part of the day to complete, the Royal Army switched from parade mode to combat march mode. The king left the front of the column and took his place amongst his troops. The men travelled in the following order. First were the *nakhtu'aa* rangers acting as the vanguard. Then came the regular infantry, the *menfut*, being led by the king himself. Then came the archers. Behind the archers was the baggage train of donkeys, accompanied by Seshrab and the other attendants. At the end of the column was another contingent of *nakhtu'aa*, whose duty was to guard the rear in case the soldiers were attacked from behind.

It was thirty miles from Khaset City to Yamu. The troops from Sapmeh and East Ament were due to join them along the march, tripling their fighting strength from 2,100 to 6,300 men, many of whom were battle-hardened veterans who had fought beside Shaweneiti and his father time and time again. How could the treacherous Governor Nesbit possibly stand against them?

It was getting hotter. Summer was coming, and with the heat came thirst. In the past, most Egyptian armies fought during the summer because that was when the Nile flooded, and since the landscape was inundated the farmers couldn't do any work on their farms until the waters subsided. Under the militaristic King Nebsenre, the troops had been fighting virtually all year round, waging a new campaign every two months.

Still, although the scheduling of battles was different, for the time being anyway, the men who had been called up for military service still led the same weary life that others in the past had led. One author wrote about the terrible life of the Egyptian infantryman...

*Come, let me tell you of the sad life of the soldier. Behold how many superiors he has: the general who sends him to his death, the second-in-command, the standard-bearer who thinks he's above everyone else, the scribe who pesters him daily with records and reports and forms, the commander of the fort who daily inspects the men, the battalion commander, the company commander, and his own squad leader. The officers go in and out of the barracks shouting "We need laborers. Get to work! Chop that wood! Carry those stones!" The poor fellow is awakened at any hour for whatever reason. He toils all day long until the sun sets. He is always hungry, his belly hurts; he is dead while yet alive. After having been released from the day's duties, he does not receive a piece of bread for his evening meal, but a small bag of grain – he is expected to make his own bread himself, grinding the grain into flour and mixing it with water to form a sort of paste, which he cooks over the fire. There is sand mixed in with the grain. He has no strength left from the labors of the day, and now he is expected to grind the grain on the stones just to make a small piece of bread for his dinner. Even when he does no work in the camp, he toils to make a meal.*

*Word comes: the army will march to Syria. The weapons in the armory are distributed to the men, but they have little else. He has few clothes and no sandals. His march is uphill through rough rugged mountains. His feet are cut apart and bloodied. He drinks water only every third day; it smells foul and has a salty taste to it. His body is ravaged by illness. He will not rest. They march, and march, and march.*

*The enemy suddenly attacks. He and his men are surrounded, showered with missiles. He is weak from the constant marching, and now must fight. All strength is gone. He is told "Quick, charge forward, valiant soldier! Win for yourself a good name!" All is confusion, his head spins, he doesn't know what he's doing. His body is weak, his legs fail him.*

*When victory is won, the captives are handed over to His Majesty to be taken to Egypt as slaves. One of the captives, a foreign woman, faints on the march, and the soldier is ordered to carry her, for all slaves are wealth and they must be accounted for and preserved. His knapsack drops, another grabs it while he is burdened with the woman. His wife and children are in their village; he dies along the route and does not reach it. If he comes out alive, he is worn out from marching.*

*Be he on the march or in the camp, the soldier suffers. If he leaps and joins the deserters, all his family are imprisoned. He dies on the edge of the desert, and there is none to perpetuate his name. He suffers in death as in life. A big sack is brought for his body, and is buried in foreign soil. He does not know his resting place. His soul never reaches Heaven.*

After two long hot arduous days of marching westwards along the dusty pebble-strewn roads, King Shaweneiti and his army reached the border of royalist territory.

The river separating the rebel province of West Ament from the royalist-controlled province of East Ament was only two hundred feet wide. Any preparations that Nesbit could undertake would be plainly visible on the opposite shore. Moreover, the opposite shore was easily within arrow-range of Shaweneiti's archers, who had a maximum range of 400 feet.

But there were no enemy soldiers, no barricades, no entrenchments, nothing. It looked as if Nesbit wasn't ready or even expecting an attack at all. The opposite shore was mostly flat farmland dissected into various-sized squares and rectangles by earthen dikes. There was a grove of date palms in the distance. There was a village not too far away, but there were no signs of activity. It looked so deceptively peaceful.

"Do you see anything?", King Shaweneiti asked as he intensely scanned the landscape.

"Nothing, Your Majesty", said Colonel Mebydos of the East Ament Regiment. "There's not a sign of any defense. I don't like it".

"We will make camp here tonight. Bring forth all of the archers from all three regiments and have them take position here upon the riverbank. Send a company of *nakhtu'aa* ashore to sweep the opposite side", commanded the king.

"Right away, Your Majesty".

The archers were called forward, all 1,500 of them, and a company of a hundred rangers clambered onto one of the barges that lined the king's side of the shore. The barge was then sent forward, the drivers using long poles to push their way across. When the men reached the opposite shore, they immediately raced towards the village. When they got there, the villagers didn't put up a fight. There were no weapons, no entrenchments, no spider holes for hiding. But there was something odd: where were all of the men? All who were left in the villages were children, women, and elders. When asked where they had all gone, all of the villagers gave the same response: "They left".

Shaweneiti realized that all of the young men of the village had been conscripted into service, yet he didn't actually see any soldiers present. "Make camp", he called out. "Tomorrow, we will cross the river and press on to our objective".

Under the guard of the archers, the remainder of the army set about erecting their tents, preparing their evening meals, and refilled their leather water bottles. Tomorrow, either in the morning or the afternoon, the army would arrive at the rebel-held capital. They would finally get to grips with the man who had so villainously slain their former king and had very nearly slain his son. They were fully expecting a fight. Some of the men were eager to get stuck into a good scrap, while others spent the evening hours composing love poems to their wives and sweet-hearts at home. Most of the men didn't sleep.

Seshrab was wide awake. As he looked up at the clear black night sky ablaze with stars, his mind whirled with a million frantic thoughts. Tomorrow, definitely tomorrow, there was going to be a battle. Tomorrow, people were assuredly going to die. Yet he himself never considered that he would be in any actual danger. After all, he wasn't a soldier, he was a scribe, an official of the palace staff. He and the other attendants would certainly be kept in the rear far out of harm's way, while the soldiers of His Majesty's Royal Army did their bloody work. Even so…he was still anxious and nervous…and he wondered what tomorrow would bring.

Morning.

Even before the sun was up, the army was roused up from their tents. No more time could be lost. The Royal Army needed to take the city of Yamu this very day, and secretly, King Shaweneiti was personally relishing the prospect of grasping the man who had arranged his and his father's murder and killing him with his own bare hands.

Dozens of water craft had been assembled for ferrying the troops across, as there were no bridges which spanned the Nile during this time, and even if there were any, they would likely be swept away into rubble with the next year's flood. For several weeks, under the now-dead Nebsenre's command, barges, rafts, rowboats, *anything* that could float, were gathered together for this undertaking. To any casual observer, it was blatantly obvious what was going to happen. Waging a war was not a subtle enterprise.

Shaweneiti waited for all of the men to cross over onto the enemy's shore. As soon as he was certain that all of the men and baggage had crossed to the opposite bank, he called out "Assemble for marching! We're moving directly to the capital of Yamu. Be on guard for an attack. They're waiting for us".

The men formed up into the standard marching position that they had assumed on the way here, and now set off towards the capital of West Ament. The men were tired, but morale was high. By the king's reckoning, his army outnumbered Nesbit's by nearly three to one. He was confident of victory. He would sweep aside the traitor's puny army like sand blowing in the wind.

It was eight miles to Yamu if the army travelled in a straight line from the landing point to the capital. It was very hot. The soldiers' feet were getting raw, having walked without wearing their sandals to avoid shredding the leather on the rough sandy gritty roads. Blisters and blood were a common sight. Every two miles, the men stopped to drink and tend to their weary and cut-up soles. On the second rest stop, when the army had reached the half-way point, the king held up his hand as a signal to halt. The monotonous shuffling and knocking sounds which accompany a large assemblage of marching men came to a disrupted and clumsy stop. There were a few muffled groans of tiredness and aches, and a few loud exhales snorted out through noses. As the men busied themselves tending to their aching tired feet, or wiping the sweat out of their eyes, or taking a well-needed sip of water…

"FIRE!!!" someone shouted.

Everyone instantly halted and their heads whirled in every direction.

"Your Majesty", shouted one of the company officers, running up from the column's rear, "there's a large fire burning to the northeast".

"The northeast?" asked Colonel Mebydos of the East Ament Regiment. "We just came from there". Then his eyes widened, and he turned to his king. "The ships!"

"Nesbit knows we're here", said Shaweneiti ominously in a low voice.

"Your Majesty, should we turn back?" asked the company commander.

"How *can* we go back with the ships destroyed?!" sniped Colonel Ankharis of the Sapmeh Regiment. "We're trapped! We've got no way to escape. We must make a defensive stand right here. Prepare for battle!"

"No!" said King Shaweneiti. "We go to Yamu as planned. Fighting here may not ensure us victory and Nesbit will surely escape. The city of Yamu has to be captured and Nesbit has to be killed. As soon as that is done, with their commander dead and the capital city in our hands, our enemies will lay down their arms. If we fight them here, we'll be too exhausted to take Yamu, and we may be attacked by more of Nesbit's troops while we recover. It won't take long for Nesbit to see the smoke. At this moment, we have no other option but total victory. Get the army up. No more rest stops. We march on Yamu now!"

The frantic call quickly spread to get the army moving as fast as they could. The troops once again shouldered their burdens and heaved their shields and weapons, and quickened their marching pace. Nervous glances were exchanged between them.

The royalists marched the rest of the way without stopping, always looking over their shoulder to see what was coming up behind them. The troops could plainly see a large cloud of dust rising up from the ground keeping pace with them.

At last, with one more mile to go, they could see their target in the distance – Yamu, capital city of the province of West Ament.

The army took no time to pause and survey the landscape, but kept moving. Shaweneiti analyzed the area as he marched with his troops. As they marched, a call came from the rear – enemy troops had been spotted behind them, and were approaching fast.

Shaweneiti and his soldiers in the front ranks could clearly see that the West Amentites had prepared defenses around their city consisting of trenches and earthen walls, and they could only guess at how many hundreds or thousands of men lay behind those embankments. The king got a sinking feeling in his stomach, but he had been in hard battles before, and this one would not be any different. "Advance to within 500 yards of those earthworks, then halt".

As Shaweneiti's army drew nearer and nearer to its destination, a sense of dread began to build up inside the minds of his troops. Five hundred yards from the entrenchments, the army stopped; they were safe from arrow fire at this position. There were clearly men behind the embankments – the royalists could see the enemy's spears sticking up above the earth, and they could see archers lining the town walls, ready to rain their arrows down on the army should it advance too close. Yet, nobody on the enemy side moved.

Shaweneiti had assumed by now that he was outnumbered, but he didn't know by how much yet. He had a very good idea what was going to happen next – both enemy forces were going to attack the royalists from two directions simultaneously. "Form square!" Shaweneiti shouted. "Baggage and archers in the center, infantry on the outside. Get rid of the animals – they'll only be a hindrance to us once the battle begins".

When Seshrab heard this, his heart jumped into his throat. He could barely breathe. He had earnestly believed that, as a non-combatant, he'd be kept in the rear out of harm's way. And yet it was clear that there were enemy troops to the rear, as well as to the front. He would not be able to sit at a safe distance and watch the battle passively from afar – he'd be right in the thick of it. His breathing became labored, his body started trembling, and he couldn't think straight.

"Your Majesty", said Colonel Mebydos, "in order to form square, with so much taking up the center, that means that the infantry will be stretched unusually thin".

"I'm aware of that", the king replied.

"Not *too* thin, I hope".

The donkeys had their supplies removed, and were driven off with slaps and shouts. They fled blindly into the countryside, undoubtedly to be captured by enemy soldiers or starving peasants. Then King Shaweneiti turned to Seshrab, whose face had blanched with terror. "I need all of you to help", Shaweneiti said to Seshrab and the other attendants, a great deal of urgency in his voice. "If our enemies break through, we're all dead, every one of us, including you. Stay in the center with the baggage. Keep down and do not wantonly expose yourselves. I may have need to call on you later, but pray that I will not be forced to take such measures. Doctor, you and your assistant remain in the center where it is safe. This is going to be a very bloody day, and I will need all of your skill to save my men".

The archers hurriedly stuck their arrows into the ground so that they could be quickly retrieved. Meanwhile the infantry took position around them, forming a protective wall, their officers driving them on with curses and threats, urging them to get into position faster. Seshrab and the others crouched down while the archers made ready. He was becoming more and more scared by the minute. He looked to his left, and saw that his friend Djoser was visibly shaking. Seshrab reached over and tapped him on the shoulder. "Is this…is this your first time?"

Djoser brokenly shook his head and gulped. "No. I did this once before".

Seshrab was surprised. He had no idea that Djoser had been in a battle. He had never spoken of it or even hinted at it. "Where? When?"

"When Khaset City fell to Nebsenre's army. I was there when it happened…I saw things".

"If you did this before, then why are you scared?"

"Because I know from experience *exactly* what's going to happen in a few minutes, that's why".

"Is it as bad as I think it is?"

"Worse".

As the second body of enemy troops approached closer and closer from the Royal Army's rear, the men squinted to see if they could identify them. There was something strange about their appearance. They didn't look Egyptian.

"Great gods, they're Libyans!" exclaimed Colonel Mebydos.

"How many?" asked Shaweneiti.

"Thousands of them!"

"Which tribe?"

"I don't know, Your Majesty. They're too far away to tell".

These warriors were the Imukeheku, one of the most powerful of the Libyan tribes. Theirs was the tribe that was the nearest to Egypt's border, and the tribe that the Egyptians had fought most often against. Due to prolonged contact with their Nile-dwelling neighbors, the Imukeheku had become heavily Egyptianized. They worshiped Egypt's gods, they dwelt in Egyptian-style houses, they fought with copies of Egyptian weapons, and fought with Egyptian military tactics. The Imukeheku chief even bore the customary five royal titles of the Egyptian kings.

But they looked different. The Libyans were foreign people, not only in terms of nationality but in terms of appearance. They had white skin and blue eyes, but they had coarse black hair like the dark-skinned Nubians to the south. The Libyans grew their hair long, which they combed backwards and greased with olive oil or fashioned them into dreadlocks. The Libyans fought nearly naked, with nothing covering their bodies except a tight loincloth that barely covered their private parts. Many men had black tattoos of various geometric designs covering their bodies. The Libyans had fought wars against the Egyptians for centuries. The Egyptians loathed and detested the Libyans, who they regarded as being little better than cavemen; the sight of them and mere thought of them filled them with disgust. The Egyptians called the Libyans *hestyw* – "barbarians".

Seshrab couldn't describe how he felt when he saw the Libyans suddenly emerge from the wavy haze of the heat radiating off of the baking ground. He had never seen such people before. They advanced as a single massive horde towards the royalist position. Then, about 500 yards away, they suddenly stopped. They began rhythmically banging on their cowhide shields with their spears, barking out their chants and their war songs as they did so in their strange language, trying to intimidate the royalist soldiers into pissing their legs. A few of them did.

Seshrab knew several languages, but he didn't understand a single word of Libyan. It was a good thing, too, because if he knew what these painted savages were screaming out, he might have lost all hope. Slamming on their shields, rhythmically stomping their feet, and swinging their weapons around in the air, they voiced in unison their threats and oaths of the coming victory, their bodies and minds thoroughly possessed by bloodlust – *Today is the day of blood! Today is the day of blood! There is no escape for you. There is no hope for you, for I have come for you, and today you shall die. You shall die! You shall die! Fight beside me my brothers, stand beside me in battle. My shield will guard you. My spear will guard you. My courage will guard you. My determination will guard you. We are one path, we are one heart, we are one mind. We are the sons of Earth. We are the land, we are the water, we are the sky. In battle you shall see the truth of my soul. My brothers give me strength, my ancestors give me strength, my spirit gives me strength, Earth gives me strength. How can you stand against such power? You are foolish to think that you shall win this day! Prepare yourselves, for I shall be savage upon you as the lion is savage upon the antelope. I will kill you! I will kill you! I will kill you! Do not have hope of victory. You are doomed to fail. You are doomed to be slaughtered. I will make you feel pain! Pain! Pain! Forever!!!*

In front of the mass of Libyan warriors stood the Imukeheku chief, resplendently garbed as befitting a member of royalty. He was clothed in a large ornate floral-pattern cloak that was wrapped around his body and fastened above the left shoulder. On his arms and hands, tattoos were plainly visible. Around each upper arm, he had a large gold arm brace. Only the chief wore a beard; everyone else was clean-shaven. The beard itself was confined to a large long tuft extending off of the chin and was a deliberate imitation of the false beards that Egyptian kings wore. His long black hair was fashioned into thick dreadlocks, two of them hanging down on his chest and wrapped with leopard fur, and the remainder tied behind his head in a ponytail. He carried a long spear and a large oval wicker shield covered in zebra skin. He raised his arms up slowly, still gripping his spear and shield, and his attendants unfastened his cloak and pulled it off. As they stripped him, it was seen that the chief, like his men, wore only a loin cloth in terms of actual clothing, and elaborate geometric tattoos covered his entire body. As a mark of his status, he also had a pair of belts decorated with large gold disks crossed over his chest in an X.

The Libyan tribal chief then barked out a command to his army, and the men reshuffled into a triangle-shaped formation. As soon as they did this, the West Amentites who had formerly held their defensive positions behind the earthen barricades came out from behind the protection of these parapets, shields up to avoid being shot with arrows, and likewise formed into a triangle-shaped formation.

To King Shaweneiti and many of his veterans, the enemy's plan was obvious. He tried to remain calm and composed on the outside so as not to alarm his men, but in his gut, he was shaking with dread. He now regretted that he had been so overconfident about sweeping away Nesbit's puny army like sand in the wind.

Shaweneiti, standing in the center with the archers and with Seshrab and the attendants cowering low nearby, gave his orders. "Soldiers, our enemies are going to try to split us. They will attack us with all of the fury that they can muster. We are outnumbered. We have no escape from this place. We either leave in victorious triumph or we die. Archers, shoot when ready. Infantry, stand your ground firmly. Don't give them a single inch, don't take one step back. If just one man falters, we are beaten. These men will not show mercy to us today. Don't give them any in return. Stand your ground bravely. I am with you".

The Libyan chief raised his spear to the sky, and with a great single roaring voice, the entire Libyan army broke into a flat all-out mad-dash charge, barreling straight towards Shaweneiti's men, spears leveled like thousands of sharp-bladed battering rams. An instant later, Nesbit's West Amentites did the same, charging Shaweneiti's men from the opposite side. "Hold fast, my sons!" shouted Shaweneiti. "In the name of the gods, hold fast!"

What strategy does one employ when you're outnumbered, have no hope of escape, and are being attacked from both the front and the rear simultaneously, your enemies are equipped to crack through your formation, and surrender is not an option? – dig in your heels, say your prayers, and fight like lions. Fight and kill like you've never had to before. It all comes down to who wants it the most.

There was no need for any orders to be given to the archers – they had done this many times before. They knocked their arrows into their bowstrings, and waited for their enemy to come within 200 yards of their position. The archers drew their bows upwards, the front half towards the West Amentites, and the back half towards the charging Libyans. The enemies came within range. The archers all shot at once.

1,500 *phthifts* sounded in the air as arrows sailed into the sky, arcing, and then descending downwards with a deadly purpose. There's a strange unique sound that arrows make when they make contact with a target *en masse*. There is no word for it, but perhaps it is just as well, for what word in any language could possibly convey that horrible sound? There soon came a distorted gut-sickening cacophony of thuds, thwacks, bangs, rips, and cracks, intermingled with strange thick wet sucking sounds, and of course screams of pain. It temporarily broke both sides' momentum. It slowed them down slightly, but it didn't stop them.

The archers prepared for another volley, and hit both sides again with 1,500 barbed shafts, causing even more casualties. By now, the enemy on both sides was less than a hundred feet away. "Infantry, prepare to throw javelins!" called out the company commanders. "Ready…throw!"

The infantry hurled their javelins, leveled their spears, and then readied themselves to receive the impact of the enemy's charge. "BRACE YOURSELVES!!!" yelled out one of the captains. A few of the men closed their eyes.

There was a loud splintering smash of broken spears and broken shields. Spears were slammed into bodies at full force. Thankfully, both attacking groups had lost a great deal of their momentum, so at the moment of impact, the two defending lines didn't split as the wedges collided into them, but rather bent inwards, with the royalist square now forming an hourglass shape. No matter how hard the men braced themselves, they were pushed back, and the ground seemed to give way under their feet. The impact knocked the wind out of them, and spears and javelins collided with flesh. Many in the front ranks were killed within the first few seconds of combat, but the lines held firm. The fighting was furious and hellish. Everywhere there was the thrusting of spears, the smash of wood and leather, and the screams of dying men.

From the relative safety of the interior of the square, Seshrab looked on in a mixture of terror and awestruck amazement. He kept his head down, but he still tried to keep aware of his surroundings. He felt like a frightened gazelle, his eyes always darting this way and that, searching for danger, searching for spears sailing through the air or arrows sharply cutting through the wind. His body was shaking, and he couldn't stop it. Every second that passed, he felt that he was surely going to die. He couldn't think. His entire brain was clouded over with fear. He now existed solely on his senses. The terrible sounds of the battle were loud and ringing in his ears – the scraping and rasping of metal against metal, the scratching sound of bracing against leather, the hollow thuds of shields banging into one another. And then there were the acrid smells of sweat and urine, and the beating boiling heat of the hot summer sun smashing down on everyone like a red-hot sledgehammer only made everything worse. The fighting made a large cloud of dust which hung suspended over the ground like a brown low-lying fog, and Seshrab found it difficult to breathe. He kept coughing, which didn't alleviate the butterflies in his stomach. He was torn between two primal emotions – taking cover in some sheltered place, or running away. As Seshrab remained hunkered down in the center, even though he was relatively safe, he felt this powerful urge to run, to crash through the battle lines and run away as far away as he could as fast as he could. Why? He would surely be killed if he tried to do it, but he was feeling it all the same. His chest felt heavy, as though his heart weighed twenty pounds. He took in deep, heavy sucking breaths, which made him cough harder because of the overwhelming dust of the battle. From his position in the center, Seshrab understood why the Egyptian military drilled and re-drilled and re-re-drilled so much. It was to prepare them for such events as these.

In contrast to Seshrab, terrified with fear and frozen in hectic panic, His Majesty King Shaweneiti was the complete opposite. The king was in the center as well, not far from where Seshrab was. However, in contrast to his chief scribe who was crouching down on the ground in a fetal position, *Nesu* stood straight and tall, in full view of everyone on both sides. His face appeared stoic and calm, showing no fear but rather an uncompromising determination and resolve. He had been directing the battle from this position, giving orders to this company or that and directing the archers where to shoot. Meanwhile the priest who accompanied the army was kneeling, loudly chanting prayers and mantras.

Yet despite his prayers and entreaties for divine aid, the situation was now getting desperate. Many of his infantry had been killed. The lines were weakening, and both the Libyans and West Amentites were slowly pushing forward. If something wasn't done right now, the lines would crack, the enemy would rush in, and everyone would be killed.

Shaweneiti turned to Seshrab and the other attendants. "Our defensive lines are weakening", he said sternly. "I must order you into the fight. Grab a shield and any weapon that you can find, and stand in the battle line with the soldiers".

Seshrab was practically beside himself with fear, but he had no time to question or protest. He realized the danger of the situation. If the Libyans or West Amentites managed to split the lines and get inside the square, they would slaughter the royalists from the inside out, since the interior had the archers and attendants, and the front-rankers with their long spears could not turn around easily.

Seshrab armed himself with a spear and shield. "Defend yourselves against our enemies. Fight for your lives, men", were the king's parting words, and then he left, making his way to the other side of the square to survey the situation there.

The attendants scattered to either side of the square, some going off to fight the Libyans, and others to fight the West Amentites. Seshrab was confused and panicked. He didn't know which way to turn. The cacophony of the battle erupted around all sides, and the horrendous sounds of agony and screaming were everywhere, and over everything was the unbearable searing heat of the sun. He had lost sight of Djoser, who had been standing next to him, but now disappeared. Seshrab knew that he needed to fight. He was terrified of the Libyans – savage bloodthirsty barbarians whom he imagined would do horrible things to him – and so he left to fight against the West Amentites, whom his fear could get a better grasp around. He found an exposed gap in the battle line and quickly raced in to plug it, and right away he was met by a wall of enemy spears. His immediate instinctive reaction was to hold his shield high, duck his head behind it, and madly stab and jab his spear, hoping that he'd hit something. This went on for about three seconds, when he heard a splintering crack, and suddenly his spear felt much lighter. He knew without even looking at it that someone had chopped off the copper spear-point, and now all he was left with was an eight-foot wooden pole.

Seshrab was then possessed by something. Whether it was courage, bloodlust, or desperation, he couldn't say, but regardless of what it was, Seshrab felt a great fury of adrenaline and a sense of purpose rising within him. Using his long pole, he kept thrusting forward, keeping the enemy spearmen at bay. He kept hammering their shields, going BANG! BANG! BANG! in quick succession. He could feel his heart pounding, the blood rushing through his veins. The sounds of the battle seemed to die away. All that he was aware of were his immediate surroundings, and it seemed as though the rest of the attacking and defending lines disappeared, and their sounds blended together into a long, distorted dream-like warp. Seshrab was overcome with a feeling of power. He'd never felt anything like this before in his life, not even when he was beating Imhotep senseless with his own scepter. This was something more, something of a much more immense magnitude than that event. It was an extreme sensation, "extreme" being the operative word. It was extreme rage, wrath, fear, sadness, and glee all rolled together.

By now, the battle had dragged on for nearly an hour. Shaweneiti had lost almost half of his men by this time. All around the defensive lines, there was a wall of bodies. Casualties were getting heavy on both sides, and the fighting was becoming increasingly desperate and savage. But at that moment, the tide began to turn. The Libyans had been marching non-stop ever since midnight. By now, it was noon, and the Imukeheku warriors were exhausted. They had marched for eleven hours, and had been fighting an intense battle in the hot boiling sun for the last hour. They were tiring. The royalists facing the Libyan attack could feel it slackening off. Shaweneiti could sense it as well. They weren't attacking as forcefully as they had before. Over the still immense sounds of the battle, Shaweneiti shouted to his men facing the Libyans "Your enemy is weakening! Press them harder!"

His men were tired as well, and they would have liked nothing more than this pushing match to be over. However, they followed the orders of their king and they began to liven up their attack. By now, the men were existing solely on adrenaline, and they had to keep up the pressure. If they were to slacken, they might very well collapse from exhaustion. Their bodies would give out from under them. With somewhat renewed vigor, the royalists pressed themselves against the Imukeheku.

The gamble worked. By now, many of the Libyans were too tired to continue fighting, and their attack collapsed. They began to slowly back away while the royalists continued to stab at them with their long spears, many of which had been reduced to sharp splintered staffs. A large number of Shaweneiti's troops had been forced to fight with their secondary weapons – their axes, maces, and daggers which hung at their side – and fought the Libyan barbarians at very close range. In the fury of the assault, several of his men were forced to fend off the savages by shredding at their faces and bodies with their teeth and fingernails. Yet the determination and discipline of the royalists began to turn the battle to their advantage. The Libyan attacked stopped – the warriors turned around and retreated. The men wanted to chase after them, but Shaweneiti prevented them. "No! Hold your positions!" The reason why he did this was because the other royalists were still fighting the West Amentites, and they were not going to retire as the Libyans had done. Not only that, but he did not want his men to expend their energy pursuing the Libyans. No, better to let them go and keep his men in fighting condition. He knew that this battle was only half-way over.

After the Libyans fell back about thirty yards, Shaweneiti shouted, "The line facing the Libyans will split in half, with each half falling in beside the flanking lines". And so, the line of infantry which had been facing the Libyan attack split into two. The left half then swung to a right-angle, linking up with the left side line, and the right half did the same, joining the right side line. Now the royalist army was in a U-shape, and the archers in the middle had a clear shot at the retreating Libyans. "Archers, kill the barbarians!", Shaweneiti ordered.

By this time, the archers only had a few arrows left. Many of them had none and were ordered to join the infantry line armed with axes and clubs, but the handful of archers that still had a few shots left would leave a well-felt impression upon the backs of the retreating Imukeheku warriors. Those royalist archers who had any arrows left raised their bows for the final time, and released the last of their deadly shafts into the air. It worked. As the Libyans retreated, being in a state of complete exhaustion and having no desire to fight further, they were suddenly hammered with a volley of arrows through their ribs, shoulders, and spines. That did it. The retreat now broke into a full rout, and the Imukeheku tribesmen fled the field. The Libyans were out of the battle.

With the Libyans no longer a threat, Shaweneiti could now concentrate entirely on the West Amentites. "Flanking lines!" he called out. "At my word, you will swing and close on both sides of the West Amentites. Archers, grab some weapons and shields and join the infantry". With the rear freed up, the archers, who were now completely out of ammunition, raced to where many of their comrades and enemies had fallen, and they picked up whatever shields and weaponry they could get their hands on. After they grabbed what they could, they joined the main line infantry.

"NOW!!!"

And so both flanks and their "attachments", using the angle junction of themselves and the line attacking the West Amentites as a hinge, began to swing forward upon the West Amentites like a pair of doors and eventually crashed onto the West Amentites' flanks.

The West Amentites saw to their incredible disbelief and surprise that they were now being attacked on three sides. They had not seen or heard anything of the Libyan retreat since they were too busy fighting the royalists. The reality of the situation began to dawn on the enemy troops. If the royalists were now attacking the West Amentites with all their strength, it must have meant that the Libyans were finished. Somehow, the tide of the battle had abruptly turned. They were no longer the attackers, but the defenders. A twinge of fear began to grip at the hearts of the West Amentite soldiers.

With the rear freed up, and with his royalist soldiers now attacking just one enemy, King Shaweneiti knew that it was now *his* turn to join the battle line. There was no longer any need to stay in the center and coordinate multiple defenses from multiple directions. Now, there was just one direction and one enemy. The time for staying in the rear was over. He surveyed the situation, determined where the fighting was the fiercest, where he was most likely to be killed, and knew at once that he must fight *there*.

His Majesty, armed with a shield and his royal mace, crashed through his own lines, pushing people out of the way. Among those whom he shoved aside was Seshrab, miraculously still alive with nothing left of his spear than a splintered stump. Seshrab and the king were now standing side-by-side. In a furious and insane display of bravery, wrath, and power, Shaweneiti began to bash and smash at the West Amentite attackers with his mace like a madman. "Fight, my sons!" screamed Shaweneiti, whacking people to his left and right. "Hold back nothing! Give them all that you have!"

And so Seshrab and the rest of the royalist infantry pressed themselves harder upon the West Amentites, not so much killing them but rather pushing them together. The royalists advanced slowly upon their enemies from forward and both sides, a few inches at a time, which meant that the enemy troops were being squeezed together with increasingly little room to maneuver.

By now, the battle had lasted for one and a half hours. Both sides were tired, but they maintained themselves. However, it appeared that the West Amentites were behaving with an increasing air of desperation. Shaweneiti could feel it. "Hit them harder, men! They're breaking!"

After a few more minutes, men from the West Amentite side began to run away to the safety of the city gates. There was now a crack in the dam, and Shaweneiti knew that the harder he and his men pushed, the greater the likelihood that the dam would collapse altogether. And it did. In no time, the entire West Amentite line broke into a retreat.

"*KILL THEM ALL!!!*" roared out the king's voice over the sounds of the battle.

Like some unholy beast within, the royalists, who were themselves on the verge of collapsing into unconsciousness due to the battle and the incredible heat, suddenly gained a new vitality, and in a single bone-chilling chorus, they all let out a mighty war-charge. It was like listening to a thousand lions roar.

With their enemy in full retreat, the royalists spared no venom. It was five hundred yards from their positions to the city gates, and for half of that distance, the retreating West Amentites had no protection from their archers stationed atop the city walls. The royalists, including Seshrab, who was bloodied and battered but still alive, surged forward as if the gods had replenished their strength. No longer tired and weary, adrenaline and a sheer desire for savage killing gave them their unearthly power. They bounded across the dusty sandy plain like cheetahs pursuing fleeing gazelles, tightly gripping their axes and maces; most of their spears had been broken. Some of them came upon their retreating adversaries so quickly through their leaps and bounds that they actually physically collided into them or tripped them over. Then, they savagely pounded or chopped them to bits.

But then, the royalists made a mistake – they ventured into the enemy archers' kill zone. As soon as they passed the 250-yard mark, the archers atop Yamu's walls released a deadly volley of arrows. The royalists had no idea what hit them. Suddenly, out of nowhere, death rained from the sky, and men began dropping all around. For Seshrab, it was something out of a nightmare. He had seen arrow volleys, but he had never been on the receiving end of one until now. Arrows came down all around him like a fury. Abruptly, all of the courage and bloodlust that he had experienced evaporated from him and the only thing that he could think of was fear. He stopped running after the enemy troops, hunkered down under his shield right there in the middle of the open field, and began screaming uncontrollably, and he screamed louder every time an arrow slammed into his shield with a loud sharp *THWACK!*

"Shields up! Keep going after them!" Shaweneiti shouted to his men as he ran, the arrows zipping through the air. In the background, one of the men was impaled by three barbed shafts and dropped to the floor, while another standing nearer to the king was struck by one arrow in the face and a second went through his throat. Men were dropping dead everywhere. The remaining soldiers raised their large shields above their heads like sunshades to protect them from the arrows while they still pursued their enemies as they fled towards the gates, the royalists following hotly behind.

The king spotted Seshrab cowering in terror under his shield. With anger swelling up within him, he rushed over while arrows still flew through the air, some missing him by only a few inches, put his mace in his left hand while still gripping his shield's hand strap, and then grabbed Seshrab by the throat and yanked him up off the ground. "Get up! Get up and fight or you're a dead man!" Seshrab was overwhelmed with fear and bewilderment, like a frightened deer, but he did what his king told him, and he and the king raced towards the gates side-by-side with their shields held high, protecting each other.

The West Amentites now made it to the city gates, which had been opened by the men inside to allow the soldiers to escape to safety, but there were so many of them and they couldn't squeeze in through the comparatively narrow doors. Shaweneiti's royalists were in hot pursuit, hacking and clubbing men down as they went. When they reached the gates, panic set in. The archers on top raked the royalists with a withering barrage of arrows, and many were run through from above. Shaweneiti himself led the charge, and he let out a great roar of rage, holding his mace up high. One West Amentite turned around to see the king coming straight at him. He had no time whatsoever to react, and Shaweneiti, with all of his strength, brought down the solid diorite club with full force on the man's head. His skull was smashed to bits, bloody brains spilling out everywhere, and his lower jaw hung loosely and limply from his crushed skull while one open eye drifted lazily off at nothingness, and the man fell to the ground. The man's blood had splattered everyone in the near vicinity, the king included. Shaweneiti and his men hammered the fleeing West Amentites, massacring them at the gates with a primal animal fury. Arms flew downwards and downwards, the gleam of blood-covered copper in the sunlight glinting as the strikes came down, down, down. Everywhere were the sounds of broken bones, of ripping flesh, of dripping and splattering blood, of screaming, of choking on one's blood, of whimpering desperation, and the savage animal-like growls and roars of men possessed by the wrath of Sekhmet, the ravenous goddess of bloody rage whose murderous fury was unstoppable, who even the other gods feared. The scene at the gate was one of unimaginable slaughter.

"Get inside! Push them! Push them inside!" shouted Shaweneiti. "Get men up on the wall to kill those archers! Kill them! Kill them!" he kept shouting it out, drilling it into the minds of the men like a religious mantra – *Kill! Kill! Kill!*

At last, the royalists broke through.

To Seshrab, the battle was a dizzying whirling blur. Things were happening everywhere all at once. The royalists were *inside* the city now. Already, soldiers were clambering up the walls to get to the archers. The West Amentite bowmen were being beaten and hacked to bits, and some were thrown off of the walls, plummeting to the ground below. The royalists had gone frenzied. Eager to destroy the West Amentites, the men hacked down every moving thing in their path. Seshrab gazed around him in incomprehensible horror. The scenes that he witnessed, the things that he saw the royalist soldiers do to the people of that town, the things that he did not think that people were capable of doing to each other. It was beyond cruel, beyond savage. To him, it seemed like an unimaginable exercise in madness. Madness! That was the only word that he could think of to describe it all.

The soldiers raced through the streets, even into the buildings, smashing down doors and hacking and stabbing the people who had taken refuge inside. The streets were slippery with blood, urine, and discharged feces. Shaweneiti and Seshrab pushed through the narrow winding alleys. The king advanced straight towards the largest building in the town – the governor's palace. That was where Lord Nesbit and his followers were making their last stand.

"I want him!" shouted Shaweneiti to his men. "I want him myself! I want him alive! No one is to touch him but me!"

The royalist soldiers surrounded the palace, a large mansion surrounded by a high brick wall with a gate. The gate was wide open; Nesbit had left it open to allow any of his retreating men to make their stand in the palace. Some of Nesbit's attendants were getting ready to slam the gate doors shut, but King Shaweneiti barged through them, swinging the doors fully open. One of the attendants was knocked to the ground, and was immediately impaled by a royalist spear. Shaweneiti charged into the open courtyard of the governor's mansion, not stopping, and immediately met a large body of armed men standing guard in front of the door of Nesbit's house. Nesbit himself was nowhere to be seen. The king seemed unconcerned with the large number of men arrayed against him, and went straight at them, alone, without losing any momentum. In a wild blind fury, he spun and whirled, slashing and whacking with his mace, moving like leaves blowing in the wind. His own men followed close behind, and lent their own helping hands. In no time, the defenders were all slain and Shaweneiti, using his heavy stone mace, smashed down the fragile cedar door with a single mighty swing.

"*NESBIT!!!*" he screamed out walking inside, pacing through the halls, kicking open doors and looking in. "Come out here, you coward!!! Your army has been beaten! Your town is in ruins! Your subjects are even now being slaughtered! You are finished! You are done! There is no escape from this place!"

Then, he turned to one more door, kicked it open, and saw what he was after. It was a bedroom. There he was – Lord Nesbit, Governor of West Ament, along with his family. They were all cowering in terror in a corner.

Seshrab came in immediately after him, panting, followed close behind by a few blood-covered soldiers. Shaweneiti pointed to his newfound prisoners. "Tie them up! Take them outside".

Some of the soldiers rushed over and ripped the expensive linen sheets from the bed, shredded them into strips, and used them to tie their hands behind their backs.

King Shaweneiti walked outside into the hallway, and out the front door. Standing a short distance from the doorway, only a few feet from the smashed and bloody corpses of those men who were the last line of defense against the royalists, the king boomed out, "It is over, my sons! We have him! Victory is ours!!!"

There was a great shout of hurrahs and huzzahs from the men, echoing loudly around from everywhere. For Seshrab, he was glad that it was all over.

Around now, the adrenaline which had fueled the king's royal fury throughout the fight started to crash, and the king's whole left arm began to pulse with throbbing surges of pain with each and every heartbeat. Shaweneiti glanced under his shield at his left arm, which had been tightly bandaged and wrapped after it had been slashed open by that assassin's knife several days earlier, and over this padding was a thick leather bracer which extended from the wrist to the elbow. Even so, he didn't like what he saw. There was no damage to the arm armor itself, but the whole inside was soaked through with blood.

But he couldn't tend to his injury now – he had a much more important matter to take care of first.

Lord Nesbit, Governor of West Ament, had been defeated. King Shaweneiti had explicitly instructed his men that he was to be taken alive. Enemy leaders were hardly ever killed on the battlefield. Instead, every measure would be taken to ensure that they would be captured rather than killed, and for very good reason. The ritual killing of the enemy commander was not merely an execution; it was an extremely sacred act drenched with powerful religious energy and symbolism. The sacrifice of the enemy leader would be an act demonstrating the king's legitimacy as Horus incarnate, and reaffirm the power of the Egyptian king over his enemies.

The treacherous Lord Nesbit was brought before the king in the blood-splattered courtyard of his mansion. The bodies that were there had been dragged away and heaped into a bloody slippery pile. Nesbit's hands were tied behind him with strips ripped from his own bedsheets, and was forced to kneel on the ground, his head bowed in submission. All the while, the surviving women of the town were releasing such unworldly and disturbing wails and utterances that sounded not of humans, but rather like the shades of the dead, calling forth another soul to come down into the earth with them.

King Shaweneiti stood there, tall, powerful, and imposing, gripping his mace in his right hand. The priest who had accompanied the royalist army here was standing next to him. Nesbit knew exactly what was coming next. So too did Seshrab, who decided at this point that he did not want to see what was assuredly going to happen, and he quickly turned and walked away.

King Shaweneiti reached down with his left hand and strongly gripped Nesbit by his hair – he had real hair, not just a wig over a shaved head – and yanked Nesbit's head so that the doomed man could look directly at the king, and the king could look directly at him. Shaweneiti turned his body somewhat to the side and swiftly raised his right arm upwards, tightly gripping his mace – the classic "smiting posture". Then, using every muscular fiber in his entire upper body, he slammed the mace down with full force onto Nesbit's skull. The impact shattered the man's head into pieces, and a sharp breaking *crunch* sound could be heard by everyone nearby. Blood and brains splattered everywhere. Shaweneiti let go of the body and Nesbit's corpse slumped onto the floor like a slab of meat.

Now, the priest who had been standing near Shaweneiti this whole time rushed over with great haste, stooped down, and scooped up the blood in the sand. Shaweneiti pulled his blood-splattered *nemes* crown off, revealing his shaved head, knelt, arms spread outwards crucifix-style to receive the divine blessing, and closed his eyes. The priest, using two of his fingers, dipped them into the bloody mixture, and then painted a large red circle on Shaweneiti's forehead. This mark was the symbol of the sun. The sun god Ra was King of Heaven, the undisputed ruler of the sky world. The Egyptian king was the undisputed ruler of the mortal world, and was therefore Ra's parallel on earth. The sun was also symbolic of the king's power. Just as the sun stretched its rays over the earth, so too did the Egyptian king stretch his hands over the land. His reach was inescapable. There was no place to hide. He was all powerful, all present, and even Almighty.

Nesbit's family prostrated themselves on the ground before Shaweneiti, the god-like red sun of victory boldly decorating his forehead. Blood was still dripping off of his mace. At last, the traitor's wife spoke. "Your Majesty, I beg of you, please grant us allowance to bury my husband our lord, according to our holy rites, before you put us to death".

Collective punishment was the norm. Just as a whole company would be beaten for an infraction committed by one soldier, so too would an entire family be punished for the crimes committed by one of its household. In the case of treason, the entire family – men, women, and children – would be executed. There were practical as well as symbolic reasons for doing this. Practically, there existed the possibility that the surviving members of Nesbit's family would take revenge for the death of the man, regardless of the fact that it was he who had initiated the conflict. Symbolically, the man's memory and his presence on this earth would be visible by the mere presence of his family. Just as the name and legacy of a dead artist lives on with his paintings, so too does the name and legacy of a criminal with his surviving family members, for their mere existence was proof that he had once dwelt upon this earth, and they forever carried with them the stigma of the crimes that he had committed. The Egyptians believed that sin and immorality were contagious, like a virus, and that if one person in a family conducted himself with evil, other members of that family would be lured into that life as well. Therefore, for the good of all, and to keep the disease from spreading, the entire household had to be exterminated. It was a code that was not questioned by anyone. Nesbit's family awaited Shaweneiti's answer, knowing what their own fates would be regardless of how he decided.

To Shaweneiti, the answer was clear. Nesbit was a conspirator, traitor, and blasphemer. He had slain the king, the living god of Egypt. This man was not entitled to an afterlife, and even if he did somehow cross the threshold into the beyond, then he would surely be damned when he was brought before the jury of the gods to account for his actions while alive, and his heart weighed next to the Feather of Truth. Why bother putting the gods through the effort of judging a man guilty of so many heinous crimes? Why make them waste their time?

"No", Shaweneiti replied sternly. "He will remain as he is, mutilated on the ground, exposed to the open air, so that vultures and jackals can pick at his corpse. He will not be buried and will have no second life. This is my decree".

At this, they began to sob and cry, not for their own fates but lamenting the damnation of their family's leader. Shaweneiti gave a flash of his eyes to his men, and the soldiers came and carried the family away – the wife, a teenage son, a child daughter, and an infant son – to their execution.

As they were being taken away, Shaweneiti put his cloth headdress back on and took a few moments to ensure that it was positioned properly. Then, he turned towards the captured Libyan commander, kneeling on the ground. His arm braces and gold disk belts which he had crossed over his chest had been snatched by a royalist soldier. The chief imagined that the same grisly fate that befell Nesbit would happen to him, and he began sing-chanting his death prayer to himself, waiting for the killing blow. His blood would make the ground sacred.

Shaweneiti grabbed the man by his long dreadlocks and yanked him upwards, and he let out a yelp that was a mixture of pain and fear. Shaweneiti was still holding his mace. The Imukeheku chief readied himself to meet his fate, and he tried to the best of his ability to do so bravely, still singing in a shaky voice, but fear and panic were clearly written on his face.

"What is your name?" asked Shaweneiti sternly.

There was a pause. "Bokhor", he replied, "Chief of the Imukeheku".

"The man who stands beside my enemy on the battlefield is my enemy also", began the Egyptian king in a powerful commanding voice. "If I had been killed and my father had survived when Nesbit sent his men to murder us, and if my father had defeated you today, he would not hesitate to smash your brains out onto the sand. But I am not my father. You were not the one who conspired against my father and myself, and you only joined my enemy's side because he likely promised you riches. Because of that, I shall not kill you". Shaweneiti let go of his hair. He looked at one of his officers standing nearby. "Cut his ropes".

As the officer reached forward with his knife and sawed through the cords, the Imukeheku chief began brokenly thanking the Egyptian king for sparing his life. "Thank you, Your Majesty! Thank you". He was about to stand up when Shaweneiti snarled at him.

"Do not stand! Bow before me, and pledge your allegiance!" he shouted, pointing to the ground.

The chief quickly knelt, and prostrated himself in deference, both hands pressed against the ground and his head bowed low. "Praise and glory to you *Nesu*, King of Lower Egypt. I, Bokhor, Chief of the Imukeheku, swear peace, friendship, and fealty to Your Majesty. Never shall my people take up arms against Egypt while King Shaweneiti reigns".

Shaweneiti kicked him away onto his back. "Go back to your own lands, and take your barbarians with you. Do not cross the border between our two realms ever again". Pointing at him with his bloody mace, "I, Nesu Shaweneiti, have decided to grant you mercy. Do not make me regret it".

The Libyan chief slowly rose, uncertain of what to do next.

"Go now!!!", Shaweneiti shouted.

The Libyan leader took off with the remainder of his men, moving westward towards the Libyan border. Shaweneiti's officers were stunned.

"Your Majesty, you're letting them go?", asked Col. Ankharis, who was standing nearby.

"You disapprove of my benevolence, commander?"

"No, Your Majesty! It's just…it seems unwise to let your enemies live".

"The Western Barbarians were not my enemies". Shaweneiti pointed to the lifeless body of Nesbit. "He was".

The king then knelt in the blood-splattered sand, bowed, and held his hands open and aloft towards the heavens. "Praise to the almighty god Ra, King of Heaven. Praise to the almighty god Horus, son of Ra, for granting me vengeance upon my father's murderer. Praise to the almighty god Montu, god of war and master of battles, for granting my soldiers victory. Praise to the almighty goddess Wadjet, overseer of Lower Egypt, for giving me her protection. I give my undying thanks to you, o gods, that we have emerged victorious on this bloody day".

The Battle of Yamu was over. Shaweneiti had his revenge.

# CHAPTER 9

*On the battlefield of Yamu, His Majesty Nesu Shaweneiti emerged victorious over his enemy, the treacherous Lord Nesbit, who had ordered and arranged the murder of His Majesty's father. I myself fought in the lines in service to the king's command. With Nesbit's death, the province of West Ament was added to His Majesty's domains, whose lands now stretched from the center of the Nile Delta westwards to the borders of Libya. Upon the field, the king paid homage to Ra, Horus, Montu, and Wadjet for granting him victory. He concluded a treaty with the Libyans, in which they swore never to attack Lower Egypt as long as Shaweneiti reigned as King, thus protecting Lower Egypt's western border. With victory achieved and peace established, His Majesty and his army returned to Khaset City with great pomp and celebration, and the king bestowed honors upon his soldiers.*

King Shaweneiti had entered the Battle of Yamu with 6,300 soldiers: 4,500 infantry, 1,500 archers, and 300 *nakhtu'aa* rangers. When the battle was over, two-thirds of his army lay dead and nearly everyone else was wounded. Shaweneiti and his men were outnumbered two to one, cut off and surrounded in enemy territory with no chance of retreat. At the end of that harsh hot bloody day, both enemy armies had been crushed. One of their leaders was dead and the other had pledged lifelong peace. The rebel province of West Ament was now under royalist control and the Libyan frontier had been secured. On paper, it was a major decisive victory, but try telling that to the 4,000 soldiers that His Majesty fought with who would not be marching in the victory parade and who would not be going back to see their families again.

The greatest loss that the Royal Army suffered was the death of Col. Horahauty, the commanding officer of the Khaset Regiment. He was an experienced and highly capable officer who had faithfully served as one of Gen. Nakhtibre's subordinate commanders for many years. Nakhtibre considered Horahauty to be a worthy replacement to lead the troops if he and his son should both perish. It had happened when the West Amentite line had broken and routed, and were falling back to the protection of the city. As the Royal Army pursued them, they came within range of the archers lining the walls, and their advance temporarily halted. Horahauty attempted to rally his troops to continue the pursuit when an arrow found its mark in his thigh, cutting the femoral artery. As he futilely attempted to stop the bleeding, he was struck four more times in other parts of his body, and he died within seconds. Colonel Horahauty's death was a heavy price for winning this victory, and in this hostile time with the earth shaking with the trampling footsteps of marching armies, the king of Lower Egypt needed experienced and talented commanders like him. His death was one that he could ill-afford at this moment.

Now the necessary-but-grisly task of counting the dead needed to be carried out. Not only did the number of royalist casualties need to be accounted for, but also the number of enemy dead needed to be precisely recorded as well. In addition to carrying out this daunting chore, an exact accounting also needed to be made of all of the goods which were to be taken by the army. All captured loot was to be initially turned over to the king. He would in turn divide it into three portions: one would go to the priests and temples in thanks to the gods for granting him victory, the second would be sent to the royal treasury, and the third would be partitioned amongst the soldiers. Plunder might include weapons, armor, jewelry, livestock, grain, household furniture, and even enemy prisoners who would be sold as slaves.

Lord Nesbit and his entire family were dead. Seshrab, who had seen enough killing for one day, decided that he would not watch the executions, and he walked off to be by himself for a bit, someplace where he could clear his head of everything which had happened that day. Yet where could he go? Everywhere throughout the city was the blood-red image of death. Still, he needed to get away from all of it, at least temporarily. Or at least he thought he could.

Seshrab, splattered all over with blood from the battle and covered with bruises, quick-walked out of the mansion's courtyard just before Lord Nesbit met his death, taking care to walk around the mass of dead rebel soldiers that lay hacked to pieces around the gate of the mansion's perimeter wall. He slowly passed through the gate and made his way through the blood-covered streets of Yamu, and surveyed the scene of wholesale slaughter and carnage.

Dead bodies were everywhere, either whole or in pieces, sprawled out in the middle of the streets, slumped in piles against walls, hanging out of windows, almost all of them lying in un-natural distorted contorted positions, many with horrid looks and expressions on their death-frozen faces. The streets and alleyways were thoroughly soaked with blood, standing in small puddles formed by depressions in the streets' surface. Here and there were severed arms, some of which were still gripping weapons, or severed heads, or the top halves of human torsos with the bottom halves lying a certain distance apart, or internal organs strewn about with their sickening slippery glisten. Many wounded, their hands or arms cut off, or with deep gashes across their heads, or desperately trying to keep their livers and intestines from falling out of their open bellies, crawled, wriggled, and writhed around like human maggots, crying, moaning, and screaming, their voices all mingling with one another like souls in torment. Throughout it all was the ever-increasing pungency in the air of blood, raw meat, urine, and discharged human feces. Several fires had broken out within the city, and some of the soldiers had formed makeshift fire brigades to put them out before they spread. The smoky rasping smell of charred timber and plaster combined with the unmistakable acrid sour stench of burning hair and cooked meat pervaded the lungs and stung the eyes. And the hot glaring sun was still beating down hard on everything below. A disjointed part of his mind wondered if all of this was some horrid twisted dream. Seshrab was still holding onto his blood-splattered shield and his broken splintered spearpole. After a few moments of staring slack-jawed at the sight before him, his hands went limp and his shield and spearpole dropped to the ground with a muffled thud. He slowly descended, slumped down into a corner, and stared.

Who knows how long he sat there, his fists tightly clenched over his mouth, his breathing heavy, measured, and deliberate, his eyes wide and unblinking, staring at everything and nothing.

Then…

"Chief Scribe?…Chief Scribe?…Seshrab?"

At first Seshrab wasn't sure if what he was hearing was real, but he slowly turned his head. There, standing above him, was King Shaweneiti, tall and imperious, covered from head to toe with the blood of his enemies, looking down upon him.

Seshrab didn't say anything. He just blankly looked at him.

"Seshrab, are you hurt?"

Seshrab hurt all over. His body was sore, his back ached, his shoulders ached, his arms ached. He felt light-headed and dizzy. The adrenaline was crashing, and as its numbing effects slowly slacked off, he began to hurt more and more. His whole body had taken a hard beating during the fight, and he had physically exerted himself far more than his body was used to. But the king's question began to jog his distracted mind back to its proper place, and he started to check himself. Yes, both of his hands were still there. Yes, both of his arms, too. He felt across his chest and up and down his curled-up legs. Lots of bruises, and a few cuts, but no broken bones. No major injuries. "No", he said looking up from his fetal position in the corner. "No, I'm alright".

"Then *get up*. You are my chief scribe, and I have a job for you".

Seshrab began to get his bearings, and he slowly haltingly stood up with abrupt jerks, his joints stiff, his muscles and bones sore, and stood to attention as he ought to in the presence of his lord and sovereign. "What would you have me do, Your Majesty?"

Meanwhile, the suffering unfortunates crawling around in the streets were still wailing and screaming around him. A few called out for the king to help them while others begged him to kill them and put them out of their misery. His Majesty ignored them.

"The battle is won. Now, we must tally the price of this victory. You will count all of my courageous dead. Each of my soldiers who lost his life this day must be accounted for so that he may be praised and honored for his valor. See to it that all of my sons are collected and counted. Never mind about the enemies' dead — they'll be taken care of later. I shall appoint several of my men to assist you. Do you understand everything that I've just said to you?"

"Yes, Your Majesty".

"Are you sure?"

"Yes, Your Majesty, I understand…count the dead…your dead…not theirs".

"Good. Get started now. Several troops shall join you shortly".

"As you wish, Your Majesty".

The king turned and began to set off, but after just one or two steps, he halted, and looked slightly over one shoulder. "Earlier, you had said to me that you had never seen a battle before?"

Seshrab didn't say anything. He just slowly nodded, his mouth hanging open.

"Don't ever forget what you see here today". And the king walked off as the wounded and bleeding people of Yamu groaned and called out for mercy or death, clawing up at the air, reaching out to him as he walked off to attend to other business, leaving Seshrab standing there, alone, surrounded.

After a few minutes, a platoon of twenty of the king's men approached where Seshrab was standing. Several of them had suffered various injuries and were bearing bloodied bandages upon their arms, legs, heads, and bodies. Yet in spite of their condition and their tired state, the men were in high spirits. They were alive, and how glorious it was to be alive! In their exultant frame of mind, all was right with the world.

"Chief Scribe Seshrab!" one of them called out. "The mighty warrior himself! You made it!"

"Of course he made it!" another of them replied smiling. "He's a Canaanite, and Canaanites are a warrior race".

"Congratulations! You made it through! Well done, man! Well done!" called out another, patting him heartily on one shoulder.

Seshrab was uncertain as to how to respond to this chummy back-slapping. His whole body hurt, he was bloodied and bruised, his mind was swimming, and he was surrounded by horrid sights, sounds, and smells. These twenty men had endured exactly what he had, and yet they didn't seem all that worse for wear. Quite the opposite, they were in good cheer.

"I'm glad to see that you're well", said Seshrab. "I imagine that you are used to this sort of thing, otherwise you'd not be so light-hearted".

"Oh, this is all in a day's work for us old soldiers", one said. "But it's no different for you either, eh? After all, you Asiatics fight battles against each other all the time!"

"Well, other Asiatics perhaps, but…".

At this, some of their eyes began to widen. "Wait a minute, just wait one minute now…Are you saying that this is your first time? You've never been in action before?"

"No…no, never".

"Well, I'll be!" one of them hollered. "I didn't think anybody was unbloodied in these times! By the gods, quite an introduction then for you, wasn't it?"

"Yes, yes it certainly was". Seshrab was starting to feel very uncomfortable with this conversation.

"You know, for a man who's never held a spear before in his hand, you did alright", one of them said. "Yes, sir. For a first-timer, you did just fine".

"Thanks".

"Anyway, enough of the comradely pleasantries", finally announced the leader of the group. "His Majesty had told us what he intends, and we're here to help you. After all, you can't do this job all by yourself, now can you?"

"No, no certainly not…It's…it's too much…it's too…".

"Seshrab are you alright? Are you feeling unwell? Do you want to sit down for a bit?"

"No, I…uh…I…"

"I think he's going to faint! Remember, he's not used to this sort of stuff. Seshrab, sir, if you feel you need to unburden your belly, don't try to hold it in – just let it all out. I did the first time".

"I think I'm…" and Seshrab immediately doubled over and wretch-vomited all over the ground, heaving and wheezing.

"There, that'll do it", one of the soldiers said. "Get it all out of your system. You'll feel better".

"I remember my first engagement", one of the men reminisced. "I was sick as a dog for three days straight afterwards".

"Afterwards? My first time, I threw up even before the battle started", said another.

"Hey, enough chatter! Get this man some water!"

One of the men who was carrying a leather skin slung over one shoulder passed it over and Seshrab washed the bile out of his mouth. However, a horrid lamentable chorus immediately arose all around this small ensemble. Several of the enemy wounded had seen the water bottle and now called out for it. *"Water! Water! Please, give me water!"*

"SHUT YOUR TRAPS, YOU DAMNED VERMIN!!!" snapped one of the soldiers and kicked one of them in the face.

"Come on", said another of the men. "We can't waste time chatting. We've got a job to do. The sooner we get it done, the sooner we can get some rest".

Seshrab walked down the main street towards the city's gate as if in a daze, in a daydream. He shuffled in a very peculiar un-natural stilted way, his feet incoherently sloshing through puddles of blood. In the gate's immediate vicinity, there was a huge pile of interwoven slippery carcasses with all manner of hideous nightmare-inducing renderings done unto them. Seshrab was forced to walk on top of them to go outside to the battlefield beyond the town. Already, the pounding sun and heat had made the bodies swell and stink.

As he climbed and clambered over them, he gasped at the sight that crashed upon his eyes. The whole field before the town seemed to be carpeted with corpses, decapitated heads, severed arms and legs, internal organs strewn about here and there, and an immense quantity of blood. The air was thick with the buzzing swarms of flies. Vultures were already circling overhead, their black forms silhouetted sharply against the hot cloudless sky, while others were busily ripping apart the bodies, harshly cawing and squawking to each other.

The most macabre thing of all, at least to Seshrab's mind, was the disposition that many of these bodies were lying in. In the middle of the battlefield, there was an absolutely massive pile of corpses, massed upon each other, except for one spot directly in the center, shaped like an hourglass, which was perfectly clear. This was where the royalist army had made its stand. They stood their ground and the enemy had not broken through. Over half of King Shaweneiti's men were lying dead or wounded in the ranks that they had placed themselves in. The remainder of the royalist dead were scattered about in various grades of thickness, some sparsely strewn about, while others were closely packed together.

Seshrab and his associates got to work sorting out friend from foe, the living from the dead. The dead didn't seem real. Yes, they were human-shaped, but they seemed *false* somehow, like mannequins or statues. Around him, surviving soldiers gathered together to strip the dead of whatever loot that they had on them. Both the king's physician and his assistant had survived the battle, and right away, they began to tend to the wounded, although they felt as if they were performing an impossible task. Surely many of them were doomed.

Seshrab turned his glance to see one of the men holding a large knife and sawing off the hands of the corpses. "What are you doing?! There's no need to desecrate the dead!"

"It's standard procedure", said one of them. "To count how many enemy troops have been killed, one hand is cut off of each dead body. Less dead weight to carry".

Seshrab decided not to push the matter further. As he examined the corpses, trying to determine who was who, he turned over one of the bodies. He immediately recognized him.

"Djoser!!!" he cried out.

His fellow scribe, the man that he had shared a room with, and the first person that he felt any sort of bond with since he arrived in Egypt, was now lying lifeless on the blood-covered sand. He had fought in the front ranks against the Libyans, and he had been killed.

Seshrab had been numb so far. The horrid sights around him had overloaded his brain, and aside from a spell of vomiting, he had no reaction. But now an abrupt change occurred. Now, he collapsed down on the ground and started crying. He tried to lift up Djoser's body, but despite Djoser's small size and thin build, Seshrab now found him to be surprisingly heavy, and he could only lift him up a few inches. He cradled Djoser in his arm, tightly pressing his limp lifeless ragdoll form against his chest. The soldiers who had been assisting him heard his shout and hastily ran over to him to see what was the matter. They saw Seshrab sitting down cross-legged surrounded by a sea of dead bodies. When he saw that Seshrab was crying and holding one of the corpses earnestly, they stopped, remaining a respectful few feet away. "Sir, did you know this man?" one of them asked.

Seshrab, sniffling, looked up, away from Djoser's body but not looking up at the king – just sort of blankly staring off. He whimpered, sniffed, and responded "He was my friend...Gentlemen, help me with this one".

And with the greatest care, all of them gingerly lifted Djoser's dead body, and stepping very carefully, brought him towards where the other royalists laid, and very gently set him down as neatly as possible. One of them found a cloak somewhere on the field, and covered Djoser up so that the buzzards, the flies, and the sun wouldn't get to him.

The king and his men rested in Yamu for the rest of that day and the following day. Word soon spread throughout all of Egypt, both north and south, of King Shaweneiti's great victory. The Battle of Yamu would surely go down in legend as one of the greatest battles ever fought. Stories were passed from one person to the next about the long march, and about how the Libyans snuck behind the army and destroyed the king's ships so that he had no chance of escape. They told how His Majesty was completely surrounded. They spoke of the vile cruelty of the West Amentites, people who were surely in league with the dark god Set, and about the ferocious barbarity of the Libyan savages, men who fought naked and covered their bodies with tattoos. They described the bloody clash of the fighting itself. The battle had become so desperate that His Majesty was forced to have the servants and the camp attendants join the battle lines alongside the regular infantry! They relayed how the Western Barbarians had been put to flight, and how in a swift stroke, Shaweneiti swung his whole army upon the forces of Nesbit – suddenly, the enemy was on the defensive, and the king was pressing the attack! They spoke of the king, valiant and courageous in battle, more like a lion than a man, smashing people to his left and right with his royal mace. Exaggerated stories were told of the king's mighty strength, how he completely cleft three men in half with a single blow, and about how the gods favored him by making him invulnerable. They told each other that the arrows would bounce off of his dark sun-weathered copper-colored skin as if it actually was made of copper, and about how the enemy spears would not penetrate him, but instantly became blunt. They told how the West Amentites fled for their lives in the face of his strength, of how the city was broken into, of the fighting in the streets, and the capture of the vile enemy commanders. They spoke of the king's ferocious determination and resolution when he smote Governor Nesbit, and of his genial mercifulness when he spared the Libyan chief's life. How becoming a king! How royal! How noble in expression and deed and voice!

What these stories and tales did *not* tell were the stories of men who had their intestines ripped out while they were still alive, of men who had literally been torn to pieces, of how everyone on both sides, even the king, was splattered with the blood of hundreds of men. They did not speak of those who had their arms and legs chopped off. They did not speak of how the royalist troops went on a rampage through the city of Yamu and slaughtered the entire city's population – men, women, and children. They did not speak of the king's soldiers grabbing squealing babies from their cribs and cradles and then smashing their skulls against brick walls. They did not talk of people being thrown out of windows, of having their throats slit open, of being manually strangled to death and having their spines twisted and snapped. They did not speak of the horrible stench of that place, the horrible vomit-inducing smell of congealed blood, exposed internal organs, urine, and human feces in the hot beating summer sun. They did not speak of how King Shaweneiti ordered the death of Nesbit's wife and children, and how the children screamed and cried when they saw their mother's head cut off with an axe, the blood shooting out of her vessels like hot red fountains, and of how the children screamed out when the soldiers pinned them down to the ground to hold them still and repeatedly stabbed them through with their spears over and over again until they stopped screaming. No, the stories never talked about those sorts of things.

Seshrab lay on the floor of a burned-out house in the shade of a broken wall. He was tired, light-headed and light-bodied, and the room that he was in seemed to sway and spin around him. He did not want to think, and yet his mind raced and whirled. Every swaying and flickering shadow in the room reminded him of some horrible and terrifying sight that he had seen on that bloody day. Every single second, he could hear the battle raging around him, he could hear the ringing of weapons, the great yelling and shouting of the soldiers, and the agonizing screams and cries of terror of the people as they were butchered and slaughtered. Whether his eyes were open or closed, he could still see them. Whether his ears were open or covered, he could still hear them. *Great god El*, he thought to himself, *I beg of you, let me forget. Let all of the memories that I have be killed. I don't want to remember anything of it.* He had heard stories about people who had experienced things which were so horrible that they were blocked from their memory. He wanted the same to happen to him, but El did not grant his request. He remembered.

He could not really remember what he himself had done during the battle – that part at least was a bit of a blur. He knew that he had gone into the fighting, and he knew that he had fought hard, but as for individual events, it all sort of blended together. However, he *did* remember some of the faces of those that he met, some of the faces of the men who were arrayed against him, the faces of the men who tried to kill him, and the faces of the men that he himself had killed. He remembered finding Djoser's bloody mutilated corpse lying on the field. He remembered that he had cried, and Seshrab cursed himself for not having said something appropriate and meaningful to him beforehand.

Seshrab had spent the past two days carrying out the laborious and macabre task of counting the dead. The census of the fallen had left him numb as he was required to count each individual royalist corpse one-by-one. In some cases, he wasn't sure if different parts of bodies belonged to one person or different individuals. The royalist soldiers were laid out with dutiful care in neat precise rows. As for the bodies of the Libyans, the West Amentite soldiers, and the unfortunate peasants of Yamu, they were all dragged together, piled into heaps, and set on fire. This was an extremely serious thing. Egyptians were resurrectionists. They believed that the body would literally rise again during the time of the Final Judgment. Therefore, the body needed to be preserved – hence, mummification. The dead could only be granted their second life as long as the body was intact. If the body was destroyed, the soul was damned, never to be granted an afterlife. Nesbit had rejected obedience to the king, he ordered the assassination of Nebsenre and his son, and his men had fought against His Majesty. Egyptians, including Shaweneiti, were avid adherents to the old adage *He who is not with me is against me*, and Nesbit's fate had been sealed three times over. Egyptians also believed in collective punishment. Nesbit, his family, his soldiers, and his subjects had all been killed and all of their bodies had been destroyed. Shaweneiti damned and cursed them all to have not only their bodies die, but to have their souls die as well. For them, there would be no Heaven or Hell or any afterlife. There was nothing. No executions or tortures ever devised by the most sadistic minds could compare with the idea that a person would deliberately deny another person a second life – that was infinitely worse than any earthly punishment.

On the day after the battle, King Shaweneiti began making preparations to return to Khaset City. His Majesty knew that he needed to appoint a new governor to rule this province, but right now, he had more pressing matters to concern himself with. The most daunting task of all was how to go about burying all of the dead bodies of his royalist troops. In former days when the Egyptian army went off campaigning into foreign lands like Nubia, Libya, or Canaan, any dead bodies had to be brought back home because the dead always had to be buried on Egyptian soil. Shaweneiti briefly considered whether he should bring the dead soldiers back to Khaset City for a proper burial, but he quickly shot this idea down as foolish. The logistics were too immense. There was no way that he could transport 4,000 corpses back to the capital city. There were only 2,000 soldiers under Shaweneiti's command. Many of them had suffered horrible injuries during the battle, and were unfit to work. No, they would be buried right there, outside the city, in a soldiers' graveyard. After all, West Ament was Egyptian soil, too.

Seshrab was still lying where he was all day, eyes closed. Although his eyes were firmly shut, he could still see all of the macabre and horrid sights from the battle he fought in two days ago, and he could still hear those abominable sounds. Then, through the frantic desperate curses of terrified men, through the deafening clashing of weapons on shields, through the screaming of scared children calling out for their dead parents, he heard footsteps approaching him and pause nearby. "Chief Scribe? Sir?"

He let out a tired groan. "Yes, what is it?"

"His Majesty wants to see you".

Seshrab opened his eyes and saw a wounded royalist soldier. The soldier's left arm, his shield arm, was in a sling – he had taken some very hard hits – and he had a bloody bandage wrapped around his forehead. Seshrab tried to get up, but his whole body ached and his bones creaked. The soldier bent down and helped him get up using his one good arm. "Where is the king?" Seshrab asked.

"I'll bring you to him, sir".

King Shaweneiti had set up his command post in Nesbit's burned-out palace. During the time that Lord Nesbit was the governor and essentially the self-appointed monarch of West Ament, his estate had been one of the most lavish in all of northern Egypt. His house was splendidly decorated with exquisite paintings and artwork, gaudy and expensive solid wood furniture, and valuable antiques. Nesbit obviously had a taste for the finer things of life. Now, his palace was a blackened ruin. The wonderful frescoes that had been painted on the walls were all charred and discolored. His well-polished cedar wood furniture had been turned into charcoal and ashes, and many of his possessions had been irreplaceably destroyed. Nesbit's remaining valuables had been confiscated by the king as trophies of war, and would be apportioned out according to His Majesty's favor sometime in the near future. Such was the penalty for treason.

Seshrab and his escort came to the king. The soldier saluted and left. Seshrab tried his best to stand at attention. "You summoned me, Your Majesty?"

The king looked up. "How are you, Chief Scribe?" he asked. The king had fresh bandages around his left arm, and it was suspended in a sling around his neck.

"Tired and weak, Your Majesty".

"You had a hard day yesterday. So did everyone. I too am tired and weak from the fighting, but I cannot afford to rest – there is too much to be done. The soldiers were impressed by you, Seshrab. They told me that you fought well yesterday. For someone who has never been in a battle before, you did good work. You should be proud of yourself".

"I can't really remember what I did, Your Majesty. If the soldiers say that I fought well, I'll take their word for it".

Shaweneiti now had to get to the point. "I need you to do some things for me".

"What would you have me do, Your Majesty?"

"We will be leaving in a few days", said the king. "We need to secure as many barges and ships as soon as possible to ferry the army across the river. We also need many donkeys to carry the supplies and the plunder for the men. The great heat is already causing the corpses to smell foul, and I have heard the jackals howling all night. I have decided that I shall dedicate the battlefield as a cemetery for my soldiers. The sand will protect them and it will also serve to slightly dehydrate the bodies, and therefore preserve them for their second life. We cannot bury them in mass graves – the bodies need to be separated from each other with sand all around them, otherwise they will rot where they touch. But we cannot dig 4,000 individual graves as we are. There are only 2,000 of us left, and many of them are so horribly injured that they are in no condition to work. I fear that a good many of them will not survive more than a few days. So, here is what you must do. I need you to send some general messages, to be spread throughout the domains that I currently rule over. We need food, medicine, and salt. Send word throughout all of West Ament to have the villagers of this province come here with their shovels and hoes, whatever digging tools that they have, and have them assist in burying our honored dead. We need a large number of donkeys to carry supplies and the wounded who are too sick to walk. We also need boats to transport the army across the rivers. Do you understand and remember what I have just told you?"

"Yes, Your Majesty – food, medicine, and salt for the men, workers to dig graves, donkeys, and ships".

"Good. Get working on those messages right away. The sooner you dispatch them, the sooner we can leave this wretched place and get back home".

"Yes, Your Majesty". Seshrab bowed and left.

Seshrab did what he was told. Knowing the danger of disease and the need of the Egyptians to preserve the bodies of their dead, he decided that the most important letter, the one that he should send first, would be to the newly-conquered people of West Ament. This letter informed the province's inhabitants that Lord Nesbit was dead and that His Majesty King Shaweneiti was their new master. The letter commanded them to all come to Yamu bringing with them shovels to bury the dead as well as food, medicine, and salt.

The nearest village was half a mile away. The Royal Army did not have any donkeys – they were all let loose and chased away before the battle began. The message would have to be delivered in person by men who had to walk there. Seshrab himself could not go since he was too busy, so he asked if there were any soldiers fit enough to do the task. He needed three: one to carry the message, and the other two to act as guards to make sure that the messenger was protected and to ensure that the message was delivered. All three would be heavily-armed to intimidate the people and to assure their compliance with His Majesty's wishes.

Within about two hours, the first of the villagers started dribbling in from the surrounding countryside, mostly women and children under the age of thirteen. Almost all of the men had been pressed to join Nesbit and his army in defending the city – all of them were now dead. They were all carrying tools of some sort or another.

It took all day, working non-stop, to dig all of those graves due to the immense number of corpses. Under normal circumstances, these processes would be methodically performed by highly-trained embalmers under sterile conditions over a certain period of time. Now, there was no time to take such luxuries. The dead soldiers were hastily "field dressed" by amateurs, getting it over and done with as quickly as possible. Afterwards, they should have been placed into canvas body bags to protect them from the sun and air, and also to cover up their appearance, but the army didn't have any body bags. So instead, the corpses were buried deep in the sand to protect them from exposure to the elements and to slow down the process of decomposition. Once they were laid in the pit, salt was dumped on them, looking like white lime powder, and then the graves were filled in.

King Shaweneiti stood beside Seshrab watching the spectacle unfold. The battlefield looked like a swarm of ants or a hive of bees busily working. "I insist that the dead be interred with full honors. Once the burial is complete, we shall hold a proper ceremony".

"Yes, Your Majesty".

"I want you to write another letter. Send word to the royal goldsmith in the palace. Tell him that I want him to make 2,000 flies".

"*Flies*, Your Majesty?"

"Just send the message. He'll know what I mean".

"Yes, Your Majesty", replied Seshrab, puzzled.

After several hours, all 4,000-something bodies of the royalists who fell at Yamu were buried, their grave lines arranged in precise neat rows. There were no tombstones or grave-markers of any sort. His Majesty ordered those who were fit to stand to arrange themselves nearby for the cemetery's dedication and for the funeral service of the dead.

"Today, my brave soldiers, we mourn our fallen comrades. It is fitting that due respect shall be given to those who have passed on into the land of the spirits. It makes my heart glad to know that there are no cowards among you. You are all in my favor, and I am in your debt. Many of you have fought beside me since I was young. We have journeyed together on many campaigns and have known many hardships. The life of a soldier is not an easy one, and it is not one which I can recommend to all people. Only those who have strength, both physical and emotional, can do what has been done here.

"This place is called Yamu, the capital of the province of West Ament. It was on this spot two days ago that we proved our strength to ourselves, to our friends, our family, and our gods. The all-seeing ones know our worth, and they know the great worth of those whom they have received into their company.

"This place is very important, and the times which you live in are also very important. In the past, our kingdom was great and powerful and our wars were fought against foreign enemies, but now we fight amongst ourselves. Our enemies are our fellow Egyptians, people of our own blood, people who in the past we feasted with, played with, and labored with. What we saw here two days ago is proof of the vices which have plunged our land into turmoil. Since these dark times descended upon us nearly a century ago, thousands of Egyptians have perished in battles fought amongst ourselves. The great battle which was waged here two days ago is merely the latest in an innumerable number of battles which have been fought on our own sacred soil. Today, my sons, we stand upon the battlefield which saw the deaths of many of our dearest friends. I now ask that we have a moment of silence in remembrance of them".

Everyone bowed their heads, including Seshrab and the king. For a minute, the field was silent. Perfectly silent. Not even the wind.

Seshrab wanted to think about Djoser, but his mind was a blank. It was almost as if his brain would not let him remember his face. Seshrab then realized somewhat to his shock that he couldn't remember what his friend Djoser looked like at all. How could that be? It wasn't as if the two had been apart for so long. They had known each other only a couple of days ago. Yet now, it was a blank. Seshrab vaguely remembered Djoser's shape, but he could not remember any specific details. Perhaps El had granted his request. Little by little, he was forgetting.

The king spoke again. "I have commanded that this battlefield is to be dedicated as a cemetery for the fallen. It has been left up to us to continue the work for which they gave their lives. These dead must not have died in vain. They died to bring us out of this darkness which Egypt has known for nearly a hundred years. Let us work together to bring that dream into reality, to make Egypt whole and free and strong once again, to recreate the Egypt that our forefathers knew, the Egypt that was the light and the envy of the whole world".

Shaweneiti raised his arms. "Almighty god Ra, lord of the sky and king of the gods. Almighty god Osiris, god of the dead and master of the Underworld. Almighty god Montu, god of war, master of battle, smiter of armies, and destroyer of nations. Almighty goddess Sekhmet, the ravaging princess of wrath. Almighty god Thoth, the all-wise and all-knowing. Almighty goddess Isis, healer and protector. Almighty god Anubis, who conveys the spirits of the dead from this life to the next – I, King Shaweneiti, call upon you. I ask that you accept my soldiers into the land of eternal paradise. May their hearts weigh lightly upon the scales of judgment, may their sins be washed out so that they be made strong and upright in the next life. May they have all things good and pure on which the gods live. May they know happiness, peace, and prosperity forever. In the name of the gods, let it be done".

The soldiers bowed their head yet again in reverence, bidding farewell to the fallen for one last time. Soon, they would be leaving.

King Shaweneiti had sent word back to his provincial governors that the army had been victorious and would return shortly. The people were to make all necessary preparations for their arrival. Barges and boats had been prepared to ferry what was left of the army back, first across the narrow strait to the province of East Ament, and then afterwards to Khaset Province. From thence, the army would march to the capital of Khaset City. As Chief Scribe, Seshrab was entrusted to oversee all of the administrative details of getting the army back on its feet. The troops and attendants had to march eight miles to the coast.

The eight-mile march to the river might as well have been a hundred miles. The sun was still burning hot. The journey was deliberately slow, less than a mile per hour, and the army stopped every ten minutes for water and rest. The officers repeatedly promised them that they could be at ease soon enough. "Stiffen yourselves, my brave fellows!" called out Col. Ankharis of the Sapmeh Regiment, who had been wounded but was still able to walk. "Soon, there will be a great celebration held in your honor. There will be music and feasting and dancing girls!

And all of you can rest in soft beds". He tried to sound up-beat, but secretly, he was worried that many of his soldiers might not survive the trip.

Like he had done with the sick and injured miners at Hathor's Mountain, Seshrab set up a transport system for those wounded who were unfit to walk, consisting of a canvas cot being suspended in between a pair of donkeys. The wounded would be carried to the ships waiting at the river on these large mobile stretchers. King Shaweneiti, who was not usually given to excessive displays of emotion, merely smiled and simply said "This pleases me".

Finally, after marching all day long, they reached the river. "We will camp on the riverbank tonight", said the king. "Tomorrow, we will take ship and march in the victory parade back to Khaset City".

The next day.

As the column advanced up the main highway towards the capital, soldiers banged on gigantic kettle drums, and the people waved multicolored ribbons. King Shaweneiti, in true royal style, was carried on his golden litter by four burly stern-looking attendants as they made their way back to the royal palace. The men tried their best to stand straight and tall, to bear their wounds with dignity, but many of them could barely walk. Seshrab, who walked behind the king's litter (the king's most important subordinates were privileged enough to do this) wondered if the king should have just come back home more quietly.

Then he saw King Shaweneiti seated atop his shimmering gleaming golden litter draped with the red velvet curtains. *No,* he thought. *That wouldn't be his style. Shaweneiti is a king, and a king needs to look and act like a king.* Seshrab looked around him, and saw the wounded soldiers trying their best to walk, to remain stoic, to not show how much pain that they were in, to try not to wince, to try not to cry. *Yes, this is what kings do...unfortunately.*

Bringing up the rear of the advancing column was a large train of treasure bearers carrying all of the loot that they had plundered from the enemy dead and from the city. Seshrab was marching near the front with the king, so he couldn't see them, but he knew what was there. After all, he was given the tedious task of listing and cataloging every individual item that was brought back. It took him two whole days to do it. He thought about the items that were now being carried back to the city as trophies of war: bracelets, necklaces, pendants, rings, and a wide variety of other objects. Some of them were owned by Governor Nesbit and his family, but others had been personal possessions which were formerly owned by the people of Yamu.

The parade stopped in front of the royal palace. The king's litter was very carefully placed down on the ground. He stepped off, fully garbed in his complete royal regalia, and raised his hand towards the crowd in a combination of greeting and blessing. The crowd cheered. Standing at the gate of the palace were several guards as well as the royal goldsmith. He was carrying a large box made of cartonnage.

"People of Khaset City", began Shaweneiti, "several days ago, our army won a great and wonderful victory on the field of Yamu. The tyrannical despot Nesbit, who had arranged my father's death, has been defeated. His entire army was put to death, and Nesbit himself has been slain. His Libyan allies have pledged eternal peace. The province of West Ament is now under royal control, and our western border has been pacified. People of Khaset City, behold your victorious heroes!"

The crowd cheered loudly.

"This was a hard-fought battle, and it shall be sung about for years to come. All who fought in this battle have proven their worth as men. Therefore, I shall do something which has seldom been done in the history of our nation. I hereby decree that everyone who fought at the Battle of Yamu is to be given the Golden Fly".

The crowd murmured amongst themselves. The only items that could be called "medals" in the Egyptian military were small golden medallions in the shape of flies, given for "persistently biting the enemy". A soldier could only win one of these "Golden Flies" per battle, and he had to show incredible distinction. Understandably, given that Egypt frowned on individuality, the Golden Fly was seldom awarded to a single person, unless the formations had somehow broken up and combat had dissolved into individual fighting. Mostly, these awards were given to particular *units* that had distinguished themselves. However, King Shaweneiti had just announced that everyone who participated in the battle was to be given one of these Golden Fly medals. This was practically unheard of. The general awarding of medals to an entire army had only happened on two or three occasions in Egypt's 1,500 year-long past. But then again, the Battle of Yamu was not like most battles.

King Shaweneiti signaled the royal goldsmith to come forward. Escorted by two heavily-armed palace guards, he approached carrying a massive chest mounted on a sled, and bowed respectfully to His Majesty. He then opened the lid, revealing the precious contents inside: two thousand Golden Fly medals, each one about an inch long, with a thin golden chain fastened near the flies' heads.

The first men whom Shaweneiti bestowed medals upon were his two surviving regiment commanders, Colonel Ankharis and Colonel Mebydos. He addressed each of them by name and then said "In recognition of your gallant behavior at the Battle of Yamu, I hereby award you the Golden Fly".

Since Seshrab had fought at Yamu, he too would be awarded this prestigious honor. The soldiers were still talking about how he had behaved during the battle. Some said that he fought with a raving fury, as if he was possessed by the goddess Sekhmet herself. Several others commented that his battlefield wrath was due to his inherent violent Canaanite temperament. Regardless of the reasons, for a man who had never fought in a battle before, they were highly impressed with him. Even the veterans voiced their approval.

After Shaweneiti bestowed his rewards to his generals, His Majesty approached Seshrab and held up the medal, spreading the string in a wide loop. "Seshrab of Hebron, Chief Scribe to His Majesty King Shaweneiti of Lower Egypt, in recognition of your gallant behavior at the Battle of Yamu, I hereby award you the Golden Fly". The king then placed the medal around Seshrab's neck. Seshrab looked around at the wounded soldiers and officers, men who had fought beside their king for many years, and as he fingered the golden insect that hung around his neck, all he felt was shame.

One by one, King Shaweneiti personally went down the line. Every soldier, servant, clerk, and attendant, everyone who had been present on that hot dusty bloody day, was given a medal. The entire process took almost three hours. When he was done, he turned to the crowd and said, "Behold these great and valiant men! Honor them and praise them as heroes, the victors of the Battle of Yamu!"

The crowd cheered again.

"My brave soldiers, my valiant sons, you have served me and my father more loyally than any man can ever hope. You have been away from your family and friends for far too long. Therefore, I hereby decree that you are presently dismissed from active service. Go back home to your wives and your children and sleep once more in a soft bed. Do not think of where you shall march tomorrow, or what battles you may fight in the weeks or months to come. For you, your service is done. Your king thanks you for all that you have done in his name and in the name of his father. His Majesty is eternally grateful to all of you", and he bowed to them.

At this, his soldiers, his tired weary bloodied men, loudly cheered and shouted his name over and over again.

Then, the king re-mounted his golden litter, and accompanied by his servants and attendants and a small troupe of guards, they entered the royal palace. When the last soldier passed through the portal to the palace's courtyard, the immense gates closed, and the crowds dispersed.

At the Perah, the main doors were flung open and the attending guards bowed as the king and his entourage came through the entrance hall. Horemheb, Chamberlain of the Palace, was there to greet His Majesty. Horemheb was the head of the palace staff, in charge of all of the servants who worked there – all of the butlers, maids, repairmen, cooks, and cleaners answered to him. His job was to make sure that the palace was running smoothly at all times. Horemheb was twice Seshrab's age, with a chubby build and a somewhat boyish face, and he walked with a lot of swagger and purposely spoke with a deep powerful voice. "Welcome back, Your Majesty", said Horemheb, bowing. "The courtiers are awaiting your arrival in the throne room".

His Majesty silently nodded in reply.

As the glittering doors of the throne room were opened, Seshrab saw the nobles and courtiers arranged on either side of the red stone walkway leading up to the elevated dais. The room was well lit and smelled pleasantly of various perfumes. After being where he had been, Seshrab thought that it was the most beautiful smell in the world, like a heavenly garden. A wonderful feeling of calmness swept over him. It was good to be back in familiar surroundings. *I'm home*, he thought.

The king was greeted with bows and applause, but King Shaweneiti, as usual, was cold and aloof, rarely smiling, rarely showing any emotion. Seshrab had thought that the king would be pleased and warmed by such a kind gesture as this, but was surprised to see that the expression on Shaweneiti's face was anything but pleasurable. There was always a dismissive seriousness about him. He slowly walked up the stairs of the *dais* and looked at the throne, briefly brushed his fingers against the red velvet cushion, then turned and sat down on it. "I thank you for this warming display of loyalty. However, I am very tired and I wish to rest. All of you are dismissed. Resume your duties. Yet, I ask my wife to remain behind, that I may speak with her".

Seshrab thought that the king was being a little rude, but still he obeyed the king's command and departed for his quarters. He was looking forward to lying on his cot again after being so long away from it. A restful night's sleep would do him much good, for he needed to resume his clerical duties as soon as possible. *First thing tomorrow*, he thought, *I'll have a meeting with the other scribes to catch up on how things are, but as for today, I need some rest.* He was also contemplating whether or not he ought to pay a visit to the court physician. He had been having horrible nightmares for the past few days, bizarre and macabre thoughts would intrusively crash into his mind without his control, and he also found it difficult to concentrate, which was worrisome because he needed to be able to keep his mind clear in order to do his job. Every now and then his heart rate would dramatically increase, and he sometimes found it difficult to breathe. Perhaps a few nights in his own bed would amend this peculiar condition.

Everyone left the throne room, leaving only King Shaweneiti's wife behind. As Seshrab walked towards one of the side doors, Queen Neferet's eyes briefly clicked towards him, and then drifted off again.

Queen Neferet was a quiet demure woman close to Seshrab's age. She was the younger sister of Queen Meret, who had been married to Shaweneiti's father Nebsenre. Seshrab had very rarely seen her during the whole time that he worked in the palace. Her and her sister lived tucked away in a small apartment within the Perah, and Seshrab hardly ever went there.

While he was alive, Nebsenre was a beast to his wife, Queen Meret, whose name cruelly meant "beloved". The rough and gruff army general often treated her like one of his subordinate commanders, shouting orders and cursing at her. If things were not done exactly to his standards of perfection, he would sometimes strike her. She would often be seen in the palace with marks and bruises on her face and body, yet nothing could be done. He was, after all, Horus incarnate, the living god of Egypt, or so the temple priests proclaimed. When he was murdered by Lord Nesbit's assassins, Meret did not cry.

Meret's sister Neferet, whose name meant "beautiful", did not cry either. She had been married off to Nebsenre's son Shaweneiti at the same time that her older sister was forced to marry the general-turned-traitor who had killed her father. Neferet had no love whatsoever for her husband, but then again, Shaweneiti didn't have any love for her either – he merely tolerated her as being convenient. She had given birth to a daughter, but after that, the two of them were never intimate. They didn't even sleep in the same bedroom. This was somewhat worrisome, since the royal family (the current one anyway) needed to be preserved, and the only way to do that was through heirs, preferably sons. King Shaweneiti was in his late 30s and he had no sons. Time was ticking away.

Neferet could have been very beautiful, indeed, as her name suggested. Her body was well proportioned – not too fat, and not too thin, her breasts were just the right size, her hips were perfectly round and wide enough – and her features were not unpleasing, but she was lonely and depressed, and this caused dark circles under her eyes, and to have a perpetually ghostly downcast expression. Her skin was very pale and gaunt, in contrast with her jet black hair and large dark brown eyes. The fact that she always dressed in flowing white robes enhanced her spectral appearance.

A few seconds of awkward and somewhat intimidating silence passed by. Then, addressing his wife, he said "I have returned", firmly, straightly.

Another two or three seconds of silence. "Yes, my lord", she replied.

"Were your orders obeyed in my absence?"

"Yes, my lord".

"Were there any troubles in the palace?"

"No, my lord".

Shaweneiti breathed in deeply through his nostrils. He waited a second or two. "And how are you?"

"As always, my lord".

Seshrab's room was located all the way down at the end of the long hallway of the Servants' Quarters – the very last chamber, or "cell" as the small rooms were actually called. Aside from the small oil lamps which sporadically dotted the walls, the hallway was dark, dusty, and ominous. As he walked down the corridor, the sounds of his shuffling footsteps ricocheting around the plastered walls, he heard muffled voices coming from inside several of the rooms to his right and left, some male, some female.

He was now approaching his door, getting larger and larger as he came closer to it. Then, his heart started pounding again. Odd, these sporadic bouts of elevated heart rate had been occurring somewhat regularly since Yamu. For a fleeting instant, Seshrab wondered if he might be coming down with something. But this was more than just a quickly-beating heart – he also felt a growing sense of apprehension and nervousness. Why should he feel so anxious about going back to his own room? After all, shouldn't he get calmer and more relaxed the closer he got to his own bed, which was the one thing that he had been looking forward to more than anything else? The closer he got, the worse he got. His heart raced, his breathing became heavier, and his body started shaking.

As he reached for his door, he hesitated, and it just hit him why he was feeling this way. He knew that it was there, because he had passed by it several dozen times. His head slowly turned to the left and looked directly at it. It was the door that lay adjacent to his, the door to a room where he used to sleep on the floor.

It was Djoser's room.

Seshrab turned slowly towards it, facing it directly. With heavy footsteps, he approached it and cautiously pushed the door open with a loud creak. From where he stood, his eyes scanned inside. The square window, which sat in the middle of the wall facing out into the open courtyard of the palace lit the room up brightly – good for a scribe like him. All of the contents, everything, was exactly the way that he had left it when he accompanied the army on the march. Every minor inconsequential object that lay about the place seemed to have a dozen or so memories attached to it.

It was now that the full realization of Djoser's death struck Seshrab like a battering ram. His legs suddenly gave out from under him and he collapsed to his knees onto the floor with a sharp thud, his left arm stiff and straight horizontal, the hand tightly gripping the doorpost, his right hand bracing himself against the floor, and loudly and openly wept. He sobbed and wailed, and the tears poured from his eyes. All of the muscles of his body tightened, especially around his cheekbones and jaws. He cried and cried.

The noise of his sorrows caught the attention of the occupants of the nearby rooms. The loud sounds of someone crying were unmistakable. Sporadically, doors on the right and left of the hallway opened in a disorganized unison and heads poked out with puzzled and worried expressions. The sound of Seshrab's crying echoed down the long hallway, and it became distorted and unearthly, sounding like the mournful doloration of disembodied damned souls. When the various servants saw what was causing the noise, their expressions immediately changed from perplexment to altruistic concern. They rushed out of their little cells and fast-walked or ran toward where Seshrab knelt gripping the ground. They slid and skidded towards him and bent down, throwing their arms around him, young and old, men and women, butlers, maids, cooks, and handymen. They tightly grasped him around his back and about his shoulders, looking on him with pity and empathy. A few wondered to themselves whether or not they should try to pick him up, but they decided not to – don't push him.

"We heard the rumors when Djoser was not seen among the victory parade. We suspected then that he had gone west", said one of the kitchen servants. They clutched him tighter. "We all feel his loss…*all* our losses. There are four thousand others who are missing from their beds today, who will not see their families, who will no longer know the kindness of love and friendship. Djoser was a good and kind lad. You were his friend. I am sure that his heart did not weigh heavy upon the scale".

It was now that they instinctively determined that he should be picked up off of the floor. Using a little coaxing, Seshrab gradually rose, shaking. "Come", said the kitchen servant, "we'll take you to your room".

The servants regarded Seshrab very highly. They would not have shown such care and compassion to just anyone, especially not Imhotep the Toad. One of the servants opened the door to Seshrab's room, and he was brought inside. Seshrab could barely see through his tears, but after he wiped his eyes and looked around through the bleary wavy wash, he saw that his room had been all made up and prepared for his arrival. A large tray of fruit and bread lay upon the small nightstand located next to his bed, along with some wine. Sitting upon the bread was a note which read *Welcome back Chief Scribe Seshrab.*

"You did this for me?" he asked.

"We felt it would be a decent gesture", one of the maids commented.

Seshrab turned around and looked at them, somewhat smiling. "Thank you. Thank you, all of you. You are all so good to me".

"Are you feeling better?" another one of them asked.

Seshrab nodded. "Yes...yes I'm feeling much better now".

"Well, you've had a long journey. You should clean yourself up and get some rest. We'll try not to disturb you for the rest of the day". They smiled and left, getting back to their business, and closed the door.

Seshrab walked over to the nibble tray. "They're such good people", he mumbled out loud. He didn't have the heart to tell them that he didn't feel hungry. He was more tired than hungry. His body still hurt from the battle, and from the long eight mile walk back to the river, and the walk from the river to Khaset City. He ached. He collapsed onto his bed and immediately fell asleep.

Seshrab awoke a few hours later, his heart beating fast and sweating. It was almost dark, sunset. He looked around, expecting to see fearful sights, for that was all he saw while he was asleep, and saw that his tray of food and wine were still there. The lamps were still lit from when he arrived. He slid off of the bed and moved towards the food, grabbed the tray, then plopped back down on the edge of his bed and started munching away.

About five minutes later, a knock came at his door.

"Yes?" he called out, food still in his mouth.

The door hesitantly opened. It was one of the junior scribes, Khepermoses, a mere stripling of about 13 or so. He had stayed behind during the king's invasion of West Ament to help out around the palace. "Good evening, Chief Scribe. Are you well?"

Seshrab swallowed and took in a few deep breaths. "Yes, I'm feeling better, thank you".

"That's good. We were concerned about you". A short pause. "Sir, you are to come to the Perah".

Seshrab now got more alert. At first he thought the king wanted him to do some business. Then he thought, *Oh no, what if the king heard about me crying and wants to talk to me about it? What if he doesn't approve?*

As if reading his mind, the young scribe said, "Don't worry. It's not the king. Really, sir, you are such a worrier. Everywhere you look, you see dread. You're always wondering if you've done something wrong or if you're going to be reprimanded or punished in some way. You're obsessed with bad consequences to all of your actions. It's a very unhealthy frame of mind. You would be best rid of it".

"Thanks, I'll try".

"Anyway, the king did not summon you".

"Then who did?"

Seshrab stood outside the door to the room. This was a part of the palace which he had only been to a couple of times in the past, and only to deliver a quick message. He had never actually been summoned to come here. *What reason could there be? Well, best to get it over with.* He knocked on the door to announce himself, and then opened it.

"Excuse me…but, um…I was told that you wanted to see me", he said.

Queen Neferet sat on the edge of her bed. "Come. Sit with me for a while and keep me company".

Seshrab was unsure of what exactly to do, but even so, he nodded and approached.

"Here", she said, indicating that he should sit directly next to her on the bed.

An inner voice was screaming inside Seshrab's mind that this was a bad idea and he needed to get the hell out of there as fast as possible. "Your Majesty, I shouldn't. It would not be proper".

She smiled a little. "Don't worry, it's not like that. I did not bring you here to have you make love to me. I have so few people here who see me. You seem like a good man. Stay here for a while. Let me know that I'm alive".

Seshrab now felt sorry for her, and ashamed that he originally thought that she had summoned him here to have sex with him. He nodded his head, and sat down on the bed next to her.

"For the time being", Queen Neferet said, "do not think of me as your queen. Think of me as just another person. I know that my husband does…*Husband*" she sneered spitefully. "Be open and free with your speech. Tell me who you are, and where you come from".

Seshrab cleared his throat and shifted. He still felt a bit uneasy about this. "I am a Canaanite by birth. I come from the city of Hebron, located high up in the hills. Because of the altitude, the air is cooler there than in the hot dry valleys below. It has a population of 5,000 people. Much of the landscape surrounding the city is covered with grape vineyards and fig farms. My father is a prosperous merchant, and my brothers work for him".

"You have brothers?"

"Yes, two of them – Danel and Yasib. Danel is the oldest".

"Are you the youngest of your father's sons?"

"Yes, I am the youngest".

"How old are you?"

"Twenty-one, Your Majesty".

"Please don't call me that, not now, not here".

"I'm sorry".

"What about your mother and father?"

"My mother's name is Donatia. My father's name is Ibiran. They've both been very good to me…I miss them all terribly every day. I'm sorry every day for what I put them through".

"Unfortunately, the past cannot be changed", she said. "What has happened will be. Enough of such sad things. Tell me more about your home. Did you enjoy living in Hebron?"

Seshrab shrugged. "It was alright, I suppose. For most of my life, I had not travelled beyond the walls of my home-town. Hebron was all that I knew. Whether it was good or bad, I didn't know, because I didn't know any better. It wasn't until I was a young man that I saw more of the world…but I'd rather not talk about that. Too many bad memories".

"Yes, I know. I have bad memories, too". Here she paused, as if not certain if she ought to proceed further. "I was here when the palace fell, when Nebsenre and his rebel army attacked us. Both myself and my sister saw our father and mother killed before our eyes. Nebsenre, the great general, who was called a hero by the people, he put his axe into my father's neck, while his soldiers stabbed my mother to death in front of me. That was one and a half years ago. One and a half years. It seems like yesterday…and it seems like a thousand years".

"For me, my old life in Hebron seems so long ago", said Seshrab. "Much has happened since then".

"Do you miss your old home?"

"Yes, but there's no hope of ever going back there. I miss my family, my house, all of the things I left behind. Don't misunderstand me, this is a good place to be…but…".

"But it's not home" she concluded.

Seshrab nodded.

# CHAPTER 10

*Shortly after His Majesty returned with his victorious army to Khaset City, he performed the necessary rites to guarantee the journey of his father's soul to the afterlife and his body's eventual resurrection. I was informed by my fellow scribes of the funerary rites accompanying the burial of an Egyptian king. Much of what they said was strange to me, as Canaanites such as myself do not believe in such things. The funeral procession went to the tomb where Osiris-Nebsenre would be laid to rest, which was within the necropolis that lies to the west of Khaset City's walls. His Majesty was accompanied by his wife Queen Neferet and her sister Queen Meret, who was formerly married to the king's father Osiris-Nebsenre. He was also accompanied by numerous priests, attendants, and soldiers. At the place of entombment, the final sacrifices and prayers were offered. In his will, Osiris-Nebsenre had set aside a parcel of land for the priests. In return, they were ordered to maintain the tomb and temple, watch over the king's body and possessions, give daily offerings to his soul, and pray for his soul's salvation in the time of judgment. The coffin was then laid in the tomb, and the entrance was blocked up.*

For three days, the king's bedroom had been off-limits to everyone in the Perah except close family and a select handful of attendants. Armed guards stood vigilant and attentive outside the door, having been given strict orders that *nobody* was to be allowed access to the royal bed-chamber unless they had permission to be there. No one was to disturb him, and nothing was to be touched. For those three days, that particular section of the palace was unusually quiet. Nobody passed down that corridor. Nobody wanted to.

The king's private quarters lay within the center of the second floor of the Perah. The room was stuffy because there were no windows, but that was the price of security. Too many kings in this age and before had met premature ends at the hands of rebels and assassins.

For three days, he had laid there upon the soft mattress stuffed with ten thousand goose feathers, draped with the bedsheets made of the most exquisite pure white linen, and ringed with the thick heavy bedcurtains of luxurious royal blue. On the small tables on either side of the bed, small incense sticks and lamps filled with aromatic oils burned, designed to ward away evil spirits and to guard against any unhealthy miasmas that may be contaminating the air. Lying nearby and scattered in various places around the whole room were numerous protective charms and amulets, just in case. Every once in a while, somebody would open the door to make sure that the incense and the oils continued to burn, and to check that a fire hadn't broken out. Those few who were permitted to enter the room were always accompanied by at least two guards who were armed to the teeth. Upon opening the door, the pungent odors of incense and the thickness of the vapors were overwhelming. The burned-out incense sticks were replaced, and the exhausted oil lamps were re-filled. As a final caution, the attendant pulled open one of the bedcurtains very slightly and peeked inside the shadowy enclosure, just to make sure that he was still there.

Yes, he was still there, lying in the center of the bed perfectly straight, his arms crossed over his chest, the exquisite white linen bedsheets pulled over his face.

King Nebsenre's body had laid in-state within the Perah as part of the customary three day mourning period, as was mandated by both state and religious law. Afterwards, the body would be brought to the embalmers. The embalmers themselves were never allowed inside the palace. After all, the "Men of Anubis" handled corpses, and as such they were "unclean". Instead, the body would have to be brought to them.

Seshrab was not present during any of these proceedings, as he was still with the Royal Army recovering from their bloody victory at Yamu. However, most of the other scribes had remained at the palace, and they continued to perform their day-to-day services under the direction of Queen Neferet, King Shaweneiti's wife, who had been put in charge during the king's absence.

While the newly-crowned King Shaweneiti and his army marched west, others in the palace were negotiating with the embalmers concerning the dead king's mummification and funeral. Shaweneiti had ordered that the gold which had been found upon the assassins would be used to pay the embalmers for their work. However, many more matters needed tending to: the coffin, the goods to be laid in the tomb, the funeral services, etc. Everything required payment and paperwork.

Seshrab and the other scribes had prepared all of the necessary documents prior to his departure with the army. Most of it was pretty formulaic – all they had to do was to copy the standard forms and contracts which were used in these circumstances. There were literally hundreds of specific details that needed to be attended to involving things which Seshrab simply did not understand. Yet he had no time to ask questions – the army was going to march out the next day, and he needed to be ready – so he simply copied the contract terms word-for-word and stamped his seal on them. He promised himself that he'd inquire about these matters in more detail later when he had the time. Then, he packed his bags for the upcoming invasion.

Seshrab had been away with the army for two weeks, and much had surely taken place in the palace during the time that he was gone. He was certain that, upon his return, there would be a massive back-log of work with his name on it. The day after he came back to the palace, his first task was to acquaint himself with everything that had been going on during his absence. He convened a meeting with the other scribes in the Perah's council room. In addition to Seshrab acting as the chief scribe, there were seven other scribes who worked in the palace: Amunimhet, Atenmoses, Khepermoses, Nebrenuisis, Senedj, Senwasret, and Thoth-hotep. Most of these men were around Seshrab's age in their early to middle 20s. Khepermoses was the youngest of them, being just 13 years old, and Senwasret was the oldest at 34. The chair where Djoser had formerly sat stood empty, although its very empty presence seemed to deafen every other sound in the room.

"Good day, gentlemen. I would like to thank all of you for coming", began Seshrab as he settled into his chair at the end of the table. "Before we begin with today's business, however, I should like all of us to have a few moments of silence in remembrance of our fallen comrade and friend, Djoser. He was the first to explain to me the inner workings of the palace, and he was the first to extend his hand of friendship to me. I shall miss him dearly for the rest of my life, as I am sure will you, also. Let us now bow our heads in remembrance, and silently offer up whatever prayers are in our thoughts to his memory and his soul".

The other scribes respectfully bowed their heads, a few closed their eyes, and wordlessly annunciated their prayers to the heavens. Scarcely a breath or a heartbeat was heard.

"And now gentlemen, to business", Seshrab began, shuffling a little in his chair to get more comfortable. He expected to be here for a while. "The reason why I have asked all of you to attend is to make me appraised of everything that has been going on in the palace during my absence which would require my attention. So… what happened while I was gone? Is there anything that I need to know about?"

"Sir, while you and Djoser were away", began Senwasret, "the body of King Nebsenre continued to be laid in the Perah throughout the customary three-day mourning period. The day after the army departed Khaset City, the body was taken out of the Perah and delivered to the embalmers to be prepared for burial".

The steps needed to prepare the king's body for burial were lengthy. Even now as the scribes spoke, it was still undergoing the various preservation procedures that would be needed to ensure his "second life". The entire process would take nearly two and a half months to complete.

"Was the assassins' gold delivered to the embalmers, as the king requested?" asked Seshrab.

"Yes", interjected Khepermoses, "but it only partially covered the cost. The remainder had to be paid for with other means".

"How much?"

"Uh, just give me a second, sir", and he began shuffling through a portfolio of papyrus documents. "Ah, here it is", and he handed it to Seshrab down at the end of the table.

As Seshrab glanced at the receipts, his eyes steadily grew larger and larger. "They asked for all of this?!"

"It is a dead king we're talking about, Chief Scribe – what did you expect?" commented Senwasret.

"Even so, it's very high!"

"These are tough times, sir – people need to get their money any way they can. When uncertainty increases, prices increase too".

"You know", commented Nebrenuisis, "you'd think with all of the warfare and the poverty and everything else that's going on in the world these days that the embalmers would have plenty of business and they could afford to cut their costs. After all, it's not exactly like there's a *scarcity of death* out there, eh?"

"True...*but...*" began Senwasret, "with life so uncertain and with most people just a hair's breadth away from starving to death or being murdered by roving gangs of bandits or being killed in battle, most people don't have the necessary cash to pay for a proper funeral. Mostly, the best that you can hope for is to be chucked into a pit and hope that a pack of feral dogs won't dig you up".

"I mean, come on Nebrenuisis, we all know how much even a 'basic' funeral costs" added Khepermoses. "When the person's royalty, you'd practically have to mortgage your house in order to pay for one".

"Alright, alright, I'm sorry I brought it up!"

"And also, how often does a king die?" asked Khepermoses.

"These days, *quite often*, actually".

"They come and go so fast, I can't keep track of them anymore", commented Atenmoses.

"You know damn well what I meant", snapped Khepermoses. "Compared to ordinary people, who can't afford to pay for funerals for the most part, kings are few and far between, so the embalmers have to charge accordingly. That's why they jack up their prices. Not to mention that the embalmers themselves might be dead tomorrow and they need to get their cash now while they can still get their hands on it".

"Alright, enough, enough", said Seshrab, putting an end to this before it went any further. "Regardless of the cost, was the price paid in full?"

"Yes", replied Khepermoses.

"Good. I imagine that the work on his body is still progressing".

"The embalming process has only recently begun, sir", said Atenmoses. "It will take over a month for the body to be prepared, and more time to get his tomb and burial in order. That ought to give us some time to go over the details of his burial goods, his funeral procession, and his entombment".

"Well, we did draft up a preliminary list, didn't we?" asked Khepermoses.

"Yes, I have it here somewhere", responded Atenmoses who now began to look through his own stack of paperwork.

"Wait, that was only a *preliminary* list?" inquired Seshrab incredulously. "Surely that was the finished contract, wasn't it?"

"Oh no, sir, that was only the basics. There are still many more details that need to be straightened out in the meantime", replied Atenmoses.

"Gods, I thought that we had settled all of that. What else needs to be done?"

"Well, for starters", began Thoth-hotep, "his funerary goods need to be prepared and catalogued. Then there's the matter of making sure that his tomb is ready for burial. Then there's the actual funeral ritual itself, which is rather involved. Then we have to have guards employed to protect his tomb from robbers, although personally I think that may be a futile enterprise".

"This is a thoroughly foreign business to me", said Seshrab sinking backwards in his chair as the true daunting nature of this began to sink in. "I had no idea things would be this complicated".

"But, sir", began Senedj, "you were the one who prepared the documents for the king's mummification and burial. Surely you must have seen all of the details that needed to be tended to".

"Indeed I did, but I scarcely knew what I was copying. I was too pressed for time to take note of the hundreds of points that needed to be addressed. All I did was simply copy the forms and put my seal on them".

"Well it's important that all of it is there. Everything needs to be accounted for, point-by-point. We Egyptians need to bring whatever would be needed for our second life: food, clothing, furniture, tools, everything that we could use in the world beyond".

"Yes, otherwise we would be impoverished, helpless, and hopeless for all eternity", chimed in Senwasret.

"I would have thought that in the afterlife, everything would be provided for you", said Seshrab thoughtfully.

"Maybe *your* gods are that beneficent, but not here".

Seshrab took in a deep breath. "Alright, it looks like we'll be here for a while. Let's go over the arrangements for the dead king's mummification, funeral service, and burial".

"For starters", began Nebrenuisis, "into the tomb is to be placed one *deben* of gold and another *deben* of silver".

"Do we even have that much after we paid the embalmers?"

"Yes…just about".

"Oh gods".

"There must also be containers of beer, wine, dried fruits, and lots of other things".

"Speaking of 'lots of other things'", said Seshrab, "as a non-Egyptian, I find many of the terms and details of the mummification and entombment procedures to be extremely perplexing. For instance, why is it necessary that there have to be all of these little statues and figurines placed in the tomb?"

"Those are the *shabtis*", said Khepermoses. "They help the soul of the dead in the afterlife".

"And why must there be so much turquoise? Do you know what people have to go through to get that much turquoise?!"

Everyone there shrugged and stared blankly.

"Hopefully, you'll never know. It's not pretty, I can assure you. And what about this part here? This is an itemized list of what look like medallions and amulets of various sorts".

"Yes, those are the funerary amulets", answered Senedj. "For protection, to keep away bad luck and evil spirits. They have to be placed upon the mummy and within the tomb in a very specific order. They need to be added in for each step in the mummification process".

"Which is rather lengthy, right?", asked Seshrab.

"Yes, very lengthy. Everything has to be just so in order to preserve the body for the afterlife".

"I hate to sound like an ignorant clod", began Seshrab. "But can you please explain to me just what exactly mummification is? I mean, I've heard the word several times, and I think I know what it means, but I'm not sure".

"Mummification is a procedure for preserving the body so that it can be resurrected at the time of the Final Judgment", said Thoth-hotep. "The afterlife is temporary – the second life is what's important".

"I'm not sure I follow".

"In the Final Judgment, the gods will reward the virtuous, the great, and the good by raising them up from their graves and granting them everlasting life. The body needs to be preserved in order to allow that to happen, otherwise there can be no second life".

"That's really what you believe?", asked Seshrab incredulously.

"It's the truth!" said Amunimhet, clearly hurt.

"But what about the good people whose bodies *aren't* saved? What happens to them?"

"They perish", replied Atenmoses.

"That doesn't seem fair".

"Since when has life *ever* been fair? I don't like it any more than anyone else, but that's the way it is".

"What exactly has to get done? Nothing is explained in any of these papers", asked Seshrab.

"That's no surprise", said Atenmoses. "The embalmers keep mum on that sort of thing".

"Why? If I'm paying for it, don't I have the right to know exactly what they're doing with my money?"

"No…you don't", said Senwasret.

The room went awkwardly silent.

"If you want to know what goes on behind closed doors in the embalmers' tent, I'm afraid I can't provide that information to you", said Thoth-hotep. "None of us can. You see, none of us have actually *seen* a mummification, and I don't know anybody who has".

"Neither do I", said Amunimhet. The rest of them likewise shook their heads in agreement.

"The art of mummification is a closely-guarded secret known to only a select few", said Senwasret, "and none of them are willing to talk of anything that they do. Such knowledge is strictly forbidden for anyone to know except for those who were initiated into it – the so-called 'Men of Anubis'. And let me tell you, there are some pretty lurid rumors about that crew. Some of the speculations about what exactly they do are really wild".

"The reason why there are all of these guesses, rumors, and suppositions is because none of them have ever written down the process of mummification", said Thoth-hotep. "Mummification is such a sacred thing that the knowledge of its procedures has never been made public. Very few people are permitted by the priests to become 'the Men of Anubis', or even to be inside the tent where the various rituals take place. The procedure also takes place far away from the city so that the smells don't disturb anyone nearby. On top of all that, associating with dead bodies makes you *unclean,* so being an embalmer is a rather lonely profession – not too many friends".

"So you see, sir", said Amunimhet, "we can't really help you. I mean, we can guess all that we like, but none of us really know".

"Well…I've heard stories", said Atenmoses.

"We all have", added Khepermoses. "First, they slice you open and pull all your guts out. Then they cover you in salt to dry you out".

"No, no, you skipped a step!" said Amunimhet. "After they slice you open and pull out your innards, the person who did it is beaten to death with rocks right there on the spot!"

"What?!" exclaimed Seshrab, getting increasingly antsy. "Why on earth would they murder him?!"

"Because, sir, he violated the law by desecrating a corpse", Nebrenuisis chimed in matter-of-factly. "Anyone who deliberately defaces a human body is punished by stoning – that's the law".

"The body must be intact in order for it to be resurrected at the Final Judgment", Senwasret explained. "Damaging the body in any way, regardless of the reasons, greatly risks the body's ability to be resurrected, and so the offender must be punished severely. However, you can't actually make direct contact with him, for he is unclean, and if you touch him with a bat, a mace, or an axe, the contamination will radiate itself into your own body and you will become unclean, too! So, the only way to execute him is by either shooting arrows, hurling javelins, or throwing rocks at him. The law clearly states that the offender must be stoned to death".

"You see?" continued Amunimhet. "They cut you open, rip out your guts, and then they die!"

"Yeah, well I heard that they don't do that", commented Atenmoses. "I heard that they just throw gravel and pebbles at the guy. The law says that a person who desecrates a body must be beaten with stones, but the law doesn't say how big those stones have to be".

"Gods, I love a good legal loophole", said Senwasret, snickering.

"I heard that they pull out your brain through your nostrils", said Khepermoses.

"I heard that they don't actually remove the brain at all", interjected Senedj. "It's just a sensationalist urban myth".

Seshrab's heart rate started to increase. *No, not again.*

"I heard that they pour molten wax down your throat", added Nebrenuisis.

"No, it's not molten wax – it's molten tree resin", corrected Khepermoses. "And they don't pour it down your throat. They pour it up your nose after they pull the brain out".

Seshrab's heart was pounding, and he was having increasing difficulty breathing. "Gentlemen, I think that's enough", he said.

"How do they even get the brain out, anyway?", asked Atenmoses, ignoring him. "I mean, the brain's huge! What do they do? Cut your nose off, pull the brain out, and then sew the nose back on or something?"

"I've wondered about that too. Personally, I don't believe it", said Senwasret. "I mean, you *can't* pull the brain out through the nose. It's just not possible. No, I think that what they *really* do is that they take a saw or a chisel or whatever, and cut around your skull and pop the top part off, like two halves of a melon, remove the brain, and then re-attach the two halves of the skull together".

"Alright, here's what I heard", added Senedj. "I heard that they take this really long metal spike, and they slam it up through your nose into your brain, and then they—".

"ENOUGH!!! STOP!!! STOP IT!!! STOP TALKING ABOUT IT!!! STOP GOING ON AND ON ABOUT IT!!! GODS, ENOUGH!!! STOP IT!!! STOP TALKING ABOUT BLOOD AND BRAINS AND GUTS AND STABBING AND SLICING AND CHOPPING AND KILLING AND STABBING AND BEHEADING AND IMPALING AND RIPPING AND MURDERING!!! I DON'T WANT TO HEAR IT!!! YOU HEAR ME? I DON'T!!! I DON'T!!!"

The room was silent. Everyone at the table was staring at Seshrab. He had bolted up from his chair, knocking it to the floor, and had slammed his writing stylus over and over again into the cedar table and had crunched and crumpled all of the papers in front of him.

Seshrab then noticed that his fellow scribes weren't the only ones there. At some point during this loud outburst, several of the palace guards who had been out in the hallway had opened the door to see what the noise was all about. Several other people who had been out in the hallway heard the yelling echoing down the corridors and popped their heads into the doorway to see what on earth was going on.

"Is everything alright here, sir?" one of the guards asked.

Seshrab didn't answer right away, then a smothering blanket of embarrassment and humiliation flooded over him. "Yes…yes, I'm fine. I'm alright, I'm alright". He picked the chair up and made a panicked show of straightening out his papers.

"Maybe you should go back to your cell and lie down for a while".

"Yes…yes, maybe I should. Sorry. Excuse me", and he grabbed his papers and carried them off, then realized that the other scribes needed them and he scurried back to the table and dumped them back onto the table and quick-walked back out the door.

The rest of the scribes continued sitting at the table. Nearly all of them were silent and frozen still. Khepermoses let out a long slow exhale. Senwasret didn't say anything – he just shook his head.

Seshrab bolted up from his bed screaming in panic, gripping his chest, wheezing, hyperventilating. As he frantically looked around the room, it took him a few seconds for him to realize where he was. He was in his cell, in his bed, in the royal palace. He let out a painful moan as he hung his head low, tightly gripping it with both hands, his nails digging deeply into his scalp. It had happened again. Great gods in Heaven, when would it all stop? He had hoped that his condition would improve with time, but nothing had changed.

There was a knock on his door. "Sir, sir are you alright? Can I come in?"

"Uh…yes…yes come in".

The door opened and it was one of the other scribes, Khepermoses, the youngest scribe who worked in the palace. "Did you have another nightmare, sir?"

"Yes, yes but I'm better now".

"Are you sure? I mean, you've been having these nightmares ever since you came back from the war. Do you want me to get the doctor?"

"NO!!!" Seshrab blurted out, but then tried to collect himself. "No, you don't need to get the doctor. It's not worth waking him up and troubling him over. It's just bad dreams, that's all. I'm fine. I'll be fine".

Clearly Khepermoses wasn't convinced. He knew for a fact that Seshrab *wasn't* fine, but he decided not to press the issue.

Seshrab now felt so foolish. Once again, he had embarrassed himself. "Truly, Khepermoses, I am very sorry if I disturbed you. But I don't need to see a doctor. I'm not sick – it's just bad dreams. Just dreams".

Khepermoses still wasn't convinced. "Alright, alright sir…Good night", and he began to back out of the doorway. However, as he was about to leave, he decided that he needed to say something. "Chief Scribe, sir, as you are my superior, I cannot give you orders. If you do not wish to seek help, I cannot order you to do so, but these dreams that you are having are harming you. Perhaps Canaanites like you put no stock in such things, but Egyptians take dreams *very* seriously", and then he left and closed the door.

It was now time for the funeral of Shaweneiti's father King Nebsenre. A funeral for a king was a massive and solemn public affair, and every notable "who's who" was expected to be there. As Chief Scribe, Seshrab was expected to attend and to provide an account of the proceedings. Still, he was very uncomfortable being there.

Before the assembled crowd of visitors and dignitaries, one of the attending judges announced according to law and custom, "If there is anyone here who wishes to stop this funeral or wishes to take possession of the body, let that person step forward now". If someone presented himself and made an accusation that the dead person had led an evil life, the body would be denied burial. If it was shown that this person's accusation was false, the liar was severely punished and the funeral was to go on. If no one presented themselves, the mourning family would then be called upon to recite the good deeds and qualities of the deceased.

No one stepped forward.

The procedures would continue as expected. King Shaweneiti, Nebsenre's oldest child and successor, stood before the coffin which held his father, and recited his eulogy to the assembled crowd of attendees and onlookers. "It is customary", he began, "that before the body is carried away to its final resting place, that the surviving family members of the deceased should recite the good qualities of the person's character and give a record of the good deeds that he had done in his life. Too often people's bad deeds are what are remembered, and we dwell so much on their vices that we forget their virtues. This already condemns the soul even before it is allowed to stand trial in the Council of the Gods. What good things are there to say about my father? He was a caring parent, a good commander, and was respected and admired by those who knew him best. He was courageous, spoke plainly and directly, told the truth, he was firm, but just, he rewarded those who deserved it, and punished those who deserved it. Above all else, he cared most not for his soldiers nor for me his son, but for Egypt. It was his dream that our fragmented nation be re-united into the mighty power that it was before. This was his quest. Sadly, he was never able to fulfill his fondest desire of once more having a united country. Although he reigned briefly, he was a strong ruler, feared by his enemies, and respected by his subjects. I ask the god Osiris, Lord of the Underworld, that he receive the soul of my father happily, and grant him all that he desires in the afterlife, and let him take his place in the Land of the Righteous. Hail Nebsenre, Osiris incarnate, General of the Army, and one-time King of Lower Egypt".

The crowd then repeated over and over, "Praise and honor to you, Osiris-Nebsenre".

Now that the speeches were made, the time had come to carry away Nebsenre's body to its final resting place. To the west of Khaset City was the necropolis, the "city of the dead". Cemeteries were usually located on the western side of the Nile River or on the western side of a city due to the west's connection with death. It was believed that the souls of the dead went westward with the setting sun. Osiris, the god-ruler of the Underworld, also presided as the overseer of the West. Just like many other peoples, the Egyptians had their own euphemisms regarding death. Rather than saying someone had "passed away" or "made the final journey", whenever someone died the Egyptians said "they went west".

While he had been alive, Nebsenre had ordered the construction of a tomb within Khaset City's cemetery as soon as he became King. There were several large cemeteries in Egypt where royalty and nobility were entombed. However, rather than laying him to rest beside other kings and dignitaries, King Nebsenre's body would be laid to rest within the town's common cemetery, alongside the graves of his beloved fallen soldiers whom he had commanded in battle. It was, perhaps, more fitting that way.

The majestic pyramids of Giza are one of the iconic images of Egypt, but these massive structures were built early in Egyptian history, during the 3rd, 4th, and 5th Dynasties who had reigned centuries ago. By the end of the 12th Dynasty, pyramids had fallen out of fashion – they were too large, too expensive, and too time-consuming to construct. In an age when a king's lifespan had been significantly shortened due to revolts, assassinations, and civil wars, he needed to have his final resting place erected in a hurry. Therefore, Egyptian kings were now mostly entombed within smaller flat-topped mausoleums. The Egyptian word for "mausoleum" was *per-djet*, meaning "the eternal house". The Arabs who occasionally visited Egypt to trade saw these tombs and called them *mastabas*, "benches", due to their boxy rectangular shape. During the Second Dark Age, the lack of central authority in Egypt as well as a general contempt for law and order led to a massive surge of grave robbing and grave desecration. Tombs were broken into, the grave goods plundered, and even the mummified bodies themselves were deliberately destroyed by thieves to find jewelry and other valuable objects. Therefore, during this time, Egyptian kings began to transition from above-ground tombs to secret underground tombs. These were almost exclusively excavated in Upper Egypt, which had a higher elevation and possessed more hilly rocky terrain. In Lower Egypt, with its relatively flat ground located only a few feet above sea level, a high water table, and the rich Nile Delta which flooded over every year, burying bodies underground simply wasn't practical.

Nebsenre's funeral procession was led by a herald, announcing the king's death, and reciting various prayers and incantations to help him on his journey to the afterlife. Afterwards came women, professional mourners, who tore their clothes, pulled at their hair, and covered their faces with clay and threw sand on their heads; these last two acts were a way of empathizing with the dead being laid in the dusty earth. Then came four men carrying the empty royal throne litter, showing that the king no longer sat upon it. Then came men bearing various offerings such as bread, cattle, jars of food, and beer, all of which would be sacrificed to his soul upon their arrival at the tomb. Then came the priests dressed in the skins of leopards and cheetahs burning incense in copper holders. Behind the priests was dragged the large funeral barge itself, dragged on a sled, with the coffin laid upon it; Shaweneiti walked beside it. Then came those who carried the king's possessions to be buried with him in his tomb; Seshrab walked amongst these men a respectful distance behind his master. At the end of the procession was a body of soldiers to make sure that the men in front didn't carry off the king's goods for themselves. All of the members of the funeral procession wore strips of white linen tied around their heads as a symbol of mourning.

It was only a short walk to the cemetery west of the town's walls. The whole way, crowds of peasants lined the road on both sides, kneeling, bowing, praying, and lamenting. In front of Nebsenre's small tomb was a small mortuary temple where sacrifices and offerings would be made to the soul of the dead king. It was a small square room with an altar in the middle, and a half-sized statue of the dead king above it seated in a stone chair atop a stone block. Not exactly grand or awe-inspiring, but it served its purpose. A stele stone was erected outside the temple's entrance engraved with a biography of the great man, detailing his life and accomplishments, and bearing an invocation to his spirit.

In the king's will, he set aside a parcel of land for the priests. In return, they were ordered to maintain the tomb and temple, watch over the king's body and possessions, give daily offerings to his soul, and pray for his soul's salvation in the time of judgment. It was believed that the dead person's soul needed constant nourishment, just like the physical body. So every day, food, water, and beer were to be placed inside the temple upon the altar. Within the temple was a miniature model of the funeral barge, the one which would carry the king's soul into the afterlife, and would also carry the essence of the offerings given, since the actual physical offerings couldn't be transported into the other world. Atop this boat were a small miniature sarcophagus and a large jar. The sarcophagus carried the soul, and the jar carried the offerings needed to nourish the soul in the afterlife. This model boat was a bridge between the mortal world and the divine world, by travelling back and forth collecting the food, water, and other goods given to Nebsenre at his shrine, and bringing them back to him in the afterlife. Every day, the heavenly ship made this spectral voyage.

Nebsenre's coffin was carried off of the funeral barge and was borne into the mortuary temple. Here, the priests would perform the last of the sacred rites upon the body before it was laid to rest in the tomb and sealed up. Shaweneiti presented the sacrificial offerings, stating "An offering given by the king to Osiris, Great God, Lord of the West, Lord of Busiris, Lord of Abydos. I hereby give invocation offerings of bread, beer, oxen, birds, alabaster, clothing, and all things good and pure which the gods live on. This offering is made for the *ka* of my father, Nebsenre, Osiris incarnate".

Once the final prayers were spoken and the final offerings and blessings were made, the time had come to carry the body into the tomb's burial chamber. The hallway extending from the mortuary temple to the burial chamber was decorated with paintings and spells concerning the dead man's actual journey into the afterlife. Nebsenre's painted wooden anthropoid coffin was laid into a larger rectangular box-like wooden sarcophagus which had been painted outside and inside with various spells and prayers meant to ensure the soul's and body's survival in the afterlife and the second life. The lid was lowered, and the joint was sealed shut with molten tree resin. Then all of the various funeral goods and personal possessions were placed around the tomb, heaped and stacked in piles, so that Nebsenre would not be deprived of any of the things he had known in his mortal life.

As soon as the last of Nebsenre's worldly goods was brought into the tomb, the burial chamber was sealed. A shrine to Anubis, the jackal-headed psychopomp who conveyed the souls of the dead from this life to the next, was placed in the hallway outside the burial chamber's bricked-up entrance to guard it against intruders. The Anubis shrine consisted of a large hollow wooden box decorated in gold leaf, and on top was a cartonnage reclining statue of a jackal, the sacred animal of Anubis. The statue was coated in black resin, the same resin that was used to coat the mummy. The Anubis shrine was called "the Shrine of Secrets", and for good reason. Firstly, the large shrine protected the entranceway to the sealed burial chamber and all inside was supposed to be kept secret. Secondly, mummification was a secret art, and placed within this shrine were the tools used in the mummification of the king. Mummification implements could only be used once, and so they were laid to rest with the body that they helped to prepare.

Finally, the hallway was bricked up, and the dead man's *ka* statue was placed in front of the sealed entranceway.

Seshrab had been trying to hold himself together as best as he could through all of this. Nobody likes funerals, but being in that cemetery, with the crowds of wailing crying spectators pressing in on both sides, and surrounded by the aura of death, it was too much. He had to step away. He needed air.

Later that day, after everyone had returned to the palace, Seshrab had another of his episodes. Thankfully it happened in private, so nobody saw him, but this was it. This was the last straw.

Seshrab walked up to the door of the court physician's quarters and took in a deep slow breath. For a moment or two, he wondered if he ought to do this. *You're weak*, a voice in his head snarled. *You're the only one who has this problem. Be a man and suck it up!* But he had heard these voices before, and he knew that they were holding him back. He needed help, and he shook the noise out of his mind. He came this far, and he needed to go all the way. He knocked on the door.

Seshrab could hear the doctor get up from a chair and walk towards the door. The door opened and the doctor stood in the open passageway. "Ah, Chief Scribe. What can I do for you today?"

Seshrab stood there in the hall, stiff as a board, his eyes looking down or off to the side, anywhere but directly at his face.

"Sir, is there something the matter?"

This needed to end: the nightmares, the panic attacks, the feelings of dread, the sudden uncontrollable outbursts of rage. It needed to stop, and so Seshrab looked up at the court physician, and with every pound of inner fortitude that Seshrab could muster, he uttered the words "I'm sick".

# CHAPTER 11

*After His Majesty Nesu Shaweneiti laid the body of his father Nebsenre in his tomb within the necropolis of Khaset City, the time came for him to undergo the mysterious and sacred rites which would imbue him with the divine essence of the god Horus. Within the Temple of Ra, His Majesty was transfigured into His Divine Majesty, the living god of Lower Egypt, and he adopted the regal name Khemshawre, by which name he would be known to all from then on.*

"How is he?"

"His mind and his soul are greatly troubled, Your Majesty", replied the court physician. "Nightmares, horrible thoughts, unstable moods. Some within the palace think that his wits are failing. They're afraid of what he might do".

King Shaweneiti shook his head. "No, his wits are not failing, doctor…not yet. I've seen this many times before. This is not the work of a rotting mind or an evil spirit. Some men simply cannot bear what they have seen and done. You were right to tell me of his visit to you last night. Yet the fact that he appealed to you for help shows that he's not too far gone. His condition can be amended provided it is treated delicately. See him every day, and keep talking with him – talking helps. Seshrab is too valuable an asset to be lost. Especially now. You are dismissed".

King Shaweneiti had been reigning as King of Lower Egypt since his father Nebsenre was assassinated, but his official coronation hadn't taken place yet. Tradition dictated that the monarch could only be crowned at the beginning of a new season, so he had to wait until the appropriate time had come. That time was now.

This was the beginning of the season of Akhet, the time when the Nile would flood. The Egyptian calendar of 365 days was divided up into three seasons each spanning four months. It began with the season of *Akhet*, "Flood" (mid-July to mid-November), during which time the floodplain around the river would be covered by water. Since the farmers had nothing to do while the waters covered their land, it was during Akhet that most wars were fought, but under Nebsenre and Shaweneiti, the men had been fighting battles virtually all year round. Afterwards came *Peret*, "Growth" (mid-November to mid-March), when the Nile at last receded and farmers could plant their seeds and watch them grow. Finally came *Shemu*, "Harvest" (mid-March to mid-July), when the crops would be gathered and stored.

However, the old reliable rhythm of the seasons was becoming ever-more mercurial and changeable. The Nile River, which used to flood and recede exactly according to schedule year after year, hadn't flooded for the past two years, and in the years prior, sometimes it flooded and sometimes it didn't. Droughts and famines were becoming more common. Egypt, once known as the breadbasket of the world, was experiencing hunger and starvation on a scale that it had not known since the age of the pyramid-builders came to an end. The severity of life was further compounded by the civil war that had been ripping Egypt apart for the past ninety years. Famine and disease are the unwanted bastard children of conflict.

Traditionally, the coronation ceremony for Egyptian kings took place in the city of Ankh-Tawi at the Temple of Ptah, the god of creation. Just as the mighty Ptah created all things upon the earth, so too would he create a living god out of a mortal. The ceremony of *apotheosis* in which the king would be transfigured from being just an ordinary man into a god was a secret one done behind locked doors. There were no windows in the temple to ensure that no one outside could look in and observe the secret ceremony, with its mysterious ways and arcane rituals known only to the priests who worked inside its walls. Everyone who worked inside the temple, whether they were priests, attendants, guards, or scribes, was sworn to secrecy, pledging a sacred oath to never reveal the temple's mysteries to anyone on the outside on penalty of immediate death.

Unfortunately, the city of Ankh-Tawi was now deep in enemy-held territory, and no Lower Egyptian king could travel there in safety. Due to the Temple of Ptah being out-of-bounds, the kings of the 14th Dynasty who ruled from Khaset City had merely gone a few steps outside of the royal palace to the Temple of Ra, which lay within the city right next to one of the main gates, to be coronated there. Ra was, after all, the king of the gods, and Horus was his son. Therefore, shouldn't it be only natural that the king of Heaven bestow his blessing upon the king of Earth, transforming him into his son and making him Horus incarnate?

In addition to his upcoming coronation and transfigurement, other matters weighed on King Shaweneiti's mind. With Colonel Horahauty having been slain at the Battle of Yamu, Shaweneiti still needed to appoint a new commanding officer to lead the Khaset Regiment. With Lord Nesbit dead, he needed to appoint a governor to rule West Ament Province, and he needed to appoint a commander to take charge of the military affairs of that province as well. Finally, he needed to appoint a vizier to assist himself in the overall governing of the kingdom. Of these, the last was the most difficult. Shaweneiti himself had served as Vizier when his father had been King, but his role abruptly changed when his father was assassinated. Ever since then, that post had been vacant, but the problem was that the office of Vizier was always held by a member of the royal family; peasants and even aristocrats were excluded. However, there wasn't anybody available of suitable royal stock to hold such a high office. Shaweneiti only had one child, a toddler daughter named Atentjehenet. His half-brother Montunakht was the same age. This was ample reason why the royals typically had large families, partly to ensure that there was an heir to continue the dynasty, and partly to staff the most prestigious offices with the king's family members. These were troubling times. If anything should ever happen to him, who would take care of his daughter and half-brother?

At this time, His Majesty made a decree. "The Season of the Flood approaches", King Shaweneiti announced in the Perah before his assembled officers and attendants. "Just as my father before me, and the others who wore the crown before him, I shall enter the Temple of Ra that I may be officially crowned as *Nesu*, King of Lower Egypt, and undergo the sacred mysteries which shall transform me from a mortal man into the living god of Egypt. This important matter must be delayed no longer. I therefore order that word be sent to the priests in the temple to prepare for my arrival, which shall be in three days' time".

Three days later, King Shaweneiti left for the Temple of Ra in a grand procession of pageantry accompanied by many guards and servants. The priests in the temple had been made aware of His Majesty's coming and they were given ample time to ready everything for his arrival. The Temple of Ra was where General Nakhtibre had been crowned following his successful takeover, taking the regal name Nebsenre, and it was also where he was cruelly murdered prior to his grand campaign to invade and conquer West Ament. This was where Shaweneiti had offered his sacrifices to the god Ra to give him favor for the upcoming fight – favor which was evidently granted. The great god clearly looked well upon him. Hopefully now, when he needed Ra's help more than ever before, that favor would not be withdrawn.

Shaweneiti approached the large central gate in the middle of the high brick wall which surrounded the temple's courtyard and struck the great copper gong which hung from the wall to announce his presence. The gate immediately opened, and the priest bowed to him.

"I have come here to this holy place to receive the blessing of Ra, King of the Gods, King of Heaven, that I may be made his son".

The priest bowed again and led His Majesty inside, whereupon the gate promptly closed shut behind them. His Majesty would be allowed to enter the temple and no others; everybody else who had accompanied him would be forced to wait outside the walls. What strange rituals would occur within was for no one's eyes to see.

King Shaweneiti was led through the vast colonnaded hall and towards the Holy of Holies, the sacred chamber which held the monumental idol of the god Ra. It would be within this little room, closed off to everyone but the few priests who worked here, that the great miracle would happen.

There were several priests dressed in their finest robes assembled within the sacred chamber. "Remove your garments entirely, and stand before the god openly, so that you may be humbled before him and his awesome power", announced the chief priest.

Shaweneiti soon stripped himself of all of his clothes and articles and stood naked before the assembled body of holy men.

Then, two priests dressed up like the falcon-headed god Horus, son of Ra, poured holy water upon Shaweneiti's head four times from four separate earthenware vessels. "With this holy water", they annunciated, "you are washed and purified in the eyes of Ra. As the almighty god Ra was born out of the primeval waters, you are reborn in the eyes of Ra".

Once he had been ritually cleansed and purified, Shaweneiti donned his royal robes and knelt before a priest dressed as Ra. Shaweneiti's hair and eyebrows were caked with blue paint from crushed lapis lazuli while his face was painted with gold, since the gods were reputed to have skin of gold and hair of lapis. Through these things, he was made immortal.

Then from the priest of Ra, Shaweneiti received his father's golden *ankh* necklace, which was hung around his neck. The ankh represented the power of life and death, and only gods had the right to wield such power. "With this symbol", the priest spoke from behind his falcon-headed mask, "you are bestowed with the power of the gods. You are no longer Shaweneiti, son of Osiris-Nebsenre. You are my son, beloved Horus, my most favored one, who shall sit at my right hand, and you shall be honored and worshiped in the eyes of men".

Shaweneiti bowed. "I am your son and you are my father, great one, and I shall honor and obey you".

"Stand before the assembly of the gods that you may be presented to them", and the incantations proceeded: "Blessed is the son of Ra in the eyes of Mut, Queen of the Gods, who now bestows her favor on her son, Horus incarnate. Blessed is the son of Ra in the eyes of Khonsu, the god of the moon, who rules the tides and the rhythm of the seasons. Blessed is the son of Ra in the eyes of Ptah, the god of creation, who molded all things on earth out of the primordial clay. May the son of Ra create for himself a reign befitting him as the son of Ra and King of Egypt, with great buildings and monuments, and a legacy that will shine as the sun shines in the sky. Blessed is the son of Ra in the eyes of Montu, the god of war, who shall stand beside the son of Ra in battle and protect him against his enemies' weapons, and grant him victory over all of Egypt's foes, for he shall be feared by all enemies, and they shall prostrate themselves before him in servitude and submission. Blessed is the son of Ra in the eyes of Nefertum, god of healing. Blessed is the son of Ra in the eyes of Nekhbet, the goddess of Upper Egypt. His power shall extend from one end of Egypt to the other as wings that stretch over the sky. Blessed is the son of Ra in the eyes of Wadjet, the goddess of Lower Egypt. The cobra of his crown shall spit venom into the eyes of his enemies. Blessed is the son of Ra in the eyes of Set, the god of foreign lands. Never shall foreign adversaries invade Egypt's borders whilst the son of Ra reigns. Never shall there be disorder, discord, and chaos in his kingdom whilst the son of Ra reigns. Never shall the deserts overwhelm his kingdom whilst the son of Ra reigns".

Then, all of the costumed priests turned towards the priest garbed as the falcon-headed god Ra. "Almighty Ra, King of the Gods", they recited, "your son Horus shall live on earth in the form of Nesu Shaweneiti, King of Lower Egypt. We are satisfied with him in life and peace. He is your son, of your flesh, of your vigorous seed. You gave him your *ba*, your power, your influence, your magic, your crown, even when he was still in the womb of the mother that bore him. The lowlands and the mountains belong to him, all things that the heavens wrap around, and everything which the sea encircles. We give him dominion over the lands in peace. We give him all life and good fortune on our part, all food on our part, and all sustenance on our part. He is at the head of all men as King of Lower Egypt, seated upon the throne of Horus on earth like Ra sits on his throne in Heaven forever and ever".

In all documents and inscriptions, the king's name was written within a symbol called the *shen-ren*, "the encirclement of the name". The *shen* was a circular ring-like symbol meant to represent a loop of rope tied into a knot, and which denoted protection or guardianship. This *shen* ring was held in the gods' hands, and anything which was placed within the boundaries of the *shen* would be under that god's personal protection. Placing a person's name within this enlarged *shen* ring ensured that no harm, either physical or spiritual, would come to the bearer of that name. Egypt's monarchs were the only ones who had their names written within the *shen-ren*.

Upon his coronation, the king would be transfigured, imbued with the divine essence of the god Horus himself, and thus became Horus Incarnate, Living God of Egypt. Upon his coronation, the king was required to assume a new identity, since his old name identified him as a mere mortal, and a new name was needed for he was no longer the same person. The king was not allowed to choose his own throne name – that name was decided by the priests, under divine guidance of course. "You are reborn and renamed in the eyes of the gods and men", said the chief priest. "You shall be known to gods and men as *Khemshawre*, for Ra is the Creator of Light, and you shall be a light in the eyes of your father".

"Hail, His Most Divine Majesty", the assembled priests called out, "Nesu Horus-Khemshawre, ruler of Lower Egypt by the grace of the goddess Wadjet; Son of Ra; Horus incarnate; Horus the avenger of his father; living god of Egypt; he of the Great House; maker and issuer of laws; the golden one; the eternal one; presider of the nation's wealth; he who is victorious over all of his enemies; he who displays the royal regalia; he who propitiates the gods; bringer of life, prosperity, and health; powerful of strength; sacred in body; magnificent in appearance; he whose rule is undoubted, unquestioned, and enduring as Ra endures as the ruler of Heaven. May he live, prosper, and be in good health".

"Here I stand upon the earth", spoke the newly-crowned Nesu Khemshawre, "arisen out of the primordial waters, and came into being upon it. May I be exalted upon it so that you, my father, great Ra may see me and favor me. I have come to you, o father. I have come to you, o Ra! Grant that I may seize the sky and take possession of the horizon. Grant that I may subdue my enemies and provide for my people. Place the shepherd's crook in my hand so that I may lead my people, my flock, and that the heads of Lower Egypt may be bowed before me. I charge my opponent to stand up, for the gods have favored me. I shall strike him down, for I am protected by the gods".

The high priest concluded the ritual. "Nothing is lost to you, and nothing ceases for you, for behold you are more renowned and more powerful than all upon earth", said the priests. "You are god on earth, the living god of Egypt. O almighty Ra! Raise our king up to you! Embrace him, for he is your son and our lord. He is King, he is the Lord!"

Outside the temple, the restless crowd grew ever more impatient. The rituals, whatever they may be, were taking too long. What was going on in there? When will he come out?

"LOOK!!! THERE ON THE ROOF!!! HE COMES!!!"

Standing atop the roof of the Temple of Ra, flanked on either side by the priests who had invested him in his awesome divine power, was Shaweneiti, now reborn as Khemshawre, Son of Ra, Horus Incarnate. His face had been painted with gold, and he wore the most splendid and most pure of white robes. Hanging around his neck was the shining golden ankh, which he had been forbidden to wear until then, and would continue to wear on his body until his death. Horus had come to earth.

The crowds knelt, bowed, and prostrated themselves before their divine lord and savior. "Hail Horus, Son of Ra! Hail Horus, Son of Ra!"

But then came more shouting, this time from further off in the distance. There was some commotion coming from the rear of the crowd. The word soon spread amongst the gathered masses like a wildfire. "THE NILE IS TURNING!!! THE NILE IS TURNING!!!"

The Nile River had turned red! Red from churning mud and silt, red from a strengthening current. This could mean only one thing – the Nile was flooding! For the first time in years, the life-giving river would rise! There would be no famine this year, no hunger. The land would be green and good again! Shaweneiti was blessed in the eyes of the gods. He had their favor. He was *Khemshawre*, "Ra is the Creator of Light". He would make the light glow. He would bring Egypt out of the dark.

# CHAPTER 12

*Following his coronation, His Divine Majesty Nesu Khemshawre undertook his first overtures in diplomacy. He renewed the peace treaty with Nesu Wahibre, King of Upper Egypt. He also renewed the treaty that he had made with the chief of the Libyans following his victory over them at the Battle of Yamu. He also renewed the treaty with the Canaanites who controlled Canaan and Sinai so that Egypt would continue to have access to the copper mines of Sinai in exchange for giving the Canaanites a steady supply of Egyptian goods. As Chief Scribe, I prepared all of these treaties.*

*However, as I had put my name on these official documents as Chief Scribe, and as copies of these documents were distributed throughout much of Canaan, my identity and my whereabouts now became known to those who lived there. One of these documents was sent to the king of Hebron, my former master. When he saw my name upon that sheet of papyrus, all of the rage that he bore against me returned. He vowed my death, even if he had to invade Egypt itself.*

Now that Nesu Shaweneiti had become Nesu Khemshawre, Horus Incarnate, Living God of Egypt, he was the full-fledged potentate of his domain. The first item on the royal agenda was to shore up his rule by establishing positive relations with his neighbors. He would try to do it without bloodshed. No part of Egypt, not even those parts under Khemshawre's control, had a permanent standing army. Soldiers could not be kept in the field indefinitely. They had homes, farms, and families to attend to. Khemshawre had to try diplomacy. Thankfully, he was a lot better at it than his father was. To his father Nebsenre, diplomacy was about making threats, but to him, it was about making deals.

Khemshawre's first task was to make contact with his "brother king", the king of Upper Egypt, King Wahibre of the 13th Dynasty. For the past few decades, both the northern and southern Egyptian kings had agreed to recognize each other's authority over their respective halves of the country. This relationship needed to be maintained in order to preserve the peace between the two. Wahibre's capital in the town of Lisht lay on the western side of the Nile about forty miles south of the Nile Delta's southernmost point. Lisht had been a royal center for generations, especially during the 12th Dynasty, which the current 13th Dynasty claimed to be directly descended from. The tombs of King Amunimhet I, who was the founder of the 12th Dynasty, and his son and successor King Senwasret I were located there. Yet while Wahibre reigned as the king of the south, his unimpressive royal realm consisted only of the town of Lisht and the land immediately around it, and absolutely nothing else. Real power within Upper Egypt lay in the hands of the regional warlords. For safety, His Divine Majesty would communicate with his "brother king" in the south through a series of official envoys who would conduct negotiations in his name. King Khemshawre signed the documents by stamping them in clay with the official scarab seal which bore his new throne name. The documents were proofed and co-signed by Seshrab, the king's chief scribe.

After dispatching letters to King Wahibre, Khemshawre journeyed west to the city of Yamu. There, he would conduct business in-person with Bokhor, Chief of the Imukeheku tribe, whom His Divine Majesty had so decisively defeated at that place the previous year and had coerced into pledging peace. Khemshawre also intended to use the trip to survey the western frontier's defenses and to further instill royalist control over the province of West Ament. Seshrab accompanied the king on this trip. It was very hard for him at first to go with his lord and master westwards again, to the same place where a great and lamentable battle had been fought not long ago. The city still bore a great amount of damage from the battle, but it was being rebuilt and a great deal of construction was underway when the party arrived.

Upon arriving in Yamu, Khemshawre selected one of his ablest ministers as West Ament's new governor. Shortly afterwards, messengers were dispatched across the border into Imukeheku territory bearing the official scarab seal of His Divine Majesty, ordering that Bokhor, his Libyan vassal, must come to Yamu to reaffirm his earlier pledge of subservience and obedience to *Nesu's* will. Within a matter of days, Chief Bokhor arrived and prostrated himself at His Divine Majesty's feet, pledging peace, obedience, and friendship. To ensure that the Libyans remained pacified, Khemshawre ordered a new regiment to be raised to defend the province – the West Ament Regiment. One of the men who fought at Yamu, a battalion commander named Djedkherure, "Ra's voice speaks", was promoted to Colonel and was made the commanding officer of the West Ament Regiment.

With matters on the western frontier well in hand, Khemshawre and his entourage returned to Khaset City to carry out more business there. He now turned his attention east to Canaan. In the past, the Canaanites agreed to allow Egyptians access to the copper mines of Sinai in exchange for rare Egyptian goods. Egyptian cargo ships brought spices, perfumes, rare gems, large bolts of linen fabric, and large bundles of papyrus paper up the eastern Mediterranean coast to the various Canaanite ports. In these warlike times, with copper urgently needed for the production of weapons, the copper trade was occurring with greater fervency. The Canaanites didn't mind, for they were obtaining shiploads of rare goods in exchange for copper. Egypt was tearing itself apart in civil war and impoverishing itself at the same time.

Khemshawre's diplomatic ventures with the various Canaanite potentates would prove to have unforeseen side effects. The Canaanite city-states were small and in close proximity to one another. News travelled quickly through the caterpillar-like spread of gossip. As Chief Scribe to His Divine Majesty, Seshrab was required to sign his name on every official document. The king's name and seal were enough, but just for good measure, the chief scribe had to sign his name on documents as well, acting as a witness.

After a few weeks, word of the trade agreements between Egypt and the Canaanite states reached the city-state of Hebron. The ruler of that city, King Sihon, sat in his palace, wine goblet in hand, his mind already tipsy with strong drink. Then the messengers arrived carrying news from abroad. Amongst the various correspondences which were delivered into Sihon's hands was a papyrus scroll sealed with the great scarab seal of His Divine Majesty Nesu Khemshawre, King of Lower Egypt, Son of Ra, Horus Incarnate, so forth and so forth. Ah yes, this must be a trade contract – he had been expecting this to show up sooner or later ever since he heard that a new king sat on the throne. It was not addressed to King Sihon personally, but was a general contract which had been dispatched to many of the kings and lords in the area. This document was merely the first draft, and as such it described business in rather broad terms – the specifics would need to be determined later through further negotiations. Lawyers would need to be brought in by both sides to go over the finer points.

King Sihon cursorily scanned through the lines of text, not really all that interested in what he was reading. Then, he came to the end and saw the seals and signatures. The largest was the name and royal cartouche symbol of King Khemshawre, King of Lower Egypt. However, in smaller print underneath it were the words SESHRAB, CHIEF SCRIBE, WITNESS.

*Seshrab.*

*That name…that horrible damnable name!*

With that name visible on that piece of paper, the hate came surging back up within him. He remembered the rage that erupted from him all those years ago when he learned that Seshrab had escaped from the palace dungeon. He immediately had the jailer responsible for guarding him killed on the spot for his incompetence and threatened to kill more of those in the palace if he was not found soon. He ordered Seshrab's family arrested, imprisoned, and tortured to confess Seshrab's whereabouts, but they knew nothing. Search parties were dispatched along the major roads for several miles, but there was no sign of him. King Sihon didn't like receiving bad news. With Seshrab's family of no use to him, he let them go, but warned them that he'd be keeping an eye on them just in case their missing son tried to contact them. The search possies who failed to turn up any sign of Seshrab's whereabouts or path of travel were cursed for bumbling fools and were thrashed out of sight. In his palace, Sihon stewed on this young upstart who had evaded his bloody anger and who had made a fool of him and his court, and promised that he'd kill the boy if he ever got his hands on him. Yet after a while, his anger died down, and he found new targets for his ire, and in time, the teenage scribe who had the impertinence to defy him was forgotten. After all, he was probably dead by now.

And then, months later, King Sihon paid an official royal visit to the seacoast city of Gaza to meet with its lord, King Ariyak, to discuss business. Negotiations between the two heads-of-state had been in the works for some time, carefully laying the groundwork and playing the delicate dance of diplomacy, and this would be the first face-to-face meeting to talk about matters in-person. The meeting went very well on the first day. Things were proceeding exactly according to plan. But on the second day, things took a dramatic opposite turn. The second round of tete-a-tetes between the two potentates had just begun when King Ariyak's three children came into the hall. A man named Saul of Jericho, a minor-ranking official within the court who served as the tutor to the royal children, could not be found in the palace. He had not made his presence known at the customary place and time to teach them their lessons, and nobody else in the palace had seen him that morning. The sudden absence of this man troubled King Ariyak incredibly, and he immediately went straight to the man's quarters, accompanied by several heavily-armed guards as well as his personal doctor, fearing either foul play or perhaps the man might be lying sick in bed. Not wanting to be out of the king's sight and hearing, King Sihon followed.

The room was empty. It had been completely cleaned out, except for a small note lying on the bed. Maddeningly, the note did not give any reason for Saul of Jericho's departure. Instead, it contained a series of heartfelt statements thanking King Ariyak for his kindness and wishes that he should have a long reign and that he and his children should be healthy and prosperous.

King Ariyak was beside himself with bewilderment, wondering why on earth Saul would inexplicably sneak off in the middle of the night. Was he not happy here? Was he not provided for in every way? Was he not an honored member of the king's household? King Sihon asked Ariyak why he was so distressed by this man's departure. This fellow, whoever he was, was clearly not as loyal and reliable as Ariyak had supposed. Ariyak replied that the man had ingratiated himself into His Majesty's company and had performed his duties splendidly. Ariyak had saved this man from the gutter when he asked for a job in the palace, and soon proved that he was an intelligent man who could read and write, and was highly educated in a number of fields, which was all the more remarkable for his young age.

That caught King Sihon's attention. The questions began. A young man of such high intelligence and skill languishing in the gutter? Yes, he was begging in the streets before King Ariyak took him in out of kindness and gratitude. How long had he been in Gaza? He had been in the king's service for such-and-such a time, and had been in Gaza for such-and-such a time before that. Prior to then, nobody in the city had seen him before.

The dates fit too well. The description fit too well. It was too much of a coincidence to be merely a coincidence.

"There is no such person as 'Saul of Jericho'", said King Sihon to King Ariyak. "That young man is really Seshrab of Hebron, a wanted criminal who escaped from my palace dungeon and is now living as a fugitive from the law. He is a rebel and a traitor, and he deserves death for his crimes".

"What?!", replied Ariyak. "I cannot believe that of him! He was too full of kindness and compassion to be as you say!"

"I am not mistaken! He was young, but he was well educated and highly skilled. He served as a scribe and accountant in my palace. He rose against me and defied my power. He was arrested and imprisoned, but somehow escaped and fled from Hebron. Then, a young man arrived without explanation in your city very shortly after he vanished from mine, and soon demonstrated that he was possessed of great intellect and education. Yes, I say that this fellow deceived you into taking him into your confidence. He is not Saul of Jericho – he is Seshrab of Hebron, liar, deceiver, crook, swindler, rebel, and traitor, and his life is worth no more than a dead dog! He is my enemy and he has escaped my justice! And you had this dangerous criminal under your roof all along? That looks poorly for you. We have lately been drawing close to each other in partnership, partners in peace and partners in war. Together, side-by-side, Gaza and Hebron shall prosper together and shall stand beside each other in battle against our enemies. Seshrab is my enemy. Therefore, I urge you, King Ariyak, great and wise king, to lend me men to assist me in hunting down and capturing this villain and bringing him to justice".

But King Ariyak just stood there, and stared at him.

"Sire, I know that these things must be difficult to believe, but I assure you—".

"No", said King Ariyak.

King Sihon was caught off-guard by this. "What, Sire?"

"No…No, I won't…No, I will *not* help you. I say again, I will *NOT* help you! This man, this 'Seshrab' as you name him, was one of the finest and most respectable people that I ever knew. His presence within my house was a joy and a treasure. He never gave me any offense, and he treated all about him with great kindness and courtesy. He was the finest teacher my children ever had. They are the most educated people in my kingdom, thanks to him. One day, they shall be great kings and queens, thanks to him. I know how to read and write, thanks to him! My entire household owes that man a debt that I fear I shall never repay. And you *dare* to call him 'villain'? Then, sir, I call you '*liar*'! I call you '*scoundrel*'! I call you '*detestable damnable dog*'! *GUARDS!!!*"

The armed men who had accompanied King Ariyak now stepped forward and imposingly brandished their weapons.

"King Sihon is no longer welcome within my house! *Get him out of my kingdom!!!*"

In a flash, the armed men laid well-muscled hands on either side of King Sihon and bodily dragged him out of their king's sight. "Let go of me! Take your hands off me! I am a king! A king, damn you! Damn you all! You will regret this, Ariyak!!! I swear by all the gods, you will regret this!!!" And they threw him out the door!

King Ariyak stood there listening to King Sihon being carried off, his curses and threats ringing in the halls, and lowly muttered to himself, "Good luck, Seshrab".

Prior to his visit to Gaza, King Sihon had completely forgotten about the young man who had dared to defy him. Now, he was all that Sihon could think about. He vowed that he would never rest, he would undertake any effort, march any distance, and pay any price to have Seshrab's head on a plate.

True to his word, King Sihon used every resource at his disposal to track Seshrab down. He had learned of Seshrab's presence in the port-city of Ezion-Geber, and afterwards learned that Seshrab had been hired as an accountant for a turquoise mine in Sinai. However, there were many turquoise mines in that region, and the king was unable to find out which one Seshrab was posted to. So, he sent a general letter to all of the mine operators in the area, asking if they knew of anyone who fit Seshrab's description. No mention was made of any crime to avoid scaring Seshrab off, and also to avoid having anyone kill Seshrab before King Sihon could get his hands on him. One of these letters eventually found its way to Hathor's Mountain. Seshrab was called into his boss' office and told about the letter, and was told that a response had already been dispatched, saying that there was indeed a youth who fit the letter's description. When Seshrab found out that King Sihon was still looking for him, he told his boss and the workers that he would personally go to Hebron to see the king in person, and then fled in the opposite direction to Egypt.

Unbeknownst to Seshrab, when King Sihon received the mine boss' letter, he gathered a small military force and raced to Hathor's Mountain. Upon arriving, his troops captured and imprisoned the mine workers and King Sihon confronted the mine boss Iuniyrapet, demanding that Seshrab be handed over. Iuniyrapet replied that Seshrab had already left for Hebron nearly two weeks earlier. The king replied that he didn't believe him, and the camp was ransacked. When Seshrab wasn't found, King Sihon again demanded where Seshrab was and where he went, but everyone replied that they did not know. In his rage, King Sihon had everyone there killed and the camp was burned to the ground. Seshrab's trail had gone cold.

But now, months later, it became glowing red hot. Seshrab's whereabouts were now plainly clear. King Sihon knew exactly where Seshrab was and what position he held. The king of Hebron sent a letter to King Khemshawre informing His Divine Majesty that Seshrab was a fugitive, a wanted criminal, who had assumed many false names in order to obscure his identity. He ordered the king to hand over Seshrab immediately, promising that if he did so, he would make it worth his while. If not, then there would be war. As soon as King Sihon dispatched the letter, he mustered his army and prepared to invade Egypt.

Two weeks later.

Seshrab was in one of the rooms in the palace going over the records of something or another, when a messenger burst in panting. "Chief Scribe, sir, His Divine Majesty orders you to appear before him immediately! He awaits you in the throne room. Please sir, go to him now! He is very angry!"

Seshrab raced to the throne room as quickly as his legs could move, his feet slamming and skidding on the paving stones. At last, he came to the throne room via the right-side door, and opened it. There was Khemshawre, seated. Flanking him on either side were three armed guards. One of them was Captain Nebikhamu, the commander of the Palace Guard. The king had a very stern look on his face.

As soon as the door swung open, his head snapped bird-like towards the sound's direction. He didn't say a word, but as soon as Seshrab saw his master's face, he knew he was in for trouble.

"Your Divine Majesty, I heard—".

"You will stand at attention in the presence of your master!" he barked.

Seshrab was startled by this, and immediately obeyed. He rushed to the front of the *dais*, and stood rigidly at attention. *He sounded like his father just then,* he thought.

Khemshawre looked down at Seshrab from his perch for what seemed like an eternity. His left elbow leaned on the throne's arm rest, while his right hand, clenched in a fist, tapped onto the right armrest every two or three seconds like a cat flicking its tail in agitation. This went on for about ten seconds, although it seemed like much longer. The silence, punctuated rhythmically by those sharp whacks, and the Egyptian king's expression made Seshrab sweat.

"Do you remember when you first came to the Perah?" the king finally asked.

It was an odd question – of course he remembered. "Yes, Your Divine Majesty".

"It was during the reign of my divine father, was it not so?".

"Yes, Your Divine Majesty".

"Do you recall *why* you came here?"

"Yes, Your Divine Majesty".

"Say it".

The demand was a bizarre one. Khemshawre had been fully aware of Seshrab's background ever since he had arrived – Seshrab had plainly told him of it. He had confessed to everything. Something was off about all of this. "I had come to you after days of wandering, seeking refuge".

"Refuge from what?", asked the king. "Or should I say, from whom?"

"Your Divine Majesty, it was from my former master, Sihon, King of Hebron, who sought my death".

*"And still does"*, he intoned ominously. Then, he held up a piece of paper, which had been tucked on the side of his body. "I have just received a letter from him, Seshrab of Hebron, or should I call you Saul of Jericho? Or perhaps Zacharias of Lakish?"

The color dropped from Seshrab's face.

"Your life, it seems, has been a very colorful one indeed. Your former master's anger has not abated over these many years. On the contrary, it has grown all the stronger. Now, it is an obsession. He has been hunting you ever since you escaped from King Ariyak's court in Gaza. He has discovered that you are in my service. He knows that you are here, in my country, in my city, in my palace, in my very home under my very roof! King Sihon desires your death above all things, and no amount of gold, silver, or precious jewels can buy off his wrath! He demands that I hand you over to him immediately...*or else*". Here the king paused, letting what he said sink in. "He also states that he's willing to make it worth my while to cooperate with him. He promises peace and trade, and even a military alliance against our enemies as long as he remains alive. He promises wealth and goods and assurances that he will not attack, provided I deliver you to him". The king let that sink in, too. "Have you nothing to say to all of this?"

Seshrab gulped. He wasn't sure if he could or should say anything. It appeared as if the king's mind was already made up. "Your Divine Majesty, I...I trust that I have not done anything to displease you while I was in your service".

"No, you have not. In fact, you have performed your duties very well".

"Does Your Divine Majesty wish to send me away?"

Khemshawre remained silent for one or two seconds. "The king of Hebron is sending an army to attack us. He has threatened to sway the rebel lords who occupy the eastern half of the Nile Delta to join sides with him. If they join his army, I cannot be certain of victory. The Royal Army of Lower Egypt has suffered greatly and I cannot afford to undertake another military campaign until it has recovered in strength. King Sihon does not want my kingdom or my head – he wants *you*. I can either hand you over to him, in which case he will promptly turn his army around and return to whence he had come, or I can refuse his demands and face his wrath".

"Your Divine Majesty, I would wish to remain in your service. I have done well, as you said. Please, do not send me away. Do not send—".

Khemshawre shot up from his throne, crumpled up the papyrus letter, and threw it at Seshrab's face. *"PEOPLE HAVE DIED BECAUSE OF YOU!!!"* he screamed at the top of his lungs, his lion-like voice echoing thunderously in the colonnaded chamber, the reverberations of the sound waves distorting the voice and making it sound deeper, larger, like a large flesh-eating beast.

Seshrab had never seen the king act this way, except in battle. And then the king's words dawned on him. Seshrab's eyes widened, and he began to shake. He frantically thought of his family, his friends, and the people that he worked alongside. Horrible images raced through his brain of seeing everyone who was dear to him slaughtered.

Khemshawre slowly sat back down on his throne. He let Seshrab stand there, alone with his thoughts for a few seconds. "I am glad that you understand the seriousness of the situation. And make no mistake, it *is* serious. But it still leaves me with a problem – what am I going to do about you?”

“If I may ask, what is your answer, Your Divine Majesty?”

“I don’t have one…*yet*. I have a lot of thinking to do. However, I must make sure that you don’t run off the way that you did with the Hebronians, the Gazans, and with those poor unfortunates at Hathor’s Mountain. You will remain here, and you will be kept under watch to *ensure* that you remain here. The other scribes will take over your duties”.

Khemshawre snapped his fingers, and the six heavily armed men who had been standing by the throne descended from the *dais* and surrounded Seshrab. Two of them grabbed him by the arms.

The king pointed outwards. “Take him to the dungeon, and keep him there until I have decided otherwise”.

As he was being pulled away to the palace’s prison, Seshrab called out, “Your Divine Majesty, master, I beg you! Do not send me away! King Sihon will kill me! Do not let me die! I am a good servant! I’m loyal to you! Don’t let me die!” and they pulled him through the door out of the throne room, and closed the door behind them.

The guards brought Seshrab down the long smokey hallway. Captain Nebikhamu opened the door to his cell, the very same cell that Seshrab had been thrown into when he first came to the palace when he was suspected of being a spy, gave him a short shove inside, and slammed the door behind him, bolting it shut. Then, Capt. Nebikhamu turned to the other five guards. “All of you, stay out here and don’t let him out, no matter what. Only *Nesu’s* word can set him free”.

For the next two days, Seshrab remained in that dark dirty prison cell. Food and drink were brought to him every morning, but he had no appetite. He just lay there on the floor, blankly staring up at the ceiling. At night, when the guards re-opened his door to take back the cup and plate, they saw that the food was still there, not moved by even an inch, and Seshrab would be in the exact same position, silent. There was evidence of tears. He didn’t try to escape. He didn’t even try to move.

Two days after his confinement, a group of six guards unlocked his door and entered his prison cell. All of them were armed. “His Divine Majesty wants to see you”, one of them said.

Seshrab slowly craned his head in their direction and vacantly stared at them with bleary eyes. *Alright, let’s get this over with.*

They brought Seshrab back to the throne room. There was his master, the king, a determined and scrutinizing look upon his face. His eyes locked onto the Canaanite scribe who approached him. For a few seconds, the two remained as they were. Seshrab's guards were drawn up close to him, just in case he tried anything.

Abruptly, King Khemshawre called out "How large is the Hebronian army?"

The question caught Seshrab off guard. "Um…small. Only a thousand men, Your Divine Majesty, if even that".

Khemshawre thought for a moment. "What is their status? Are they well-trained?"

Again, Seshrab was perplexed. "Not compared to your army, Your Divine Majesty. They are of average ability for Canaanite forces, they being more-or-less equally armed, equipped, and trained to each other. There are a handful of professionals, but the majority are fighting farmers who trade their tools for weapons when the king calls them".

"Well led?"

Seshrab thought. "Not particularly. The soldiers are only as courageous as their leader".

"And how is their leader, King Sihon, in battle?"

"I have never seen him in battle, Your Divine Majesty, but I have heard that he is headstrong and reckless, and he punishes soldiers for failure even if they were following his orders".

Khemshawre huffed. "Typical. How are the Canaanites armed?"

"Similar to the Egyptians, Your Divine Majesty. Minimal or no body armor. Copper axes and spears. Wicker shields covered in cowhide. Standard for Canaanite warriors".

The king thought again, this time longer. Seshrab could tell that his master was processing all of the information, but he failed to comprehend why his master would want to know all of this. After a minute or so, sitting silently on his throne, deep in thought, Khemshawre said "I have not yet received word of the Hebronian army's movements, but I suspect that they are still marching towards Egypt. Soon, they will arrive at the Wall. As you know, I do not yet rule over the eastern districts, and the lords of those places cannot be trusted to act favorably towards me. They might resist the Hebronians' approach, or they may allow them to harmlessly pass through their lands, or they may even join sides with King Sihon in the hope that they can drive me from my throne. Regardless, my realm is now threatened. Contrary to my wishes for peace, and contrary to the promises which I made to my soldiers of their services being finished, I must call upon them once again to take up arms in my name. The Royal Army will assemble, cross into Sinai, and intercept the king of Hebron before he can cross the border into Egypt. Perhaps I can persuade King Sihon to turn his army around and return back to his city. If not, there will be a fight".

Seshrab thought that he misheard him. "You…will fight the king of Hebron, Your Divine Majesty?"

"Only if I cannot avoid it. From what you have just told me, this battle, if there be one, will be a minor affair. Nothing like Yamu", and the king gave a slight smile of recognition.

All of a sudden, Seshrab began to feel better. "Thank you, Your Divine Majesty, for coming to my aid".

"Do not thank me", said the king as he rose and walked down the steps of the dais towards him. "Thank your fellow scribes, thank the butlers and maids, thank the bath attendants, thank the cooks, thank the guards, and above all, thank my wife. Gossip travels fast in these confined surroundings. Ever since I put you under arrest two days ago, all of them have been pestering me day and night – I have been relentlessly bombarded with their incessant pleas on your behalf. Apparently, they like you. It was out of their appreciation for you that I relented. Someone who is so kindly thought of by so many ought to be well-attended to and retained". Khemshawre put his hand on Seshrab's shoulder. "You are free from your confinement, and I wish you to remain in my service", and he smiled.

Seshrab smiled too.

"Do not smile just yet", the king cautioned. "You are still my chief scribe, and as per your duties, you are to attend upon me. You go where I go. That means if I march off to war, you march with me".

Seshrab could feel himself getting antsy again. He could feel it coming on. *Oh gods, not now! Not here! Not again! Not now! Not like this!*

"Seshrab, look at me", said the king.

"Your…Your Divine Majesty, I…I don't think—".

"Seshrab, look at me", he repeated in the exact same voice.

Seshrab tried hard to follow his king's wish.

"Look at me. Concentrate on my face. Here, take hold of my hand".

Seshrab reached out and clasped the king's outstretched palm.

"You know what to do. Deep breath in, hold for three seconds, breathe out".

Seshrab tried. The guards began to look nervous.

"There's no need to be concerned", the king said to them, his gaze still firmly fixed on Seshrab's trembling face. "He knows what to do. Here, follow me", and the king started breathing in deeply.

Seshrab started falteringly to mimic him, and eventually kept time with him.

"Feel my hand. Feel the fingers of my hand, my palm, my knuckles. Know where you are…You are here".

Seshrab gripped the king's hand tighter. Slowly, very slowly, he began to come down.

"See. You can do it".

"I'm…sorry, Your Divine Majesty".

King Khemshawre shook his head. "There's no need to apologize. A man who catches mosquito fever doesn't apologize for being sick – it's the mosquito's fault, not his. A man who has seen what you have seen doesn't apologize for his memories. You are not the first person to be shaken by the sights of battle, and as long as men kill each other, you won't be the last".

Seshrab was unsure of what to say, until at last he said "Thank you".

"Do you remember when you accompanied me back to Yamu to renew the peace treaty with the Libyans? You were very scared at first to go back there, but I assured you that nothing would happen, and nothing did. We watched the city being rebuilt, there were no terrible sights, sounds, or smells, and nothing unpleasant occurred. We stayed there for several days, and then we left. You remember?"

"Yes, I remember".

"Where I go, you go. It doesn't mean that you have to pick up a spear and go into the lines like you did before. If what you've told me about the condition of the Hebronians is true, there might not even be a battle. In fact, I wouldn't be a bit surprised if they all turned around and ran away at the mere sight of me", trying to cheer Seshrab up.

"Your Divine Majesty…I don't think that I can do this again".

Khemshawre nodded. "Some men can't. But I have been a soldier my whole life, and I know *for a fact* that you're one of those who can".

# CHAPTER 13

*With his realm threatened with invasion, His Divine Majesty mustered his troops once more and disembarked from the coast. I accompanied my master upon this expedition. After sailing eastwards, he and his men landed within the westernmost part of Sinai and awaited the approach of the Hebronian army, led by my former master King Sihon. There, with troops arrayed on either side of the field, I braced myself for the coming fight. Whether the day would end in victory or defeat, on that day old business would be settled at last.*

Upon the Royal Army's return to Khaset City, the king had dismissed the troops, saying that there was no more need for their service. The soldier thanked him for that, since it had been a long, long, time since they had seen their homes and their families. But now, Egypt was threatened by invasion from the east. Once again, with some reluctance, Khemshawre was forced to call upon his brave soldiers, his "warrior sons", to once more pick up their shields and their weapons and march off to fight Egypt's foes. Of course there were grumbles, there were curses, there were shouts and screams, but in the end, those who were called upon to do their duty sighed and accepted the king's command. After all, to them, this was not Horus-Khemshawre, Living God of Egypt. This was their own beloved Shaweneiti, "the boy", the darling of the army, who had been bred to battle since he was a child. How could the soldiers possibly ever refuse him?

If the Hebronians penetrated through the Wall, the vast swamplands that lay on the border, and crossed into Egypt, they might make a pact with one of the warlords of that region, and then combine their forces, and then would become an even bigger threat that King Khemshawre would have to deal with. No, in order to keep the risk to a minimum, the Royal Army would have to go around these rebel-held eastern territories and land in Canaan, somewhere on the northern coast of the Sinai Peninsula, and intercept the Canaanite army *before* it could cross into Egyptian territory. Ever since Khemshawre was young, he had contended with battles and campaigns fought within Egyptian territory, largely against other Egyptians. Now, for the first time in his career, his soldiers would be fighting against a foreign opponent on foreign soil.

For this campaign, His Divine Majesty mustered up an army of 1,000 men – he felt that such a number would be sufficient enough to deal with the Hebronian army, which, by all accounts, was much less-disciplined than his own force. Only one-quarter of Khemshawre's men were experienced battle-hardened veterans, while the remainder were new recruits. For these men, this would be their first campaign…and possibly their last.

King Khemshawre, fully armored in copper and carrying his shield and diorite mace and with his father's leopard pelt draped about his shoulders, stood at the head of his men. "Soldiers, brave comrades in arms, I promised you peace. I assured you that you could return to your wives, your families, your homes, and your crops. I had promised that you could lay aside your spears and your shields, and awake each day knowing that you would not need to fear the dread of battle. I am truly sorry for this. I seek no glory, honor, land, or plunder in calling you to march off to battle. Rather, we must face the onslaught of a foreign foe bent on invading my realm. The Canaanites, *those wretched Asiatics*, have assembled an army and are marching to invade. They believe that my offers of peace and friendship have betrayed weakness. They have promised to join sides with the rebel lords of the east, and together, they will overwhelm us like the Nile's flood. Therefore, to safeguard our lands, our homes, and everything we hold dear, we must go on the offensive. Once more, we must march to battle, boldly and aggressively. We must strike him before he strikes us. We must overwhelm and destroy him before he destroys us. We must cross into foreign enemy soil before our beloved Egypt suffers further blood to be shed into it. You all remember the words of my father. You all remember that he warned us of the enemy at the gate. He warned us that Egypt, weakened from turmoil and civil strife, would be carved up by its enemies. We have fought them off before, and we shall do it again. They have failed before, and with you marching beside me, they shall fail again. Soldiers, march!"

Once more, there was pomp and celebration as the army left the rendezvous point at Khaset City and marched north to the coast. Seshrab accompanied them. This would be his second military campaign with the Royal Army of Lower Egypt. They took ship for most of the journey. Seshrab oversaw the loading of supplies and men, keeping close tabs with a stack of documents pertaining to one logistical detail or another. Then they set sail, heading east to the rising sun.

The eastern half of the Nile Delta was a wild and violent place. Numerous factions constantly battled against each other, either to defend against attacks or to advance into someone else's territory. Nobody within that part of the Nile Delta acknowledged Khemshawre, or indeed any monarch of the Fourteenth Dynasty, as their master. If he was to set foot within their lands, there was a very high likelihood that he would be imprisoned or killed on the spot. So rather than going through these lawless domains, fighting battles and sieges all along the way, and severely depleting his fighting strength, Khemshawre and his troops would travel by ship and go *around* them.

When he was alive, King Nebsenre had been planning a grand campaign to conquer this part of Egypt as soon as he had secured his western flank, but he was slain before he could carry his plan into action. His son and successor Shaweneiti, now Horus-Khemshawre, had decided to leave well enough alone. He had been more focused on consolidating the territories that he ruled over rather than occupying himself with military adventures. The eastern provinces could wait until a later time, or at least that was what he had hoped. But his enemies had other ideas. Plans never survive contact with the enemy.

Still, although His Divine Majesty had decided not to raise his war-club against the eastern provinces, he nevertheless needed to keep a close eye on them, for the fighting and turmoil which raged there might very well spill over into his own lands. There was also the possibility that some foolish or headstrong warlord might get the notion into his head to invade his realm, and he needed to be ready for that. There were several local despots that the king needed to be wary of. One was the ruler of the province known as Far Eastern Land. This had once been the easternmost province of Lower Egypt, guarding the kingdom against incursions by the Arabs and Canaanites. As such, this province was strongly defended and all of the settlements were fortified against attack. Now, it was an independent state, and its governor had become very rich by exacting heavy tariffs on trade goods coming into his lands. Consequently, he also had a large army to protect his riches. Yet it was unlikely that this man would turn his host westwards upon *Nesu*, for he was occupied with more immediate concerns.

The royal fleet continued to make its way eastwards, hugging the coast, when it approached the place where the eastern-most branch of the Nile River emptied into the Mediterranean Sea. Situated at the mouth of this branch of the Nile River was the city of Per-Amun, "the House of the god Amun", one of Egypt's major shipping ports. Observing from the deck of the ship, Seshrab could plainly see that the city was heavily militarized. Per-Amun was one of the most well-fortified cities in all of Egypt, and with good reason. Its situation at the mouth of one of the Nile's branches made it strategically and economically important, and as such it was under constant threat of attack. A massive stone wall augmented at regular intervals with towers surrounded the entire city, and it also housed a large garrison of soldiers. From the decks of the ships, Seshrab and his companions observed that the city walls were bristling with troops. It appeared that the entire male population of the city had been conscripted.

At one time, the rich port-city of Per-Amun had been the capital of Far Eastern Land. However, things had changed. One man ruled almost all of the province, but at some point during the Second Dark Age, Per-Amun had broken away and declared itself to be an independent city-state under the rule of its own warlord. Ever since then, decades of near-constant warfare had ensued between the provincial governor endeavoring to re-establish control over this separatist city, and the inhabitants of the city fighting to preserve their autonomy. A large cemetery lay outside Per-Amun's walls stretching for a considerable distance, were there lay buried the thousands who had perished in the numerous attempts to re-take the city. The war was not over yet. Per-Amun was constantly under the threat of assault, and as such the city was heavily guarded at all times, always on the lookout for advancing armies on the horizon.

There was another man within this part of the Nile Delta who had audaciously assumed the title of "Prince of the North", and he claimed absolute unquestionable rule over all of northern Egypt, including His Divine Majesty's lands in the west. Every once in a while, he would send an inflammatory insolent message to the royal court in Khaset City demanding that they acknowledge him as the true ruler of Lower Egypt and pay homage to him. These messages were almost always ignored. This man may have talked big, but as of yet, this jumped-up self-proclaimed autocrat had not made any serious attempts to enlarge the small territory which he ruled over in Egypt's northeastern corner, ruling from his headquarters in Djanet, which was only a minor town. For now, the Prince of the North's main antagonist was the governor of the province of Far Eastern Land, who was himself engaged in a near-constant state of war with the rebellious separatist city of Per-Amun.

After two days of travel by sea, which the Egyptians called the *Wadj Wer*, "the Great Green", the ships sailed past the Wall, the area of marshes which marked the border between Egypt and Canaan. For the most part, the Wall was impenetrable, but armies could still punch through if they were determined or stubborn enough.

After the ships sailed past the border swamps, Khemshawre ordered the captains to pull ashore. The signal was given, and the boats swung towards the beach. The ships pulled up to the beach, and the soldiers disembarked, their feet touching foreign soil for the first time. The *nakhtu'aa* were sent ashore first to secure the landing zone and to scour the area – they reported that all was clear. The rest of the soldiers then left the ships, carrying their supplies and tents with them. They gazed around to get their bearings and to see their new temporary home.

The main coastal highway known as "the Way of Horus" ran along Sinai's Mediterranean coast, dotted here and there by small fishing villages. King Khemshawre knew that this route was the most likely path that the Hebronian army would take. The landscape along the seashore was flat, but just on the opposite side of this coastal pathway, the sand heaved and swelled like an earthen ocean. The entire landscape was devoid of life, with not even a thorn bush to be seen. No cover, nothing to hide behind, except the sand dunes which rose upwards.

The caravan route seemed like the most obvious path that the Hebronian army would take. It briefly entered into the king's mind that the Canaanites might try to surprise him by swinging around his position and attacking him through the sand dunes, attacking his right flank. King Khemshawre knew full-well that it was very easy to hide even large numbers of men in terrain like this, with the sand dunes blocking the enemy's view until the last moment. Sand dunes were good places to conduct ambushes. However, he quickly dismissed the idea. He knew from experience that sand dunes were difficult if not impossible terrain to fight in, whether attacking upwards or downwards.

Khemshawre turned to the soldiers. "Rest, and make ready. Archers, take position atop those taller sand dunes to gain a vantage. The Canaanite army will approach upon us in due time, but we will see them long before they see us. I do not know when they will come, but when the time comes, we will make our stand here".

Two days later.

It was a hot and dusty day. There was a slight breeze coming down from the north, blowing a thin sheet of brown sand over the ground, hanging tentatively at knee-level like a khaki mist. The sky was clear and burning. The rest of the men were lounging in or around their tents, trying not to exert themselves due to the heat, saving their strength for the coming fight, not knowing *when* or *if* it would ever come.

King Khemshawre looked outward. This was a good position. This hill, although rather low, overlooked a large part of the valley. This would be the route that the king of Hebron would have to take. The mosquito-infested swamps which guarded the eastern approach into Egypt were several miles to his rear. From atop this rise, the Canaanite rabble could be easily spotted as they made their approach towards the border. Of course, the individual soldiers themselves would not be seen at first. No, the first thing that would be seen would be a massive cloud of dust rising up into the air on the horizon, the natural by-product of a large number of men marching through dry dusty terrain. Their position would be located hours before they would actually come into view. By the time the enemyn troops were seen, Khemshawre would have his plans all worked out and his men would be ready for whatever came their way.

Sure enough, a large cloud of dust appeared on the horizon. No simple trade caravan could kick up something like that. Such a cloud of dust could only be raised up by the trampling feet of hundreds or thousands of men.

Khemshawre then looked at Seshrab, who was standing not too far away. "They're coming", he said.

Seshrab nodded in understanding.

"Hebron is a long way from here. It's a long way to travel for revenge. Your former master must hate you greatly in order to travel so far and to dare take the risk of entering my realm".

"I had hoped, Your Divine Majesty, that King Sihon would put me out of his mind and go on with his life".

"Time only heals *some* wounds, not all of them. For others, the passage of time only causes the injury to become infected, and it worsens the pain. With every year that passes by, the hatred grows until it is all consuming, like sepsis spreading through the body. Hatred has contaminated Sihon's body. His heart can think of nothing else but killing you". Khemshawre then looked at his men, seated on the ground, many of them holding their shields over their heads like sunshades. "It may be that a battle is to be fought here", and then he walked away.

"Your Divine Majesty, I do not wish men to die for my sake. Perhaps King Sihon may be compelled to withdraw and leave peacefully".

The king stared at him, unblinking. "Even as you speak your words, you doubt them. You and I both know that King Sihon will do no such thing. He has not come all this way merely to talk. No doubt, he will demand that I hand you over to him, and if I do not, he will attack. If I were in his place, that is what I would do. He will not be persuaded to withdraw. Do not speak of such foolishness again", he said curtly, and then pointed away. Seshrab was dismissed.

The king turned to his soldiers who were resting on the ground. "The enemy has been sighted on the horizon", he said to them. "They will be upon us in four or five hours. Take position behind this hill, so that you will be unseen by the enemy as it approaches. Then, when I give you the word, you shall make your presence known".

Now the pre-battle panic set in. Heart rates quickened, senses were heightened, and minds raced. Even so, it would still be a few hours before both sides closed action.

Seshrab looked at the dust cloud materializing on the horizon. *He's coming*, he thought. All of the emotions which he had felt years ago when he was on the run now came flooding back to him. Today, right here on this spot, old business was going to be finished. One way or another, it would be settled once and for all. Seshrab was glad of it.

For the next four hours, Seshrab, King Khemshawre, and a small handful of troops stood atop the summit of the low hill which rose overlooking the valley, carefully observing the approach of the Canaanite army. Vague at first. Then, discernable human forms, silhouetted dark against the light bare ground.

"Hmm…about five hundred men, I'd say", spoke Khemshawre to himself. "Not much of an invasion force. Did you not say they numbered a thousand men?"

"Yes, Your Divine Majesty. But Canaan is a warlike place. He assuredly could not take his entire army, or else his city would be left defenseless".

"That would explain why King Sihon planned on recruiting the eastern provinces to his banner. He knew that he had no hope of conquering us with such a small force as his own". Khemshawre continued to observe the Hebronians as they advanced closer and closer to his position. "They march poorly. No order at all. No discipline".

"Nothing like your great and powerful host, Your Divine Majesty", said Seshrab, trying his best to give subtle flattery.

"Even so, I shall not make presumptive statements about sweeping them away like sand in the wind. Even a disorganized rabble can still inflict great damage. They will approach near us in a few minutes. I must be sure to give *His Majesty* a proper reception when he arrives".

Khemshawre walked towards his soldiers who had taken cover on the opposite side of the hill. Calmly, without shouting, he plainly said to them "The enemy is here. Do not make any noise. Stay low so that you will not be spotted as they come up the valley. Let the enemy think that we are few, let him become confident and careless. I am hopeful that I shall avoid a fight, but if there is one, know that I do not doubt we shall win victory. You new men, heed the words of the veterans. Follow their instructions, maintain discipline, and fight with fury, and you will have no reason to be afraid. Remember, I am with you here today, and I will fight just as hard for you as you will for me. I expect all of you to do your duty. Now, ready yourselves for battle".

Despite their king's confidence and his encouraging words, many of the new troops appeared nervous. A few of the veterans patted them on the shoulder saying things like, "You'll be alright, son. This shouldn't be much of a fight, you know. This will be over and done with in just a few minutes. After all, they're only wretched Asiatics".

The Canaanite army advanced up the narrow dusty caravan road, drawing up closer and closer with each passing second. A reckless gaggle of armed men carrying all manner of weapons and shields of varying sizes and shapes, all mixed helter-skelter together in a single disorganized mass. From their perspective, to their front, they could see a small group of men standing atop a low hill. There appeared to be only fifty of them or thereabouts. One of them seemed to be their king, for he was armed and dressed much more splendidly than the others, and one other man seemed to be wearing plain clothes and wasn't carrying any weapons at all. Was he, perhaps, the king's vizier? An advisor of sorts? Maybe a translator? His personal attendant?

King Sihon of Hebron marched at the head of his troops. He was easily distinguishable from his men, dressed in a long flowing robe and decked out in a massive gold necklace. From where he stood, he could make out the distinct height, width, and proportions of a man who had once been a mere boy in his service, someone who had slighted him, someone who dared to defy his will. It was...*him.* The Hebronian ruler smiled even as his heart seethed with hot dark blood. The Egyptian king had agreed to terms. At last, his life's goal would be fulfilled. And if the Egyptian king would wish to fight it out, there was surely little that his small troupe of fifty or so bodyguards could do. This fight would be a pushover.

The Canaanite army approached closer. Then, about 300 yards from the hill, King Sihon called out to his men to stop.

There was silence.

Another shout was heard in the valley below, and the Canaanite army spread out and assembled into battle formation.

"Your enemy comes to meet us", stated Khemshawre. "I shall go forth to speak with him. You will approach beside me".

Seshrab suddenly surged with fear. He didn't like the idea of getting too near to the man who tried to execute him once before, and would now demand his head on a plate. "But, Your Divine Majesty, what if King Sihon tries to capture or kill me? Would it not be better for me to remain behind here?"

Khemshawre glared at him. *"You will approach beside me"*, he repeated with a much sterner tone.

Seshrab bowed meekly. "Yes, Your Divine Majesty".

Khemshawre turned to his soldiers. *"My brave sons, NOW! Advance!!!"*

Now the Royal Army emerged from cover and advanced to the front, thundering in step, dust rising at their ankles, the hot sun glinting off of their copper spearpoints. From below at the Canaanites' position, the haze of the heat made the Egyptians look like they were underwater. The ethereal spectral image of the wavy lines of troops undulating down the hillside was unreal, surreal. The Canaanites held their ground while the Egyptians continued their approach, weapons braced tightly in their fists. There were many more than just fifty bodyguards. There were hundreds of them…no, more! There had to be a thousand men assembled into ranks!

Khemshawre and his chief scribe Seshrab at his side advanced towards the Canaanite army. Despite the knowledge that the royal host was marching behind him, Seshrab's heart was pounding. He had not been this afraid since he fought that terrible battle at Yamu. As hot as he was, he felt chilly, the shaking skin-crawling chills of nervousness. Should the Canaanites suddenly charge, he would almost surely be struck down and killed within the first few seconds. Moreover, he carried no shield or weapons. He advanced, walking towards the army on foot, defenseless, like a sacrificial lamb.

At a distance of a hundred yards, the Egyptian army stopped. There was silence for a few moments. Seshrab, King Khemshawre, and King Sihon slowly and cautiously advanced towards each other, through the middle of the hundred yard no-man's-land that separated the two armies. As they advanced closer to each other, Seshrab got a better look at the troops that had marched here, behind their ranks of sharpened spears and hide-covered wicker shields. These were men of Hebron, his home-town, and despite not being back home for several years, Seshrab still recognized many of their faces. They were his next-door neighbors, his acquaintances and associates, the fathers, uncles, brothers, and cousins of the children that Seshrab had played with when he was younger. Some of them had come to the house to have dinner with his family, while others had been his father's customers or business partners. It was one thing to go to battle against strangers. It was quite another to fight, and possibly kill, people that you personally knew.

The two sides drew up to each other, and halted. They studied each other in silence for some seconds. King Sihon bowed respectfully but not very convincingly. "All hail the great and powerful king of Lower Egypt. Praise and honor upon you", he said to Khemshawre.

"All hail the great and powerful king of Hebron. Praise and honor upon you", Khemshawre replied with burdensome formality.

Then, King Sihon said "Great king, you have something which belongs to me".

"I doubt it, Your Majesty", replied Khemshawre.

King Sihon studied Seshrab's appearance, garbed in Egyptian style. Seshrab gazed down at the ground, not wanting to look at him. "Kneel in the presence of your master!" the Hebronian king shouted.

Seshrab did not kneel. He looked at King Khemshawre anticipating a response, but the Egyptian king said nothing.

"Did you hear me?! I did not discharge you from my service. Therefore, under the law, I am still your master, and you must obey me. Now *kneel!!!*"

"This man stopped being your servant when he left. He's my man now" said Khemshawre. "King Sihon, you came here for some purpose. Speak of it".

"You know very well what my purpose is!" he spat. "That man has committed treason against me and he has escaped justice! For years, I have pursued him, hunting him, and now I find him here! That man must pay for the wrongs that he has done to me! I will have blood for such an offense!!!"

Khemshawre looked at him, unblinking, for a few moments. "Yes, I agree".

*WHAT?!!!* Seshrab thought.

"Yes, you shall indeed have blood". Then, in a lightning quick move which caught everyone by surprise, Khemshawre whipped out his royal mace and slammed it into King Sihon's skull with a nauseating *crunch*. His head was smashed in like a melon, with blood and brains splattering the sand. Seshrab, who was standing directly next to the king, was wide-eyed in shock. A collective gasp shot from the Canaanite army, along with a few startled shouts and screams. The Egyptian soldiers didn't say a word.

"Stay here", the king said softly to Seshrab, his body trembling. Then King Khemshawre, alone, advanced boldly towards the Canaanite host, clenching his bloody mace, leaving a trail of blood-drops every few feet in the sand. He strode in wide determined steps towards them, unflinching, unfearing.

The Canaanites were unsure of what to do. They did not charge upon him, but remained fixed where they stood, though, true to mention, a few of them, especially those who were nearer to him, staggered back a little in terror. Who was this man who feared not his own death? The king advanced until he was only a few paces away from the front-line troops. One man against an army of five hundred. His predatory eyes surveyed the herd of trembling antelope standing before him. Meanwhile, his army remained menacingly perched atop the slope, ready to come barreling down towards them in an instant.

"Your king is dead", loudly declared King Khemshawre, loud enough for everybody on both sides to hear, his eyes glaring at the shocked Canaanite rabble standing before him with carnivorous lion-like hunger. "If Hebron wishes to fight over its king's death, then come at me! Come at me now! But know this – if you strike me down, my soldiers will come upon you, and they will not rest until each one of you lies dead in this sand. If any of you takes even one single step towards me, I assure you, I promise you, nobody here will escape alive. Now...*which one of you wishes to die first?*"

The Egyptian king was standing only a few feet away from them. The Hebronians did not move. They frantically glanced at each other and shuffled their feet, waiting for somebody to say or do something. Then, as if with one collective thought, they gave their answer. The entire Canaanite army slowly and sheepishly turned around, and began the long march back to Hebron. Nobody said a word.

King Khemshawre stood there for a minute or two, watching them amble off in retreat back to their homeland, having accomplished nothing. They left the body of King Sihon where he lay crumpled in the dirt – not one of them had bothered to retrieve it. Khemshawre looked down upon the fat man, the front of his skull smashed inwards, and walked away.

The king walked towards Seshrab, who remained exactly where he left him. "Stand at attention in the presence of your master", said the king, parodying King Sihon's own words.

Seshrab did so, gladly.

"You have lived your life in fear. You shall not be afraid anymore. Now, we will go back home".

Seshrab was overjoyed when he came back to Khaset City. Never in his whole life was he so glad to see its walls and gate looming up in front of him. Never was he so deliriously happy to see the acres and acres of grape vineyards that lay spread out beyond its walls. Khaset City was more than just a temporary staging ground for a portion of his life. Now, it was home, a real home.

When they got back to the palace, Seshrab excitedly said, "Forgive me, Your Divine Majesty, but I cannot attend on you for a while. There is something that I must do".

King Khemshawre knew instinctively what it was. He smiled. "Alright, go and tell them".

Tired as he was, Seshrab raced through the corridors of the Perah and down the long hallway of the Servants' Quarters. He collided into his door, bursting it open and snatched up a piece of paper and his writing set. Knowing that he was safe from harm now, Seshrab decided to send a letter to his family back in Hebron.

*My dear beloved father,*

*I am Seshrab, your youngest son. I am alive and well, and am in the service of the great king of Lower Egypt, Nesu Horus-Khemshawre. I greatly apologize for not writing to you sooner, but I was afraid. King Sihon doomed me to death, all because I stood up for what I believed was right. I have had both good and bad fortune in the years that followed. The king of Lower Egypt has proven to be a good and gracious master, and I have been made his chief scribe. I know that I am safe under his protection. On my behalf, the Egyptian king met King Sihon upon a battlefield and slew him with his own hand, and his army was forced to withdraw. I no longer have any reason to fear, and I feel that a great weight has been lifted off of my shoulders. I no longer have to worry or constantly look behind me, and so I can write to you now. Do not grow anxious over me. I am in good health and in good spirit, and for the first time in a long time, I feel at peace.*

*Your loving son,*
*Seshrab*

After writing the letter and sending it off to be posted, he returned to his cell, lied down on his bed, and closed his eyes. That night, he slept the first full night's sleep in months.

One and a half months later.

Some injuries take longer to heal than others. Some people heal faster than others. Some people *never* truly heal.

Seshrab had been keeping up his daily appointments with the palace doctor, just as the king had mandated. Little-by-little, his condition was showing signs of improvement especially since King Sihon's death. Seshrab's nightmares, though by no means vanished, were coming less frequently and they had taken on subtler tones. His "episodes" were also becoming more manageable, not as severe and crippling as they once were. Deep breaths, count to three, deep breaths again. Feel the surfaces around you. Know where you are. You are here. You are safe.

Seshrab had heard no reply from his letter. With every day that passed, he grew anxious for the mail, but there was none. Then, one day, one of the servants, a maid, came to Seshrab's cell.

"Yes?"

"Sir, His Divine Majesty wants to see you. He says it's very urgent. His exact words for you were 'Lay aside whatever you are doing and come to me this instant'".

"Is he in the throne room?"

"No sir – in his private bedchamber".

Seshrab immediately rose and jogged down the hallway and through the various corridors of the palace. The king's bedroom was on the second floor of the palace. It was the second-largest room, second only to the vast throne room, which sat directly below it. Seshrab rushed up the stairs, panting, and was surprised to see the king standing *outside* his bedroom door. "You…", he wheezed, "…you said you wished to see me, Your…Your Divine Majesty?".

"Pause for a minute to catch your breath, Seshrab", he said. "I will not conduct my affairs with someone gasping for air like a fish taken out of the water".

"Yes, Your Divine Majesty".

Seshrab was graciously allowed to collect himself for a while.

"And now, to business", said the king. "I have called you up here on a matter of great importance. I don't want to use the throne room – it's too public. My private bedchamber is exactly that – private. I decided that this place would be more fitting. I have a gift that I wish to present to you".

"A gift, Your Divine Majesty?"

"Yes. Go inside and you shall find it".

Seshrab, unsure but obedient, opened the door.

"FATHER!!!" he shouted gleefully.

There, standing in the room, was the old bearded man, a great smile on his face beneath his chiseled wrinkles. The two of them flung their arms around each other.

"Oh, my son! My son!"

Seshrab started to cry. He did not notice that the king had quietly closed the door and walked away. He decided it would be best to leave them alone.

"Did you receive my letter?"

"Yes, I received your letter! Oh my son, you are alive! Alive! For these past years, for all this time I had believed that you were dead. And now you are here. The gods are wonderful. El has resurrected my son. My son was dead and El gave him life again! I cried and I wept. I prayed constantly, begging the great god El to grant me favor, to convince him to bring you back from the dead, and to trade my own life in exchange. But my prayers were not answered until now". The two sat down on the king's bed. "How are you?"

"I am well", said Seshrab smiling.

"Yes, you look well. You've grown plump since we last saw each other".

"I was only a boy then. I am a man now, father".

"Have you taken a wife? Do you have children?"

"Not yet. I am…not sure I'm ready for that".

"Well, all in time, all in good time. Talk with me. Tell me everything!"

Seshrab told his father all about what had happened to him since he escaped from King Sihon's dungeon. He relayed his story of his suffering in the desert, how he wandered about in the wilderness for many days until he came upon the city of Gaza. He explained to his father that he took a new identity, Saul of Jericho, because he was worried that there might be a warrant out for his arrest or death. For two months, he lived the life of a street beggar, eating scraps and garbage, and never taking a bath. Seshrab said that this was the lowest that he felt, even more so than being in King Sihon's dungeon. He confessed that he often cried during this time period.

Then his narrative picked up. He explained in a somewhat excited tone about the necklace caper, about how he had captured a thief who had stolen the king's necklace – ripped it right off of his neck in front of everyone in broad daylight! – and wished to return it. Except that he was mistaken for the thief, and he was beaten into unconsciousness. When he awoke, he was inside a dank and dark prison cell. He explained to the guards who he was, and was brought before King Ariyak to account for himself, and was eventually placed in his service for a time.

Seshrab spoke of his escape, of his journey southwards with the Arab nomads, of his time in Sinai as an accountant at the turquoise mine on Hathor's Mountain, and finally of his time in Egypt. He tried to recount the stories with as much detail as he could remember. He spoke of how he had fought in a battle at a place called Yamu, and that he had acquitted himself well in the fighting, and that he had even been awarded a medal for bravery by the king himself. Finally, he finished his tale by letting his father know of the fatal meeting between the king of Hebron and the king of Lower Egypt. His father thought that this was all very thrilling. "My, what a life you've led" he responded.

Now it was Seshrab's turn. "What of you and Mother and my brothers? How are they? How is Hebron these days?"

"Your brothers, your mother, and I are well. When…when you first escaped from King Sihon, the city guard came to our home and tore our house apart looking for you. They demanded to us over and over again where we were hiding you, but we told them over and over again that you had not returned and we had no idea where you were. Then we were all arrested and brought before the king, who accused us of lying and harboring a wanted fugitive. He beat us and tortured us. When he was finally convinced that you were not here, he let us go. That was the last I heard about you for years".

"What other news is there from home?"

"These are troubling times, my son. There is great consternation and anxiety in the air we breathe in Hebron. The Amorites are on the move again. They've invaded Phoenicia, and there is word that they are pushing further south. Everywhere people point to the north and say to each other 'Watch the horizon – the Amorites are coming!' It's come to the point where mothers scold their children saying 'Be a good girl or boy, or the Amorites will get you!' Sooner or later, they may come knocking on our house's door. The stories of what has happened are garbled and unclear. They claim that the Amorite warriors are armed with weapons that do not bend or break in battle, that they can shoot arrows farther than anyone else, and that they travel in strange wheeled carriages affixed to mighty snorting beasts. Some say that it is the end of the world descending upon us".

"It is not the end of the world, father. The world will go on for many thousands of years. The apocalypse which will engulf us will not come until all of us and hundreds of generations that come after us are long dead. The destruction that the Amorites bring is not the hand of El, but the hand of man. Besides, Hebron is far away from Amurru. There will be time to prepare, should they come".

"Yes, I suppose you're right. Enough of this. Let's speak of more pleasant things". And so they continued chatting for hours, talking about everything. The sun had gone down and neither of them had noticed.

Eventually the door opened and King Khemshawre stood in the doorway. "I trust that this has been a pleasant day for both of you".

"Father, I want to introduce you to my master, Nesu Horus-Khemshawre".

"We already had the pleasure of meeting", said the king, a little smile on his face.

Seshrab's father bowed, and then began to kneel, but the king prevented him. "Thank you, Your Majesty, for saving my son".

"Your son Seshrab is a good worker. You should be lucky to have a son like him, and I hope to have a son such as him one day. But it is getting late. It is night already, and your son must be well-rested for the duties that he must tend to tomorrow. You may stay in the palace tonight as my guest".

"I'll see you tomorrow morning, father", said Seshrab, and they hugged. "Goodnight".

The following morning, it was time for Seshrab's father to leave. When the two of them met again, Seshrab's father said to him, "My son, now that King Sihon is dead, you can come back home. Your brothers and your mother miss you very much. It would do them good to see you return. This place, Egypt, is all fine and nice, but it is foreign land. This is not your home. Hebron is your home. Let me take you back, back to Hebron".

Seshrab shook his head. "No, father…My place is here".

"I don't understand, but I can see that you are comfortable and safe here and you have made this place your new home". The two embraced.

"It was wonderful seeing you again, father".

"And you son…I'm so very proud of you".

"Goodbye".

# CHAPTER 14

*His Divine Majesty Nesu Horus-Khemshawre returned victorious from his campaign against the king of Hebron. King Sihon was dead, and I was assured that I would remain in His Divine Majesty's service as long as I performed my duties faithfully.*

*After his return to Khaset City, His Divine Majesty deemed it best to remain at home, governing his provinces and issuing laws and decrees. Several of the rebellious eastern provinces sent embassies to the royal court to propose agreements of friendship, and possibly even negotiate alliances with His Divine Majesty. However, while he received this welcome news from the east, it was also during this time that he began to receive distressing news from the south.*

The so-called "Hebronian War" ended in victory, even though it certainly wasn't much of a war by anybody's standards, but nobody in Lower Egypt was sweating over the niceties. His Divine Majesty's army suffered no casualties, and the only loss on the enemy's side was the enemy commander, slain by Nesu's own hand. King Sihon was dead, and a wave of relief overwhelmed Seshrab of Hebron. The much-welcomed arrival of his father in the royal court was a wondrous gift. For the first time in years, Seshrab had news of his family, and his family had news of their son. His father, mother, and his two brothers were all alive and well, and his father was relieved to find out that his son was under the protection of His Divine Majesty the king of lower Egypt. Seshrab was doing well for himself in his new life as a high-ranking member of the royal court, and his father was proud of him. As far as father and son were concerned, all things were right with the world.

Seshrab's master also felt much more contented than he had of late. Khemshawre's plans to strengthen and consolidate his holdings in the Delta had temporarily been put aside due to this aggravating distraction with the Canaanites. True, the eastern provinces were still in rebel hands, but they had not joined forces with the Canaanite aggressors as Khemshawre had feared, and there was little suggestion that they would be causing trouble. Far from it, in fact. The visual demonstration of King Khemshawre dispatching an invasion fleet to crush the Canaanite army upon Canaanite soil demonstrated to the eastern warlords that His Divine Majesty had ample means to bring the eastern provinces to heel through military force if he so desired. If he wanted, the great warrior king could easily send his soldiers into the eastern provinces and crush them one-by-one. The fact that he *didn't* do that was very telling to the eastern warlord governors. King Khemshawre didn't want war – he wanted peace. Furthermore, his decision to go on the offensive and repel the Canaanites before they could enter Egypt put him in good standing with the eastern lords. In their minds, Khemshawre was willing to fight to protect all of Egypt's lands, even the lands that he didn't personally rule over, even lands that were controlled by his rivals and enemies. He was willing to fight and possibly even die to safeguard all of Egypt against the hated foreign foe.

Of course, that wasn't the *real* reason why Khemshawre dispatched his troops into the westernmost fringes of Sinai. King Sihon of Hebron had threatened war and he threatened to bring the rebel eastern provinces to his side. King Khemshawre had no choice but to go on the offensive. The venomous serpent needed to be crushed to death while it was still inside its egg before it could hatch and bite Nesu on the ankle. That, and that alone, was the reason why His Divine Majesty gave the order to march.

To the eastern warlords, they realized that they need not fear the dreaded king of the north. Here was a man that they could work with, a man they could make deals with. In their usurped halls of borrowed and stolen power, some of them began wondering whether it would be to their advantage to be under Nesu's protective wings.

Meanwhile, in Khaset City, His Divine Majesty set to work catching up on old business, which involved a great deal of reading. He read reports from the cities and provinces that he controlled, he read petitions from the people humbly beseeching him to personally grant this or that favor, which he either imperiously granted or denied, he read reports concerning the military situation of the provinces and the vast howling barbarian wilderness beyond, and he read reports concerning the goings-on within the rebel lands which lay outside his border. He also passed the time doing much writing. He composed and issued various laws, decrees, edicts, and proclamations concerning this or that. He issued a statement that all of the taxes were to be lowered by half in order to give the poor farmers and land-owners within his realm a chance to recover their fortunes. This greatly pleased the people, but greatly distressed Kawaset, Secretary of the Royal Treasury, who repeatedly complained that the royal coffers were nearly empty. War is an expensive business, and Lower Egypt had been in a near-constant state of war for years. On top of that, the lavish expenses for King Nebsenre's funeral and burial had inflicted such a severe blow to the kingdom's finances that Kawaset predicted it would take years to recover. And now, the taxes were being cut to just half of what they should be? Never mind *years*, the recovery would now take *decades*. There were cheers of joy outside the palace walls, but inside, there was a lot of discontented grumbling.

A great deal of civil renewal was put into motion. Khemshawre decreed that the roads and water dikes were to be repaired, and that surveyors be sent out to re-assess people's property boundaries. The dockyards on the Mediterranean coast were to be refurbished, and His Divine Majesty's ships were to be repaired and renovated. He gave orders that the provincial garrisons were to be strengthened and the border settlements were to be fortified. New walls, towers, and entrenchments were laid out, and the laborers went to work cutting and laying bricks and mortar, digging defensive ditches, and erecting barricades and embankments. The water cisterns, grain granaries, and provision storehouses were replenished so that the settlements might better withstand a siege. And if they should come under direct attack, stockpiles of arrows, javelins, and sling stones were slowly incrementally increased and housed within the town armories. Even so, Khemshawre made it very clear, at least in private, that he desired no further conquests or expansion of the royal realm. The renewed focus on defensive rather than offensive objectives ought to have been proof of that.

Within the Perah, as His Divine Majesty ambled about through the business of state, Horemheb, Chamberlain of the Palace, entered the room where the king resided. "Your Divine Majesty, a messenger has arrived at the palace. He bears documents attesting that he has come as emissary from the warlord of Ati to discuss an agreement of friendship between yourself and himself".

"Indeed?", responded Khemshawre. "That is welcome news! Has he been searched?"

"The gate guards checked him upon arrival. He's not carrying any weapons".

"Good. Bring him in at once – I'll meet him in here. And summon Seshrab so that he may be present for this meeting. I wish there to be a record of this".

"Certainly, Your Divine Majesty", responded Horemheb, and he left.

A few minutes later, Seshrab popped into the doorway bearing his ink palette, several brushes, and a satchel full of paper. "Your Divine Majesty, I was told that you wished for me to be present at a meeting to take notes?"

"Yes indeed. We are shortly to receive an important visitor, and I wish for you to be a witness and record what is said".

At that moment, a stranger walked down the hallway escorted by four guards and accompanied by Chamberlain Horemheb.

"Your Divine Majesty" began Horemheb, "here is the man that I told you of"

"Thank you, Chamberlain. He may enter. Guards, two of you shall remain outside the door, the other two shall come within. Chief Scribe, take your seat".

The man entered the room and bowed respectfully to the king of Lower Egypt, the two armed men flanking him, ready to split him open just in case he tried anything. Meanwhile, Seshrab went off to one side and took his seat, readying his paper and pen. The visitor had a dignified bearing and was very well-dressed in the best white linen trimmed in gold braid. Around his neck hung an elaborate golden and bejeweled pectoral, and on one hand was a large gold ring. "Hail to His Divine Majesty, Nesu, King of Lower Egypt. May you prosper and be in good health. I am Nakhtkare, emissary to my master Lord Petifre, lord-duke of the province of Ati, and lord-mayor of the city of Busiris. I have been empowered by my master to discuss affairs of state in his name. I carry his great seal, and you may treat my words as if they were his words. His Lordship has heard many tales of your strength of military might, the wisdom and fairness of your justice, and the benevolence of your rule. Within your domain, you have known the blessings of peace and prosperity. As my master's lands lay next to yours, he wishes that positive relations may be initiated and maintained between us. Let there be only calmness and contentment reigning over your lands and ours, from this moment, forever".

King Khemshawre smiled. "Your master speaks very eloquently, and his resolve to win my affection and clasp my hand in good faith shows wisdom. Clearly Thoth has shown great favor to him to bless him as much as he has. What terms do you propose?"

"An official pledge of friendship between our two nations, an assurance of peace made by both sides towards each other, disarmament along the border which separates our lands from yours, an agreement of trade partnership, and allowing freedom of travel between our two lands".

"Does your master ask for nothing else?"

"No, great king. Nothing more".

King Khemshawre turned to Seshrab. "Did you write down all of that?"

Seshrab was still scribbling, and then stopped. "Yes, Your Divine Majesty".

"Good. Your master is very accommodating to have made his terms so simple. Now, I have some terms of my own to offer. There shall be peace between our two nations, as you have proposed. Likewise, there shall be a disarmament along the border of our lands, which shall be undertaken by both sides at the same time, to ensure that neither side has an advantage over the other. Finally, there will be freedom of travel and commerce across the border and throughout the area of both of our respective domains. But know this. A mere proclamation of friendship between our two sides is insufficient. I desire more than your master's friendship – I want obedience. I shall permit Lord Petifre to remain in his office as the ruler of the province of Ati. He shall continue to rule over those lands as he rules now, enacting his own laws and decrees, creating and collecting taxes, and all of the other powers and responsibilities of his station. But your master shall not merely be a good neighbor – he shall be my vassal and he must acknowledge me as his lord and master. As my vassal, I shall be duty-bound to protect him and come to his aid in any way in his time of need. My army shall instantly march to his defense at his request to safeguard his lands from any threats. If his people are hungry from famine, I shall be duty bound to give his people food to prevent them from starving. However, with benevolence comes obedience. While your master has the freedom to make his own laws, such laws must never contradict my own – my word always has supremacy over his. If I were to issue a law over not only the lands that I rule over directly but also the lands of my vassals, I expect such a law to be immediately obeyed and enforced. If I decree that he must muster his troops so that his army and mine may join forces, he shall do so without any hesitation, and his troops shall be placed under my command. These are my terms".

King Khemshawre let that sink in. The messenger was clearly taken aback and distressed by the king's demands. "Your Majesty, I was—".

"Your *Divine* Majesty", Khemshawre corrected.

"Pardon – Your *Divine* Majesty – I was sent to your court to negotiate a treaty of friendship, peace, and trade, but this is…more than what I had expected".

"There is much in life that is unexpected. Truly, did you earnestly think that I would agree to all of your master's terms without proffering any of my own? Surely, either yourself or the lord of Ati must have anticipated that I would ask for *something* in exchange for so much *friendship*", spitting out the last word. "I have agreed to all of the terms that your master has proposed without any haggling or compromises. For that, you should be grateful that my acquiescence was so easily obtained. But such agreement is contingent on your master subordinating himself to my will in the manner that I have just described. In order for him to remain as the master of others, he must formally acknowledge me as his. That is the price of peace".

The messenger quavered. Khemshawre stared at him, stern and unblinking, anticipating a response. Seshrab nervously glanced back and forth between the two speakers. The two guards stood firm at the door, their hands on their weapons, just in case.

"Your…Your Divine Majesty…I cannot give an answer. I must depart from here and return to the city of Busiris and inform my master Lord Petifre of your demands. He shall send word whether or not your terms are acceptable to him".

"No", came Khemshawre's reply.

The messenger was stunned. "I'm sorry?"

"No. You shall not leave here without giving an answer. You shall not return to Busiris to appraise your master of these developments. There is no need for your master to lend his voice to these discussions. As you told me when you first arrived, you *are* your master's voice. His mouth is your mouth and his words are your words. You are your master's official envoy, his legate, entrusted by him to act reliably in his name as if he himself were here, and that I may treat your words as if they were his own. You carry his seal-of-state to stamp official documents with his name and make them legally binding. Your master has granted you the authority to make decisions on his behalf in his name. Make use of that authority, otherwise you are nothing more than a common messenger delivering a letter. You have offered your terms, which I have agreed to. I have offered mine…which you *must* agree to. Otherwise, the deal's off. There will be no peace, there will be no travel or trade, and there certainly will be no *friendship*".

The messenger shook. He knew he had no alternative but to sign. The Royal Army was mighty, and Nesu's wrath was well known. The last thing that the great and beautiful city of Busiris needed would be to incur the Son of Ra's displeasure. "Your Divine Majesty…I accept the terms".

Khemshawre smiled. Seshrab smiled. The two heavily-armed guards who stood blocking all forms of escape smiled. The messenger wasn't smiling.

"Then we are agreed. Peace and friendship. Chief Scribe, will you please draw up the treaty between our realm and theirs? Two copies please".

"Yes, Your Divine Majesty. I shall get to work on it immediately", and Seshrab gathered up his things and walked out the door, which the guards opened for him, and which was promptly slammed shut behind him, and the two men resumed their stations.

"My chief scribe – he's a very bright man", said King Khemshawre. "So are you, too, as it happens. Agreeing to what I asked for was very likely the smartest decision that you ever made".

After a couple of hours, Seshrab returned with two copies of the treaty, which both parties looked over to make sure that everything was written exactly as it should be. It was all there. Both King Khemshawre and the messenger Nakhtkare stamped their seals at the bottom of both documents. Afterwards, Seshrab affixed his name and seal to it as a witness.

"There, the business is done", said Khemshawre. "Sir, you may return to Busiris and report to your master Lord Petifre of Ati that your mission was successful, that the king of Lower Egypt agreed to all of the terms that he proposed, and also report to him that he is now my vassal, with all of the duties and perks that such a position entails. If your master is distressed to learn that he is now my vassal, console him by reminding him of all that he has gained from his vassalship. I have given him everything he asked for and more! He is under my protection, but he is no longer his own master. Understand".

"Yes, Your Divine Majesty".

Khemshawre signaled to the guards to open the door, and as he led Nakhtkare by the shoulder towards it, he added "I do not think I need to explain to you what would happen to your master and his lands if he were to break his covenant of faith and friendship with me. But just in case Thoth has momentarily withdrawn his favor, know that your capital of Busiris sits very close to the border of my realm. It would not be any inconvenience upon me to dispatch my great host to your citadel within merely one or two days and invest it. Know that I do not take lightly those who break their word. I wish you a safe journey back to Busiris" and closed the door behind him.

"Your Divine Majesty", began Seshrab, "I'm uneasy about this. Suppose the lord of Ati were to take this agreement poorly. What then?"

"He cannot refuse this treaty. His hands are tied. By his own error, he made his messenger a legate rather than keeping him as just a messenger. Empowering his envoy to speak on his behalf and make decisions in his name has cost him his liberty. If he were to disavow the treaty, he would be breaking his word. He will not raise his hand against me".

"If you wished the lord of Ati to be subservient to you, then why not just demand his subjection? Why settle halfway for making him a vassal?"

"It is not settling – it is prudence. The lord of Ati is a strong, headstrong, and prideful man. If I were to demand his servitude, he would immediately resist and raise arms against me. He will not subject himself to the humiliation of being a subject, but he might be a bit more amenable to being a vassal. I have granted all of his requests, I have given him everything that he asked for, and in exchange, all I want for him to do is kiss my ring. Naturally I would prefer for him to be subservient to me and for the province of Ati to be absorbed into my realm, and naturally he would prefer to maintain his total independence and autonomy which he has exercised so far. This arrangement between us is, as it were, a happy medium".

Sure enough, word was soon proclaimed that the neighboring province of Ati was now a vassal state of the kingdom of Lower Egypt. True to their word, both King Khemshawre and Lord Petifre pledged peace and friendship to each other, and both sides demilitarized the border which adjoined their two lands. The garrisons that guarded the riverfront were dispatched elsewhere, and the fortifications were either repurposed into other things or else they were torn down and the building materials recycled for other projects. Commerce increased between the two, as was promised, and goods easily flowed back and forth across the border.

Word of these developments travelled swiftly throughout the remainder of the north. The news of the reduction of the mighty lord of Ati, the most powerful leader within the center of the Nile Delta, from being an independent warlord to now being a vassal of the king of Lower Egypt soon spread to the halls and strongholds of the other warlord leaders in the central and eastern parts of northern Egypt. It caused a definite reaction.

Several weeks after news of the treaty was announced, Horemheb, Chamberlain of the Palace, came rushing through the corridors. "Where is the king?" he demanded of everyone that he encountered. "I need to speak to him immediately!"

"I think he's in his bedroom", said one.

Instantly, Horemheb rushed upstairs and knocked on the door. "Your Divine Majesty, are you within?"

There was heard a shuffling from inside and the door opened. "Yes, Chamberlain, what is it?" the king asked rather groggily. Evidently he had been sleeping and the knocking woke him up.

"Your Divine Majesty, I have come to tell you that several emissaries from the eastern provinces have arrived at your gate. They beg leave to be admitted to your presence so that you may hear what they say".

The king sighed. "Very well, I shall attend on them in the throne room", Khemshawre responded. "Have the visitors wait in the reception hall until I have made myself suitably presentable".

"Of course, Your Divine Majesty".

After about ten or fifteen minutes, the group of three envoys were permitted into His Divine Presence as they were escorted into the throne room. Each of the three men were tall, well-proportioned, pleasantly-featured, and wearing exquisite clothing – clearly they had been chosen by their masters to make an impression. The three men approached the royal dais, where Nesu sat upon his throne in his regal glory, ringed by imposing armed guards, and bowed to him.

"Who comes here seeking my ear? Let them approach and make themselves known", Khemshawre announced.

The first man approached. "I am Khayu, emissary to the lord of the province of Far Eastern Land. Your power and your might are great, and news has arrived in our lands that you have made a treaty of friendship with the lord of Ati and have placed him and his lands under your protection. My master, the lord of Far Eastern Land, also desires great Nesu's friendship and protection. More so, we desire military aid against our foe. I have come here to request Your Divine Majesty join forces with my master's army and together make war upon my master's enemy, the lord-governor of the city of Per-Amun, who has revolted from my master's rule and falsely claims independence. Their disloyal and mutinous actions are an affront to order and the rule of law, and repeated attempts to reclaim the city by force have failed. But with Your Divine Majesty's aid, we can surely crush these rebellious enemies and these traitors and bring them all to the end that they deserve".

At this, the second man approached. "Do not listen to this man's lies and boasts, great Nesu! I am Neferka, official emissary of the lord-mayor of the city of Per-Amun, whom this fellow so basely slanders as a den of traitors, rebels, and mutineers. Per-Amun is a free city, a freedom hard-won by the blood and sacrifices of its people. For too long, we endured the crushing subjugation of the lord-governor of Far Eastern Land, demanding heavy taxes, confiscating our lands, restricting trade, imposing ever-more draconian laws against us, and sending troops into our streets to enforce his will. By will and endurance, we threw off our suppressors and declared ourselves an independent city-state, an independence that we have maintained with the deaths of our own people and the slaughter of any and all who may force us back into subjugation. I have been sent here by my master to request Your Divine Majesty to wage war against my master's enemy, the governor of Far Eastern Land, so that we may preserve our independence from his tyranny. In exchange, we offer wealth, goods, very favorable trade and shipping agreements, and of course our eternal friendship and gratitude".

The envoy from Far Eastern Land audibly scoffed at this. "Indeed" was the only response he could muster.

"Do you have something to say?"

"Well, considering that the entire state of Per-Amun comprises only one city, and considering that your back is against the sea and your belly faces towards my armies, and considering that none of the other lords of the region support you, I dare say that 'friendship and gratitude' are the only meaningful things which you can offer. And I don't think that Nesu will risk going to war for the sake of your friendship".

"Bold talk from someone who has tried time and time again to conquer us and who has failed every time! I've lost count of the number of times you've sent your armies against us, and every time we slaughter them! May I remind you that the city of Per-Amun used to be the capital city of your province until we drove you out, and you were forced to set up a new headquarters in Hut-Waret? We may be small in number and small in size, but we were strong enough to cast you out, and we were strong enough to repel every armed force that you sent against us, and we are strong enough to continue to hold you back as long as we breathe!"

"And yet, for all of your defiant rhetoric, here you are now, sticking your hand out, begging for help. If you really were as strong as you say, you could continue to hold off our advances without any assistance".

"By that same token, you too betray your weakness and impotence by entreating His Divine Majesty to lend you his troops so that you may defeat us all the easier, because you know for a fact that you cannot do it on your own. So now here you are, as you say, sticking your hand out".

"Enough, enough!" called out Khemshawre. "You've been arguing for less than a minute, and I've endured your cattish bickering long enough already. I will not give any decision on this matter now, and I will not be cajoled or badgered into choosing between you". Then he paused and pointed to the third man, standing a little in the back. "You there. You have not said anything since you arrived. Who are you and why have you come here".

The third man approached. "I am Sekhemre, and I am no messenger, envoy, or emissary. I am the lord of the province of Kha and master of the city of Djedet, sacred sanctuary of the fish goddess Hatmehit. I am here to request Your Divine Majesty join forces with me to defeat our common enemy, the man who boldly calls himself 'the Prince of the North', who rules over the province of Ampehu from within his fortified stronghold of Djanet, who daily threatens to invade and conquer my domain and all of northern Egypt, whose insults and insolence can no longer be borne with patience".

"Insults and insolence are not sufficient cause to wage war", replied Khemshawre. "Let the ignorant and the foolish prattle on as much as they will, for then all about them will know them to be ignorant fools, and their boasts and threats will be dismissed as easily as the nonsensical ravings of an imbecile or a madman".

"Sire, you did not let me finish. In exchange for your aid, I do not offer mere professions of friendship and gratitude. I offer something more. If you assist me in destroying the Prince of the North, I shall not be merely a friend, an ally, or a vassal, but shall be your loyal and faithful subject, and my lands will become your lands. The entirety of the province of Kha, which I have ruled over as its lord and master for many years, shall be delivered unto you and placed into your hands. Kha will be another province of your royal realm, the taxes and duties collected from them to be yours. My coastal harbors that stand upon the fringe of the Great Green shall be bases for your merchant vessels and your fleets of warships. My soldiers who currently pledge their loyalty and allegiance to me shall serve no one but Nesu. Destroy the Prince of the North, and all of this I shall give you".

The other two envoys were speechless. The king, too, was amazed at what was just said to him. Then, the other two envoys regained their wits. "No…no! Your Divine Majesty, do not listen to this man!" said the ambassador from Far Eastern Land. "He is giving you a gift of mud wrapped in gold! The province of Kha is a worthless swamp that stinks of fish. Were it not for the nearness of the seacoast, Kha would be of no use to anyone. So much has been placed on the value of the water that they neglect the value of the land. Yes, destroy the Prince of the North! Destroy him! He is our enemy too! But to accept this so-called 'gift' of a worthless province is beneath your consideration".

"Beneath consideration, indeed!" snapped the envoy from Per-Amun. "As you heard him say, Kha possesses many armed troops. If Kha becomes absorbed into the royal domain, they shall become the king's troops! The Royal Army of Lower Egypt is already great and powerful. Nebsenre conquered two provinces, and surely would have conquered more had he not perished when he did. His son and successor conquered a third, and then afterwards repulsed an invading horde of wretched Asiatics. Now, the lord of Ati, who had been able to maintain his independent state against all who opposed him, has lately pledged himself as Nesu's vassal. With each advance, the might of the Royal Army becomes mightier. If Kha becomes another province of the royal realm, thousands more shall march under Nesu's banner. And if the province of Ampehu falls before the royal host, as surely it must, then those lands would be added to Nesu's domain's as well. Isn't that the real reason why this bothers you? Ampehu stands next-door to your own lands. Your province, as it is named, stands at the extreme east of Egypt. If His Divine Majesty should conquer Ampehu, there would be no escape for you should he turn his hungry eye on you. The populations of those provinces would be ample recruiting stock for the Royal Army. You would be hopelessly outnumbered, and your subjection would be assured. Look at what the Royal Army did at Yamu, the fame of that battle echoing up and down the length of Egypt, in which His Divine Majesty, with a force of six thousand men, repulsed not one but two armies which attacked him simultaneously, destroying one and mauling the other and sacking the city of Yamu to boot! If he could accomplish so much with the force he led then, then think now on what he may be able to do if his army numbered twice as many men! Think about what he will do to your lands and your own army if Ampehu were to be used as a springboard for his operations".

"I suggest you take your own advice", said the envoy from Far Eastern Land, "and think carefully of what His Divine Majesty will do to you if Kha falls within his sphere. Kha is home to many ships, ships that can be used to wage great battles on the open waves, ships that can be used to transport armies across the water, ships that can be used to blockade and besiege troublesome seacoast settlements such as your own. So far, Per-Amun's saving grace is that it stands upon the water and can therefore be resupplied by sea in the event of a landward siege. If the ships of Kha come into His Divine Majesty's hands, and if he decides for whatever reason to turn his attention upon you, then you will be trapped between the jaws of a crocodile. With the vast army upon the land and the domineering navy upon the water, you have no escape, and your people must either surrender or starve".

This back-and-forth would have continued on for some time. But during the midst of this squabbling, Horemheb poked his head through one of the side doors of the throne room and gestured if he could be allowed to approach. King Khemshawre saw him and nodded. The portly Horemheb ambled up the stairs of the dais and whispered something into the king's ear.

Immediately, Nesu's face changed from one of irritation and tired resignation to one of great concern and alertness. He stood up from his throne.

"Gentlemen", he began, "the three of you have given me a great deal to think about, but know that I cannot make a decision of such weighty consequences so soon. I shall need time to consider all that was said and to determine the best course of action. I shall retire to confer with my officers and advisers on what is to be done. In the mean-time, you are royal guests, and you are to be treated as such. Every reasonable accommodation shall be made for you during your stay here. Gentlemen, I bid you farewell".

The three envoys bowed to the king of Lower Egypt as he left the throne room with his guards and Horemheb trotting by his side. None of the three men who had arrived were satisfied with the outcome, but at least they weren't sent packing. No doubt, the bickering and squabbling amongst them would continue as long as they remained within the Perah's walls.

Meanwhile, King Khemshawre quick-walked through the halls, the guards marching around him in step, and the chubby Horemheb trying to keep up with His Divine Majesty's military pace.

"How long ago did it happen?" he demanded.

"Two or three days, perhaps", Horemheb responded.

"I had thought that I'd hear word sooner about something like this! Don't we have any spies or observers within Khensu?"

"No, Sire, we don't, at least not to my knowledge".

"That was an oversight. Summon Colonel Ankharis, Colonel Mebydos, and Colonel Djedkherure, as well as the governors of Sapmeh, East Ament, and West Ament to come to the Perah immediately. Dispatch the fastest runners. Tell them it's an emergency. And send for Lord Petifre of Ati as well. After that, call for a meeting in the council room immediately. Send for Captain Nebikhamu, Kawaset, Imeni, and Seshrab. Also send word to the governor of Khaset to be present as well. I want you to tell them what you told me".

"Yes, Sire".

In a few minutes, the king, Horemheb, Seshrab, Captain Nebikhamu the commander of the palace guards, Kawaset the secretary of the treasury, Imeni the secretary of grain and livestock, and the governor of the province of Khaset were gathered together in the council chamber. There was a tense feeling in the air. Something was happening.

"Gentlemen", began the king, "Horemheb has just shared some very unwelcome and distressing news. Tell them".

Horemheb loudly cleared his throat. "A little while ago, rumors started coming into the city that something had happened to the southeast. Two or three days ago, Sekheperenre, Governor of Inebu-Hedj, who controls access to the southern entrance of the Nile Delta, conquered the province of Khensu".

*Say-khepper-enray,* Seshrab sounded out the name in his head. He was getting a nagging feeling of déjà vu. *I know that name. I've heard that name before somewhere.*

Horemheb continued. "His army stormed and overwhelmed the provincial capital of Khem, and killed the warlord who ruled there".

"Up until the present", interjected the king, "relations between ourselves and the rebel province of Khensu had been peaceful – they did not bother us, and we didn't bother them. Khensu lies immediately south of the province of West Ament, and therefore, the taking of this province is an immediate threat to the royal realm. Of all of the warlords of Upper Egypt, he's the most ruthless of the lot. Even the king of the south dares not stand against him. He has already expanded his reach across the northernmost part of the river, and now, for the first time, he's encroaching into the Delta. I am concerned that this person will continue to expand his reach and possibly make an attempt to breach the borders of my realm. Therefore, I order that our military positions be strengthened and defenses of Khaset City are to be put into order. The number of palace guards on shift at any given time are to be increased, and the number of soldiers garrisoning the city as a whole are to be increased. Any questions?"

Everyone shook their heads.

"Then let us get to work", and everyone was dismissed.

Little by little over the ensuing days, the provincial governors and the provincial military commanders who were summoned to the palace arrived. The last to come were the governor and regimental commander of West Ament, who had the furthest to travel. Once more, a meeting was called in the council room, and Khemshawre appraised them of the situation.

"I have cause to suspect that Lord Sekheperenre may have designs upon my kingdom", the king continued. "Khensu lies upon West Ament's southern door, and it would not be any difficulty for him to send his army marching northwards along the riverbank to invade that province. I therefore order that the entirety of West Ament is to ready itself for invasion. All of the city and town garrisons are to be on full alert. Colonel Djedkherure, you will immediately mobilize your regiment and have them ready to march at a moment's notice. I also want daily intelligence reports on whatever activities are occurring within Khensu, no matter how trivial they might appear. Understand?"

"Yes, Your Divine Majesty".

"To Lord Petifre and to the governors and military officers of East Ament and Sapmeh, you too are to make all preparations for a possible attack. Likewise, I expect daily reports from each of you on activities to the south. In particular, I want regular reports on whatever activities are occurring within the lands of Sapi-Res and Ka-Khem, since those lands are closest to yours".

Just then, there was a pounding on the closed door.

"What is it?!" demanded the king.

It was Horemheb. "Your Divine Majesty, news just arrived at the gates. Sekheperenre and his army have stormed the city of Iwnu and have seized possession of the whole province of Hekat".

The king stood silent for a few moments. "Thank you" was all he could say. Horemheb nodded, and left, closing the door behind him.

"Gentlemen, the situation has just become more urgent. Two provinces have fallen to this man in as many weeks, and there might be more. Return to your provinces immediately and carry out my instructions".

Everyone got up and left. Even Khemshawre left the room. Horemheb was outside the door waiting for him. "Your Divine Majesty, what is to be done?"

"I've given instructions to the lords and military commanders of the provinces to ready themselves for an attack. I'm to receive daily reports of Sekheperenre's activities. I will also send a message to Sekheperenre himself, ordering him to halt his advance".

"What about the envoys?"

"I haven't decided on who I'm going to send yet".

"No, Sire, the envoys, the emissaries from the east. They arrived two weeks ago and they've been sitting around the palace waiting for you to give them an answer about what they want".

"Oh, I had completely forgotten about them! I forgot they were even here! Summon the three of them to the throne room – I'll meet them in there".

In a couple of minutes, the four men were in the throne room. Curiously, the king was not seated upon the throne. The envoys found him pacing about in the hall. "Gentlemen, approach! I must speak with you at once".

The three men advanced, curious and expectant.

"Gentlemen", the king began, "you arrived in my court over two weeks ago requesting my assistance in various military ventures. I was not able to give you a decision at that time, and since then, I have kept you waiting. For that, I apologize, but I trust that your stay here has not been uncomfortable. Regrettably, due to recent developments, I must send each of you back to your lands empty-handed, without any promises of military aid on your behalf against your respective enemies. However, this much I will say to you. I am uncertain as to how much you are aware of what has been going on within these walls, but if you are ignorant as to all of this, some alarming news has come to my ear. Lord Sekheperenre, the most powerful warlord of Upper Egypt, who controls the cities of Ankh-Tawi, Giza, Dashur, and Saqqara, has invaded the Nile Delta and has conquered the provinces of Khensu and Hekat, and it appears that he will not stop there. Therefore gentlemen, I must advise the three of you to return to your lands immediately and make all preparations to repel a possible invasion. Gentlemen, you are dismissed".

The message given, the king promptly turned around and stormed out of the throne room, leaving the three eastern envoys stunned. But that reaction didn't last for long. In a few moments, their wits returned to them, and they hurried out of the palace as fast as they could.

As the three men hurried back to whence they came, King Khemshawre got onto his next task – composing a letter ordering Sekheperenre to stand down and advance no further beyond his present position, or else face military action. The letter needed to make its message keenly felt. A weak response to the recent developments betrayed a weak ruler and a weak military position. The message needed to have teeth to back it up. It needed to be stern, but not too stern. An inflammatory letter full of threats might have the opposite effect and goad Sekheperenre into attacking His Divine Majesty's lands anyway just to see if Nesu really was as tough as he claimed to be and to prove that even a living god was no match against his army.

*To Sekheperenre, lord of the province of Inebu-Hedj, and master of the cities of Ankh-Tawi, Giza, Dashur, and Saqqara:*

*News has lately come of your assault and conquest of the provinces of Khensu and Hekat, of the destruction of the capitals of those lands, and of the slaughter of their people. The advance of your army into the north has not gone un-noticed by myself and those who serve under me, nor has it escaped the notice of the free states of the eastern parts of the Nile Delta. Even now, all are readying themselves to stand against you, should you continue to press your army further northwards. You have advanced far enough. Stand your ground and march no further. If you persist and if you continue to send your army into lands beyond Khensu and Hekat, you will be opposed.*

*Nesu Horus-Khemshawre, Son of Ra, Horus Incarnate,*
*King of Lower Egypt*

With the message written, Khemshawre knew that he would need somebody to deliver the letter. He could not go himself, not without an entire army to protect him, and he did not want to send the whole of the Royal Army southwards against Sekheperenre, no matter how much the prospect secretly delighted him. Still, since the messenger would be travelling into hostile territory, that messenger would need an armed escort of adequate number to ensure that he entered and departed Sekheperenre's lands safely. The lord of Inebu-Hedj would not take kindly to being told "This far, and no further", and the king could not be certain of how severe his reaction would be. But who could he pick for such a dangerous mission? It had to be someone whose words and very presence carried weight, someone who commanded respect, yet someone who was also not inexpendable should the worst happen. One of the governors? No, he needed them to see to the administration of the provinces and to ready the provinces for defense. One of the regimental commanders? No, he needed them to take charge of their military forces and get ready to march at a moment's notice. One of the officials of the palace staff? Captain Nebikhamu? Horemheb? Kawaset? Maybe even Seshrab? No, none of them seemed suitable for the task he had in mind. After pondering this for some time, he finally had his answer. He began writing a second letter…

*To Lord Petifre, Governor of Ati, Lord-Mayor of the city of Busiris, and Vassal to His Divine Majesty Nesu Horus-Khemshawre:*

*As per the treaty which was signed by you vicariously through the hand of your envoy, I am your lord and you are my vassal. As such, you are given the freedom to govern your lands in any way that you see fit, and in exchange, you must pay homage to me as your overlord, and obey any tasks which I may give you. It is at this hour of decision that I have a task for you. It is my command that you are to journey into the lands held by Lord Sekheperenre and to deliver my message to him, which I shall give you. For your protection, you shall be accompanied by a large entourage of armed bodyguards. Lord Petifre, you are the strongest ruler of the central Delta. Your name is known and feared. You are a man that the other warlords respect, and I cannot think of anyone else better suited to act as my emissary in this circumstance than yourself. You are to demand that Sekheperenre give you an answer to my message then and there and not delay. Once his reply has been received, you are to return with all haste to Khaset City and report to me what his answer is.*

*Nesu Horus-Khemshawre, Son of Ra, Horus Incarnate,*
*King of Lower Egypt*

Lord Petifre had left not even half an hour ago – the messenger might still be able to catch him on the road back to Busiris. Khemshawre sent word to the governor of Khaset to select twenty strong, healthy, and well-trained men from the provincial regiment to gather together at the city armory, where they were to be fully armed and armored for combat and were to be kitted out for a long overland expedition to the south. Afterwards, they were to make their way to the city's gate to await the arrival of the king's messenger.

Next, Khemshawre picked out one of the palace pages, and told him to take the two letters and rush out and find Lord Petifre immediately, give him the two letters, and tell him to hurry back to Khaset City to link up with his armed escort, and from there on continue southwards to Lord Sekheperenre's lands.

It took a while, but the boy the king dispatched eventually found Lord Petifre on the eastern road. He was just about to board a ferry boat to cross over the river into Ati when the messenger ran up to him and grabbed him by the arm, and told him that he had come from the Perah and that the king needed him back at Khaset City at once. The boy handed Lord Petifre the two letters, stamped with Nesu's official scarab seal bearing his royal cartouche. Lord Petifre, who had been sent out of the Perah to warn the people of his province that war might be coming, asked the ferry captain for a piece of paper, a pen, and ink, but the ferry captain didn't have any. Exasperated, he went to all of the nearby huts asking the local riverside peasants for paper, ink, and a pen, but none of them were any help.

Finally, he spotted a merchant leading a caravan of three donkeys laden with satchels of goods tied to their backs. Lord Petifre ran up to him and hurriedly asked the man if he had any paper.

"Yes", he said, "but only a few sheets".

"Just give me one! I only need one! Give it to me! And ink, do you have ink?"

"Yes", the man responded. "I'm on my way to do business in the market".

"I need to borrow this for a moment".

The man was about to protest at having his goods wrenched from him, but this fellow was dressed like a nobleman and he seemed to be either desperate or crazy. "Keep the damn thing! I'll buy another one!" and the merchant got himself and his caravan out of there as fast as possible. Heaven knows what this lunatic might do!

After Lord Petifre finished frantically scribbling out his note with a piece of straw that he found, he handed it to the ferry operator. "Take this letter immediately to the city of Busiris. Deliver this note *IN PERSON* to my steward at the governor's palace in Busiris – he'll know what to do. He must get this letter, it's very important!

Here, take this as payment", and he pulled off both of his golden bracelets and handed them to the man. With that done, Lord Petifre turned around and hurried back along the road to Khaset City to meet up with his military escort.

The ferry boat operator, who couldn't read or write, had no inkling of what the letter said. He was very poor, business was shaky, and his day-to-day livelihood was precarious. He was usually paid in grain or salt for his services. Gold was a rare and exotic thing to behold in his hand. Paper didn't sparkle in the sun, but gold certainly did. Paper was worthless to him, but gold wasn't. With glee, he stuffed the two golden bracelets in a burlap sack and shoved it under the prow. Then, he casually flung the hastily-written note into the river and for a second or two watched it float downstream. After all, paper was worth nothing.

Back at the Perah, King Khemshawre was eventually informed from the returning page that he had found Lord Petifre and delivered the two letters to him, that he had returned back to Khaset City, and had left soon afterwards for the south accompanied by the armed guards that His Divine Majesty had waiting for him. Khemshawre was relieved. Things had been moving very fast, but now he felt like he was getting a handle on things. Lord Petifre was a strong-willed authoritative man. The other eastern warlords respected him and made sure to stay on his good side. If anybody could talk Sekheperenre down from continuing his northward advance, it would be him.

Several weeks went by, and there was no word. True to the king's command, the provincial governors had been sending daily intelligence reports to the Perah on the condition of the nearby territories, but all of them stated that there was nothing out of the ordinary. Khemshawre breathed a sigh of relief. *Perhaps it's done*, he thought. *Lord Petifre delivered my letter, he gave his speech, and Sekheperenre backed down. That's that. It's finished.*

Still, Lord Petifre should have been back by now. His absence was becoming worrisome. Khemshawre was at a loss as to what could be delaying him for so long.

And then, one day…

"Your Divine Majesty, a messenger has arrived at the palace, carrying a package and a note. He comes from the court of Lord Sekheperenre".

As soon as those words left his mouth, there was heard a commotion in the palace. There were shouts, yells, and screams.

"What is that?! What is all that noise about?!" the king demanded, and he went out into the halls to see what the problem was. There were armed guards rushing through the halls towards where the noise was coming from.

Eventually, they encountered some people coming from the place. Several looked disgusted and sickened. "Oh gods, it's horrible! Horrible!" one of them called out.

The king and his guards soon became aware of a faint fetid odor emanating from the direction of the Perah's reception hall. Khemshawre knew that odor very well. He had spent enough time on the battlefield to know *exactly* what that smell was. They entered the reception hall to see a crowd of people arranged tightly in a circle. They were all looking down at something, but the king couldn't see what it was from where he was standing.

"Make way! Make way! Make some room!" the guards called out, pushing people out of the way as the king approached.

And then he saw it.

It was a large box made from cartonnage, a storage box, an ark, the sort that was used mainly for carrying grain or salt. But the box felt unusually light. Even so, there was clearly something inside – the people who took it from the messenger could hear something knocking around in there. The box had been fastened shut with twine wrapped around it, and a small note was stuck underneath the cording with the words *For Nesu's Eyes Only* written on it.

Despite the package being addressed to the king personally, Horemheb, Chamberlain of the Palace, had gotten inquisitive and opened it, and immediately gasped with horror. There were other people nearby who shrieked when they saw the box's contents.

Khemshawre recognized it – the hair, the features, the eyes. The glazed cloudy dead eyes.

Inside the box was the decapitated head of Lord Petifre resting upon a pile of twenty severed hands. Also within the box were two letters: one was torn in half, and the other was intact and tied with string. Upon closer inspection, the two ripped pieces of paper were the left and right halves of the letter that King Khemshawre had written addressed to Lord Sekheperenre ordering him to stand down. The king then retrieved the other letter, pulled off the string, and unfurled it…

*I, Nesu Sekheperenre, King of Lower Egypt, received your late embassy demanding obedience to your will. Your demands are refused. Your lacky, Lord Petifre of Ati, is not anyone I fear, for no living man has cause to fear a dead man. You have sent armed troops into my lands, and they are now food for vultures and jackals. Your spies have been uncovered by my spies and have all been arrested and put to death. I lead a great and mighty host, and I have conquered many lands. I have added Khensu and Hekat to my realm, and my generals have lately taken Ka-Khem and Sapi-Res. I shall add the lands of all who oppose me to my domain. Submit, and you will be my servant. Resist, and you shall see the last of your days.*

# CHAPTER 15

*Word soon arrived in the royal palace of Khaset City that the emissaries of His Divine Majesty had all been put to death, and that Sekheperenre had taken possession of the provinces of Ka-Khem and Sapi-Res. Finally, Sekheperenre challenged Nesu's power by claiming that he, not Horus-Khemshawre, was the true king of Lower Egypt. Following Sekheperenre's false declaration of power, His Divine Majesty declared that Sekheperenre was an enemy of the king, and prepared for war.*

War.

It was the one word that nobody living in Khaset City wanted to hear. Once more, the dreaded sounds of battle would be ringing in people's ears. With the coronation of His Divine Majesty, and with a renewed focus on civil affairs and diplomacy, many had hoped that they would be free from the sound of marching regiments, at least for a while. But it was not to be. The enemy had other ideas.

During the Second Dark Age, war was the norm and peace was the exception. The fighting had been going on for the past ninety years, and despite everyone's high hopes for peace, it didn't look like the fighting was ever going to stop. In Egypt, entire generations had been born and died in these turbulent fiery times. This was all that they knew. This was the way things were. It was the way that they *always* were. It was the normal way of the world.

The great warrior king of the north, Nesu Khemshawre, had also grown up in this world. He had been born and raised in combat. He had gone on campaign with his father since he was a child. He had been fighting battles since he was 14. He had been commanding entire armies since his late 20s. He and his beloved troops of the Royal Army of Lower Egypt had fought in more battles than he could remember. He himself had long ago stopped keeping count of the hundreds of people that he had personally butchered and slaughtered with his own hands. And yet, for all of his battlefield prowess, Khemshawre had hoped, perhaps naively, that it didn't always have to be this way. He had big plans for his royal realm once he became a living god. The regiments would stand down, the soldiers would be sent back home to tend to their families, houses, and farms, and His Divine Majesty would place a greater emphasis on civil affairs rather than military affairs. The crook of care was just as important as the flail of wrath, but most of the great and powerful within Egypt only seemed to be interested in the second option.

Now, against his hopes, Khemshawre was compelled to once again call upon his brave martial sons to defend the royal realm. Lord Sekheperenre had defied His Divine Majesty's will. He had advanced into Lower Egypt and had taken control of several border provinces despite Khemshawre's clear warning to back off. He had cruelly slain Khemshawre's emissary Lord Petifre and all of his bodyguards. Finally, Sekheperenre had boldly challenged Nesu's right to rule and had dared to declare himself to be northern Egypt's true master. There was no going back from this. Sekheperenre needed to be destroyed.

In theory, the Royal Army of Lower Egypt numbered 8,400 men plus an additional number of Atian allies. In reality, it only numbered a fraction of that size. His Divine Majesty had ordered that the ranks were to be replenished with replacement troops, but that would take time. He had likewise ordered that a new regiment was to be created and manned to defend the westernmost province of West Ament, but again, that would take time. And now, war was once again on the horizon. There was no more time.

Word of what had happened to Lord Petifre, of Sekheperenre's defiance, of the conquests made by his troops, and of his threats to conquer the kingdom of Lower Egypt and place the cobra-headed *nemes* crown upon his head quickly percolated out of the rooms and hallways of the Perah and into the remainder of the royal palace complex. Like a perverse osmosis of terror, it soon spread from there to the general population of Khaset City. Afterwards, it wasn't long before everybody in Khaset Province knew of what had happened.

Panic.

The people knew all too well what was entailed in the ominous threat of Lord Sekheperenre's army. The coming war would not be fought on some distant far-off battlefield on the frontier. Instead, the coming battles would be fought through the farms, villages, towns, and cities of the royal realm, and the three martial muses of fire, destruction, and slaughter would rage in all their revelry.

Within the halls and chambers of the royal palace in Khaset City, the atmosphere was hectic and frantic. Reports were coming in from all quarters on the whereabouts and activities of Sekheperenre's army, of the number and disposition of the king's own forces, of supplies and provisions, of the best avenues for advance and retreat, and of the best places for attack and defense. Finally, preparations were being hastily made to fortify the city and even the royal palace itself in the event of a siege, the fear of which, although no one dared think of it, was continuously gnawing at their stomachs.

Within the Perah's conference room, the same room that so many war cabinet meetings were held, King Khemshawre met with his military officers, intelligence agents, and civilian dignitaries about what was to be done. Seshrab was present, recording the minutes. The king's two pet greyhounds, white Osiris and black Set, sat on the floor beside him, alert and uneasy. They might not have been able to grasp what exactly was going on, but they knew that it was causing their master immense worry, and they wanted to be there for him. Despite the urgent air of the meeting, Khemshawre was grateful for their company.

"The siege began two days ago", said one of the men. "The city was caught unprepared and didn't have sufficient time to bring in all of its stores for a prolonged siege. But Busiris is a formidable stronghold. Its walls and towers are sturdy, and the city is defended by a sizeable garrison of troops. It will require much work on Sekheperenre's part to break through. However, outnumbered as they are, and with the immense forces that Sekheperenre has brought to bear on them, it will only be a matter of time before the city falls".

"How much time?" asked the king.

The man shrugged. "Two or three weeks. Maybe four at most, but certainly not more than that".

"I wish to state also", said another man, "that Sekheperenre invested the city with only part of his army, while the remainder of his troops pushed through the provinces of Ka-Khem and Sapi-Res. Once these separate forces rendezvous at Busiris, Sekheperenre's total strength will be perhaps three times as great as that which currently has the city besieged. Once these forces link up, loss will be assured".

"Sire, a treaty was signed between us and Ati. Ati is your vassal, and you are required to come to their aid. We can't sit and wait for Sekheperenre's forces to be depleted from a prolonged siege. As we just heard, the siege is not likely to last that long, and Sekheperenre will almost assuredly crush Busiris within a week or two".

"We need to attack Sekheperenre *now* before the remainder of his troops arrive on the scene", said Colonel Ankharis, the commander of the king's Sapmeh Regiment. "If we attack him now with everything we've got, we have a chance. We can knock out Sekheperenre's various contingents one-by-one. However, if we delay, then that will give him time to gather his forces, and defeating him in open battle will be next to impossible".

"Even as we are now, we don't have enough troops available to immediately take the offensive", said King Khemshawre. "Most of my veterans were lost at Yamu. The majority of the men who now march under my banner are untrained raw recruits who know barely anything of warfare. The troops of the Khaset Regiment are insufficient to send off to the front. We will need to gather our forces together to take the offensive against Sekheperenre, but that will take time. I've already dispatched messages to the governors and commanders of East Ament and West Ament to send whatever troops they have, but it will take days for them to come here".

"Sire, we need troops in the field right now! Today!" urged Colonel Ankharis. "The sooner we can put an army on the march, the better. We need more men, every available hand".

"I have dispatched a runner to the court of King Wahibre of Upper Egypt in the city of Lisht. It will take time for him to get there, since Lisht is far behind enemy lines and he must evade capture by Sekheperenre's forces. Wahibre is Sekheperenre's lord and master, and Sekheperenre is his vassal. He is duty-bound to obey his king's word. My brother-king of the south and I have an agreement with each other. We both acknowledge each other as the rulers of our realms, and there is mutual respect between us. Sekheperenre may not have listened to me, but I am hopeful that Wahibre's word carries more weight with him. I have also dispatched a messenger westwards into the lands of the Imukeheku tribe, to the great camp of Chief Bokhor. He is my vassal, and likewise so are all of his people. If I call upon him for aid, he is required to obey. I expect him to bring several hundred or even a thousand of his warriors to fight on our behalf".

"Can we trust the barbarians to keep their word?" asked Horemheb, Chamberlain of the Palace. "They are still bitter about the losses which our army inflicted upon them that day, and of forcing their chief to submit to you. If you send them a message calling upon them for help, they would think it fitting to refuse to come and let us suffer for it".

"Or worse, they might even be tempted to join with Sekheperenre and fight on his side!" said Colonel Ankharis.

"Yes, I've considered that", said the king. "The troops from West Ament have been standing guard upon the western border to protect those lands against the barbarians should they become hostile again. I hesitate to recall them to fight with me, and thereby leave our western border undefended. I need to keep the West Ament Regiment in place until I can be assured of the Libyans' compliance. That leaves only the troops from East Ament, Sapmeh, and Khaset Provinces available.

I've sent word across the northern fringe of the Delta towards the lands of the eastern warlords. They were entreating me earlier with overtures of friendship, so let's see if they are willing to now come to a friend's aid. I have told them that Sekheperenre is bent on being master of the entire Nile Delta, which means that their lands, too, are in jeopardy and likewise so are their lives. Hopefully, the threat of a common enemy will be enough to join in a common cause against a common threat".

"It's also equally possible, Sire", said Colonel Ankharis, "that Sekheperenre may sway them to become his vassals and subjects with the promise that they can remain in their offices, with all of the perks and privileges that this entails. If we can dispatch messengers asking the eastern warlords to join our side, then so can he. In the meantime, we must wait for their reply? And for the Libyans' reply? And for King Wahibre's reply as well? We wait and wait for an answer which either may or may not come? Meanwhile, the situation in Busiris becomes ever-more desperate, and Sekheperenre becomes ever-more stronger. We have to launch an offensive right now while there's still time. Give the order, Your Divine Majesty. Order me to the front! Order me to take my regiment to Busiris and attack Sekheperenre's army. Give me leave to destroy their supply and communication lines, destroy their food stocks, and cut off all hope of reinforcement".

"Your so-called 'regiment', Colonel, which formerly numbered 2,000 troops, now barely numbers 500 men. If you take your regiment against Sekheperenre's host alone, your defeat and your deaths will be assured. Even if I dispatch all of the troops under my command today, it still won't be enough. As much as it pains me to say it, we are not as strong as we used to be. We need reinforcements, we need the Libyans, we need the eastern warlords, we need every man". The king then took in a deep breath. "So it therefore seems that I have no other choice but to issue a drastic order – *full mobilization via forced conscription.* Every adult male from teenager to elder will be forcibly inducted into the Army whether they like it or not. They are to take hold of whatever weapons that they can get. The armories will be emptied out, every spear, shield, dagger, javelin, mace, axe, bow, and arrow will be parceled out to the men. Even so, it still won't be enough. Some of them will have to carry makeshift weapons into combat: pitchforks, sickles, shovels, hammers, wooden clubs, even kitchen knives strapped onto the ends of broom handles. I understand, gentlemen, how desperate this is, but these are desperate times, and we cannot afford to neglect military necessity for the sake of personal appearance or humiliation".

The men gathered there seemed to understand.

"Gentlemen, unless there is anything further to discuss, let us be about our business. Chief Scribe?"

"Yes, Your Divine Majesty?"

"Draft a decree ordering full mobilization of the adult male population for immediate military service. Any male who no longer bears his sidelock-of-youth must serve in the Army effective immediately. Once that decree is made, I will sign it, and copies will be distributed through all of the provinces which I rule over. Half of the conscripts are to remain behind to defend the provinces against attack by Sekheperenre's troops, the other half are to rendezvous at Khaset City immediately to receive armor and weapons. Understood?"

"Yes, Your Divine Majesty".

"But in the meantime, Your Divine Majesty", said Colonel Ankharis, "what do we do *now*?"

Khemshawre stared. "Unfortunately, Colonel, in the meantime, we cannot do anything".

On the same day that Lord Petifre and his bodyguards were ruthlessly and perfidiously butchered, Sekheperenre dispatched two of his battle-captains to separately take one-third of his troops and take possession of the border provinces of Ka-Khem and Sapi-Res. He himself would lead the remaining third against the province of Ati, with the goal of capturing the city of Busiris. Busiris was a great prize, one of the largest and most well-fortified cities in Lower Egypt, and it was located near the Nile Delta's exact center. Ideally, the city would be captured intact, and it would be used as a springboard for launching offensives elsewhere throughout Lower Egypt. However, if the city had to be destroyed, oh well, then so be it.

Ka-Khem and Sapi-Res fell quickly. The defending armies of the local warlords were defeated and the survivors of the slaughter were forcibly inducted into Sekheperenre's army. With every victory, the fires spread, the bodies piled higher, and the number of troops which he commanded became greater. No one within the kingdom of Lower Egypt knew precisely how large Sekheperenre's force was, but everyone was convinced that it was just as large, if not larger, than the Royal Army of Lower Egypt.

The province of Ati was invaded the day that Lord Petifre's decapitated head arrived in the royal court in Khaset City. Sekheperenre's army, which he personally commanded, swept up the length of the province as quickly as possible through forced marches, sacking and plundering every village that they passed by and forcibly conscripting the peasant population to serve as slave labor. Within a day,

Sekheperenre's army appeared outside of the provincial capital city of Busiris. The city was well-fortified with impressive stone walls and towers. Assaulting the city would be unnecessarily costly in lives, so Sekheperenre resolved to surround the city and lay siege to it, starving it into submission. In Egypt's hot climate, food and fresh drinking water would be more valuable to the besieged inhabitants than gold.

Before the siege began, a messenger was speedily dispatched out of Busiris across the border into Khaset Province, and he informed King Khemshawre of what was happening. Ati was the king's vassal, under the king's protection, and he was duty-bound to come to its aid. He dispatched messengers to Nesu Wahibre, King of Upper Egypt, urging him to order Sekheperenre to halt his attacks. He sent messengers to the western Libyans ordering them to furnish all of their warriors to come and fight alongside his army. He sent messengers to the eastern warlords of the Nile Delta urging them to join hands in defense against a common enemy who was hell-bent on their conquest and destruction. All the while, Busiris suffered while looking desperately to the western horizon to catch sight of the glorious regiments of the Royal Army of Lower Egypt marching to their rescue.

But days passed, and there was nothing. The siege dragged on, the casualties increased, the defenses were weakening, and the supplies of food, medicine, and clean water were running low. Most dis-hearteningly of all, there was no sight of the Royal Army.

For His Divine Majesty, waiting in his palace chambers, there was also no word. None of his letters had been answered, and the silence was maddening. Yet for Colonel Ankharis, the commander of the Sapmeh Regiment, who had been pacing back and forth in the palace for days, what was even more maddening was standing around and doing nothing. Peasant levies had been drifting into Khaset City in drips and drops ever since his king's decree was issued declaring full mobilization. Many of them had never held weapons before. Their training was quick and rudimentary, teaching them only the absolute bare basics. The longer the delay in sending them to the front, the more they could be trained, and likewise the better odds they had of surviving. However, the longer they delayed, the more likely Sekheperenre would assemble the full might of his army and crush Busiris by storm, and when that happened, there would be nothing stopping him from crossing the border into Nesu's kingdom, and then the Royal Army would be entirely on the defensive. The Royal Army needed to attack now, *right now*, while there was still time. Once again, Colonel Ankharis went to his king entreating him, begging him, even *demanding* that he launch an offensive.

"No, Colonel! The Royal Army is not numerous enough or strong enough to go on the offensive!" Khemshawre boomed. "I lost many of my best troops at Yamu. I have raw untrained draftees standing in the ranks now, men who barely know how to march in step and stand straight in formation, never mind knowing how to handle weapons or knowing anything of tactics or strategy. If we send them off to the front now, they'll be massacred, and then there will be no one left to defend the provinces or the capital when Sekheperenre launches his offensive against us. We have to stage a progressive delaying action, stalling for time, giving ground little-by-little so that we can create the breathing room for reinforcements to assemble and come to our aid. Then, and only then, our combined forces can go on the offensive against Sekheperenre's rebel army".

"But that will take weeks, maybe months, and in the meantime the situation will have become worse. And who knows if the reinforcements are even coming?! Have you heard *anything* from the Libyans? Or from the eastern warlords? Have you received any messages from King Wahibre ordering Lord Sekheperenre to stand down? And even if the king of the south were to issue such an order, who's to say that Sekheperenre would even listen to him? King Wahibre barely maintains control of just one single town, you control four entire provinces. If Sekheperenre refused to heed *your* warning, then he's certainly not going to heed his!"

"Enough! We must wait for more men! We cannot launch an attack yet. I must gather more troops, and that will take time. I decide when we march, not you!"

More days passed, and there was nothing. Then, a messenger was brought to the palace – a Libyan. He was brought under armed guard, and the men who stood on either side of him were clearly not happy about being there.

"Your Divine Majesty", one of the men spoke, "this barbarian was sent to Yamu to speak with the governor of West Ament. The governor ordered this man to be brought under guard to speak with you directly". Now he turned to the tattooed long-haired man. "Tell him! Tell your king, your lord and master, what you told the governor!"

The man hesitated. At this, King Khemshawre, growing aggravated and impatient, grabbed the man by the throat while his two dogs Osiris and Set snarled and growled. "Tell me what do you have to say", Nesu demanded.

"Great king", he choked out, "I must report…that…due to difficulties, the Imukeheku cannot stand with you against the pretender Sekheperenre".

"Difficulties?! What difficulties?! I ordered you! I commanded you! What possible 'difficulties' could you be facing to prevent obedience to my will?!"

"Sire, we face hunger. The harvest has been poor, and there aren't enough men to bring in the few crops. We are under attack by our neighbors, the Sepedu and the Esbetu. Our calamities are so numerous that—".

Unable to listen any more, Khemshawre smacked this man hard across his face. The dogs barked and snarled. "What is the *REAL* reason?!" Khemshawre yelled. "What is the true reason why my orders were disobeyed. You will tell me now!"

"My lord, I have already said!" quavered out the man's voice as he lay on the floor, the armed men around him bracing their clasped hands on their dagger handles.

Khemshawre reached down and once more grabbed the man by his neck and forcibly lifted him up to his feet. "Answer me, or I shall snap your neck right now!"

"THEY WERE PAID OFF!!!"

Khemshawre paused. "Who paid them?"

The man was silent.

"*WHO PAID THEM?!*"

"*…Sekheperenre…*"

Khemshawre flung the man back to the ground. "Send this serpent back to the hole that he crawled out of!"

Later that same day, Khemshawre received more bad news. A letter arrived from the court of King Wahibre, King of Upper Egypt. The king of the south refused to render assistance to his "brother king of the north". Sekheperenre was his vassal, and he would not wage war upon his vassal.

"The reinforcements are not coming!" said Colonel Ankharis. "King Wahibre is sitting on his hands, and the Libyans have turned their backs on us! The eastern warlords refuse to send any help. They're on the fence waiting to see who emerges victorious, and they will only pledge their support to the winning side. We cannot delay any longer! Reinforcements or not, we have to attack *NOW!* Stay behind and see to the defenses if you wish, gather up the stocks and stores, assemble whatever troops you can and ready yourselves for a long defensive campaign. But know I intend to attack, and if you will not take the offensive, then I will! Give me command of the army! Put the new recruits and the draftees under my direction. You say we don't have enough soldiers? You give me the peasants, and I will *make* them soldiers, one way or another!"

Khemshawre couldn't help but grin. He could hear his father's voice in the fury of this man's throat. *Boldness, always boldness,* Colonel Ankharis used to say. Defense was never in Ankharis' nature. *Forwards, ever forwards.* "My father did very well to make you one of his officers – the Lion of Sapmeh. Very well. We will march to the front and relieve the siege of Busiris. Bring over the Sapmeh Regiment to Khaset City, along with all of the peasant levies that you can take. I will personally lead the Khaset Regiment. Choose amongst the battle-captains within your regiment who shall be best-suited to command the conscripts. Teach them everything that they need to know in the little time that they have between now and the coming battle. We march to the front tomorrow".

Colonel Ankharis smiled.

# CHAPTER 16

*After being abandoned by all of his allies in his hour of need, King Khemshawre mustered his army and marched against Lord Sekheperenre to relieve the siege of Busiris, the capital city of His Divine Majesty's vassal the lord of Ati. There, upon the field before that mighty city, a great and terrible battle was fought...a battle which cost His Divine Majesty greatly.*

The soldiers, torn, bandaged, and bloodied, raced back and forth loading up their pack donkeys, shouting and cursing to work faster. All unnecessary objects and hinderances were cast aside in heaps to speed their travel. They had to get out of there *now* before Sekheperenre's troops finished looting and plundering and came back to end what they had started earlier that day. King Khemshawre, battered and bruised, gazed around him in shock, disbelieving what he was seeing around him. All the while, towering billowing black smoke rose out of the fiery ruins of the city of Busiris.

"Do you think he surrendered?" asked one soldier to another.

"Are you crazy?", his comrade replied. "Colonel Ankharis would *never* surrender!"

"Stop your chattering and get back to work!" barked their captain, one of the few officers who had survived. "They'll be on us any minute! Toss that junk over the side and burn it so that they don't get their hands on it! Move!"

The river crossing back into Khaset Province had been a miserable affair. Despite the best efforts of the men to stay calm in the face of looming danger, there was a lot of noise and scared voices as they shoved and pushed into each other, they shouted and cursed, and men slipped and fell into the river and had to be pulled out. Their hap-hazard conduct in trying to get into the boats and push them off the shore would have been comedic were it not for the seriousness of the situation. The king stood powerless as he watched all of this. He knew it was hopeless to say anything to them to get their heads together. Fear had gotten hold of them. A king, not even a god on earth, can simply order fear to go away.

Finally, the entire royalist force was back across the river and were now within the province of Khaset. Despite the fact that they had been up for over twenty-four hours without any sleep, a combination of fear and adrenaline kept them awake. Now they had to get back to Khaset City as quickly as possible and ready the capital's defenses. Word soon got around amongst the nearby riverside villages that *Nesu's* army had returned, and it certainly did not look triumphant.

"Is that the last of them? Are all of the men and supplies across?" Khemshawre asked one of his surviving officers.

"Yes, Your Divine Majesty", he replied.

"Good. Destroy the boats. I will not allow Sekheperenre any means across the river". He turned once again to his men. "Spread this message throughout the province", commanded King Khemshawre to his officers. "The enemy approaches. Abandon your homes and possessions, carrying with you only whatever weapons and provisions that you can, and seek shelter within the walls of Khaset City, and there you shall be protected. Go now!"

The officers saluted and then raced off, barking out orders to their subordinates and their relay runners.

In truth, Khemshawre had no intention of protecting these people. What he really wanted was to quickly augment the size of his army so that it could at least marginally compete against Sekheperenre's vast host. The men who had been left behind when His Divine Majesty marched out to confront the great pretender had been the very old, the very young, or those who were physically unable to march or fight. Now, Khemshawre would need to call upon even these poor souls to aid him in his hour of need. The enemy would surely come any day. In fact, they were probably even now following the retreating soldiers' trail.

Khemshawre couldn't afford to grant his men any time to sleep. Once everyone was across the river, they had to keep moving, and despite their weariness and battlefield wounds, they moved at a brisk pace. Moving as fast as their legs could carry them, they made their way northwards to the capital. Everywhere that they went, they spread the word to the villagers to join them at the capital to make their stand against Sekheperenre's army.


Back at Khaset City, Seshrab had not accompanied the army on its march into Ati. He had been ordered by His Divine Majesty to remain behind and take part in the organization of the palace's defenses, should the worst come to pass. Seshrab had been very busy while the army was away working with the palace staff to ensure that it was secure in the event of an attack. All of this was done under the direction of Queen Neferet. With the king gone, she was the one in charge, and although she wouldn't dare say it out loud, there was a part of her which hoped that he'd never come back.

Command came easier to her than it did for other women of her station. Her husband and his father were frequently gone on campaign, leaving either her or her older sister Meret running the palace's affairs. The two of them enjoyed these respites from their husbands' presence, and after Nebsenre's assassination there was only his son that they'd have to face.

Seshrab marveled at how both Queen Neferet and her sister handled themselves in a time of crisis. "Your Majesty, forgive me if I may sound impertinent or insolent", he began, "but you conduct yourself admirably in the face of danger".

"Thank you, Chief Scribe", replied Queen Neferet. "After all, I am the daughter of one king and the wife of another, and a queen should be seen to be steadfast, especially in seeing to her home. The kingdom may belong to the king, but the palace belongs to the queen. The man rules the family, but the woman rules the house".

Seshrab laughed out loud. "Yes, I know! I remember when I heard that old expression for the first time, when I visited a fisherman's hut near Giza. He may have been the patriarch of his household, but within the four walls of their home, his wife was the undisputed lord and master".

"Is that the same in your homeland in Canaan?"

"No, hardly! In Canaan, the man is master. Women simply do what they're told".

Queen Neferet cast Seshrab a look. "How terrible", she intoned.

"Well, not so terrible", Seshrab replied. "The man is expected to take care of everything. Every decision is his, and the blame and punishments for making bad decisions are also his alone to face. He's expected to do everything for his family and provide for them in every way. Their salvation rests entirely on his shoulders. If all goes well, nobody praises him, because he's doing merely what a man is expected to do. But if he neglects his family, or if he fails to provide for them and protect them, then he's spat on for being an incompetent dolt. A marriage can get broken up if the woman asserts that her husband has not lived up to his duties and responsibilities, leaving him with nothing. Being a patriarch isn't all that it's cracked up to be".

Queen Neferet smirked. "Indeed. You yourself don't seem to be the *incompetent* sort. No, you look like you handle yourself very well".

Seshrab wasn't sure what to say. "You...you *flatter* me, Your Majesty".

"It wasn't meant to be flattery, merely an observation", she replied. "You've been employed in the palace for some time. Nearly a year, I think. We have all seen how you carry yourself here, how you handle the tasks assigned to you, and how you cope with things which are unpleasant. If what you say is true about the men of Canaan, and I have no reason to doubt you, for you would never be so foolish as to lie to me, then I think that you would do very well as the head of your household. You are intelligent, capable, clever, and kind. Any woman would be grateful to have a man such as yourself as her husband".

Seshrab openly blushed. "Thank you, Your Majesty".

"Enough chatter, you two!", chimed in Neferet's older sister ex-Queen Meret. "We were told to prepare for the worst, and there's still a lot of work to be done. This is not the first time that my house has been threatened, but I pray to the gods that it's the last".

"Yes, yes I have delayed long enough", said Seshrab. "I must continue overseeing the preparation for the defenses" and he went off to attend to business. Queen Neferet watched him as he departed.

She turned back to see her older sister Meret sternly scowling at her. "Stop", said Meret gravely. "Stop it now".

"What?"

"Do you think I'm blind? I see the way that you look at him. Even *he* does, but like you said, he's a very smart young man, and he's smart enough to know that your thoughts are dangerous. If you're entertaining any *notions* in that head of yours, put them out of your mind now. We live in a hard world in a hard time. Members of royalty don't last long here. Indeed, it's nothing short of miraculous that the two of us survived as long as we have".

"We weren't always royalty" countered Queen Neferet. "Remember that we were commoners, too, before our father became King".

"Well we aren't commoners anymore", replied Meret, "and with an increased station come increased expectations, and we are expected to carry ourselves with at least an outward showing of dignity. That means you play the part of a loving dutiful wife, no matter how detestable the thought is to you. You have a daughter to think of, just as I must always think of my son. Whatever I do, I do for his sake, just as you will do what you must for her sake. Think of your daughter the next time you're entertaining ideas of secret dalliances with one of the king's servants. How will your little girl fare in this world after her mother gets her throat slit for treason?"

Queen Neferet didn't have an answer.

Ever since the king left with the forces under his command to relieve the enemy's siege of Busiris, people in the palace and in the city had been uneasy. This wasn't like the king's grand campaign into West Ament the previous year when the Royal Army marched off with great pomp and celebration, flanked on either side of the main highway by cheering crowds. Nor was it like the king's audacious maritime expedition where he and his men marched north to the seacoast, boarded ship, and sailed off to the westernmost parts of Canaan to defeat King Sihon. When the boats cast off from the piers, the local dock workers and fishermen hailed the king and his men as they embarked for unknown shores. This time it was different. The departure of the army for Ati, to come to the aid of the king's vassal and relieve the siege of Busiris, was not marked by cheering crowds and waving pennants. The few people who stood by the roadside to watch these untested soldiers being led off to battle were silent and sullen. Perhaps, inwardly and secretly, they knew what was going to happen. Drafting the entire adult male population into the military was a desperate stop-gap measure to make up the short-fall in numbers, but Khemshawre had spent enough time on campaign to know that there were great risks in sending raw untrained peasants off to the front. He knew full-well from hard-learned experience that most of them would not survive their first battle.

Word reached Khaset City of the army's return even before the army had been spotted. In time, the townspeople saw the battered smashed remains of the king's troops returning up the main north-south highway through the vast fields of grape vineyards. The men were bedraggled and fear-stricken, and interspersed amongst them were crowds of civilian refugees carrying whatever personal possessions that they could haul on their backs or carry in baskets and bags. They all had nervous, anxious, worried expressions. Some of them were calling out for family and friends who had become separated in the crowd, some were praying, and others were crying. They were accompanied by whatever precious livestock that they could take with them – a few goats, a few geese, and maybe one or two donkeys here and there. The messages that came into the city were alarming. "The army is lost! Great *Nesu* retreats, and the enemy advances! Withdraw within the walls of Khaset City and beg the gods for your lives!"

As the troops made their way up the road towards the capital through the vast sea of grape vines, battered and bleeding, tired and exhausted but still shuffling forwards in a forced hurry, Seshrab heard the calls from within the palace. He rushed out to see the army returning as a mangled mess. The number of men who came back was far smaller than the number that had left. By Seshrab's quick estimate, only about one-third or one-quarter of the men had returned. It was difficult to gauge the exact number, though, because the troops were mixed up helter-skelter with the civilian refugees.

"Where's the rest of them?" Seshrab wondered aloud. "Where's the rest of the army? Where's the rest of the army?" he called out to the troops who passed by, but nobody paid any attention to him. Finally, he physically grabbed one of the soldiers, a shell-shocked fellow with a bloodied bandage wrapped around his head and with one arm limply hanging in a hastily-improvised sling, and demanded to him "What happened?! Tell me what happened?!".

"We *lost*, that's what happened" came the reply.

"Lost?! We were *slaughtered!*" responded another.

"We were outnumbered and out-matched. Damned levies turned their backs and ran. It was a massacre".

"Colonel Ankharis of the Sapmeh Regiment was killed. He took some troops and led them on a suicidal charge against the enemy lines to allow the rest of us time to escape".

"Make your peace with the gods, sir. You'll be seeing them soon. We all will", and they walked by.

Finally, Seshrab saw the king himself in the middle of the column. "Sire! Your Divine Majesty!" Seshrab called out and ran up to him.

Khemshawre didn't stop walking. "What are you doing here?" he demanded in a low voice.

Seshrab was taken aback by the king's stern tone. He hadn't heard His Divine Majesty talk this way in some time.

"You're supposed to be inside the palace working with the rest of the staff on preparing the defenses".

"Yes, I was doing that, Your Divine Majesty", replied Seshrab, keeping pace, "but I heard the commotion and I wanted to see what was happening".

"What's happening is that, for the first time in my life, I *lost* a battle. Within only a few days, or perhaps as soon as tomorrow, Khaset City will be under siege, and we must be ready for when they arrive".

"Sire, Colonel Mebydos of the East Ament Regiment arrived with his troops at the capital shortly after you left. He wants to know what you want him to do".

"Where is Colonel Mebydos now?"

"He's in the Perah".

"Good. I need to talk to him immediately".

The king and Seshrab entered the Perah and saw the place enveloped in an atmosphere of desperate confusion. Captain Nebikhamu was waiting for him at the door. The king's two greyhounds Osiris and Set were also waiting eagerly for their master to come home. They were whimpering, and they even tried licking his bruises as he walked.

"Your Divine Majesty", began Capt. Nebikhamu, "the full contingent of guards has been posted to permanent watch. Sufficient stores have been brought inside the palace. Windows are being barricaded shut. I've been giving the staff some training in the handling of weapons. The kitchen workers and the repairmen seem to have taken to it rather well, but the others are having a hard time getting to grips with things".

"They'll need to learn fast. The enemy approaches now. The city will be under attack any day. Assemble all of the palace staff in the throne room for an emergency meeting. And send for Colonel Mebydos, my wife, and her sister".

"Yes, Sire, immediately", and Captain Nebikhamu rushed about in and out of all of the halls shouting. "Pass the word, emergency meeting in the throne room! Emergency meeting in the throne room!"

Little by little, the palace staff came into the great colonnaded hall – the high-ranking officials, the subordinates, the lowly servants. Colonel Mebydos, Queen Neferet, and former Queen Meret were there as well. There was a great amount of commotion within the throne room as people demanded answers. The king hurriedly ascended the steps of the dais, followed closely by his two dogs, but he didn't sit down – he didn't have *time* to sit down. He hadn't even bothered to change his dirty bloody clothes or wash. "Silence! Silence!" he called out. "I have bad news. The army has been defeated. The city of Busiris has fallen and the whole of the province of Ati is now in Sekheperenre's hands. There are no other troops or defenses between us and the enemy. Sekheperenre's army will be at our gates in perhaps one or two days. Make all preparations to secure the palace against being breached. Stock up food, water, bandages, and weapons. Get your personal affairs in order, and ready yourselves for battle! Dismissed!"

Some of the workers were stunned speechless, others were frantic and hysterical with panic. Seshrab just stood there, numb, as the remainder of the palace staff hurriedly exited the throne room. Then, he too slowly slunk off, not sure what to do. All he wanted at that moment was to go back to his room and curl up on his bed, and wish for everything to just go away. Deep breath in, hold for three seconds, deep breath out.

"Colonel Mebydos, stay – I must talk with you" said the king as he descended from the steps to speak with the man directly face-to-face. "Colonel, after a lifetime of victories, for the first time, I have experienced defeat. Nothing stands between the capital and Sekheperenre's army. The enemy will be upon us soon, and despite all preparations made to repel the enemy's advance, I fear that Khaset Province might be lost. Colonel, you have served me and my father well. We have fought in many battles together, and you have distinguished yourself greatly. Leave your troops here with me to defend the city. As for yourself, return to East Ament Province immediately, and take charge of the province's defenses. Make your stand there".

Colonel Mebydos had tears in his eyes. "Sire, I…I cannot".

"You disobey me?"

"My regiment is here. My king is here. I must also be here, standing beside you, in victory or defeat".

King Khemshawre was overcome and embraced the man. "Go to East Ament. Make your stand there. And tell Colonel Djedkherure of the West Ament Regiment to prepare all military forces to repel an attack against his province. The two of you are to coordinate your efforts as much as possible. I hereby promote you to the rank of General, and furthermore, I appoint you as Supreme Military Commander of the Royal Army of Lower Egypt. If, by chance, we meet again in this life, then we will laugh and smile. But if not, know that you are a brave and loyal man, and I think it a great privilege in my life to have known an officer like you. Now go, and fight your battles without me".

The newly promoted *General* Mebydos, barely able to restrain himself, stood at attention and saluted one final time. "Sire, it has been the greatest honor of my life to have known you", and then turned around and departed the palace.

Now, King Khemshawre turned to his wife, Queen Neferet who was standing off to the side with their daughter Atentjehenet. Her older sister Meret was standing close by with the king's half-brother Montunakht. Both children were now barely 2 years old.

"I have neglected you terribly", he said to her. "I beg you for your forgiveness, and I beg forgiveness from your sister for the poor way in which both myself and my father have treated her. I deeply regret it, I regret everything. I am sorry that I was not a better husband to you, or a better father to our child. If we emerge out of this, I promise you, things will be different for you. Things will be different for all of us. I promise".

At that moment, a messenger burst into the throne room. "Sire! Sire! Sekheperenre's army has crossed the river and has landed in Khaset Province. They will be within sight of the city in just one or two days!"

"Thank you. Dismissed" said the king, and the man took off.

Khemshawre turned to his wife again. "Remember what I said. I mean it. I promise".

News of the advance of Sekheperenre's army struck the capital's population like an earthquake. Everyone knew that there would be another battle soon, and many instinctively felt that this one would not end well. The troops within Khaset City were rapidly descending into an armed rabble. Seshrab had never seen them like this before. In the past, he admired the Royal Army's discipline, training, precision, expert drill, and their unwavering power. Now, he saw all of that evaporate away like a puddle of water in the hot sun. These were not the hardened disciplined professionals who had awed him when he first arrived in Egypt the year before, the mighty men who had fought and prevailed at the Battle of Yamu. Now, they looked and acted like bumbling raw recruits. Even the grizzled battle-scarred veterans felt the sucking falling quicksand-like sensation of fear take hold. Fear is like some contagious disease, spreading from one person to the next, and it quickly infects the whole population. When fear enters the body, intelligence exits. Fear wraps itself around people's brains and it makes them act foolishly, it makes them not think clearly, it makes them do stupid things.

At sunset, His Divine Majesty stood on the city's ramparts scanning the horizon. To his left and right were soldiers and civilians, old veterans and new recruits, all of them waiting in restless anticipation for the distant sound of war drums. The combined total of his army numbered 20,000 men, including both the professional soldiers and the people that he had press-ganged to fight at his side. It was the largest army that he had ever commanded, if one could call it an "army". Nearly all of them were ordinary people, and many were barely teenagers.

He heard some footsteps coming towards him. "Good evening, Chief Scribe", he said without turning around or altering his fixed gaze.

"Good evening, Your Divine Majesty. I was told that you wished to speak with me?"

"Yes. Seshrab, you came to this land a year ago seeking protection from your enemies, seeking salvation from your own death. In the time that I have known you, you have served me very well. You are one of the most intelligent and reliable people that I have known. However, it seems that death has followed you once again. A great battle is to be fought here, and if you remain in this place, it's possible that you may not survive. I do not wish for a man of such quality as yourself to lose his life before he has fully lived it. You are not Egyptian, Egypt is not your birthright land. You do not have to stay to defend it if you do not wish it".

"Your Divine Majesty, are you ordering me to leave?"

"No. I'm saying that if you decide to leave, I will understand".

It was at this point that Seshrab fully grasped what the king was telling him. This was Seshrab's one and only chance to get out of the palace and out of the city before the assault began. *Nesu* had virtually granted him permission to go. If he left Khaset City *right now*, he would be safe. For a few moments, Seshrab wondered if he should go back to his family in Hebron, to leave this violent and strife-ridden landscape with all of its power-hungry potentates, its bloodshed, its starving despairing people, and the relentless mosquitoes. He could go back home.

*Home.*

Home to Canaan, to Hebron, to be with his father, mother, and brothers, to take his place in the family business, to live his days without fear. *Go. Go now, before it's too late.* Every gram of logic within his brain was telling him that getting out of Egypt *right now* was the only sensible thing to do. It was the smart thing. It was the safe thing.

It was also the cowardly thing. Seshrab had been on the run for much of his young adult life, and he was not eager to run again – he liked being planted in one place. No, he was running even before King Sihon put a price on his head, running away from a hard toiling life by being a scribe, one of the privileged positions in society. Granted, it was his father's wish, but even so, he felt a certain degree of responsibility in that choice. He could have quit. He could have chosen another path in life, but he didn't. He would never get his hands dirty or know real work, like the poor slaves who labored at the turquoise mine in Hathor's Mountain. He would never have his muscles and bones ache, and that was good, but he would also never know the satisfaction of building a house with his own hands, or growing his own fruits and vegetables, or raising his own sheep and goats on the hillside. These were the sort of things that *real* men did, and he hadn't done any of them. It was a great feeling of pride that he never knew, a feeling that he had *done* something, that he had *accomplished* something. Seshrab hadn't accomplished *anything* in his life. Looking back, being a scribe, a writer, did not seem like an honest and appropriate way to live. He suddenly felt great shame. All around him, people had worked very hard to get what they needed and to raise themselves up in the world, but for himself, things had been handed to him for much of his life without any work or effort. He had been safe and sheltered, aside from a very black period during his late teens and early 20s. It was hard, cruel, and brutal during those years, and yet, Seshrab began to think with a certain level of fondness about them now. During that time, he was his own master, and his fate was in no one's hands but his own. He had lived by wit, by cunning, and by sheer strength of will. He had survived when death around any corner seemed inevitable. During those years, he had truly lived. Now, surprisingly, he began to miss it. *What I would give to be a street beggar in Gaza right now*, he thought. *Or travelling with the Arab nomads through the deserts of Sinai eating dates and drinking goat milk.*

Seshrab now began to wonder if he had wasted his life.

Yet how many people had travelled as much as he, or seen all of the things that he had seen, or had been on so many adventures? *Adventures?* Yes! There *were* adventures! Locked in a dungeon for daring to defy a tyrant, awaiting execution, only to break out during a brilliant midnight escape! Wandering through the desert, surviving on less food than a lizard would eat, braving the heat and the sand and the elements, enduring what no other man could have! Living in disguise in a foreign city, living on the streets, surviving by his cleverness and persistence, and eventually rising up to become a member of a king's household! A sudden plot twist – the benevolent ruler is friends with the story's villain. The audience gasps. Another daring escape, and being rescued by the exotic and mysterious Bedouins, the masters of the desert, learning their strange language and their curious ways. Taking another assumed identity, he makes his way to Sinai where he works for people who do not suspect his past. Little do they know that our hero has a price on his head, and if they should find out, they would surely cut his throat. Escaping to Egypt, imprisoned as a spy, being made a servant to a living god, fighting in the front ranks in a great battle and earning great acclaim for himself! He was given a medal for his bravery by the king, who hung it around Seshrab's neck with his own royal hands. What a story! What an adventure!

Funny, when these actual events happened, Seshrab did not feel any sense of adventure, fun, or glory at the time. He was not conscious that what he was doing might be regarded by others as thrilling or exciting. It was depressing, it was grueling, it was hard, it was worrisome, and sometimes it was just plain scary. To hear a professional bard recite the tale of *The Life of Seshrab of Hebron*, it would be a thrilling drama, full of great deeds and grand speeches, highly embellished of course with poetic license for dramatic effect. The passage of time makes people feel nostalgic about their former days, however hard those days may have been. Old soldiers will regale stories to their neighbors and to little children perched upon their knee about great deeds of daring and glory. But when they actually performed those deeds, there was no glory – just sheer raw terror, and praying to the gods that you would make it out alive. Of course, they don't remember it that way now. Old soldiers *never* remember things that way.

Being in Egypt and travelling with the Royal Army, Seshrab had learned the values of bravery and courage, of always sticking by your principles and convictions no matter what. He had learned to be bold. Every ounce of logic and sense told Seshrab that the time had come for him to leave, to get out of Egypt as fast as he could and head home, but his honor said that to run away, to abandon your lord when he needed you most, was unforgivable. He might not regret it today or tomorrow, but in due time, his mind would draw upon the memory of his former master, Nesu Horus-Khemshawre, King of Lower Egypt. Seshrab would imagine His Divine Majesty facing the wrath of his enemy with one less man to fight beside him. He would wonder if his being there would have made some kind of difference. He would imagine his master killed, and wondering if he might still be alive if *he* had been there to defend him, and he would be overwhelmed with guilt and shame for the rest of his life. Logic told Seshrab to leave.

"I'm staying", Seshrab said to his master.

In the duskiness of twilight, a large cloud of smoke appeared on the southern horizon. Sekheperenre's army was burning down the abandoned villages.

"They're coming", said the king, "and there is nothing that I can do to stop them".

As the last flashes of purple, orange, and red seeped beneath the western horizon, darkness fell upon the land. The city's defenders could not see the enemy in the night, but they could see something else – campfires. A campfire was constructed for every ten or twenty people. The soldiers standing guard on the walls and towers could see them begin to light up along the horizon, only a few at first, but then more and more, spreading like a slow creeping flood across the landscape. The men had never seen so many campfires before. There were hundreds...no, *thousands* of them. It looked as if the gods had taken all of the stars in the night sky and had strewn them across the surface of the earth.

That night, the old veterans, the raw recruits, and the newly-armed civilians stood firm at the walls, towers, and gates. Nobody could eat or drink, for all of them had lost their appetites. They waited for the coming battle which was sure to happen the following morning. Waiting is horrible in war. In some ways, the fear, tension, and anxiety of the coming clash are worse than the actual battle itself. In battle, the mind and the body work automatically. There is no time for fear, there is only the instinctiveness of action and quick decision. There is brutal bloody butchery that must be done, and that takes priority over all other things, even fear. It is only after the battle is over that the survivors gradually realize what events passed, and what events that they themselves took a direct part in, and then, only then, do the emotions begin to creep back in, like groundwater seeping into and filling up a dry well.

They perched themselves upon the parapets and passed the night in sleepless worry, their minds whirling with thoughts and troubles. They reminisced on their lives, and they wondered about their deaths. They pondered whether or not they had lived good lives, or whether or not they felt their lives had been wasted. They thought about all of the mistakes and mis-steps that they had taken, they thought about all of the choices that were made, of the opportunities that were missed, of the risks that they were too timid to take, of the tasks and accomplishments that they never finished or never even started, and all of the things in their lives that they would have done differently if only they had known better at the time. Their minds frequently dwelt upon the happy care-free days of their youth when life was bright and simple, a life of friends and games and toys and glorious summer sunshine, with a loving and caring mother and father beside them at all times to nurture them and protect them against all of the evils that raged in an evil world. Most of all, they wished, hoped, pleaded, and prayed that all of this was only an illusion, only some horrible dream, and soon they would wake to discover that there was no army, no approaching battle, no threat of looming death, and they would breathe a welcome sigh of relief.

But it was not to be. Daydreams and imaginations are wonderful things. They make an ugly life beautiful. But reality is hard. And ugly.

Within the interior of the Perah, King Khemshawre spent the night within his private chapel in deep prayer and meditation. He knelt barefoot before the various images and idols of the gods and spirits of the Egyptian pantheon, his head bowed in reverence, and his arms outstretched with his palms facing upwards to receive their blessings. Outwardly he was silent and still, but in his thoughts, he was yelling and screaming, his inner voice shouting and pleading with urgent frantic desperation, begging the gods to protect him and his people with all of the vigorous vocabulary that he could think of. In the flickering orange light of the oil lamps, the little figurines of white alabaster, polished granite, and elegant blue faience ceramic seemed to move slightly, especially their faces – sometimes smiling, sometimes frowning disapprovingly, sometimes glaring menacingly, and many times with a skin-crawling demented stare. For hours, King Khemshawre mentally begged and pleaded with Ra, Isis, Osiris, Montu, Sekhmet, and all of the other gods to spare his life. He also prayed to his father Osiris-Nebsenre, the great general, to watch over him, to inspire his men with courage as he himself had done when he was alive leading troops in the field, and to give his son guidance in what he knew would be the most consequential battle that he had ever fought. He did not hear any replies.

Seshrab, who was lying awake on the bed in his cell, had no hope of sleeping that night. He had made his choice. Win or lose, life or death, he would stay. For the hundredth time that night, he rummaged through his things in his polished cedar wood cabinet, organizing them and reorganizing them, shuffling and re-arranging papers, and compulsively straightening and re-straightening the sheets on his bed. Propped up against the cabinet was his golden *sekhem* scepter, the badge of his office that marked him as a high-ranking member of the royal court. He remembered when Imhotep was still around, and he remembered the great beating that he had given that bloated toad of a man with that very scepter when he had taunted and insulted Seshrab just one time too often. Seshrab couldn't help but smirk and snicker at the memory. Yes, that was a *good time*, wasn't it?

There was a knock on the door. "Yes?" he answered.

The door opened. It was Khepermoses, one of the junior scribes, just 13 years old, just barely a man. "Sir, I can't sleep".

"Nobody can", replied Seshrab. "Come in".

Khepermoses entered the room and sat down on the bed next to him. "You worried?"

"Of course I'm worried".

"But you shouldn't be. I've never been in a fight before. This is all new to me. But this is nothing new to you. You've fought a battle before, at Yamu. And again when you went with the army to fight the Canaanites. And even before that, you've been through so much. How can *anything* worry you?"

Seshrab snorted at the naivety and ridiculousness of it all. "You might find this hard to believe, but I'm not made of such stern stuff as you may think. That fight with the Canaanites wasn't much of a fight at all, and I'd rather not think about Yamu".

"Do you still have nightmares?"

Seshrab paused. "Sometimes", he said. "But they don't come every night like they used to, and the nightmares aren't as bad as they used to be. And I don't find myself slipping into moments of panic and fear like I did before. The doctor helped me out a great deal with that. They haven't gone away completely, but I'm managing it".

"Sir, you've been a good boss during the time that you've been here. We all think so. I just felt that you should know that".

"Thank you".

"See you tomorrow", and Khepermoses got up and walked towards the door, but then he stopped and turned around. "Incidentally, the king has issued an order to everyone. He says that all of the men gathered in the city who've been awarded the Golden Fly medal for great deeds done in battle, wear these medals around your necks for the upcoming fight. He said that such men have already proven themselves to be brave and capable of doing great things. He hopes that, by wearing those medals, you can be brave again tomorrow, and inspire others to be brave too. Sir, you won a Golden Fly, didn't you? For your part at Yamu?"

"Yes".

"If that medal is some kind of magical talisman that makes soldiers brave, then you'd best put it on. We need all the help we can get", and he left.

Seshrab walked over to the cabinet and got out the little wooden box that he kept his odds and ends in, and opened it. Mixed in amongst the various items was a golden pendant in the shape of a fly hanging from a golden chain. He had won this medal for his conduct at Yamu – every man who fought in that battle was given this medal to commemorate their heroism in the face of overwhelming odds. It was hung around his neck by the king's own hand. Seshrab still remembered the words that the king spoke to him that day: *Seshrab of Hebron, Chief Scribe to His Majesty King Shaweneiti of Lower Egypt, in recognition of your gallant behavior at the Battle of Yamu, I hereby award you the Golden Fly.* He remembered how heavy it was, and he also remembered feeling that he didn't deserve it. He still felt that way. He was uncomfortable wearing it in the presence of actual soldiers, men that he believed deserved to wear this far more than he did. Yet it was the king's wish that he be awarded this distinguished honor, and it was now his king's wish that he wear it again. Seshrab pulled the Golden Fly out of the little storage box and hung it around his neck, tucking it underneath his tunic so that it would be out of the way. It felt heavy.

As Seshrab lay upon his bed, his mind restlessly whirled with many things. He thought of his family, he thought of his father, his mother, and his two older brothers. He thought of his home in Hebron. He thought of the coming battle, of the danger, of the fear. Most of all, he thought of his own death, death in all of its macabre disgusting forms. He thought of how young he was, and how wasteful it was to have such young men as himself die before they had a chance to accomplish all of the things that they wanted to. War was a robber, a brutal thief, using violent force to steal precious irreplaceable years away from people's lives.

"I hate war", Seshrab grumbled to himself as he stared at the ceiling, and tried forcing himself to get a few minutes of sleep.

# CHAPTER 17

*After retreating to Khaset City, Nesu Horus-Khemshawre made all necessary preparations to withstand a siege. Food, water, medicine, and other provisions were brought within the city's walls, the entire male population was conscripted for defense, and weapons of varying sorts were apportioned to them. Members of the palace staff were likewise mustered, armed, and hastily trained in the arts of combat should the enemy breach the city's defenses. Likewise, I myself took my appointed place upon the parapets, shield and spear in hand, ready to do my service for my lord and master on this day as I had done at Yamu. In dread, we all looked southwards for the approach of the enemy, and we awaited what would be the final battle.*

Morning.

The people of Khaset City were not eager to see the reddish glow of dawn. They knew that the coming of the sun would initiate the battle that they had been dreading for so long. They wouldn't have long to wait. In the early dawn hours, they came.

"To arms, to arms!" called out someone on watch. "The enemy approaches Khaset City! Their warriors cover the horizon! Beg the gods for your lives this day!"

From far away, they approached slowly and steadily towards the city. The royalists heard the approach of the enemy army before they actually saw it. Based upon all of the noise that they made, there had to be thousands of soldiers fighting under Sekheperenre's banner.

Alarm calls and trumpet signals resounded throughout the city's streets. "To arms! To arms! The enemy approaches! All hands to the battlements! All hands to the walls and towers! Defend the city! Defend the city!"

There was a hurried rush of panic and last-minute preparations. Men went over their mental checklists for the fifth or sixth time. They ran back and forth to collect whatever odds and ends that they needed, or to safely stash away whatever valuables that they had for retrieval when it was more convenient. *Do I have this? Do I need this?* A thousand and one worries and cares cacophonously flooded into their minds like the whispers of hateful furies. People's thoughts truly dwell upon the most peculiar things when one's life hangs in the balance. They thought of their weapons and their armor, of whether or not their clothing looked disheveled, or if the laces of their sandals were tied and fastened properly, of their families, of their friends, of schedules that needed to be made and appointments that needed to be kept, of chores that still needed to be done, of duties, obligations, and responsibilities that needed to be fulfilled, and all the while trying desperately to keep out the horrid thought of their own death which was loudly hammering at their mind's door. Some vainly hoped that all of this wouldn't be necessary – that Lord Sekheperenre would have second thoughts about assaulting the city, turn his army around, and head back for Ati. Was assaulting Khaset City really worthwhile? Was it really worth the effort? Sieges and assaults were always a gamble, and the attacking force would lose many men. Yes, the enemy army would give up even before the battle started. After all, Sekheperenre was a clever and reasonable man. He would come to his senses, and he'd negotiate some kind of settlement with the king. Then everyone could go back home and get back to work. This whole business of war and fighting was an aggravating distraction to people's lives – there were jobs that needed to be done and bills that needed to be paid. Yet even as they desperately wanted to pretend that such things were possible, they knew in their hearts it was not to be. There would be blood and death this day. Maybe their own.

The clamor soon reached the colonnaded halls of the Perah. The news of Sekheperenre's approach, though it was long expected, had no lesser fear for those within when the word finally arrived. He was here. The battle had come.

King Khemshawre, who had been awake all night praying in his private chapel, could hear the alarm calls outside the door echoing and resounding through the palace corridors. Prayer had not worked. Now sharpened copper would have to do what the gods would not. He got up from his knees and stormed out of the palace shrine. The king's two pet greyhounds, white Osiris and black Set, were faithfully waiting outside the chapel's door for him, and they anxiously followed him down the hall as the great warrior king prepared to once again don his armor.

In the Servants' Quarters, the call went through the cells that the battle had come. "The enemy is here! Prepare to defend the palace!"

Within his cell at the far end of the long hallway, Seshrab heard the calls. Despite his attempts to get at least some sleep, he had been awake all night, his stomach queasy, palms sweaty, mouth dry. This was it. Seshrab checked one last time that he was wearing the Golden Fly medal around his neck, which the king had commanded him to wear for the coming fight. Yes, it was still there, as his fingertips rubbed against the cold metal. He forced himself to get up from his soft bed, in his little room, with the ornate rug on the floor, the nightstand with the blue faience wash basin, the *sekhem* scepter, the well-polished cedar cabinet standing against the wall, and the neatly-arranged bottles of ink and the stacks of papyrus sheets and scrolls. He walked towards the door, paused, took one last look around his room, and then opened the door and jogged down the long hallway. He had chosen this. There was no going back.

In the Perah, Captain Nebikhamu and the other palace guards were passing out whatever shields and weaponry that they could spare. Some of the shields had been hastily crafted from wickerwork and leather skins the previous night. Some of the spears were nothing more than sharpened broomsticks, while legs from chairs and tables had been fashioned into clubs. "Assemble in the reception hall and await the king's commands", they said.

Seshrab was one of the last people to take his place in line getting his gear, which amounted to a flattened grain winnowing basket covered with a sheet of rawhide and a couple of arm straps made from rough scratchy rope, and a wooden pole that had been sharpened and fire-hardened. As Seshrab received his improvised shield and spear, his heart pounding and his breathing labored and shaky, thoughts of his service at the Battle of Yamu unavoidably came barreling into his brain. He remembered the hard fighting that he had endured on that unbearably hot day, the mind-numbing terror, the blood, the screaming. He had hoped that all of that was behind him, but it was not to be, not in this world anyway.

Seshrab made his way with the rest of the crowd to the reception hall where everyone was gathering and making what might be their last tearful goodbyes. They were all there: Horemheb, the chubby chamberlain who didn't look so high-and-mighty anymore; Kawaset, the secretary of the treasury, the bookish accountant who looked so out of place holding a wooden club; Imeni, the official in charge of grain and livestock who had been active in provisioning the city for a long siege; and the other scribes who worked under Seshrab's direction: Amunimhet, Atenmoses, Khepermoses, Nebrenuisis, Senedj, Senwasret, and Thoth-hotep. They all looked very nervous.

Seshrab walked up to them. "So…" he began.

There was an awkward silence between them. "Yeah" was all that Khepermoses could say, nodding.

"Are you ready for all of this?"

"I don't know", said Amunimhet. "What about you, sir? Are you ready?"

"I think so…I hope so. I, uh, kind of hoped that I wouldn't have to be doing this again".

"We may not have to", said Thoth-hotep. "The city is well defended. We have plenty of food, water, and medicine to withstand a long siege. I don't think that things will get so bad that they'll send us in".

And then King Khemshawre entered the hall, resplendent in his martial glory, wearing his royal blue battle shirt, his gleaming cuirass of copper scales, his father's prized leopard skin fastened around his shoulders, and carrying his shield and royal mace. Strutting by his side were his pet greyhounds Osiris and Set and behind were his wife, her sister, and their two children. Everyone immediately drew themselves to attention.

The king looked over his palace staff: the scribes, cooks, bath attendants, repairmen, maids, butlers, accountants, and civil servants. This was his personal regiment, "the King's Own". Most of them looked nervous, while others seemed apathetically resigned to their fate.

"It's time", he said. "I will not be so brash as to goad you on with soaring words full of bluster and bravado. You all know what must be done today, and I expect everyone here to do their duty. I shall take my place upon the city's parapets; you shall remain behind here. Your duty is to defend the palace. Be ever vigilant and attentive for any sign of the enemy. If the outer defenses cannot hold, then we shall all make our stand at the palace walls. If these walls fail us, then we will fall back and make our stand within the Perah itself. This royal house will be our citadel. Are there any questions?"

Nobody said anything. Some shook their heads, while others cast their eyes down at the floor.

"I know that this is a very serious thing that I am asking you to do, and I am very proud of all of you. Now, take your positions and ready yourselves for battle".

It was time to go. "Well", said Seshrab, "this is it".

"Sir", said Senwasret, the oldest of the king's scribes, "I've worked in this place for a long time. I've seen many people come and go. I've had a lot of people that I've had to work for, some better than others. You're not an Egyptian, and you're younger than me by many years, and yet I have no shame in saying that you are the best boss I've ever had".

All of the other scribes nodded in agreement.

"Thanks, guys" Seshrab said with a smile. "It'll be alright as long as we stick together. Let's go".

While the staff moved off to ascend the palace walls, King Khemshawre knelt down to pet and scratch his two beloved dogs, panting and whimpering. "My beautiful little boys", he said lovingly, "Daddy has some hard work that he has to do today. I won't be back home for a while, but hopefully I'll be back tonight to play with you and feed you your dinner. In the meantime, you take care of my family, alright?"

Then he addressed the two children, his daughter Princess Atentjehenet and his half-brother Prince Montunakht, both of whom were less than 2 years old. "I need to go away for a bit today, but I'll be back home tonight. You listen to your mothers and you do what they tell you. Remember, they're in charge while I'm gone".

"Yes Daddy", said Princess Atentjehenet.

Khemshawre patted her and his half-brother on the head, both of them looking rather confused as to what was going on but knowing in some instinctive way that it was very important. Then he turned to his wife and her sister. "Stay within the palace. Keep them safe. I will join you this evening". Then he leaned in close to Queen Neferet's ear and whispered "Keep food, water, and fresh clothes with you. If I don't come back, you know what to do". And then he kissed her…for the first time in nearly two years.

As the palace staff took their places, King Khemshawre marched down the long avenue to the city's main southern gate and ascended the battlements. As he walked along the walls with the sure determined sullen stride of a male lion preparing for a battle with a rival for its pride, the soldiers on the parapets bowed their heads respectfully to him as he passed by, occasionally met with the greeting "Your Divine Majesty". Mustering up something of their courage, some of the spearmen began to forcefully bang the butt ends of their spears down into the brick walkway in a rhythmic fashion as their king approached. Only a few did it at first, and the rhythm was slow, but then, more and more soldiers began to bang their weapons, slowly, and then faster, and faster, and soon the whole promenade along the walls erupted into thunderous martial applause. As the resonance grew and intensified, people began to shout out his name, "Hail Nesu Khemshawre!" shouted one. "Hail the Divine Horus!" shouted another, "Hail our king!" said another.

As the sun rose higher and the sky became brighter, the defenders of Khaset City saw with their own eyes the awesome terror of Sekheperenre's army. The royalists estimated that the enemy numbered 50,000 men or more – they were outnumbered at least two to one. The rebels steadily advanced up the main north-south highway towards the capital until they got about one mile away from the walls, and paused. A sizeable number of the men were carrying smoldering burning coals within large earthenware pots hanging from ropes. No doubt, they would be used for setting buildings or defenses ablaze to deny such assets to His Divine Majesty.

But Sekheperenre had other plans for the fire.

The pride of Khaset City, indeed the pride of the whole of Khaset Province, were its grape vineyards. Khaset was the center of wine production within the Delta, and Khaset wine was reputed to be the best wine in all of Egypt. Thousands of acres of grape vines surrounded the capital like a vast green leafy moat. Only a handful of narrow dirt roads cut through these grape vineyards, making them the only paths in and out of the city. That was fine for small numbers of travellers, but not for an advancing army numbering 50,000 strong who were hell-bent on besieging the place. Years before, when Gen. Nakhtibre and his son Shaweneiti had led their army against Khaset City, they had been extremely careful not to damage the grape vines too much. The grapes were important to the people here, not only for food and drink, but on a deep personal level – the vineyards were part of them. Nakhtibre knew that the people would resent him and hate him if the grape vineyards were trampled under and destroyed, so he had given strict orders to his men to leave the vines alone.

But Sekheperenre didn't have such concerns and considerations. To him, the grapevines were nothing more than an obstacle standing in his way that needed to be removed. A signal was given, and after a minute or so, the people atop Khaset City's ramparts began to see the smoke.

"FIRE!!!" someone on the walls shouted. "FIRE!!! OH MY GODS, THE VINES!!! THEY'RE BURNING THE GRAPE VINES!!!"

The townsfolk of Khaset City were aghast, horrified, and in agony at what they saw happening before their shocked eyes. An immense shouting of wrenching pain erupted from the city's population – they cried, they wailed, they screamed, they slammed their fists, they pulled at their hair, and they shouted *"Oh, gods, why?! WHY?!"* A massive shroud of thick dark grey smoke rose up as they watched their beloved vines, their livelihood and their pride, turn to blackened charred ruins. The *Sebayts*, the ancient Egyptian code of morality and philosophy, had expressly forbade such wanton senseless acts of destruction. Not even the Libyan savages would dare do something so despicably cruel.

"I want that man *dead*", said King Khemshawre, malicious intent in his tone as he glared at the burning grape vineyards and the enemy army that lay concealed behind the smoke. "I don't care who does it, I don't care how it's done, but within twenty-four hours, I want that man's head brought to me on a plate!"

It took several hours to burn down the grape vines. It wasn't until mid-day that the fires died down and the enemy army could advance up the last mile or so to the city through the burning smoldering smoky ashes. As they marched closer and closer, the people on the walls could see the enemy more distinctly. They wore armor and they carried large leather shields, axes, maces, and spears. But there was something about the spears that looked unusual – they seemed to have much larger heads on them than ordinary spears did.

Heads.

As Sekheperenre's massive army slowly approached Khaset City, the defenders on the ramparts could see that many of the spearmen in the front ranks had a decapitated human head stuck onto the points of their weapons. Gasps of shock soon gave way to occasional screams of horror and pain as this person or that person on the wall recognized one of the lifeless pallid faces as their husband, their father, their brother, or their son who had marched off with His Divine Majesty to relieve the enemy's siege of the city of Busiris. Now their heads were carried in procession by the enemy troops who had slain them like trophies won on a safari. Their bodies no longer intact, the fate of their souls was doomed. They would have no second life. They were gone forever.

But the most horrid sight of all was this: Carried before the advancing army like a macabre scarecrow was the crucified lifeless corpse of Colonel Ankharis.

The brave Ankharis, the commander of the Sapmeh Regiment – a man who was reputed to never know fear, a man who always insisted on boldness and aggressiveness, a man whom the war god Montu had bestowed his favor on for many years – had courageously given his life to save his comrades. At Busiris, knowing that all was lost, he voluntarily gathered up a hundred of his best troops and personally led them in a head-on suicidal charge against the entire enemy army to buy time for his king and the rest of the men to escape. He had accomplished his mission, and he and all of his men of the Forlorn Hope had sold their lives dearly. It was reputed amongst the troops within Sekheperenre's army that it took ten men at once to finally bring down this mighty warrior. Later, the story said it was fifteen, and afterwards twenty. Colonel Ankharis, the Lion of Sapmeh, was no more, and like a prized lion slain in the hunt, he was proudly displayed for all to see.

The sight of his dear comrade's dead body, and to see it treated so shamefully, filled King Khemshawre with grief and rage. Yet he knew it would be ruinous for the little morale amongst his defenders to display his feelings. The men would surely lose all heart and all hope to see their king broken. So, he clenched his teeth, tightened his jaws, and forced himself not to scream. However, he could not prevent the tears from filling his eyes and dripping down the side of his face.

Sekheperenre could not afford to spend a protracted amount of time on a long siege campaign. Khemshawre had undertaken a scorched earth policy as he had retreated, destroying everything that could not be salvaged. Sekheperenre's army was large and it needed to be constantly fed. Hunkering down outside the walls for weeks or months and waiting for the opposing side to starve or surrender was out of the question. Most likely, the king had taken everything edible for miles around and brought it inside the walls. If Sekheperenre laid siege to Khaset City, hoping to starve the garrison into submission, his own large and unwieldy army would run out of food long before the royalists did. No, there would be no siege. The only possible way would be to storm Khaset City, to launch a direct frontal assault, to send the battering rams and the scaling ladders forward.

During the 1600s BC, siege techniques were crude and lacking. Catapults had not been invented yet. The only techniques employed by Egyptians when assaulting an enemy fortress or a fortified city were using ladders to scale *over* the walls, pick axes to chop *through* the walls, and shovels to tunnel *underneath* the walls. Tunneling was out of the question – the water table around Khaset City was simply too high and the tunnels would be flooded. The walls which surrounded the city and the palace complex within were made of brick, not stone, so they could be cut through with hammers and pick axes, provided that the pioneers had the latitude to carry on their work unhindered. This was unlikely, as the city's garrison would surely rain arrows and stones down upon them. Sending men up the scaling ladders was always a risky prospect. The ladders were long, narrow and rickety, so you could only send up a few men at a time. The defending garrison could simply push the ladders away or stab the enemy troops as they clambered up the ladders one-by-one.

Then came the deep rhythmic pounding of the drums. *Boom… boom… boom…*The ominous man-made thunder echoed oppressively over the landscape. To the city's defenders, it was as if they could hear their own fearful heartbeats. From atop the wall which surrounded the palace complex, Seshrab's throat tightly clenched itself, and he found it almost impossible to swallow. The drums were the signal.

The battle had begun.

The drums continued their ominous thunderous rumble, like the heavy footsteps of a gigantic beast, as the rebel army advanced towards Khaset City's walls. With every pounding of those resonant kettles, they advanced closer and closer. Some of the royalists were praying out loud, chanting time-honored psalms and *sebayts* to give their hearts and minds peace and to muster up some courage.

King Khemshawre intently watched the approaching swarm steadily creeping towards his stronghold. As the enemy army approached, the city's defenders could see that the rebels were equipped with numerous battering rams and scaling ladders. The rams had been constructed from the remains of demolished buildings, the roofs of them covered with wet cow hides to guard against fire. "When they reach 150 yards", the king ordered, "hit them with everything you have. Aim closely, make every arrow and slingstone find its mark. If we don't…Just hit them and hit them hard. Understand?"

"Yes, Your Divine Majesty", they collectively replied.

The rebels were now five hundred yards from the walls, and they began to spread out. In a face-to-face ground battle between two armies, spreading your men out with plenty of space between each man was foolish and reckless because unit cohesion broke apart and an army was reduced to a collection of easily-killed individual targets. But this wasn't a ground battle – this was an assault of a fortified position, and a tightly-packed mass would make an easy target.

After dispersing, the rebels now began a steady jog towards the city's southern gate, a 250 yard gauntlet. Within a few seconds, the arrows would begin falling.

Finally, the rebels came within 150 yards of the walls.

"Prepare to shoot!" shouted out one of the archer commanders. "Ready!"

The archers knocked their sharpened bone-tipped arrows and pulled back the strings.

"SHOOT!!!"

A series of *twangs* and *thwifts* resounded from the bows. The arrows zipped down to the ground, killing and wounding some men, but not enough.

"Shoot, damn you! Shoot them!" the archer commander shouted.

The archers began shooting their arrows faster and faster. Now the rebels were less than a hundred yards from the walls. Two battering rams were moving towards the gate. Men with scaling ladders raced towards the front, so that they could get their ladders up for the rest of the infantry to scramble up to the top of the walls.

"Spearmen", said the king, "prepare to repel ladders! Bring the rocks forward!"

Prior to the battle, rocks and bricks had been gathered in wicker baskets and placed at regular intervals along the walls. They were meant to be dumped on or thrown at the attackers. In a pinch, they could also make a nasty and brutish hand-to-hand weapon.

"Hold them off and fight for your lives!!!"

And so the enemy came on, like a slowly surging unstoppable flood. The battering rams hammered away at the large gate, barred and braced with thick wooden beams and heaps of burlap sacks filled with sand and rubble. *WHAM! WHAM! WHAM!* The gate held firm, shuddering and creaking under the impacts, and a contingent of armed men stood behind at the ready, waiting to cut down anybody who would enter the breach. Meanwhile, atop the walls, the archers and slingers did their deadly work. They picked their targets carefully. With so many of Sekheperenre's men holding their shields above their heads to protect themselves against the barrage of projectiles, the archers aimed for their exposed shins and feet. It wouldn't kill them, but a crippled soldier who couldn't carry out an attack was useless, and was one less enemy that Khemshawre needed to concern himself with. Under heavy fire, one suicidal squad of men after another raced forwards to brace the scaling ladders against Khaset City's walls. Most of them were shot down by arrows or pelted by flying slingstones, but a few of them managed to make it. Atop the ramparts, the spearmen used their long weapons to push off the ladders like a boat punter using his pole to push his little craft off of the shore.

But Sekheperenre had archers of his own, and they shot their arrows up in a high arc to rain downwards onto the heads of the men on the walls. The fellow who had been standing next to Khemshawre was shot with an arrow through one of his eyes. Screaming in agony, he staggered backwards and fell off of the parapet and plunged down to his death, his body making a hard *crunch* as it hit the ground, missing the gate guards by only a dozen or so feet. And all the while, the battering rams kept hammering. The gate still held, but cedar wood was soft and easily broken. The gate guards weren't sure how long it would hold.

With the city's defenders distracted with attending to this or that matter along the walls, some of the rebel troops managed to make it up the length of the ladder, only to be pushed off at the last second and fall, suffering a broken leg or a broken neck. Others had their skulls and collarbones broken with rocks or bricks hurled down onto them. All the while, King Khemshawre raced back and forth along the wall, aiding men wherever he could, giving directions, and shouting encouragement.

Meanwhile at the palace, Seshrab and his companions couldn't see much from their position. They could certainly *hear* the battle, and they could see movement, but individual people were largely indistinct. The battle must have been horrid, but there didn't seem to be any signs of panic.

For hours the battle went on, and neither side seemed to be gaining any advantage. Khemshawre and his men were causing a great amount of damage, but so too were Sekheperenre's archers. His own defending garrison was weakening, and it was becoming harder and harder to repel boarders. A few of Sekheperenre's troops had managed to climb up the length of the scaling ladders and stepped foot onto the walls, but were almost immediately cut down and were thrown over the side to keep the walkway clear. The defenders who were holding the western and eastern walls were especially hard-pressed to repel the attack. Still, the situation at the moment seemed to be under control. So far, Khemshawre and his troops were holding their own. By late afternoon, by the king's best guess, Lord Sekheperenre had already lost several thousand of his men. But it wasn't enough. There were always more of them, and Khemshawre's archers were starting to run out of ammunition.

Then there was a loud crack.

*"SIRE, THE GATE IS BREAKING!!!"*

That grabbed everyone's attention. "Every fifth man, with me!!!" called out the king, and he led them down the stairways to the south gate. He inspected the damage – the gate was indeed weakening. A few more hits and it would come down, and the enemy troops would come streaming in through the gap.

With the walls' defenders now greatly reduced in strength, it was harder and harder to hold the enemy back. The fighting was more hard-pressed, more urgent, more desperate. More rebels were making headway clambering up onto the walls and cutting down the defenders. And all the while, there was the relentless hammering of the rams.

Seshrab and his comrades could see that things had taken a turn. The processional avenue which ran through the middle of Khaset City extended in a straight line from the city's southern gate to the palace gate, and Seshrab could see everything that was happening. He could see that many of the men had left the walls and were gathering around the gate and the stairs, he could see the fighting on the ramparts becoming increasingly frantic, and he could see what looked like armed men swarming onto the walls like humanoid ants and killing anybody that they encountered.

"This is bad", he said. "This is very bad. Get ready. They're coming".

King Khemshawre and his reinforcements stood guard at the gate, watching the wood splintering with every pounding strike. Despite the thick wooden beams bracing the gate against the assault, he knew that the doors couldn't hold for much longer. All the while, his eyes darted back and forth to the walls and towers which surrounded the city. His depleted forces stationed atop the ramparts were having a very difficult time repelling the enemy storm, and the enemy was gaining ground. He watched with horror as one of his men after another was cut down, impaled on spears, stabbed with daggers, hacked to death with axes, or had their bones broken and skulls smashed in with maces. The garrison atop the ramparts fought valiantly to hold back the onrushing enemy forces, but their bravery felt more and more like desperation. It wouldn't be long.

Then it happened. There was a loud crack, quickly followed by another, and another, and the large cedar doors of the southern gate broke from their hinges and came crashing down with a thunderous *bang!* Timbers fell haphazardly while dust, mortar, and pieces of brickwork flew everywhere.

A loud cheer arose from the rebels outside and the enemy surged forwards through the breach. Without any orders given, King Khemshawre and his contingent of troops charged forwards and battled hard to hold the enemy forces at bay. From behind their wall of locked shields, they stabbed, hacked, and slashed at anything which presented itself, but it was like trying to hold back some surging flash flood of sharpened copper blades. Normally, a narrow gateway would be easy to defend against a large number of troops trying to funnel themselves into such a small opening. However, the enemy forces not only tried to come through the gate, but they also came over the walls. They were on the walls and towers and were now making their way towards the stairs leading below. Khemshawre and the troops defending against the gate would be surrounded in a matter of moments.

The position was indefensible.

*"FALL BACK TO THE PALACE!!!"* shouted Khemshawre. *"FALL BACK!!! FALL BACK!!!"*

From atop his position on the palace walls, Seshrab gasped, eyes wide, at the horrid spectacle. The king and what was left of his men were running for their lives, with the troops of Lord Sekheperenre right behind them. They raced up the main avenue towards the royal palace. Some of the king's men bravely stood their ground and fought hard to the end, but they only delayed the enemy for a second or two and were quickly overwhelmed and cut down.

At the palace, those stationed atop the palace walls gasped with horror at what they saw. The few military officers stationed upon the palace ramparts began barking out orders. "Infantry secure the gate! Get the gate open to let the retreating troops back in! Archers, ready your bows! Cover the king's retreat! Soldiers, prepare to repel enemy troops!"

"They're coming" Seshrab mumbled aloud. "Get ready!" he said to the other scribes gathered to his left and right along the wall's length. "Don't hold anything back. If you feel not up to taking another life, remember, this isn't murder. This is survival".

The king and the surviving members of the walls' defenders ran back to the palace gates as quickly as they could while the archers stationed atop the gate and adjoining walls peppered the pursuing rebel troops with arrows, slowing them down and buying a little more time for His Divine Majesty to get to safety. Captain Nebikhamu, the commander of the palace guards, was waiting at the gate along with a platoon of his troops, and when the king appeared in the doorway, Capt. Nebikhamu physically grabbed him by the shoulder and yanked him inside. Meanwhile, a few of his men held the door open just long enough for the rest of the retreating troops to make it inside and then quickly slammed the doors closed and bolted them.

Captain Nebikhamu pulled King Khemshawre through the narrow darkly-lit gatehouse corridor, passed the guard barracks and the storage rooms, passed the second set of cedar doors, and into the open courtyard. The interior set of doors were likewise shut and bolted closed.

The king was panting heavily. His face and body were splattered with blood both from the enemy and from his own men killed beside him.

"Please forgive me for taking such liberty, Your Divine Majesty", said Captain Nebikhamu.

"It's alright. Think nothing of it".

Outside, they could hear Sekheperenre's troops pounding on the locked-and-barred door. "It's bad, isn't it?"

"Yes, Captain, I'm afraid it's bad. In fact, it's *very* bad".

Upon the palace walls, the defenders were frantically shooting arrows and slingstones and chucking down rocks and bricks at the enemy below, while others maintained their guard with long spears and sharpened poles. Some of Sekheperenre's men brought the scaling ladders up the long main avenue. The archers were directed to take special aim at those men, for without the ladders, nobody could make it inside the palace complex. Seshrab and his "squad" of scribes-turned-soldiers, armed with whatever was handy, stood at the ready atop the wall near one of the staircases, defending it resolutely, and giving aid and protection to the men and women stationed to the left and right of them. Any enemy soldier climbing up a ladder was soon met by a sharpened point stabbed into his eyes and he fell screaming to the ground below.

"The palace staff fight well", said the king to Captain Nebikhamu. "You and your officers did a good job training them".

Then they heard shouting and screaming from outside – voices of men, women, and children. They were cries of shock, alarm, desperate pleading, and pain. Khemshawre had been involved in enough sackings of towns and cities to know *exactly* what that horrible shrieking noise was. He had assured and promised the people of not only Khaset City but of the whole of Khaset Province that they would be protected if they came within the city's walls. But now, Sekheperenre's troops were inside.

"Sir, the enemy is—".

"I know, Captain", said the king. "I know full-well what the enemy is doing out there. There's nothing I can do for them...There's nothing I can do".

Now they began to smell smoke. *"FIRE!!!"* someone called out. Here and there through the city, columns of grey and black smoke began to arise as the soldiers ransacked the town, plundering what they could take and burning what they couldn't. The palace staff and the palace guards fought hard to defend their square plot of ground from the encroachments of the enemy. Hundreds of rebels lost their lives trying to storm the palace walls. While some of them still vainly tried to batter down the door, others went off elsewhere in the city to find easier targets to lay hold of. By now, they had forced their way into the governor's mansion, and only the gods knew what was happening within those finely-furnished rooms and hallways. The enemy then forced itself into the Temple of Amun, located directly next to the royal palace. Sacred ground meant nothing to the sacrilegious, especially when loot was to be gained. Temples were storehouses for great wealth, and Sekheperenre's troops, many of whom came from the poor, lowly, and dispossessed, had no qualms about violating holy places to rob them of their riches and to slaughter any holy men who stood in their way.

"Sire, they're breaking through!" came a call from atop the palace gate.

Despite the gallant efforts made by the defenders to hold the enemy at bay, the cedar doors which led to the palace courtyard weren't intended to withstand a direct assault by a hostile army. Several of the rebels took wooden timbers, the very same timbers that had been used to shore up the main gate on the city's south wall before the gate broke down, and used them as impromptu battering rams to hammer the cedar doors down. They were holding firm for the moment, but they wouldn't last.

Then the wooden brace which held the doors shut cracked and broke in half and the cedar doors gave way. But the enemy who impulsively rushed forwards was surprised to discover that there was a second inner set of doors leading into the courtyard, and these doors were also bolted shut.

But there was another, more unpleasant surprise for these unfortunate souls.

The gatehouse corridor between the inner and outer doorways was narrow and dark, with a vaulted ceiling above. In the center of that ceiling was a trap door from which the gatehouse defenders stationed above could rain down all manner of horrid forms of death and misery upon anyone caught below, and today, the defenders had something special planned. The ravaged grape vineyards of Khaset City which had been turned into smoldering ruins by Sekheperenre's vile henchmen would exact one final act of vengeance from beyond their charred graves – *boiling hot grapeseed oil*. From above, a massive copper cauldron of the stuff was dumped onto the enemy troops below, searing and sizzling their exposed flesh and burning out their eyes as they screamed and hollered in agony. With everyone packed in so tightly, there was no hope of avoiding it, and they thrashed and writhed in torment.

It was a superb hit, but with the enemy having breached the palace's outer doors, they knew that this was merely a parting shot. It would only be a matter of time before the enemy would break through the inner doors and make their way into the palace courtyard. From there, they could enter the palace itself. Gradually, Sekheperenre's troops turned more and more of their attention upon the palace, and the enemy assault was renewed.

Once more, desperate times called for desperate measures. "Horemheb!" called out King Khemshawre.

The paunchy chamberlain, armed with a wooden club and a wicker shield, leaned over the parapet. "Yes, Your Divine Majesty?" he called out.

"It's time to bring out the wine".

It had come to this. "Yes, Sire. Right away".

The palace had a sizeable quantity of prized Khaset wine held in massive ceramic jars. As part of the siege preparations, these large wine casks were to be used as a last-ditch improvised defense against an intense enemy assault. They were tied about with rope and rags and were soaked in flammable resin, and they had been positioned at regular lengths along the wall. Now, it was time to put them to use. The order was given – light the fuses, and hurl them over the side.

"This pains me immensely, as I am very fond of Khaset wine", said King Khemshawre, "but in times of great peril, one must make great sacrifices".

He wasn't the only one who was pained by this. To waste Khaset City's precious wine in such a manner was more than some men could bear. It was like having their most prized possessions destroyed in front of their eyes. Some of them cried as they obeyed the king's word. After the resin-soaked fuses were lit with torches, the jars were picked up and chucked over the edge. The ceramic vessels broke, the wine was released, and promptly burst into flame upon contact with the burning resin. Those enemy troops who had been near the walls and the gateway screamed as their exposed skin burned and blistered, and they fell back to be out of the way of the blazing moat.

Even so, the king knew that such a desperate gesture would only buy a minute of time. Thousands of Sekheperenre's troops had been killed and thousands more had been wounded, but the rebel lord still had many men under his command, and he would send in the last of his reserves to make the final push.

It was time to make the last stand.

*"FALL BACK TO THE PERAH!!! FALL BACK TO THE PERAH!!!"* Khemshawre called out.

The men and women atop the walls and gatehouse hurriedly clambered down the staircases into the open courtyard and raced towards the Perah's doors. Seshrab and his fellow scribes were some of the first to make it inside. Others followed closely behind them while Capt. Nebikhamu and the palace guards covered their retreat.

It wouldn't take long for the fires to die down, and the enemy hastened it by kicking dirt and sand onto the flames to smother them. Any moment, they would renew the attack. Of course, the first place that they targeted was the gatehouse's locked inner doors.

"That's the last of them", said the king. "Captain, withdraw to the Perah – we'll make our stand there".

The palace guards dashed to the Perah's door. King Khemshawre also rushed off for a few paces, but turned around to make one last check and saw that Capt. Nebikhamu was still there, bracing himself against the gatehouse doors, like a giant trying to hold back a landslide. From within, the enemy's ram pounded hard against it. The door would break soon.

"Captain, come away!"

"No", he said with determined resolution.

"What?!" Captain Nebikhamu had *never* disobeyed him before.

"I said *NO!*" he snapped. "I live here! I live in this palace! This is my home! My bedroom is just down the hall from your bedroom. This is *my* house just as much as it is *yours*, and I will not allow any enemy to dare set foot in *my* house! Go now!"

Khemshawre took one last look at his comrade, a faithful lieutenant whom his father had fought alongside and whose loyalty had always been unquestionable, a man whom his father had made his personal bodyguard, and afterwards the leader of a troupe of bodyguards entrusted with keeping him safe. Khemshawre knew that he'd never see this man alive again, but he had no time to say any well-worded goodbyes. All the king did was raise his hand in farewell and in gratitude to his old comrade for a lifetime of faithful service, and fell back to the Perah.

Captain Nebikhamu, ever loyal, ever brave, turned back to face the growling beast that lurked outside, the beast that hammered and pounded against the doors like a raging bull elephant trapped in a cage. It wouldn't be long now. His time had come. He had chosen this.

Finally, with one last push, the doors gave way and Capt. Nebikhamu was flung physically backwards. Momentarily losing his footing and his balance, he quickly recovered and saw the whole of the rebel army coming at him through that narrow deadly space. With spear and shield, he held them off, stabbing and slashing at them as he tried to force them back. When his copper spearpoint was chopped off, he attacked them with the broken pole. When the pole was wrenched out of his hands, he pulled out his axe from his belt and started hacking and chopping away at them. One, two, three, four men he slew one after another as he beat and bore down upon them. But he was only one, and they were many. They rushed and overpowered him, grabbing his shield, grabbing his arm as he raised his axe upwards for one more strike, and they pushed their pointed sharpened blades underneath his leather cuirass deep into his belly. They cut into his neck with axes and pointed daggers, and as he slowly sank to the ground they stuck him over and over again with their spears like a team of hunters bringing down a lion.

Inside the Perah, the door leading to the reception hall was being barricaded shut with furniture, boxes, and whatever other encumbrances could be speedily brought up. This door was the only door into the Perah, and there were no windows on the ground floor. This was the only way in.

But there were windows on the second floor, and the enemy had ladders.

"Archers! Take position on the second floor and upon the roof!" the king commanded as he could hear the men outside trying to break down the door.

"Sire, they're climbing the walls! They're trying to break in upstairs! The archers can't hold them all off!"

That horrible sinking feeling entrenched itself more and more within the king's stomach, like a man sinking in quicksand. He was just delaying the inevitable. "All staff disperse! Defend the Perah against being breached! All remaining palace guards, defend the Perah's door at all costs! Defend the door to the last man!" And the king rushed off upstairs to repel any enemies who might be trying to break in. Seshrab and his fellow scribes followed close behind him.

There were now only about twenty or so members of the royal palace guards, a select unit that had formerly numbered a hundred men. This little platoon was all that stood between salvation and disaster. They knew what they had to do. They would fight and die at their posts.

Finally, the door was busted in, and the first enemy troops penetrated into the palace's reception hall. They were immediately met by a bristling porcupine of shining copper spears. This twenty-man block maintained its position resolutely within the doorway, repelling anybody who tried to enter. The fighting was hard and bloody, but it was twenty against hundreds. Little by little, the enemy gained headway, one guard after another fell to his injuries, and the last squad of guardsmen were overwhelmed, still desperately wielding their weapons against their foes even as they fell to the floor and gasped their dying breaths.

The enemy was *inside* the Perah.

Intense hand-to-hand fighting raged through the halls and corridors as the palace staff fought for their lives against the rebel army. Fierce and desperate room-to-room battles took place throughout the Perah as each individual chamber was turned into a stronghold that needed to be taken by storm. Butlers and maids fought to their dying breath. The kitchen staff armed with pots, pans, knives, and butcher's cleavers put up a heroic but doomed defense. The bath attendants threw boiling water into the faces of their enemies and rubbed caustic lye soap into their eyes, but it was all for naught. One by one, the citadels fell.

King Khemshawre had spent his whole life in the army. He had seen enough of war to know that this was a hopeless position. There was no way out. This would be his final battle.

But not everyone needed to die. It was time to put his final contingency plan into motion.

Seshrab and the other scribes had been standing near the king, shadowing him, giving him protection and hoping that His Divine Majesty's martial glory might diffuse onto them somehow. The king turned around to face his faithful chief scribe, the foreigner, the Canaanite who had come to this land seeking protection from Death. He couldn't protect him any longer. But now Seshrab could do something for him.

"Seshrab, I have a special task for you", he said, the hallways around them echoing with the clamor of battle and horrid shouting and screaming. "I know that you are a clever and intelligent man. You fought well at Yamu, which shows that you are also brave, and you *survived* at Yamu, which shows that you are lucky. Since you are smart, brave, and lucky, I am giving you one last and final order – take my wife, my daughter, my wife's sister, and her son, and get them all out of the city right now".

"Sire, I...I cannot leave you! Not now!"

"I am not *asking* you – I am *ordering* you to leave! Listen carefully! In my bedroom, behind my bed, there is a secret door. There's a hidden staircase which leads down to the sewers underneath the palace. There's an exit drain in the north side of the city wall. Take my wife, her sister, and the children, and escape out through the sewer, and get them as far away from the city as possible. I would not entrust you with so serious a thing if I didn't believe in you".

Seshrab was overwhelmed. He didn't know what to think, but in the rush of the moment, his voice spoke on his mind's behalf. "Yes, Your Divine Majesty. Yes, I will do it".

King Khemshawre reached out and firmly clasped Seshrab's arm, looked him straight in the eye, and said "You are my friend". Then he turned and rushed off to the battle.

It was then that the full realization of what Seshrab had just said hit him. He turned around and looked at the seven other scribes who were with him, men that he had grown to love as friends and brothers: Amunimhet, Atenmoses, Khepermoses, Nebrenuisis, Senedj, Senwasret, and Thoth-hotep. He couldn't abandon them. Surely, they must have known what was going to happen here.

"What about all of you?! I don't want to leave any of you here like this! I *can't* leave you like this!"

"You heard the man – you've got a job to do! Now do it!" said Senedj.

"Don't worry about us, sir", said Thoth-hotep. "You do what you have to do. We'll hold them off for as long as we can".

"We?! What do you mean '*we*'?! What about me, huh?" said Khepermoses. "I don't want to be a hero! I don't want to die! For Ra's sake, *I'M ONLY 13!!!*"

"You want to go?! Fine, go!" said Nebrenuisis. "Go live! Get out now! Get out right now while you still can! I'm staying here!"

"Come on, come with me!" said Seshrab, and pulled Khepermoses with him as they rushed down the hallway to the royal apartments.

Further on, the palace's defenders were breaking. King Khemshawre rushed forwards into the thick of the fray, fighting beside his guards and retainers. Over and over, he thrashed and bashed at the enemies in the halls, bearing down upon them with his royal mace, *the King's Own Skull-Breaker*, and it lived up to its well-chosen name. Inspired by his example, the royals began to regain their courage. The enemy wavered, the enemy fell back! The enemy was in retreat!

From around the corner of another hallway, there was heard an animalistic panting, snarling, and growling, and the rapid clicking of claws on tiled floors. The king's two pet greyhounds, white Osiris and black Set, came bounding around the corner and raced down the hallway at break-neck speed, ears backwards and teeth bared. They raced past their royal master and the men with him and charged straight into the disorderly mass of enemy troops as they tried to muster up the strength to make another push. The royal hounds roared out as they lunged at their faces and their throats, uttering demonic guttural growls as they tore open enemy necks and wrists and ripped off ears, noses, lips, and fingers. But the growling and snarling soon gave way to the harsh crunching of metal into meat joined by howls and painful whimpers that slowly died away.

The enemy troops surged forwards, stepping over the bodies of the king's two faithful dogs lying in a bloody mangled mass upon the floor. The king and his companions held firm once more against the onslaught of numbers, but there were too many. Little by little, the king and his companions were pushed back. One by one, the king's companions fell, selling their lives dearly, until only he alone was left. Great *Nesu*, Horus-Khemshawre, Living God of Egypt, the great hero of a hundred battlefield victories, the son of the mighty Nebsenre, lived to the last moment as his reputation and his name demanded and required of him. Never stopping, never ceasing, he kept battering and hammering on and on until the fatal blow came. First to the arm, then to the shoulder, then to the neck, then to the face, over and over they came as they surrounded him and stabbed over and over, downwards and downwards. They had to make sure that this mighty warrior would never rise again. He never did.

A great cheer rose up from the enemy ranks as the word spread through the palace – "*The king is dead!!! The king is dead!!!*" With renewed vigor, the rebels dashed forwards to clean up the little pockets of resistance that were left. Their next target was the line of scribes that had taken a defensive stance in the hall. This would be easy.

But the scribes didn't flee. They stood firm, a six-man phalanx of secretaries, writers, and book-keepers standing against dozens of enemy troops. They unwaveringly maintained their positions with club, dagger, and shield as the hollering rebels charged down the hallway towards them, weapons drawn.

"Gentlemen", said Senwasret, the oldest scribe, his voice quavering but resolute, "it has been a privilege to know every one of you".

At that moment, Seshrab and Khepermoses had reached the area of the palace where the queens' bedrooms were. They busted into Queen Neferet's room, but it was empty. They went to the next door, ex-queen Meret's room, and threw the door open, whereupon the two women and their children yelled out with a start.

"We've got to go right now!!! Move!!!" Seshrab snapped. "Come on, let's go! Let's go!" And everyone rose up to their feet, carrying the few parcels of belongings that the king had told them to keep with them, just in case they needed to get out. That time had come.

Seshrab leading the column, the two queens and their children being tightly carried in their arms, and Khepermoses bringing up the rear made their way down the hallway towards the king's bedroom. All around them, they could hear the clashing of battle and the screams of dying men and women, and smell the acrid stench of blood, bile, and discharged piss and feces. Then from behind them, a group of enemy soldiers appeared and they were immediately spotted. The enemy officer pointed at them and shouted "There they are! Get them!" And they charged towards the fleeing royals.

Momentarily alarmed and frozen in fear, Khepermoses snapped his head to Seshrab and yelled *"Go! Run!"*

As Seshrab and the four royals fled, Khepermoses stood his ground as the enemy troops ran towards him. *"COME ON!!! COME AND GET ME!!!"*

Seshrab, Meret, Neferet, and the two children raced for their lives down the hallway, around the corner, and down another hallway to elude their pursuers as Khepermoses single-handedly held off the enemy advance, spitting curses and insults at them the whole time, only to have the defiant voice suddenly cut off by a young man's agonizing scream, followed by silence.

Just Seshrab, the two queens, and their children rounded a corner and saw the door to the king's bedroom, a group of three enemy soldiers came up from a different direction and were now standing right in front of them. The soldiers immediately became alert and braced their weapons. Both sides locked eyes on each other and froze for a hellish eternity.

The three men were each armed with a spear and a wicker shield covered in cow hide. All three of them had blood dripping off of their weapons. Of the three, the man standing in the middle was more heavily armed and more kitted-out than the other two. Around the waist of his short-sleeved white linen tunic was a leather belt, from which hung a dagger from the left side and an axe from the right.

But what Seshrab noticed about this man the most was his face. The man had a large prominent birth mark on the right side of his face.

The two men *immediately* recognized each other. Their eyes widened, their mouths hung agape in shock and surprise.

*"You..."* gasped the soldier with the birth mark. *"I know you!"*

"I know you, too", replied Seshrab, trying to catch his breath, his heart hammering. "You're the fisherman by the river".

"You're the Canaanite traveller I met at Giza", said the man.

"You let me sleep in your house".

"You gave my family food".

There was a horrible pause for two or three seconds as both sides were unsure of what was going to happen next.

"*Please*", said Seshrab. "Please, whatever you're thinking about doing, *please don't*. Just let me go. Let us go. They're no threat to anybody".

The fisherman looked at the people with Seshrab, thinking, concentrating. Two women, probably Seshrab's age or thereabouts, and two young children, 1 or 2 years old at most. They all looked scared out of their wits. The children were gripping tightly to their mothers.

The man raised up his spear to the vertical position. The two men with him were unsure of what was going on, but they followed their officer's lead and did the same, but were nervously looking around to see if anybody was watching.

"Last year, my family was starving", said the fisherman. "You came to my house and you gave us food. You did my family a favor. So now I will do one for yours. Go, get out, me and my men won't stop you. The palace is falling and everyone in here will soon be dead. Go! Get your family out of here now before it's too late!" And the three of them stood back, making a clear path for them to get down the hallway. But they were *still* blocking the bedroom door!

"I, uh, I have to get *in there*" said Seshrab pointing.

The three men turned around behind them to see a door – an ordinary-looking door no different from any of the others. They looked back at Seshrab, the two women, and the two children for a moment, and the fisherman stepped aside. The two men with him promptly copied him.

Seshrab rushed forwards with his charges in tow, flung the door open, and raced inside, and the three enemy soldiers were surprised to see that it was a very lavishly-furnished bedroom. The three men looked at each other puzzled as Seshrab halted on one side of the large bed draped in fine linen sheets and surrounded by thick curtains of royal blue, and tried to push it. However the bed was large and heavy, and he wasn't having much luck.

No time to ask questions. The Giza fisherman, Nehem-in-netjeru, *Blessed by the gods*, turned to one of the two troopers standing with him in the doorway. "Guard the door. Don't let anyone in".

"Yes, Sergeant".

The other two dropped their spears and shields and helped Seshrab push the bed over to one side of the room. Once this was done, they could see that the bed had concealed a door in the wall, a very small door barely big enough for a person to crouch through. Seshrab pushed it open, and they could see that there was a dark narrow staircase leading who-knows where – to escape, to outside, and to salvation, one presumed.

"Quick, get in, get in!" Seshrab urged the two women and the two children, both of whom were sniffling and starting to cry. The two women crouched in through the small cramped passageway, carrying their bags of food and linens and their skins of water, and pulling the two kids with them, urging them on, telling them that everything was going to be alright and to please be very quiet.

Seshrab was the last to leave, and he turned one last time to the man who had probably just saved his life.

"Get them as far away from the city as possible", said Nehem-in-netjeru. "Keep everyone quiet, and you should be alright. I'm sorry about all of this. Good luck".

Seshrab clasped the man's hand. "You are a good man!" he said, and then disappeared into the passage and quickly shut the secret door behind him.

Nehem-in-netjeru shook his head slightly as he and his two companions stood there gazing at the little door in the wall. "No I'm not, but I'm trying to be". Then, he snapped to and remembered why they were there. "Come on, help me push this thing back where it was". And the two of them went to the other side of the large royal bed and pushed it back into its original position, concealing the tiny secret door behind the headboard once again.

With that taken care of, it was time to go. They grabbed their spears and shields and left the royal bedroom, shutting the door behind them. What was done was done.

"Alright, listen", said Nehem-in-netjeru to the two men with him as they stood outside the bedroom door. "What happened back there, that *never* happened – understood? We checked out the room, and the room was empty. There was *nobody* there, and none of us saw or heard *anything*. Right? Right?" he said, his finger pointing to the men on either side of him.

Both of them nodded in agreement.

"Good. Come on, let's get back to work. The sooner we get this business over and done with, the sooner I can get back home".

The dark staircase was barely wide enough for one person. Seshrab and the others blindly made their way down solely by feel. They had to be careful, but at the same time they needed to hurry. Even from within this closed passageway, they could faintly smell smoke and hear echoes of the clash of battle and the screams of the dying reverberating through the walls.

Finally they made it down to the bottom of the staircase and saw it opened into a sewer drain, exactly as the king had said. The long brick-lined pipeway was narrow with a low ceiling. All five of them went out into the knee-deep mucky foul fetid standing water, crouching low to avoid banging their heads. The stench of decay was overwhelming. From where he squatted, Seshrab could dimly see a tiny light at the end of the long tunnel.

"There's the opening. Come on, follow me", he whispered, his voice echoing and surprisingly loud in the cramped confined space. Leading the way, the five of them slogged through the filth, hunched over, trying hard not to gag on the stench. The narrow tunnel forced them to walk single-file. Seshrab pressed a hand to his mouth to cover up the smell, his free hand sliding along the wet slimy surface of the sewer's brick wall to guide his way forward. The two royal children, their wide eyes filled with terror, clung to their mother's skirts. Queen Meret, her regal features streaked with grime, whispered hurried words of comfort while her younger sister Queen Neferet tried to calm her trembling son. They moved in near silence, the children muffling their sobs as their mothers urged them forward.

As they carefully made their way forwards, the light imperceptibly became more tangible, but also the sound of the battle which raged above and around them became louder and louder. As they made their way closer and closer towards the sewer's exit, Seshrab could see there was a small outlet drain built into the side of the brick wall, possibly leading up to the Perah's bath room where the baths and the laundry were. There was blood trickling out of the drain. Seshrab shuddered and quickly looked away from it and kept moving.

Little by little, they could see light and smell fresh air. The faint promise of freedom spurred them on, and soon the flicker of moonlight appeared at the tunnel's end. The sewer outlet was closed off with a copper grate. Outside, rushes and tall grass obscured the view, but he could see that it was dark out – the sun had set. The flickering orange on the blades of grass showed that a fire, or possibly several fires, had broken out.

The copper grate was held in place by a simple latch lock – opening it was no problem. Seshrab opened the grate very carefully to make sure that it didn't squeak, and cautiously looked around to see if the coast was clear, the refreshing cool night air filling his lungs. From within the secret staircase, they had heard only muffled sounds of what was going on. From within the sewer line, the only things that they could hear were the sloshing of their legs through the water, their own breathing, and their own heartbeats pulsing in their ears. Now, at the sewer's outlet, they could hear much more. The battle was still underway. From their little hiding place below, Seshrab could plainly hear Khaset City in the process of being sacked, looted, and destroyed, the roaring crackling of the flames, and he could even hear the screams of people who were being tortured, killed, or driven to madness by what was happening all around them.

Seshrab, his face smeared with grime and sweat, looked around carefully. *No soldiers? No, nobody. Good.* He motioned the others behind him to follow. "Stay down, stay low, and keep quiet", he whispered. "We'll try to make it to the river. Follow me".

Seshrab opened the gate a little wider, took another look around, looked up to make sure that no enemy soldiers had suddenly decided to peer down from the top of the walls for whatever reason, and then they began to move through the little winding rivulet, using the tall grass and reeds for cover. Above them, Khaset City was aflame. They kept their heads low and moved as fast as they could.

The sewer outlet connected to an irrigation canal which fed water to the grape vineyards around the city, and from there the canal connected to the Nile River. They made their way through what was left of the grape vineyards on the north side of the city, some parts of which were still marginally intact. Concealed under the trellised vines, they made their way to the canal. They knew that if they followed it, it would lead them to the river, and freedom. The party moved progressively in stages, making their way towards one obstacle and landmark after another. The farther they got away from the city, the bolder they became and the faster they moved.

Finally, they reached the branch of the Nile that flowed nearby and found a small fishing boat beached onto the riverbank. Without saying anything, all of them rushed towards it, their eyes scanning the shoreline for any sign of pursuit. The two royal children were put in first, and they were urged in hushed tones to stay low and keep quiet. Then all of the baggage was loaded, most of which was soaked from the foul sewer water. Then Seshrab and the two queens pushed the boat off the bank and they clambered in. Seshrab was the last one into the boat and he took his place at the stern. Two oars were lying within the boat, which Seshrab pointed to. "Start paddling!" he hissed. "Hurry! Hurry!" The two queens started paddling for their lives while Seshrab kept his hands on the rudder. The Nile flowed north, and they'd move downstream regardless, but they needed to put as much distance between themselves and the enemy as they could…so, row. Row for your lives.

After a while, they stopped. Besides, the whole day had been a terrible ordeal, too much to bear, and everyone was tired and exhausted. So, they stopped paddling, and they slumped down into the boat. Their clothes were soaked, they stank from sweat and filth, they were tired, scared, anxious, and fully conscious of what their lives were now – they were homeless wanderers, people without a home and without a country. Everything that they were and everything that they knew was no more. So they hunched over in the little boat, the women and children holding each other close while Seshrab kept his eyes peeled for any signs of danger.

Seshrab turned around and looked behind him. In the night, he could see the blazing orange glow as Khaset City and the royal palace were consumed entirely by fire. This was it – the bad guys had won. It was so incomprehensibly horrible to his heart. As he watched the fire reduce Khaset City to smoldering ruins, Seshrab even thought that he could hear the screaming of all of those people as Sekheperenre's army fell upon them. Seshrab knew that it was impossible for human voices to travel that far…but still…

He turned back around, not wanting to look anymore upon that dreadful sight, with all of its terrible implications, his head hanging low. Just at that moment, he became conscious of his Golden Fly medal hanging around his neck, brushing against the skin of his chest – he had forgotten that he was still wearing it. He reached into his tunic and pulled it out, and softly touched the shining golden object. It was so tiny, yet, so significant. Only those who had done something truly heroic deserved to wear such an item. He looked down at the Golden Fly, turning it slightly back and forth in his fingers, feeling its texture, looking at it sparkle in the dim evening light. He was instantly overwhelmed with a devastating smothering sense of shame. *Bravery.* What was so brave about running away from the enemy? Why should he live while so many others died? Were they any less brave than him? Many of them were his friends, many of them had also fought at the Battle of Yamu and many other battles before that. Didn't they deserve to live too? Surely they had *earned* their Golden Fly. Seshrab was no soldier. He was just a scribe, a clerk, a paper pusher. He wasn't any braver or more courageous than any of them. In fact, he had spent much of that battle hiding behind his shield, ducking for cover from enemy spears and arrows. What brave man does that? Seshrab hated himself. He loathed, detested, and despised himself. He was a liar, a charlatan, and a coward. This little golden trinket deserved a man much better than himself to wear it. Great god El, even the king's two pet dogs deserved to wear this medal more than him!

The very sight of that medal filled Seshrab with disgust. He felt his adrenaline and his anger swell up, and he furiously ripped the golden necklace off, breathing deeply and heavily, and pulled his clenched fist backwards, ready to fling the damned thing into the river!

However, just as he craned his arm backwards, ready to hurl his Golden Fly into the Nile, from the corner of his eye he caught sight of the two royal women, Meret and her sister Neferet, huddled together, shaking in fear, their eyes heavy with tears, their faces distraught at the immense uncertainty of their futures, their children clinging tightly to them, scared and whimpering. Seshrab slowly lowered his arm, studying them intently. Strange, they didn't look so regal now. They did not have that same air of command and majesty as they had about them before, touched by some unknowable divine grace. Now they looked helpless, scared, and anxious. They looked so ordinary.

Seshrab then remembered why he was here, with them, at that moment. King Khemshawre, the mighty martial titan of Lower Egypt, a man who loved the Army more than life itself, realized when the walls of Khaset City were breached that there would be no victory this time. Today, he was going to lose, he was going to die – the gods had commanded it. Before he went to meet his predestined fate, the king issued one final order to his trusty chief scribe, a foreigner, a Canaanite – get the two queens and their children out of the city and away from harm. The king had entrusted Seshrab, and no other man than him, with this very important task. Amazingly, in the middle of a siege, threatened by tens of thousands of enemy soldiers, he had somehow managed to accomplish his mission. As the Perah fell into rebel hands, and as King Khemshawre made his last valiant doomed charge against the enemy ranks, willingly hurtling himself headlong to his own assured death, Seshrab, Queen Meret, Queen Neferet, Prince Montunakht, and Princess Atentjehenet had escaped. By the time Lord Sekheperenre realized that the four surviving members of the royal family were gone, at that same moment, they were hurriedly making their way down the Nile, towards freedom and another day of life. Seshrab had successfully carried out his king's final command.

Seshrab looked down once more at his Golden Fly still clenched in his fist, and then put the necklace back on. He would never take it off ever again.

"Our home is gone forever" said Meret mournfully as she looked to her younger sister Neferet. "There is nothing left, nothing but memories. What's to be done?"

"What *can* be done?" responded Neferet. "How shall we live? Where shall we go?"

Meret could not answer her sister's questions and fears, and Seshrab could not say anything either. He had no plan – he was improvising every step as he went along. Once again, he was on the move. Once more, he had to restart his life all over again. It all felt so depressingly familiar.

Finally, after a great deal of thought, he replied, "We will go back home".

They looked at him, puzzled. Surely he couldn't be serious.

"*My* home", he added, as if reading their thoughts. "I am taking both of you with me back to my home. I am Seshrab of Hebron…and that's where we're going".

And so, in the hushed hues of evening, the little boat drifted down the sleepy shimmering blue satin waters of the Nile River, out towards the vast open water of the Great Green, and towards the days to come.

*Sekheperenre was assassinated two months after seizing power.*

*In the year 1650 BC, the Amorites invaded and conquered*
*Lower Egypt, and the 14th Dynasty came to an end.*

www.ingramcontent.com/pod-product-compliance
Lightning Source LLC
Chambersburg PA
CBHW082053090726
47909CB00010B/3020